# LALA PETTIBONE'S

## ACT TWO

Heidi Mastrogiovanni

Amberjack Publishing
New York, New York

Amberjack
PUBLISHING

Amberjack Publishing
228 Park Avenue S #89611
New York, NY 10003-1502
http://amberjackpublishing.com

This book is a work of fiction. Any references to real places are used fictitiously. Names, characters, fictitious places, and events are the products of the author's imagination, and any resemblance to actual persons, living or dead, places, or events is purely coincidental.

Publisher's Cataloging-in-Publication data
Names: Mastrogiovanni, Heidi, author.
Title: Lala Pettibone's act two / by Heidi Mastrogiovanni.
Description: New York, NY: Amberjack Publishing, 2017.
Identifiers: ISBN 978-1- 944995-07- 2 (pbk.) | 978-1- 944995-08- 9 (ebook) | LCCN 2016946573
Subjects: LCSH Middle-aged women--Fiction. | Man-woman relationships--Fiction. | Dating--Fiction. | Los Angeles (Calif.)--Fiction. | Authors--Fiction.| Love stories. | Humorous stories. | GSAFD Chick Lit. | Humor. | BISAC FICTION / Humorous / General | FICTION / Contemporary Women.
Classification: LCC PS3613.A819942 L35 2017| DDC 813.6--dc23

*Cover Design: Mimi Bark*

Printed in Canada

# MERDE STORM

The Ides of March were about to slap the stuffing out of Lala Pettibone. And she didn't see it coming. Not at all.

On the fourteenth of March, Lala went out to dinner with her best friend. Lala and Brenda had gone to high school together in Santa Monica, California, and then opted to go to college on the East Coast, at schools very close to each other. Close enough that it took only a short drive to Brenda's campus for Lala to lose her virginity on Valentine's Day during her freshman year.

"I wish we'd had e-mail back then," Lala often mused, when she remembered the exceedingly bittersweet experience. "I could have written him a curt, brilliant, sexy missive telling him what a douchebag he was for never calling me after we had sex for my first time. I could have posted it on Facebook."

And then Lala would reflect a bit more and conclude that some things really probably are better left unsaid.

Lala lived in Greenwich Village, and Brenda lived on the Upper West Side. Neither of them had ever wanted to return to Southern California once they had escaped.

"I don't mind visiting LA," Brenda would often say.

"Me neither," Lala would agree. "But for a week, tops. After that, I start to get itchy being around so much space and sunshine."

Brenda and her husband, Frank, were significantly wealthy. They lived in an unbelievable apartment near Lincoln Center. Frank had inherited it from his parents. Lala loved to tell anyone who would listen how palatial her best friend's apartment was.

"The first time I went there? Brenda gave me a tour and, I swear to God, if she hadn't escorted me back to the front door at the end of the evening, I would have never gotten out of there. It's like a huge maze of rooms and doors and more rooms and more doors. And hallways. Hallways that go on forever. I swear, I'd still be there now if Brenda hadn't shown me the way out."

Brenda always tried to pay for dinner and anything else they did together, including spa weekends in Montauk, but Lala never let her.

"I'm not poor, okay?" Lala would huff and then feel guilty for being so sensitive in the face of her best friend's grace and generosity. "I can take responsibility for my life decisions."

Lala's life decisions had included knowing from a very early age that she didn't want to have children. Lala loved kids, but she knew she didn't have the patience to be a parent. She preferred being a fabulous aunt in the vein of Mame, and spoiling her actual nieces and nephews, along with all of her friends' kids, whom she counted as nieces and nephews too.

"They will all take turns taking care of me in my dotage," Lala would often say. "Because they all love me so much because I'm so much fun, and I never scold them or tell them 'no' unless their safety or health is threatened while they're in my care. I'll live in a charming guesthouse on their massive grounds in Larchmont, or I'll have my own suite in their fabulous townhouse on Sutton Place. Because I'm envisioning that they'll all be quite successful, largely due to the positive influence of their Aunt Lala. And I'll host weekly salons, and I'll say provocative things that sound cute because I'm so ancient. Like that weird stuff that comes out of Yoda's mouth, which is really quite endearing. *New York Magazine* will write a profile of me, and they'll come up with some kind of moniker like 'The Last of the Great Ol' Broads.'"

Lala's life decisions had also included not going to law school or graduate school. Lala spent the first decade of her post-collegiate life in Manhattan working toward a career on stage and screen.

"My success as an actress," she would often explain in the ensuing years, "was greatly hampered by my lack of any actual acting talent."

The turning point came one morning when she was dressing to go to an audition for a soap opera, and she had a panic attack that ended with her cutting every item of clothing she owned into tiny, heart-shaped pieces. She had to be stopped from leaving her building and getting into a taxi to go to the audition—wearing only a wristwatch, a necklace, and a pair of pumps—by a kindly neighbor who, mercifully, was heading down to the laundry room just as Lala was locking the door to her apartment behind her.

"Apparently, I didn't much care for the audition process," Lala would later explain. "Who knew?"

Lala's best life decision up to that fateful March 15th had been to marry Terrence. He was a playwright she met while doing summer stock, and he was sexy and brilliant. Best of all, he rekindled in her a love affair with words.

"I had written some in college," Lala said, "but it was shit. Absolute shit. Self-conscious and precious and affected. When I read that stuff now, I want to slit my wrists to avoid dying of embarrassment."

Terrence wrote beautiful works that had been produced at small theaters all over the country and in Canada. He won an Obie award for Best New American Play. He never made a solid or even decent living at his craft, but he and Lala were deliriously happy. They lived in a classic, fifth-floor walkup with a bathtub in the kitchen in the East 60s.

Lala's parents were comfortably well-off, and Lala was their only child (it was by marrying Terrence that she had gotten those nieces and nephews she loved to spoil), so they sent very generous birthday and Christmas gifts. But Lala had never lived the life of privilege that so many of her classmates from Wesleyan enjoyed.

Lala's parents had immigrated to the States from England, where the still-thriving class system had made her near-anarchist father red-faced with rage.

"I'll kill 'em," her father would declare. Frequently. More often than not, without any provocation. Whatsoever. "All of the aristos. I'll kill 'em all, I tell ye."

"That's lovely, dear," Lala's mother would chirp, never for a moment taking her eyes a millimeter away from the shenanigans on *EastEnders*. "We're feeling very *A Tale of Two Cities* again today, are we?"

Her parents taught at Santa Monica College until they retired. Her father was a mathematician, and her mom chaired the history department.

Lala and her parents had descended from non-observant Jews who had escaped to the United Kingdom from the former Soviet Republic of Georgia. It was from her grandmother's use of Yiddish that Lala first received her great gift: a love of language. She had treasured memories of her Bubbe Esther saying, "Don't *hock* me in *chanik*," in a Cockney accent that could have rivaled Eliza Doolittle's, pre-transformation.

After she met Terrence, Lala started writing again. She started reading all the books about writing that Terrence recommended. She stopped acting, and she spent lots of the time she wasn't working as an office temp to make money at the small desk in their small living room that she shared with Terrence. His side of the desk was "covered with crap, I mean, constantly." It drove Lala crazy. On the side of the desk over which Lala exercised hegemony, the stapler was never empty, the paperclips were always kept in a small porcelain cup, and Terrence's hand was always swatted if he tried to touch anything.

Lala had two short stories published in *The New Yorker*. After the first one was accepted, she sent out a letter to every literary agent in New York announcing her success, and asking if they wanted to read her collection of short stories, *Dressed Like a Lady, Drinks Like a Pig*. She got only one response. It was a form letter saying that her book was not what they were looking for, but they wished her every success with finding an agent who had more enthusiasm for her work.

"Barf," Lala said, after she read the form letter aloud to Terrence.

"Fuck it," Terrence said. "We don't need them. We've got each other, and we've got tomorrow, and so I say, fuck it, yes, indeed, fuck it, because we've got everything we need."

"At least their timing wasn't so shitty that it ruined our celebration."

Three weeks after Lala's first story had been accepted, and three days before the form letter had arrived, Lala and Terrence went to their favorite café to honor their anniversary. Two bottles of champagne later, they stumbled home and had the best sex they'd ever had. Of their lives. Their lives together. Their married lives together.

"Remember that time in Big Sur, right after we stopped dating other people?"

"I assume that's a rhetorical question."

"Of course it is."

"Like I could forget."

"Like I could."

"But married sex is great."

"It's not fair to even compare it with unhitched sex."

"Apples and oranges."

"Indeed."

Thirteen years into their marriage, Terrence was diagnosed with stage-four stomach cancer. He died in less than six months.

"I wouldn't trade the lessons I learned when Terrence got sick," Lala often said. "I just wish he didn't have to die so I could learn them."

People would frequently ask Lala if she could give them a general idea of what those lessons were, and Lala would respond that she most certainly could, "because I've given this considerable thought between daily and sometimes hourly crying jags, jags that, by the way, make me wonder if it's possible to die from crying, because it certainly feels like it's possible. My encapsulated version of the lessons would be, fucking pay attention while you have the chance. Pay attention every single damn day. Notice and cherish and honor those people and those things for which you are grateful. Don't assume they'll be around forever. Because you never know. Trust me on this. You never ever ever know."

After Terrence died, lots of people, from close friends to family to colleagues to casual acquaintances, asked Lala if she would be moving home now.

"I don't know what you mean," Lala would respond.

"Home," they would say. "Back to Los Angeles."

"New York is my home," Lala told them. "It was when Terrence was alive, and it is now."

Y

Lala and Brenda decided to go to their favorite Mexican restaurant on Hudson Street. The bartender knew how to create a scratch margarita that was smooth enough to make the amount of tequila that was, in fact, in it come as a big surprise when you stood up after drinking them like lemonade.

Lala had her usual problems dressing for an evening out. Or dressing for anything, really.

"I have so many friends who have excellent taste in clothes," Lala often said. "They know how to put pieces together and make these fabulous, inventive ensembles. I can barely dress myself. It's why I have so many black clothes. It's just so much easier."

Lala stood in front of the full-length mirror in her small, but very charming, one-bedroom co-op. Lala's parents had died five years before, just after she turned forty. They had flown to New York to celebrate their only child's milestone birthday, and it had been a truly wonderful and memorable visit. Clarissa and George Pettibone had more energy than many of Lala's friends. They were sweet and quick-witted and everyone loved them. Brenda threw a big birthday party for Lala at her unbelievable apartment. Two months after Lala's parents returned to Los Angeles, Clarissa died suddenly of a heart attack. Lala flew out immediately. While she was there helping her dad adjust to being a widower, George went to sleep one night and didn't wake up the next morning. It was exactly two weeks to the day after the passing of his wife of almost fifty years.

"Seriously, is that the way to go, or what?" Lala said at the West Coast memorial for her parents and at the less formal one Brenda hosted after Lala returned to New York. "My parents were in great shape right up to the end, and they adored each other, and I don't think they ever spent a night apart after they were married."

And then Lala would add, "My parents' marriage has been an ongoing reproach to my life since Terrence died. And I mean that in the very best and most loving sense of the phrase 'ongoing reproach.'"

After Terrence died, Lala alternated between long periods of having no romance at all in her life, and longer periods of dating men who lived in other cities, often cities that were quite far from New York. The winner of the longest-distance award was Danny from New Zealand. They had met through mutual friends, and they were an item for three years—if seeing each other twice a year and screwing all week can constitute being an item.

"Is anyone surprised?" Lala would ask her friends. "I'm not ready for a relationship. I don't care if it's been ten years. I lost the love of my life. I feel much more comfortable with a boyfriend when we've got several thousand miles of ocean and a very long plane ride between us."

After Lala's parents died, she sold their cute, little cottage in the easternmost part of Santa Monica and netted enough profit to buy her one-bedroom co-op in the Bancroft, one of the most sought-after locations in Greenwich Village. It was a beautiful old building with thick walls and thick ceilings and thick floors, and it had a doorman and an elevator. Lala bought a stacked washer and dryer that just managed to fit into her bathroom, and she even splurged on an interior designer who was a friend of a friend and gave her a great deal. She worked with her to create a light and warm—but above all functional and uncluttered—atmosphere.

As Lala stared in the mirror at her latest attempt to put together a cute outfit, her ancient beagle, Petunia, and her not-quite-as-old dachshund, Yootza, a sable-hued meatloaf on four chubby drumsticks, dozed on the bed. Lala had adopted them both from the ASPCA two years earlier when Petunia was nine and Yootza was five. They did not come with those names. At the shelter, Petunia was called Jasmine and Yootza was called Jerry.

"He looks like a Yootza to me," Lala said. She was sitting at a desk in the reception area filling out the paperwork while Jerry sat on her lap staring at her. "I have no idea where I came up with that. I have no idea what it means. Jerry must have told me. He must be screaming right now, 'My name is not Jerry, it's Yootza!' And I'm hearing him. Wow, that's pretty amazing."

Lala had always had pets. When she was growing up, her parents valued volunteer work as much as they treasured leftist politics, so Lala started working at an animal shelter near their house on weekends when she was just out of elementary school. As she got older, and certainly by the time she was out of college and on her own, Lala started to gravitate toward the older animals who needed homes.

"Of course I love puppies and kittens," Lala explained to the adoption counselor at the ASPCA who was overseeing her application for Jasmine and Jerry. "Who doesn't love them? They're so adorable, for heaven's sake, but my god are they a lot of work. Me, I've preferred the gray faces for as long as I can remember. My last six dogs were almost ten years old when I rescued them, and I still got another five good years with each of them, and that was especially amazing because one of them was a mastiff, and you know the big dogs generally don't live as long as the small dogs. Emily was beautiful. I had her until she was fourteen. I can't talk about her anymore, or I'll start wailing."

Lala's capacity for empathy didn't extend only to sentient beings. She always worried that the last aspirin in the bottle might be lonely, and maybe she should just go ahead and increase the dose she was taking so as not to leave the poor pill bereft of companionship.

Lala took off the light blue shirt that kind of still fit her and kind of looked okay but really didn't. She turned away from the mirror and looked over her shoulder at the reflection.

"Hmm . . . Well, okay. Hmm."

Lala walked everywhere, and she also went to the gym every day where she got her heart rate up to a level that made her sweat for at least half an hour. On alternate days she did strength training, and she always got in at least one yoga or Pilates class every week.

But Lala was short, and she loved to eat and drink, and she was never going to slow down with either of those delightful activities, so she had gotten a bit rounder as she had gotten older.

"I do like that my boobs are finally bigger," Lala reflected. She continued to stare at herself. "And I am grateful for and stunned by the fact that I don't yet have gray hair."

Yootza opened his eyes and let out a big sigh.

"Yootza, please do not roll your eyes at me. This is my true shade of medium golden brown. It has been my true shade of medium golden brown since adolescence. I do not appreciate your skepticism."

Lala sat down on the bed next to Yootza and scratched under his little chin.

Yootza had an underbite. That had sealed the deal the moment Lala saw it at the shelter.

"Mother of God, he's got an underbite!" she brayed at the staff. "Why hasn't anyone snapped this guy up before? Yeah, well, their loss."

"Mama's short, Yootza," Lala explained. She used her other hand to rub sleeping Petunia's belly. "Though Mama has unusually long legs. Mama's legs are nearly as long as Auntie Brenda's, and you know Auntie Brenda is at least half a foot taller than Mama. That's because Mama is so short-waisted. Mama's boobs just basically rest on Mama's hips. And that's why clothes tend to look odd on Mama. What time is it? I'm going to be late."

Lala stood up and marched over to her walk-in closet. It was a small space that required a stretching of the definition of "walk-in" to include taking maybe three shuffling steps from the door, but by New York standards it was something special. She pulled a pair of black pants off their hanger, and she grabbed a black top with red trim. The material on each of the pieces was comfortable, and the fit was not too tight. Lala put on a cute, little pair of red pumps and once again studied herself in the mirror.

"The red and the black. An homage to Stendhal and also the school colors of my alma mater. As you both have heard many times. I love you for always so cheerfully listening to Mama repeat herself. Did Mama ever tell you that Mama is self-conscious about many things, but her wide green eyes are not one of them? Did

Mama ever tell you that her first boyfriend in college dubbed her eyes 'just the right side of big and beautiful enough to approximate the unnerving stare of a lemur'? Which Mama chose to take as a high compliment."

Lala made big kissy noises in Petunia's and Yootza's ears.

"I'll leave the TV on Comedy Central. Don't wait up. Auntie Brenda and I have lots of fun stuff to talk about."

🍸

"Really? That's great."

Brenda smiled at her best friend. Lala often described Brenda as "Effortlessly elegant . . . which just chaps the crap out of me, frankly. She makes it look so easy. She's tall and she's got gorgeous red hair and skin like cream and you know what else is really irritating? She never works out, but she always looks fabulous. God, I love her so much."

"I am at least as surprised as you are," Lala said. "I have, and I'm thrilled to admit this, been feeling quite optimistic for rather a while now."

Lala grasped the large pitcher of Kick Ass Scratch Margaritas that was still a quarter full. She was about to refill their glasses when Felipe swooped over and gently seized the pitcher out of her hand.

"I will do this. I will attend to my beautiful ladies."

He made a graceful circle in the air with the pitcher, weaving back and forth between their glasses, not spilling a drop of the precious liquid, until the brims were nearly submerged.

"*Merci mille fois, mon trésor,*" Lala cooed. "As soon as I'm fluent in French, I'm starting on Spanish. In your honor, Felipe. *Mon trésor.*"

Felipe smiled at Lala and Brenda, before running off to join a few other waiters who had just started singing "Happy Birthday" to a table full of young women. Lala and Brenda watched Felipe grab a pair of maracas and dance.

"I realize a relationship with Felipe is probably not going to happen because of his age relative to mine, among a million other reasons," Lala said. "But I would love . . . you know, just for one night . . . or maybe a weekend in Martha's Vineyard . . ."

"Ditto," Brenda said. "In some alternate universe where I wouldn't be cheating on Frank. Oh, Lala, I'm so happy for you. I think you've found your tribe."

"I think I have," Lala said. "It's been almost a year. Everyone is wonderful in the office."

"Some more than others, right?" Brenda said.

"Some way more than others," Lala agreed, and they both grinned conspiratorially.

"We do lovely work there," Lala continued. "I think I feel at home. Do not repeat this. Not even to me. Especially not to me. But sometimes I even think I may stop being a temp and accept their offer to go on staff."

"I don't believe what I'm apparently hearing."

"Health insurance. Hello! How great would it be to not have to pay that on my own every month? And I don't come home tired at the end of every day. I love writing and editing the commentary for the pictures. The books are lovely. And you know I have no visual sense whatsoever."

"None whatsoever," Brenda said. "Not one milligram."

"And even I love the photographs. That's how lovely they are. So I come home, and I feel great, and I've been able to write more than ever. I'm working on a trilogy of novellas centering around the theme of renewal."

"Cool," Brenda said. Just as she sucked down the last of her drink, Felipe appeared as if the air around their table had miraculously created him—and another pitcher of Kick Ass Scratch Margaritas.

"Are my beautiful ladies ready for more?"

He didn't wait for an answer. He made a big circle with the pitcher until their glasses were again full.

Lala and Brenda watched him walk away.

"In the scenario going through my mind right now," Lala whispered, "I have the body I had when I met Terrence. But with bigger boobs."

"Yup," Brenda said. "So, the truth. How much of your thoughts about maybe taking a full-time, regular job at the charming New York branch of Atelier du Monde has to do with your crush on your delicious boss and the possibility of maybe marrying him and living in Paris for half the year?"

"Certainly no more than seventy-five to ninety percent. I don't know. I just have a feeling about us. Destiny? I don't know. Fate? He makes my heart go nuts."

"I'm so happy for you," Brenda said. "Especially because for a long time there everything you touched turned to shit. It just broke my heart to see you trying and trying again and again to get away from working as a temp, and you never let me or Frank help you, and you know we always wanted to, and, God, you just had one nutty idea after another to try to make some money so you could write. In hindsight, that one about hawking the energy drink was so clearly a pyramid scheme. How much did you lose?"

"I don't remember," Lala said through clenched teeth.

"We were all so worried about you. It seemed like you were being followed by this dark cloud of absolute shit."

"I remember. I was there, remember? So maybe no need to remind me? But I guess it turns out that I am what I like to call—because it's the best thing I can call myself at this point in my life—a late bloomer. A very late bloomer."

Lala suddenly got very quiet. She stayed that way for several long moments.

"After all that lovely time with Terrence," she finally whispered. "All those lovely years."

Brenda's eyes welled up even as Lala's did. Without looking at each other, they reached across the table and tightly grasped each other's hands.

"I was so lost for so long. But at least now I'm finally blooming, right?"

♥

When Lala stumbled into her bedroom it was after midnight.

Petunia and Yootza had apparently not moved a muscle since she'd left. They did lift their heads when Lala fell face forward onto the bed and landed nearly on top of them.

"Shove over," Lala muttered.

Petunia and Yootza put their heads back down and didn't move.

"Mama's sorry," Lala mumbled. "Mama imagines that the smell of tequila on her breath must be unbearably vivid to a hound's sensitive nose."

Lala hoisted herself to a seated position.

"Mama's going to eat a lot of vanilla ice cream. A ton. And Mama's going to drink a lot of water, and Mama's going to take two aspirins, or three if there are three in the bottle, because I don't want the last one to feel abandoned, or else Mama will have a wicked hangover. And then Mama is going to take you for a nice, long walk."

Lala shuffled her way out of the bedroom. She grabbed a barstool from the counter that connected her cute, little kitchen with her cute, little dining area. Lala positioned the chair so she could sit in front of the open freezer door and eat the rest of an almost full container of Häagen-Dazs. The cold from the freezer was doing a very good job of helping her not pass out.

Lala shoved ice cream into her mouth with a spoon and started to giggle.

"This is why New York is so much better than LA," Lala brayed toward the bedroom, presumably for the edification of her dogs. "You can drink to excess here, and you don't have to worry about fiddling with an app to get a ride home. All you have to do is get to the curb, raise your hand, and mumble your address before you pass out in the backseat. Suck on that, City of Angels!"

# WHEN IT RAINS

Lala woke to the sound of her clock radio blaring liberal political opinions. She gingerly reached over to the nightstand and turned off the radio without lifting her head. Petunia was at Lala's feet and was doing a passable imitation of a monster truck rally. Yootza had his head next to hers on the pillow. His snores were so delicate that they seemed like nothing more than sturdy breathing.

Lala smiled.

*Wow*, she thought. *I'm not sure, but I don't think I feel sick. Maybe I can risk trying to sit up.*

Fifteen minutes later, Lala rose, very tentatively, on her elbows.

*I don't believe it,* she thought. *I think I'm not hungover.*

Lala carefully extracted herself from beneath Petunia's chubby, beagle body. Petunia snorted and turned over on her back, her bent legs stuck up in the air. Lala slipped her feet into the slippers that awaited her on the floor. She stood up and, naked but for the slippers, sauntered toward the kitchen.

The moment, the very instant that Lala's right foot made contact with the tile on her kitchen floor, Petunia and Yootza came barreling around the corner like they were running the Iditarod.

"Ahhhhhhhhhh!" Lala screamed joyfully with comic panic at the onslaught of dogs, as she did every morning.

Petunia and Yootza pranced around in small circles. Lala pulled a covered container of kibble out of the cabinet. As always, Petunia started whining.

"Hush," Lala giggled as she doled out the kibble.

The dogs inhaled their food. Lala flicked on the old CD player sitting atop the counter. A sonorous male voice intoned in a continental accent.

"So, to review, the irregular subjunctive verbs include—"

"*Il faut que je sois . . .*" Lala said. "*Il faut que je puisse . . . Il faut que je sache.*"

Lala looked out the small window in her kitchen. The sky was crystal blue.

"What a gorgeous day," Lala said. She bent down and patted her dogs' foreheads. "Everything. People, everything, is coming up roses for me and for you."

🍷

"*Bonjour, tout le monde!*"

Lala's surging energy almost made her float into the open, welcoming floor plan of offices and conference rooms that was the US outpost of Atelier du Monde. She had walked from her place to the Chelsea location, and the air was crisp without being a bit cold. She had lifted her face to the sun, and, at one point, she almost smashed into a pretzel vendor's cart, but even the near miss with flying rock salt had not dampened her enthusiasm for life.

Everyone who heard her come in smiled at her and waved or spoke a warm greeting. Lala sidled into her chair and turned on her computer. Her desk was impeccable. There was a small, framed photo of Petunia and Yootza next to the phone.

She checked her e-mail and learned that there was going to be a staff meeting at two o'clock. And that the New York partners of the firm had been toying with the idea of instituting a Blue Jean Fridays policy but had scrapped that in favor of letting everyone wear jeans "whenever you lovely people want to."

*What a swell place to work,* Lala thought, smiling.

Lala's cousin's 20-year-old daughter had visited her from

London a few months earlier, and they had gone shopping at Banana Republic. Much to Lala's shock and against the experience of almost three decades of not being able to find a pair of jeans that made her look good—and that she could also stand to wear because they weren't constantly riding up her crack—Ava had picked out a pair that were not only on sale and comfortable, but made Lala look at least ten pounds thinner.

"It's a miracle," Lala gasped when she tried them on. "It's almost unholy what a miracle this is. I'm in a dressing room with a three-paneled mirror and fluorescent lighting, and I don't want to asphyxiate myself. I'm telling you, the devil is involved in this in some capacity."

*I'll wear my new jeans tomorrow,* Lala thought. *And I will sashay my denim-encased tuchus past a certain Gallic Adonis's office on an unending loop until he runs out and grabs my ass and covers it with kisses. What a great day this is already turning out to be. What a great year this is promising to be. What a great life this still might end up being.*

Lala pulled up the document she had been working on for a few weeks. Each page had a photo of one of the exquisite pieces in a collection amassed by a very old, very wealthy woman who lived in Montreal. The pieces were all miniature creations rendered in jaw-dropping detail. Everything in the woman's collection balanced delightfully between majestic and whimsical and no detail of reality was spared. Here was a photo of a teeny little version of the Hall of Mirrors at Versailles. Here was the Oval Office scaled to the size of a cereal box with a correspondingly small, but no less lifelike, replica of President Barack Obama. Then turn the virtual page to find a snapshot of ye olde curio shoppe in Tudor England, no bigger than a laptop.

*Where's my thesaurus?* Lala fretted. *I've got to choose at least thirty other ways to say "adorable" before lunch.*

Suddenly she froze. It had become challenging to breathe. She didn't have to look up to know he was there.

"*Ça va?*" Gérard Courtois, Vice President of Atelier du Monde, asked.

His height really was average. He was in very good shape, but not so muscular that you would want to purse your lips with a bit of patronizing disdain for the assumed oafishness that was unfairly associated with steroid use. His grayish-blond hair was closely cropped, as though he might have just been cast to play Caligula.

Lala thought he was the sexiest man she had met in a very long time. Maybe since Terrence.

"*Ça va très bien. Et toi?*"

*I can't believe we're using the familiar form of "you,"* Lala marveled for the nine millionth time since her boss had suggested they not "stand on the ceremonies" now that she was learning French. *I can freakin' not fathom how to get this stupid grin off my face. He must think I'm possessed.*

"*Très bien.* I love what you've done with the *World of Miniatures* so far. I had no idea there were so many ways to convey 'adorable' in English."

"It's a rich language, isn't it?"

"Very rich."

Gérard paused. Lala searched her brain for something charming to say and found that her library of flirtatious quips had apparently been erased by a wave of sheer lust.

*Damn,* Lala thought. *I got bupkis here.*

"Well."

"Well," Lala echoed.

"I'll let you get back to a Piazza San Marco that could fit in my pocket, shall I?"

"Yup," Lala said, smiling.

Lala watched Gérard's retreating back.

*Is that a famed Venetian public square in your pocket, Lala thought, or are you just happy to see me? Je t'adore,* Gérard. *Je t'adore toujours.*

Lala sat at the sumptuous oak conference table in the corner room. People were just starting to trickle in for the meeting. Next to her was Adele, the office manager, who bore a startling resemblance, at least in Lala's mind, to Gloria Steinem, both physically and in terms of her grace and grit. Adele was the big sister Lala never had. Though they didn't socialize outside the office, Lala was crazy about Adele. Lala hoped, dreamed, doubted that one day she could walk with as much confidence as Adele always did.

The two women stared at the other table in the room, which was decked out for a celebration. In the center of the overflowing display of food stood an excessively large bottle of champagne.

"You really don't know what this meeting is about?"

"I really don't," Adele said. "They didn't even ask me to arrange the catering. Apparently Gérard handled it all himself."

*Wow*, Lala thought. *Could . . . no . . . maybe . . . why not? Will Gérard be making a public declaration of his simmering love for me? A bold announcement? An irresistibly romantic proclamation? One that I wouldn't even think about trying not to succumb to? Immediately, right here on top of this table? Because if that's the case, I'm drinking all that champagne by myself. Wow. Maybe he really is going to . . .*

Lala tilted her head, much the way her beagle Petunia tilted her head when Lala asked her if she was Mama's precious baby girl in a grating singsong voice, and considered the possibility.

*Hey*, Lala thought. *Stranger things have happened.*

The room had filled up, and all twenty or so of Atelier du Monde's New York staff were assembled. Gérard entered with a woman Lala had never seen before.

The woman might have been a few years older than Lala. Or a few years younger. Either way, she looked terrific. She had let her hair go gray. She wore it short and swept dramatically to the side. Her black pants and white top and black and white scarf looked quietly expensive. Her jewelry was minimal, and Lala thought she could hear the earrings and bracelet whispering, in a French accent without condescension or a hint of ego, "If you have to ask, *ma chere*, you can't afford us."

Gérard cleared his throat. Everyone quieted down and gave Gérard and this mystery woman their full attention.

"I'm going to keep this brief because we have a lot of champagne to drink," Gérard began.

Everyone chuckled. The ol' reliable, big, goofy, stupid grin attached itself to Lala's face.

*He is so funny*, she thought. *And so* charmant!

"I would like to introduce you all to Marie-Laure Dermond. We have, after many, many, many months of pleading, spirited her away from *Paris Match*, and she will be our new Director of Marketing. Please join me in welcoming her."

Everyone applauded. Marie-Laure smiled graciously.

"Thank you. Thank you so much," she said. "I am delighted that Gérard has placed his confidence in me, and I am delighted that I will be working with you. Gérard tells me that you are all the best in the business. I hope that I will live up to your excellent examples. Now, enough speeches. Let us get drunk, *oui*?"

"Whoa," Lala whispered to Adele. "My kinda gal."

Everyone stood up from the table and started mingling. Lala and Adele headed for the champagne.

"How is anyone going to get that thing open?" Lala wondered.

Even as she voiced her concern, a handsome young man wearing the uniform of the catering staff came in and strode majestically toward the massive bottle.

"Is he carrying a saber?" Lala asked Adele.

Before Adele could answer, the handsome young man leaned in and wielded the sword like a master duelist.

The lip of the bottle, with the cork intact, split off in a clean break. The room erupted in applause. A geyser of liquid cheerfully bubbled out of the bottle. Lala lunged for a glass and caught as much of the champagne as it would hold.

Lala looked up from her rescue efforts to find Marie-Laure standing beside her with a glass, mirroring Lala's scoop and gulp technique. The champagne stopped spurting, and two other caterers came up to take the bottle away to pour the contents into waiting trays of glasses.

Marie Laure raised her full glass to Lala and winked.

"You are a woman after my own heart," Marie-Laure toasted.

"At the risk of sounding terse, ditto. I'm Lala Pettibone," Lala said, clinking her glass against Marie-Laure's.

"*Merci mille fois. Vous êtes très gentille.*"

"*Vous parlez français?*" Marie-Laure said.

*Damn, God love her and her dictionary-definition of a megawatt smile,* Lala thought.

"Ohhh, *je me débrouille*," Lala said, blushing.

"*Pas du tout. Vous parlez vraiment très bien!*"

"Am I blushing?" Lala asked.

Marie-Laure giggled.

"So, let us start a conversation, shall we? Tell me what I have to say to convince you to join our staff permanently."

Before Lala could gush that she was signing on immediately to work at Atelier du Monde for the rest of her life because they served champagne in elephantine bottles, and because she would be working next to her future husband, and because Marie-Laure was officially her new best friend, and maybe Marie-Laure should start planning Lala's bachelorette party right now, Gérard joined them.

*Note to self,* Lala thought. *Get hypnosis to make these shit-eating grins more manageable.*

Gérard kissed Lala on the cheek.

*I swear, I must look like I'm possessed,* Lala thought.

Gérard kissed Marie-Laure on the cheek. He stood next to Marie-Laure, and the two faced Lala, smiling.

"You have found each other already. I am so glad," Gérard said.

Lala stared at them. The blood in her veins plummeted to the temperature of a Siberian lake. In December.

They were such subtle gestures. Anyone could have missed one or both. Or interpreted either as entirely innocent.

Unless one had majored in theater in college and thus always considered herself a student of the human condition. Or unless one had been a lifelong reader of classic literature about the timeless interaction of souls and thus always considered herself a student of the human condition. Or unless one were madly in love with her boss.

Lala watched Gérard put his arm gently, tenderly, caressingly, and very briefly around Marie-Laure's waist. She watched Marie-Laure respond with equal intensity and brevity by putting her hand on Gérard's shoulder for just a moment.

Lala heard her now frigid blood pounding in her ears. She managed to retain consciousness long enough to realize that Gérard and Marie-Laure were both giving her a quizzical look. She must have been staring at them with the eyes of a lunatic.

"Yes, we found each other," Lala managed to rasp. "This is so exciting. Welcome, Marie-Laure. I wish you an absolutely wonderful, successful . . . adorable . . . time in New York."

Lala paused.

"Okay," Lala gasped. She was finding it hard to fill her lungs. "I don't want to be greedy with your time. Please don't let me keep you from meeting everyone else. We'll continue our discussion later, *oui?*"

Lala wandered, blindly, out into the reception area. She sat down. Many years later, whenever Lala would describe that afternoon, she would say that she had no idea how long she was out there.

"It might have been days for all I knew. I must have lost all sense of time and place because, I swear, I was comprehending jack shit about what was actually going on around me."

Lala stared at her surroundings, entirely unseeing. Somehow, her hand found its way into her pants pocket and grabbed her cell phone. And, apparently, it then dialed Brenda's number, because Lala found herself listening to a ringing sound and then found herself hearing Brenda answer.

Lala began to speak into her phone.

In a normal volume.

At first.

"Hi, Brenda? Can you talk?"

It was when Lala heard Brenda say, yes, she was indeed available to have a conversation with her best friend since high school, that Lala began, gradually at first and then with giddy momentum, to get louder and louder and louder.

"Wanna hear something funny? Gérard has a girlfriend! I think that's hilarious! And get this! My first impression of her is that she's lovely! I swear, my initial thought when I realized what was going on between them was to suggest a three-way."

Everyone except Lala turned to look at Gérard, who wasn't nimble enough to quash the instant raising of his brows and the instant smile that wrapped itself around his mouth when he heard mention of a possible *ménage à trois*.

"Her name is Marie-Laure!" Lala yelped into the phone, oblivious to Gérard's facial thumbs up. "How pretty is that! And there's more! She's not a cliché! She's not a . . ."

Lala swiftly cradled her cell phone between her shoulder and her chin and made air quotation marks.

". . . 'Young bimbo.' She's my age! Ish. So I can't even be pissed at him for being shallow or predictable."

Everyone had exited the conference room as Lala's words grew ever more energetically unglued.

"I had some kind of scenario playing out in my head," Lala blared into her cell phone, "in which Gérard and I had this kind of magical chemistry, and I never once asked myself why he hadn't made a move in ten months because it played into my idea that this was somehow so special that it couldn't be besmirched with actual involvement with each other, and, meanwhile, I'm a complete idiot, and none of what I'm imagining is true. And it's not his fault! He's a great guy. He never led me on. *Il faut que je* get over myself. It was all in my big, stupid head!"

The isolation spell suddenly broke. Lala covered the phone and smiled and nodded toward one of her coworkers, who was looking at her with sympathy and horror.

"It's true. I have a freakishly large head. My late husband, God love him, used to say it's because I have so much brain matter in there because I'm so smart. Which, if that's true, has gotten me exactly nowhere, right? Huh? Right? Because, seriously, it's freak-ish. When we were measuring our *têtes* . . . that's French for heads . . . in high school for the caps and mortars, I'm guilelessly walking around announcing my head was twenty-three inches in circumference like that's something normal, and all my friends are looking at me like I'm a freak because their measurements are like eighteen or twelve or something."

Lala stuck her cell phone up to her mouth and once again blasted into it. Neither of her ears were anywhere near the device.

"Brenda! Brenda, are you still there? Brenda, I can't hear you!"

With preternatural calm, Adele approached Lala. She smiled at her, and Lala smiled back.

"Lala, my dear, to whom are you speaking?"

"Brenda! My best friend!" Lala bellowed.

"How nice. May I say a quick hello to Brenda?"

"I don't think she's still there," Lala shrieked. She handed the phone to Adele.

"Brenda? Hi, Brenda, this is Adele. I'm the office manager here . . . Brenda, are you able to come over? . . . You were thinking of doing exactly that? How nice. Then we're both on the same page. Excellent. We'll see you shortly."

Lala was back at her desk working on the captions for the book of miniatures when Brenda barreled into the office.

Years later, Lala remained unable to recall many of the details of that god-awful afternoon.

"I still have no idea how I got back to my desk. I wish there had been videotape. It might have been interesting to see. I bet I looked funny, wandering over to my desk like I was sleepwalking or something. I might even be able to laugh about it now, after all this time. Probably not. It's probably too soon."

"Hey, Bren'. Whatcha doin' here?"

The rest of the staff hadn't gone back to their desks. Everyone was milling around, waiting to see what was going to happen next, but trying to look like nothing out of the ordinary had occurred that afternoon. Adele strode over and gave Brenda's hand a grateful shake. Gérard was right behind her.

"Brenda, how nice to meet you."

"You must be Adele," Brenda said, eagerly pumping her hand. "I'm so happy to meet you."

"Gérard Courtois," Gérard said.

"Gérard," Brenda gasped. She stared at him in sudden shock that she just as quickly suppressed.

Gérard grabbed Brenda's other hand and for a minute all three of them stood there in an odd kind of handheld circle of desperation and relief.

They all turned to Lala, who had gone back to focusing on her computer screen.

"I'll be with you in a sec, Brenda," Lala mumbled, totally absorbed in a full-screen image of an artist's garret in turn-of-the-century Paris. "Look at that tiny, little easel and that teeny, tiny painting on that tiny, little easel. Are they adorable, or what?"

Adele and Brenda remained silent. Until their great minds came up with a similar idea simultaneously.

Adele started, with Brenda just a moment behind.

"Lala . . ."

"Lala . . ."

"Would you be able to attend a last-minute meeting at the main branch of the library? It's starting in just a few . . ."

"I bumped into an author who was a classmate at college, and he wants to meet with a representative of a French publishing house as soon as possible to discuss a project . . ."

"Oh, wow," Adele and Brenda said.

"Maybe Lala could leave with me right now . . ." Brenda continued.

"And then you could arrange to meet with the author right after the meeting at the library," Adele concluded.

"Perfect!" they both said.

Lala stared at them for many nerve-wracking moments.

"That all sounds great!" she finally said. "Cool! Frankly, I would love to get the fuck out of here for the rest of the day."

Brenda had Lala out of her chair and into the elevator and on the street and into a cab before Lala could change what was left of her mind.

It didn't take but a few blocks of movement for Lala to notice that the taxi was most distinctly not heading uptown from the Chelsea offices of Atelier du Monde. She had been on guard since they had entered the vehicle when Brenda had furtively whispered something to the driver.

"What the fuck is going on?" Lala demanded.

"Why didn't you tell me your boss looks exactly like Terrence?"

"What are you talking about?"

"Please don't do that," Brenda said. "Please don't terrify me by not seeing what is so entirely obvious because, I swear, I do not want to have to make the decision to have you involuntarily committed. Gérard and your late husband could be twins."

Lala chuckled and gave Brenda's shoulder an affectionate swat.

"Stop! That's ridiculous! I don't see it at all."

"You stop. Seriously. They are twins."

Lala shrugged and spoke to Brenda like Brenda was the one who had just spent the entire afternoon going bat crap crazy.

"Okay, okay, don't get upset. Sure. They're twins. If you say so."

🍷

Lala sat stretched out on the loveseat in her living room. She held a mug of tea, and she was covered by a cozy comforter. Her neighbor Pyotr, a lovely gentleman in his early seventies who exuded old world charm, sat reading aloud to Lala in a chair next to the loveseat.

"But for this spectacularly wealthy diva, apparently hundreds of pairs just aren't enough. Take a walk into the shoe closet at her Malibu estate, and you will find . . ."

The front door opened. Pyotr put down the copy of *People Magazine* and helped Brenda unleash the hounds.

"They both peed and pooped," Brenda reported.

"I could have walked them myself," Lala said. "I appreciate all of this, but I think I've weathered the storm."

Pyotr pulled up a chair for Brenda, and they both sat down. The dogs jumped on Lala's lap and were settled and snoring in short order.

"Are you sure?" Brenda asked.

"I'm sure."

"You are sure?" Pyotr said.

"I am. I'll be fine. So go on and get home, both of you, okay? Thank you for worrying. Thank you for being there for me."

Brenda and Pyotr leaned forward and wrapped Lala in their arms.

"Group hug! Group hug!" Brenda declared.

Lala escorted Brenda and Pyotr to the door.

"You sure you'll be okay?" Brenda said.

"Positive. I'm going to get some writing done, and then I'll probably watch a little TV, eat a little something, and get to bed early for a change."

"Good idea," Pyotr said. "I'll let you know what happens at the owners' meeting tonight."

"Oh, shoot, I forgot all about that," Lala said. "We'll go together. It'll be fun."

"No, no, no, no, no, no, no, no," Brenda said. "You just relax for the rest of the day."

"I will inform you of everything that happens at the meeting," Pyotr assured her. "It is not necessary for you to attend. You must relax today."

"Don't be silly," Lala said. "I want to go. Those meetings are always a hoot. It's like, move over, *Melrose Place*, because life at the Bancroft is twice as sassy with half the peroxide. I'm not sure what I mean by that image or if it's even valid in this context, but it sounds clever, no? I'll pick you up at a quarter to eight."

"You are sure?" Pyotr said.

"Absolutely. The distraction'll do me a lot of good."

"Holy shit, Lala, are you okay?"

Lala peered at her upstairs neighbor, who had ambushed her the moment she entered the Bancroft's common room next to the roof garden.

"Hi, Elizabeth. I'm fine."

"Are you sure?"

"Yeeeeees?" Lala said.

"You look exhausted. Are you sure you're not sick?"

"Yeah. I'm sure. Who did the refreshments tonight? There better be some serious alcohol. Not like that bullshit punch last time that had what? Maybe point oh-oh-oh-oh-one percent booze in it?"

Lala made a beeline for the card table against the wall and was relieved to find an assortment of already opened bottles of not-at-all-bad wines. She filled a large plastic cup with Viognier.

*Okay, this is a good omen,* Lala thought. *Maybe my luck really is changing for the better.*

Lala avoided having to engage in additional dialogue about how awful she looked by making sure that her mouth was full of snacks whenever anyone approached her. For dramatic effect and to bring herself a tiny shred of amusement, she would start speaking in response to anything someone said to her, and then instantly pretend she was nearly choking because the inconsiderate person had forced her to try to converse while she was shoving food in her maw. Which, of course, necessitated gulping down big swallows of wine and refilling her cup so she could save her own life by administering a kind of liquid Heimlich to herself. Which, of course, meant Lala was well on the way to being seriously potted by the time the co-op board president entered the room and called the meeting to order.

Lala had a sudden memory of the other time that day she had witnessed a man getting the attention of a roomful of people to make an announcement, but, mercifully, she shook it off before she could do anything crazier than drink with more urgency.

*Stay calm,* she told herself. *Remain unagitated. Semper serene. Everything's going to be fine. Tomorrow is another day. Tomorrow is, in fact, the first day of the rest of your life. This wine is really not bad at all . . .*

Richard Sweetzer, the perennial shoo-in candidate for board president because no one else wanted to put up with that much crap, stood at the front of the room. He put the tips of his fingers together and leaned his chin into his hands as though in prayer. He gazed downward and spoke without lifting his head.

"God. I . . . Oh, I don't even . . ." he groaned.

Richard raised his eyes toward the ceiling, apparently unable to look at anyone directly. A current of nervous anticipation ran through the gathered owners.

"Look, there's no easy way to put this, so I'm just going to say it. Apparently the basement of our building is a quagmire of asbestos. It's pretty much gone nuclear. It's like a huge-ass Petri dish downstairs, and there is some seriously funky shit growing. Right now. Even as we speak. And I don't know how this happened, so there's no point in asking. Everything in the basement is off-limits until further notice. It's going to cost each unit at least forty thousand dollars to get us out of this mess. I'll need your checks by the end of next week."

No one moved. It seemed that even the breathing in the room

had stopped. Silence hung over the assembly until Lala's guttural wail pierced the air.

"What the fuck? Are you fucking kidding me? Fuck!"

Sleep was out of the question, even given how drunk Lala already was by the time Pyotr escorted her back to her place after the meeting. No amount of wine was going to still the voices in her head.

Lala curled up on the couch with Petunia and Yootza. The dogs' steady presence and rhythmic snoring comforted her a bit. She kept the TV on Comedy Central, and she dozed until her temp agency had opened for the day.

"Rick, I need to make forty thousand dollars as soon as possible, but definitely by next week. Prostitution, high class or otherwise, is definitely not out of the question."

"I'm already on it."

Rick's cheerful voice on the other end of the line, while clearly intended to be supportive, made Lala scrunch up her face.

"You already knew I wasn't going back to the Atelier?"

"Adele called just a few minutes ago. She said you were a gem, and they were all so sorry to see you go. If I buy you drinks, will you tell me what happened?"

"It'll have to be a lot of drinks."

"I'll call you as soon as I have something. I assume you don't want to go back to word processing?"

*Barf,* Lala thought.

"I'll take the most lucrative slot you've got. Prostitution included. And I'm available any hour of the day or night."

Lala sprawled out on the couch for another two hours. She debated eating breakfast. She debated going to the gym. She debated going back to bed. Then all the debating made her head hurt, so she closed her eyes and listened to the voices on the television. Finally, she'd had enough of her motionless confusion and despair.

*I better get my tuchus off this couch and do something positive,* she thought.

Lala took Petunia and Yootza for a long walk, pausing every couple of blocks to crouch on her heels and pet the two dogs and coo in their ears that Mama loved them and Mama would always be there to take care of them and to love them forever and ever. Whenever she stopped to fuss, Lala got teary and the dogs, picking up instantly on her bizarre energy, made a concerted effort to flee.

"Mama loves you so enormously and constantly much, my precious babies . . . Damn, Yootza, quit jerking on the leash," Lala grunted.

After she took the dogs back home and gave them a snack, Lala walked uptown to the Bide-a-Wee no-kill animal shelter where she had been volunteering for years. When she entered the lobby, she found one of her fellow volunteers, Sally, behind the desk. Sally was a fun, young gal with multiple piercings that Lala affectionately deemed "rather excessive," and Lala was quite fond of her. On that day, Sally had her head face down on the desk, and she was whimpering and sniffling quietly.

It was not the first time Lala had arrived to volunteer only to find Sally in this pitiable condition.

"Oh, no," Lala said. She scurried behind the desk and pulled up a chair to sit next to Sally. She put her arm around Sally's slumped shoulders.

"I'm okay," Sally mumbled.

It came out, "Mmm keh."

"Please, don't speak," Lala said. "I won't be able to understand a word you're saying, and that will irritate me enormously. Please tell me your asshat of a boyfriend hasn't done something douchey again."

"Nawh iss cuh cahn—" Sally began.

"Oy, such a rhetorical statement I just made," Lala said. "I thought that was obvious. Come on, sit up straight."

Sally obeyed. Lala grabbed a tissue and gently wiped Sally's face. She held the tissue to Sally's nose.

"Blow," Lala said. Sally obeyed.

"Good. Now we're going to go to the back, and we're going to find some puppies and kittens to hug, okay?"

"'Kay," Sally said.

"And then we're going to find some old dogs and cats to hug, right?"

"Right," Sally said.

"And then I'm going to take you out to lunch and remind you that you are smart and beautiful and talented, and you deserve much better than that asshat of a boyfriend."

Lala and Sally took a long lunch after spending a solid hour covering animals of all ages and sizes with loud, smacking kisses. Lala ordered bruschetta as soon as they sat down at the restaurant.

"We'll be here for a while," she announced to Sally. "What's Bide-a-Wee gonna do? Fire us?"

The two women laughed and sniffled through a shared pasta dish and three desserts. Lala told Sally about what had happened at Atelier du Monde, at least as much as she remembered. Sally said, "Yikes," a lot and kept assuring Lala that there was a great man waiting out there for her somewhere.

"You know what?" Sally said. "I bet you're way older than my mother because you make references to things that she wasn't around for like President Carter and stuff, but you don't even look old at all. You look really hot. And I'm not just saying that because I feel so sorry for you because of those humiliating things that happened with that French guy. You are seriously a babe, Lala."

"You're making me blush," Lala said. She pursed her lips in a very pleased, little grin. "P.S. I'm not sure if I should consider your enthusiasm a backhanded compliment or forehanded insult."

"Really, I've got a good feeling," Sally said. "I bet you're gonna find some great guy, and he's gonna fall madly in love with you. I think today is gonna be the beginning of a great new life for you."

"God, I hope you're right," Lala sighed.

# It's Always Darkest

When Lala walked home later that day, she was not alone.

She was not accompanied, as Sally might have imagined, by a handsome man who had come to the shelter to adopt a pet and who had ended up finding the woman of his dreams.

Lala was accompanied by a dog who looked older than his age. She gazed down at the greyhound walking so calmly and trustingly beside her.

*You sweet boy,* Lala thought.

Lala hadn't realized she had chosen to make one of her several days per week of volunteering at Bide-a-Wee the same day a transport of racing greyhounds, rescued from a Mexican dog track, arrived.

The moment she laid eyes on the dog she immediately christened Chester, she started calculating how much more she would have to earn to care for three dogs instead of two.

*I don't care,* Lala thought. *He's mine.*

Victor, Lala's favorite doorman, held the doors for her as she approached the Bancroft.

"Look whatchu got!" Victor said. Victor was a small, older man with a round, perpetually happy face, and Lala adored him.

"Chester, meet Victor, one of my favorite people," Lala said.

Victor rubbed Chester's head, and Chester leaned into Victor's hand and looked like he was smiling.

"Victor, can you do me a big favor? Can you go up and get the kids and bring them down, so I can introduce them to their new brother on neutral territory?"

"'Course," Victor said.

When he came back to the lobby a few minutes later, Petunia and Yootza were straining at their leashes. The dogs ran up to Chester and a three-way sniff-fest ensued. No growls. No bared teeth even. Just lots of sniffing.

"I'm thinking 'match made in heaven,'" Lala said. She beamed at the dogs and Victor distributed ample pats to all three.

Lala exited the building holding the three leashes. The dogs fell into a comfortable stride as a pack from their first steps outside together.

*Wow,* Lala thought. *Is my luck changing?*

Lala looked up at the sky.

*I mean for the better,* Lala silently informed the fates, heavens, universe, something. *In case that's not immediately obvious,* she added.

They walked for many blocks on all of Lala's favorite streets. They probably didn't cover more than a mile, but the walk took nearly two hours. Because every inch of sidewalk and all items on the sidewalk or adjacent to it had to be thoroughly inspected by her beasts.

People smiled at Lala and her brood as she stood patiently next to a short iron fence that was being covered with the vigorous inhalations of three very happy snouts.

"Hounds," Lala said, nodding to the dogs' admirers. "It's all about the nose."

The dogs did pick up the pace as they turned back in the direction of the Bancroft. It was close to dinnertime.

"It's funny," Lala said to them as they trotted, "without design or planning, I've ended up with three hound dogs. I like that. The nose knows."

When Lala opened the door to her apartment, the red light on her answering machine was blinking. She smacked the playback button.

"Honey, it's Rick. Don't freak out."

*Barf,* Lala thought. *Why haven't I gotten rid of that stupid machine? Why do I still have a stupid landline?*

"Crawford Dunlap is delighted to have you back."

Lala felt her breath getting choppy, and her face getting flushed.

"Deep breaths, okay?" Rick said. "They'll pay you thirty bucks an hour. And you don't have to start until ten o'clock. Okay?"

That night was not as bad as Lala thought it was going to be. She didn't sleep at all, but being in bed with three contented dogs who seemed to have known each other forever was a big comfort. Lala lay on her back and listened to them all snoring.

*Precious babies,* Lala thought. *It's going to be okay. Everything is going to be okay.*

Lala had her eyes wide open when the alarm went off at seven o'clock. And, before she knew what was happening, she started projectile sobbing.

She gulped and gasped and tried not to choke. The dogs' heads all shot up, and they were awake and on full alert in an instant. Lala couldn't bring herself to lift her head to stop the tears from flowing backward into her nose and mouth.

"Don't be scared, babies," she sobbed. "Mama's just having a little bit of a rough time. Everything is going to be okay, I promise."

Somehow she got herself to the kitchen to feed the dogs, and somehow she got herself on the couch, and at some point she ran out of tears. Lala sat there for a few minutes, reminding herself that the dogs had to be walked, but she was unable to move. Until she heard the unmistakable sound of someone peeing in the hallway.

Lala leapt off the couch. She ran to the front door and saw Yootza with his leg lifted.

"Mama's sorry," Lala wailed. "Mama's a bad mama."

Lala rushed to get them all leashed and out the door. Once in the open air, all maternal shortcomings seemed to have been forgotten. Petunia, Yootza, and Chester stared up at Lala with clear adoration.

"Stop being so kind and forgiving," Lala whispered. "You'll

break my heart."

When they got back to the apartment, the dogs amiably staked out their new napping territories to divide the available space in thirds that had before been halved. Yootza and Chester landed next to each other on the couch, while Petunia snuggled close to Lala on the loveseat.

*I should go to the gym,* Lala thought. *There's enough time before I have to go to . . .*

She put her head down on Petunia's tummy and tried to not start sobbing again.

Lala stayed there, not crying and not moving, until the last moment she could wait to take a shower and not be late for work. Petunia seemed to enjoy having Lala's face on top of her. She slept contentedly and only stirred a bit when Lala finally got up.

Lala shuffled through the lobby of the Bancroft. Victor was working that morning.

"You okay?" Victor asked.

"Appearances notwithstanding, I'm doing great," Lala reassured him. "Victor, would you be able to—"

"I would love to walk the pups," Victor said.

"God, what would I do without you? But you have to let me pay you this time."

"No."

"You have to."

"No."

"You must."

"No."

"I insist. Please."

"No."

"Victor, your kindness will make me cry."

"Don't do that," Victor said. "Don't cry."

There was absolutely none of the usual bounce in Lala's gait as she walked to midtown. The word processing center of Crawford Dunlap was on its own floor in one of the dozens of soaring office buildings that surrounded Grand Central Station.

*Just don't cry,* Lala kept thinking as the elevator made its way skyward. *You won't always feel this uncomfortable in your skin. You won't always feel so lost. Because this level of angst and* Weltschmerz *would be fucking impossible to sustain. Think of all the things for which you can be grateful. A lifelong appreciation of good grammar, for example, and to name just one.*

The elevator stopped on the twenty-seventh floor, and Lala exited. There were closed doors at either end of the elevator bank. The atmosphere immediately reminded Lala of that chamber the guy got trapped inside in *2001: A Space Odyssey* because the computer had gone nuts.

*I am so fucked,* Lala thought.

Lala pushed the button on the visual intercom next to one of the doors. The lights on the screen crackled alive, and Lala saw the face of Claire Stevenson, a reed-thin whippersnapper who was a good bit younger than Lala. And the person Lala would be reporting to, as she had in the past when she worked at Crawford Dunlap. Because Claire ran the show there.

Claire loved running the show there.

Lala saw on the screen that Claire was looking at her watch.

*What?* Lala thought. *I'm maybe three minutes late? So I'll fill out my timesheet accordingly. Sheesh. This is so fucked.*

"Hi Lalaaaaaaa," Claire's voice droned over the intercom.

The door buzzed, and Lala shoved it open. She entered a vast beehive of cubicles separated by transparent dividers. Employees were hunched over their computers.

*Smother me,* Lala thought. *Grab a pillow and put me out of my misery. Please. Somebody.*

Claire came striding out of her office, which was one of a few indented into the walls of the hive. It was a tiny space, and whenever Lala had been forced to enter it in the past, she immediately felt suffocated. Claire's office was filled with Claire's overarching pride in her position. There was a sign on the door that read "Claire Stevenson, Daytime Workflow Coordinator." It had clearly not been issued by the firm. Clearly, someone had created and printed it themselves.

*Comic Sans, bold,* Lala thought. *Could there be a more irritating font?*

"Nice to see you again," Claire singsonged.

"Thanks for having me back," Lala said.

"Come on over here. You'll be sitting next to Kim. I don't think you two have met. I don't think Kim was working with us the last time you temped for us, Lala."

A young woman with very long, black hair peered at Lala. She was wearing a deeply plunging shirt and very, very, very tight black pants. The inappropriateness of the outfit was hidden by a large black blazer. The overall effect was one of calculated sluttiness at its finest.

Kim and Lala would be sitting at desks that were facing each other. There was a divider separating the desks, but even if it hadn't been see-through, it wasn't nearly tall enough to allow any sense of division.

*Sweet mother of God,* Lala thought.

"Hi," Lala said.

"Hey," Kim said.

"Okayyyyy," Claire said. "Go ahead and get logged in, and I'll send you a job right away."

"Great, thanks," Lala said.

*I suspect my face looks like I just caught a powerful whiff of old gym socks,* Lala thought.

Lala turned on the computer at her desk. Her old log-in for the firm still worked.

*Damn,* she thought. *There is something very barfy about that in terms of the energy of the universe. The Law of Attraction is definitely dicking with me.*

Lala clicked on the network that distributed jobs to the word processing worker bees. There was a job already assigned to her. It was marked "Highest Priority." The instructions included a PDF of a handwritten document that was to be input. As soon as possible. Lala clicked on the PDF, and it appeared on her screen.

It was ninety-three pages of complete gobbledygook. Much of it in the form of charts that had arrows all over pointing to words within phrases within sentences to be inserted who knows where, and who knows in what sequence.

Lala stared at the screen. She didn't know what to do. All kinds of impulses ran through her mind as possible options.

Run.

Shout obscenities.

Flail her arms.

Sob uncontrollably.

Run out of the hive, shouting obscenities and flailing her arms as she sobbed uncontrollably.

Lala printed the PDF, set it on her typing stand, and pulled up a blank document on her screen.

*Let's just stay calm and take this one word at a time,* she thought.

Lala stared at the handwritten pages.

*Cleveland?* she thought. *Does that say Cleveland? Or does it say Cruilunt? November? What number is that supposed to be?*

Lala had hit only a few tentative keyboard strokes when her concentration was interrupted.

"So you're a temp?" Kim said.

"Yup," Lala said. She looked up briefly and smiled, then returned to the screen.

"You like it?" Kim asked.

"Oh, yeah. It is just amazingly wonderful being a temp," Lala said. She nodded without looking up.

"Flexible, I bet, right?"

"Uh huh."

"You live near here?"

"Village."

"Cool! Wow! It's expensive down there, I bet, right?"

"Oh, yeah."

Lala squinted at the writing and typed whatever made anything close to any kind of sense and braced herself for the next riposte.

"I live in Queens," Kim said.

"Mmmm."

*Sheesh,* Lala thought. *Put me in a hair shirt. Whip me with a cat-o'-nine-tails. Make the experience complete.*

There was a pause. And then it went on a bit longer. And then a bit longer after that.

*Oh, thank goodness,* Lala thought.

She allowed her shoulders to descend from her ears just a

touch.

"You have to talk to me," Kim said.

Lala looked up at her.

"Sorry?"

"You're supposed to talk to me."

"I'm . . . what?"

"You're supposed to entertain me."

Lala looked around the room. No one else seemed to have taken notice of the lunacy that Kim was hurling toward her.

*Am I being punked?* Lala thought. *Is bantering with Sausage Casing McGillicudy suddenly part of my job description?*

"Uhhhh . . . It's just that I'm on a rush and the handwriting is . . . I'm not entirely sure it's in English . . . I wish we could chat, but I'm afraid I need all my focus right now to get this job done."

Kim sneered and silently huffed. Lala gave her a big smile and went back to her screen.

Throughout the rest of the morning, Lala felt Kim's eyes on her at regular intervals. Lala refused to look up. She refused to get up from her desk to fetch a cup of tea or to go to the ladies' room. It became a point of pride for her to not give Kim any opening whatsoever for even a syllable of conversation.

And then it was almost two o'clock, and Lala typed the last period in the god-forsaken document she had created from the god-forsaken scribbles of Anthony Spaulding, partner in the litigation department. And still Kim had not left her desk to go to lunch. Lala's stomach was starting to growl. Loudly.

*Oh God,* Lala thought.

More on survival instinct than from an actual plan, Lala jumped out of her chair, grabbed her purse, and sprinted to Claire's office.

"Hi, I just sent in that job. I think I'll take lunch now."

Claire looked at her watch and frowned.

*What?* Lala thought. *Is this China? The oppressive regime is not going to allow me a break to eat?*

"Okaaaaay," Claire sighed. "When will you be back?"

"In an hour," Lala said. She tried to unclench her teeth.

At the doorway to Claire's office, Lala looked around the hive to see if there was another exit that wouldn't take her past Kim's desk. But it was too late. Kim appeared right in front of her, as though conjured by a malevolent wizard.

"You going to lunch?"

"I'm . . . it's . . ."

"Let's go together!"

"Ohhh, I wish we could, but I promised I would take my mother shopping for orthopedic shoes. Rain check?"

Kim frowned.

"Okay. Tomorrow."

It wasn't a question.

"Right. Absolutely. Looking forward to it."

Lala shot out of the elevator when its doors opened at lobby level. She thrust herself out of the revolving doors and once outside, gasped for air.

*OmigodOmigod,* she thought. *OmigodOmigod. OmigodOmigod.*

Lala looked skyward.

*I'm sorry I used you to fib, Mom,* she thought. *But there is only so much I can take. I suspect you understand.*

Lala cut over to Fifth Avenue and started walking uptown. She figured she would find a coffee shop somewhere to get an egg salad on rye.

The day was cool and comfortable. The sky was once again that clear and brilliant shade of blue that Lala loved so much. Lala noticed all of this intellectually, but she felt no joy on a visceral level.

*Omigod, Omigod, Omigod!*

She kept walking. It felt good to be on the move, and after a few blocks Lala forgot any need or even desire to eat. She reached the southern edge of Central Park and headed west to Broadway. After walking back downtown, she ended up in the lobby of the building housing Crawford Dunlap just a few minutes shy of an hour after she had bolted out of the place.

"Oh, you're back," Claire said. She looked at her watch. Lala fought an overwhelming desire to flip Claire the bird via the intercom screen. "I need to talk to you. Come to my office, please."

*Jesus,* Lala thought.

Kim looked up eagerly when Lala entered the hive.

"How was your mom's—"

"Sorry. Claire has summoned me."

"Ohhhhh," Kim said.

Lala stood in the doorway waiting for Claire to get off the phone.

"No . . . No, it's not acceptable . . . Jerry, I'm a businesswoman . . . That's right . . . Well, you better."

Claire put the receiver down and motioned for Lala to enter the sanctum.

"Why don't you shut the door?" she said.

Lala did, and then sat down in one of the two very uncomfortable chairs across from Claire's desk. Claire sighed.

"There were several issues with the document you created."

"Oh?" Lala said.

"In the future, if you have a problem reading anything, please send an instant message to me, and I will contact the attorney. Please do not contact the attorney directly."

"I'll be sure to do that," Lala said.

"Anthony was not pleased. Apparently he wrote 'felt badly,' and you typed 'felt bad.' If you couldn't read what he wrote, you should have contacted me."

Lala stared at Claire.

*Seriously, I'm being punked, right?* she thought.

"Okay, in that specific case, as opposed to all the other arrogantly illegible writing, I was in fact able to read what he wrote. 'Felt badly' is incorrect."

Claire raised an eyebrow.

"No, it's not," she said.

*Oh, honey, seriously?* Lala thought. *That much snotty superiority when you are in fact a moron? Seriously?*

"Well, if he meant that he was touching something, and he was doing a substandard job of it, then, yes, 'felt badly' was correct. But I really don't think that's what he was intending to convey. 'Bad' is an adjective. 'Badly' is an adverb."

"Anthony is a partner. He knows what words are. And there was another issue. Anthony had written 'my partners' and I's' and you typed 'my partners' and my.'"

Lala felt a sudden and very welcome sense of calm wash over her.

*Wow,* she thought. *Where'd that come from?*

Lala enjoyed spending the next few moments weighing her next line.

Claire, go fuck yourself?

Claire, you're a moron?

Claire, Anthony is a moron?

Claire, please get in touch with Anthony, and tell him I said he should go fuck himself?

Lala looked back at Claire to find that Claire was surveying her with a tight smile of triumph.

*That's it,* Lala thought. *I'm done.*

She stood.

"Claire, I think I have food poisoning. I must have eaten something bad at lunch. So rather than puke all over your desk, I'm going to head home, 'kay?"

Lala didn't wait for an answer. She was halfway to freedom when Kim appeared before her like a cloud of smoke.

"Jeez, it is unnerving how you do that," Lala said.

"Are you in trouble?" Kim whispered.

"Well, unless you can write me a check for forty thousand dollars right now, technically, yeah, I am way up shit creek without any paddles in sight. But I kinda feel good right now, so I'm goin' with that. Adios."

Lala waved a cheerful goodbye to the guards sitting behind the reception desk in the lobby. She skipped out of the revolving doors and looked around at her beautiful city.

*What a gorgeous day,* she thought. *Wow. You know, sometimes you really do just have to say, who gives a fuck.*

Lala fished her cell phone out of her purse and dialed the number for the temp agency. She was connected to Rick's line, and she got his voicemail.

"Rick, I love you, and I'm really sorry about what I just did. I swear, I'll make it up to you someday, somehow. I know I have to make money, and I know I don't know how I'm going to do that, but I am certain of one thing. If I go back to Crawford Shithole, I will do something crazy. I'm not sure what. But it will be very crazy. So in the long run, Rick, I think I'm doing you a big favor by not putting you and your agency in danger of being on the receiving end of all kinds of lawsuits for negligence."

Lala stopped to pick up an egg salad sandwich on the way home. The dogs were snoring on the bed together and didn't get up when Lala opened the front door.

Lala stood in the doorway of her bedroom and smiled.

*I am so lucky to have those three precious ones,* Lala thought.

She put the food in the refrigerator for later and went back into the bedroom to check her e-mail. One of the subject lines immediately grabbed her attention.

*Omigod Omigod,* Lala thought.

Lala had spent the past winter writing a new screenplay. It was a character-driven drama that took place one summer in Cape Cod. The protagonist was a widow in her forties who had a mad crush on a celebrated author, and, by magical twists of fate, the author was also spending the summer in Cape Cod, where the protagonist had retreated after the breakup of a masochistic love affair.

Anyone who knew Lala knew that the character of the author in her screenplay was a thinly-disguised version of Lala's favorite contemporary novelist, Jackson Platt.

"If Alexandre Dumas *père* were still alive, I would have a crush on him for writing *The Count of Monte Cristo*. But he's not, so I have a crush on Jackson Platt for writing *A Map Without Latitude*," Lala often commented to Brenda.

Lala had grown to love the characters in her screenplay as old friends. Lala had titled her work *Dressed Like a Lady, Drinks Like a Pig*.

"No, no, it's not a film version of any of my short stories," Lala explained to Brenda. "I just really like that title, so I figured I might as well get some use out of it."

*Dressed Like a Lady, Drinks Like a Pig* was the subject line of the e-mail that grabbed Lala's attention that day in the week following the Ides of March. The e-mail was from a fellow Wesleyan graduate who was a literary manager in Los Angeles. Lala hadn't known Kelly Franklin Adams at school because she was several years younger than Lala. She'd found Kelly's name and contact information on the alumni page of Wesleyan's website. After contacting Kelly with a query letter, Kelly had responded with several questions about Lala's background.

"The subtext of which," Lala told Brenda, "is you graduated when? Why don't you already have representation? Why haven't you had representation for decades already?"

Lala answered as best she could, trying to convey that she was a late bloomer with, she hoped, lots of potential, without actually writing those words. She had gone for a warm and positive tone in her second e-mail, and Kelly responded in kind. Their subsequent e-mails were increasingly cordial, especially when Lala slipped in mention of her rescued dogs, and Kelly wrote back that she had a rescued fourteen-year-old Pomeranian she absolutely adored.

Which is why Lala was so surprised when, during their one phone conversation, she had found Kelly to be surpassingly strident. But, as much as that had dampened Lala's sense that this was a match made in heaven, she had eagerly e-mailed Kelly a PDF of *Dressed Like a Lady, Drinks Like a Pig* as a preliminary step in seeing if they could build a professional relationship.

And now Lala was looking at the name of her screenplay in the subject line of an e-mail from a literary manager in Los Angeles.

*Omigod,* Lala thought. *Could my luck really be changing?*

Lala looked up at the ceiling of her bedroom.

*For the better, I mean.*

As Lala prepared to open the e-mail, she pantingly imagined a life of making a living as a writer. A life that might be close to being hers.

*Maybe Kelly can sell my screenplay,* Lala thought. *For forty thousand dollars or something. Over this weekend. That would be amazing. It'll be the first of many sales. And I'll take Rick out to dinner when I'm not writing very successful screenplays or going to premieres or dating fabulous men, and thank him for everything, and tell him I won't need to word process again, ever. God, I hate that I just used "word process" as a verb.*

"I'm two-thirds of the way through your screenplay, and I'm

sorry to say it's just not working for me . . ." Lala read.

Lala's eyes began to dart all over the words of the long e-mail. She tried to control their movements, but she couldn't.

". . . one-dimensional characters . . ."

". . . unbelievable events and coincidences leading to a cheesy ending . . ."

". . . I really wanted to like this, but I'm afraid it's not something that I can be excited about. Please understand that this is a completely subjective response. Writing isn't calculus. There are no right or wrong answers, and someone else may love this script."

❦

"I'm not kidding, Lala," Brenda screamed. "I will kick this goddamn door down if you don't open it right now! Do you hear me?"

*Everyone on this floor can hear you,* Lala thought. *People on the floor above us can probably hear you.*

"Right now, Lala! Right this second, you understand me?"

Lala opened the door and Brenda stormed in.

"Goddamn it," Lala said lifelessly. "How did you get up here without someone buzzing me? Because I would have told them to send you home if they had buzzed me."

"Think about it, genius. Victor has seen you leave the building to walk the dogs, right?" Brenda demanded. "So, he's seen how shitty you look, right? Seriously, you look like shit. I don't mean that as a criticism. So, of course Victor let me up because everyone's worried about you, goddamn it!"

"Goddamn it, you're all overreacting. I'm fine," Lala muttered. She sat back down on the couch with her dogs. "I think the tea on the stove is still hot. Help yourself."

Brenda returned to the living room with two full mugs. She handed one to Lala.

"Thanks," Lala said, not taking her eyes off the TV screen. "Can I tell you something? This show is amazing. And I frankly rue all the years I haven't been watching it. If Netflix has the entire *The Young and the Restless* oeuvre on DVD, I know what I'll be doing for the rest of the month. Look at this guy. Is he chewing gum?

He's trying to look like a badass. What is he doing with his mouth? Is he chewing gum, or is it just that actor trying to look like a badass by doing that weird thing with his mouth?"

Brenda wasn't going to look at the TV, but out of the corner of her eye she caught a glimpse of the screen.

"Wow, that is weird," Brenda said. "Never mind him! I refuse to let you distract me from what I came to say. You are clearly not capable of taking care of yourself right now and—"

"What makes you say that?" Lala said, still staring at the bizarre actor.

"You haven't returned any of my phone calls—"

"I e-mailed you. What's the big deal?"

"You look like shit and—"

"Jesus. Enough with that already. I've looked better before, I'll admit that. Hopefully I'll look better again one day. What's the big deal?"

"Lala!" Brenda screamed. "You told me in your last e-mail that the idea of never, ever, ever, ever leaving your apartment again held a certain hermit-esque appeal for you."

*Barf,* Lala thought. *I hate it when those subconscious cries for help sneak out.*

"Yeah, okay. So?" she said.

"So I've discussed all of this with Aunt Geraldine and—"

"What? Why did you worry her?"

"Because she loves you, and she would want to know what's going on with you!" Brenda screamed.

Lala sucked her lips inward until it hurt. She glared at Brenda and made a silent pledge to the death not to cry.

"I'm fine. I'll be fine."

She could barely get the words out without sobbing.

"Lala, I know you'll be fine. But why can't you let us help you be fine sooner?"

Lala knew if she said anything else, it would be impossible not to cry. Brenda seemed to know it too.

"Don't get upset, okay?" Brenda said. "I paid the assessment to the co-op board."

"Jesus," Lala whispered.

"Don't get upset."

"I'll pay you back."

"Why can't you just let me pay for it? I have the money, and you're my best friend. I know you would do the same for me."

"I'll pay you back. I'll do it as soon as I possibly can. I'll work night and day until I pay you back."

"I knew you were going to say that."

Chester the greyhound grunted and let out a very noisy burp. Lala patted his tummy.

"Do your dogs sleep through every major trauma in your life?"

"Pretty much, yeah," Lala said.

"Okay, so listen. I knew you were going to insist on paying me back, so Aunt Geraldine and I figured out a way that you could maybe do that and not go off the deep end word processing all the time."

Lala's raised one eyebrow. The lump in her throat, for the moment, lost its bullying hold over her.

"Really?"

"Yeah. There's one catch though."

"It involves high class prostitution? I don't think I have a problem with that. There is very little that I'm above at this stage of my life. I can't think of anything offhand."

"No. No blowing old men for money. Aunt Geraldine and I think it might be refreshing for you to get of town for a bit. And you know how much she would love to enjoy your company for an extended stay, so we were thinking that it might be a great idea all around if you—"

Lala leapt to her feet.

"Are you fucking kidding me?" she shrieked.

Brenda ignored her and gazed admiringly at the still-sleeping dogs.

"Wow. That's going to come in really handy for them in earth-quake country."

"Aunt Geraldine's fourplex is in Manhattan Beach!"

"Yes, I know where it is, but we think—"

"Manhattan Beach is not in New York! It's in Southern-fuck-ing-California!"

"Yes, I know, but—"

"I am not leaving my beloved Manhattan for a town that has shamelessly appropriated the name of my beloved Manhattan!"

"Stop shouting!" Brenda screamed. "Look, think about it. Maybe it's a good idea to have a change of scenery."

"Sure! A change to Paris! Not to Southern fucking . . ."

Lala stopped raving. The throat-centered bundle of tears suddenly held sway once again.

"Paris," she whispered. "Ohhhh, Gérard. Gérard, *pourquoi tu ne m'aimes pas?*"

"Lala, listen to me. You can rent out your apartment as a hotel alternative. There are websites for that. You can make major bucks doing it. And you can live rent-free with Aunt Geraldine because she said she has enough money for her next three lifetimes. You'll do that for, y'know, however long it takes until you get back on your feet."

"But it's in Southern fucking—" Lala began to yell.

Brenda grabbed her by the shoulders and shook her violently.

"Shut up and listen! No. More. Word. Processing."

Lala grabbed Brenda's arms and held them still so that they could no longer rattle her to the core. Lala and Brenda stood together as motionless as sumo wrestlers for several moments.

"Wow," Lala finally said. "Okay. There's actually no way I can deny that that would be great."

"See," Brenda said. "The sun *will* come out tomorrow." She winked. "That's very nearly a given in Southern California."

"Wait. Wait, wait, wait. How'm I going to rent out an apartment in a building with Three Mile Island downstairs?"

Brenda snorted. "You live in the Village. No one gives a shit how toxic your basement is."

# EAT HER DUST, DODGE

Brenda insisted on buying Lala a first-class ticket to LAX.

"Shut up. Okay? It's your birthday and Christmas present for the next two years, okay? Sheesh."

Brenda also insisted on arranging for a private car service to drive Lala from LAX to Geraldine's place in Manhattan Beach.

"Shut up already. Sheesh," Brenda said. "What're you gonna do? Rent a car and drive yourself? You drive for shit. You always have."

"I'll take a shuttle bus," Lala sniffed with wounded pride. "It's cheaper. I can pay for it myself. I can charge it."

"It'll take like five years to get there on a shuttle because they'll stop at like five million other places before they finally drop you off. So the private car is your birthday present for two years from now, okay? Sheesh."

Brenda also insisted on arranging and paying for a pets-only airline to lovingly transport Petunia, Yootza, and Chester to their new temporary home.

"No!" Lala shrieked. "It's a bad idea! Puppies won't like traveling! Puppies have never flown before! Puppies won't like it!"

"Shut up!" Brenda screamed. "Stop screaming! I checked it out! It's great! We'll bring them to the airport together! Puppies will love it!"

Brenda and her husband Frank, a thin, balding man a few years older than Brenda whose reserved air belied any association with the massive, dramatic Neapolitan family he had grown up in, rented a minivan so Lala could sit in the back with her dogs while they drove to LaGuardia Airport. Brenda knew Lala would be crying the entire trip.

"Mama will see her babies tomorrow," Lala sobbed. She buried her face in each of the dog's necks, going from one to the other to the other in rapid succession, looking like a dashboard bobble-head statue. "Don't be afraid, babies. It's going to be okay. Mama loves you. Mama will see you tomorrow. Mama is not abandoning you. We're traveling so we can all be together without Mama going crazy from trying to make money as a word slave. An attorney once called me that! As a joke! He thought it was funny! Because I was his word serf. His word minion. His keyboard sycophant. His data entry servant. His office temp toady who had to—"

"I think they get it," Brenda said. "Turn here, Frank."

"How many times have I been to LaGuardia?" Frank muttered. "I know how to get there."

"I'm explaining it to them because it's important to explain things to your pets, so they don't get confused or feel scared," Lala explained to Brenda.

"I understand," Brenda said. "You've been explaining it to them since we crossed the bridge. They get it."

Lala, Brenda, and Frank each held the leash of one of the dogs as they wound their way through the crowds at the terminal where Precious Pets on Planes had its welcoming lounge. Many of the people in the terminal smiled and cooed and admired the dogs.

"I wish they would stop doing that," Brenda whispered to Frank, pulling him to walk ahead of Lala and Yootza. "She'll go completely crazy at some point if too many people remind her how cute her dogs are."

"I heard that!" Lala yelled from behind them.

"There's the lounge," Frank said. "Lala! Look! Lounge!"

"I know what you're doing, Frank," Lala said. "And thank God you're distracting me because I'll go crazy if I think about how precious my babies are."

A smiling young woman wearing a pilot's uniform was standing at the doorway to the lounge. She saw the dogs approaching and got down on her heels.

"Who is adorable?" she purred.

"She seems very nice," Lala whispered to Frank.

"One of my colleagues uses this service all the time. They're top-notch," Frank said.

"I can never thank you both enough for doing this," Lala said, her voice trembling.

"Shut up and do not start crying," Brenda said.

The smiling young woman stood, after giving each dog a treat and a big hug.

"I'm Valerie. My crew and I will be responsible for getting Petunia and Yootza and Chester to Los Angeles safely and comfortably."

"Wow," Lala said. "You know their names. That's impressive."

"You must be their mom," Valerie said. She grasped Lala's hands. "We'll take very good care of them, I promise."

"Here we go," Brenda whispered to Frank.

"I heard that," Lala said, valiantly sniffling back tears.

"Why don't you all come inside, and we'll get the kids settled," Valerie suggested.

Valerie ushered them into Doggie Disneyland. Cozy beds were everywhere, next to rows of elevated and floor-level water bowls and food bowls and more playthings than Toys-R-Us has in stock the day after Thanksgiving. Petunia, Yootza, and Chester strained at their leashes.

"Let's let them go, shall we?" Valerie said. She unhooked the dogs, and all three of them barreled toward bowls full of kibble.

"Hounds," Lala said.

"Don't I know," Valerie said. "I've got four rescued bassets at home."

"You are my new best friend," Lala said.

Brenda biffed her on the shoulder.

"I'm speaking hyperbolically, of course," Lala said. "To indicate that Valerie is clearly a lovely, caring person who shares my devotion to animals."

"I share your devotion too. We have five rescued cats," Brenda huffed.

"They do," Lala told Valerie. "Brenda and Frank are wonderful people. Brenda is the best best friend anyone could ever have."

Brenda smiled.

"Great. Now I'm gonna start crying."

"Look! Ladies! Chihuahuas!" Frank bellowed.

He pointed toward a mound of little sleeping bodies in a large pen.

"Ohhh, come see this," Valerie said.

Lala looked around for her dogs and found the three of them curled up next to each other on the biggest, puffiest doggie bed she had ever seen.

"Well, some babies are apparently not having much separation anxiety," Lala pouted.

"It's because they feel safe and secure," Brenda assured her. "Because you did such a great job of explaining everything to them in the car. Repeatedly. Over and over. Until some of us wanted to scream our heads off."

Valerie picked up a sleeping Chihuahua puppy. There were dogs of all ages in the group. She handed the puppy to Lala.

"Ohhh, how precious," Lala said. She covered his little head with kisses.

"They're going to the West Coast too," Valerie said. "On their own plane. They were with a hoarder in a very small house. They were in terrible shape. A rescue group in Oregon is taking them all."

"You fly rescued animals?" Brenda said.

"Almost half our work is pro bono, I'm very proud to say."

In a theatrical flourish of mock exasperation, Lala handed the Chihuahua she had been cradling to Valerie and then whacked both sides of her forehead with her open palms. Hard.

*Owww,* Lala thought. *Easy on the special effects, Melodrama Queen.*

"Is anyone expecting me to be able to function now?" Lala demanded. "Does anyone imagine I'm not going to lose it among this much kindness and cuteness?"

"No one expects that, Lala," Brenda sighed. "Trust me. I think not even Valerie expects that, and she's only just met you."

❦

"Good thing you don't have to function on any higher level than drinking and eating and watching movies," Brenda said.

Lala and Brenda and Frank were standing in the lobby of the Holiday Inn Manhattan View. Lala had chosen the hotel for her last night in New York not because it was the cheapest, which it was not, and not because it was the fanciest, which it was not, but because it had the words "Manhattan" and "View" in its name.

Brenda and Frank were dropping Lala off there with her one small carry-on bag. All of Lala's books and clothes and personal stuff had either been shipped out to Geraldine or put in storage. Her Greenwich Village apartment was now pristinely furnished with only the things paying guests would need for an enjoyable stay.

A very nice young husband and wife had moved into Lala's apartment that morning. They were visiting from Barcelona on their honeymoon, and they would be staying at Lala's place for two weeks at three thousand dollars per week, and they were thrilled to get such a bargain compared to what hotels in Manhattan were charging. Lala's place had been booked continuously for the next six months through a website run by a woman whose voice on the phone betrayed a childhood on Long Island and a healthy serving of world weariness.

"You live in the Village," Ruth said when Lala told her about the problems in the building's basement. "In the Bancroft, for fuck's sake. No one gives a shit. We're thrilled to have you join our vacation-and-short-or-long-term-furnished-rental-hotel-alternative family. Let's make some big bucks together."

Lala had welcomed the charming newlyweds to her home. Then she had slung her small, carry-on bag over her shoulder and had commenced her farewell tour of Manhattan before she headed uptown to Brenda and Frank's place for the journey to points far west, via a certain airport in the Borough of Queens.

The dogs were already at Auntie Brenda and Uncle Frank's house because they had spent the night there, so Lala could thoroughly clean her apartment before her first guests arrived.

Auntie Brenda and Uncle Frank had been delighted to have their canine niece and nephews over for a slumber party. Auntie Brenda and Uncle Frank's five rescued cats had not.

Lala's first goodbye started in the doorway of Pyotr's apartment.

"Come in, please," Pyotr urged. "We'll have a little glass of something bubbly to toast you on your journey."

"I don't want to interrupt your morning. You must have a million things to do today. Oh, perhaps a sip for good luck."

Lala's second farewell was right in front of her when the doors to the elevator opened in the Bancroft's lobby. Lala ran up to Victor and gave him a hug. Then she immediately started pulling wads of tissues out of her bag, tapping them all over her eyes and face.

"I don't want to stain your uniform, Victor," she gasped, through sobs.

"Just think of it as a nice, long vacation," he said. Victor patted her shoulder. "We'll all be here when you get back."

Lala stopped at her local branch of the New York Sports Club to hug all the employees there who were always so nice to her.

"I bet the gyms in Southern California suck!" she brayed through sobs. "I bet they suck big time!"

Everyone in the Pilates class in the nearby glass-walled exercise studio stopped stretching their muscles and firming their cores to turn toward the lobby to see what the hell was going on.

Lala was in and out of Bide-a-Wee before anyone, Lala included, could know what hit them. She ran out the front door only a few minutes after she arrived.

"I'll be back!" she yelled over her shoulder and through her tears. "Take good care of the precious ones for me! I promise I'll be back! Sally, do not take any shit from your asshat of a boyfriend while I'm gone!"

By the time Lala knocked on Brenda's front door, she resembled nothing so much as a vine-ripened tomato on a clothed popsicle stick.

"You just can't cry this much," Brenda said. She handed Lala a margarita. "It's not healthy. Your head is going to burst right off your body from the pressure."

So, that was why Lala and Brenda decided it would be best if the decades-long best friends didn't have a sleepover together at the Holiday Inn Manhattan View on Lala's last night in New York.

"It would only be a good idea if your vision of a fun slumber party would be watching someone cry constantly. All evening and all night long," Lala had said.

"Which it is not," Brenda had agreed. "That does not sound like any fun. At all."

"Good luck, kiddo," Frank said. He wrapped Lala in his thin but muscular arms.

"I love you, Frank," Lala said. "I'm not going to cry until I get upstairs."

"That sounds like a plan," Frank said.

"Thank you for everything."

Lala turned to Brenda.

"No big deal," Brenda said. "You'll call me when you get to Aunt Geraldine's, we'll e-mail all the time, I'll plan a trip out there in a few weeks. No big deal."

"Absolutely," Lala said.

"Hey, Ladies, look at the . . ." Frank began.

Even before the first sounds came out of Frank's mouth, it was too late to try to distract them. Lala and Brenda had already, with a serenity that completely shocked Frank, stepped toward each other to hug and to cry. It wasn't loud or dramatic. It was just wrenching. They stayed there for a few moments. Frank put his arms around them both. Lala was the first to pull away.

Lala walked to the elevator. When the doors opened, she stood inside and whispered to Brenda and Frank, who were standing at a bit of distance, where she had left them.

"I'll call you tomorrow. I will also adore and treasure you both forever."

Brenda looked at Frank. Frank looked at Brenda and shrugged.

"Whadja say?" Brenda asked Lala.

*Oh, for God's sake*, Lala thought.

"We couldn't hear what you said because you were looking down at the floor and mumbling."

Lala thrust her arm between the closing doors.

"I said . . . Look, I can't yell it because that'll ruin the effect. I'll send it to you in one of those cute e-cards about eternal gratitude and friendship, and here's a virtual hug and shit, okay?"

In her room on the top floor of the Holiday Inn Manhattan View, Lala gazed at the nighttime skyline of her treasured Big Apple. She had a glass in one hand and a fistful of pretzels in the other that she pumped into her mouth between gulps of champagne.

"*I'm leavin' on a jet plane*," Lala sang quietly in her chronically off-key voice.

Lala pressed her nose against the window.

"*LA's fine, but it ain't home*," Lala sang. Her voice trembled. "*New York's home, but it ain't mine no more.*"

And then her voice found force from somewhere, and the volume rose, and the power in it almost made the tone deafness bearable, and maybe even kind of close to poignant. Kind of.

"*I am, I said!*" Lala belted. "*To no one there! And no one! Heard! At! All! Not . . . even the chair!*"

Somebody started pounding a shoe or a hammer or a brick on the opposite side of the wall.

"Uh oh. Sorry!" Lala yelled. She grabbed the bottle and poured another glass of champagne.

"That was self-indulgent," she said for her ears only. "I need some lady *schmutz*."

Lala settled on the bed and flipped on the TV to the Pay-Per-View channel.

*There better be something romantic*, Lala thought. *Something romantic with a storyline and a happy ending and with lots of shots of men's tuchuses. OMIGOD! "The Flame is Love" is on FX! When did it start? It's just starting! Not technically gal porn, but I remember the little blurb for this masterpiece in the* New York Times *TV listing. Two words. "Shameless blather." God, how fabulous.*

She scrunched herself up against the pillows in a paroxysm of delight and gazed upward toward the sky she imagined beyond the roof of the hotel.

"Thank you for your tender mercies," Lala whispered. She paused. "Were you able to hear that, Universe, God, Fate, I-Don't-Really-Know-What, or should I send an e-card?"

🍷

Lala leaned back in her window seat with her eyes closed.

*God, first class is so fabulous,* she thought. *Look at me. I'm an island unto myself.*

Lala remained supine until the very gracious members of the cabin crew began their pre-takeoff beverage service.

"Would you like a glass of champagne?" the air host asked.

Lala hoisted her chair to a sitting position.

"Yes, thank you. A glass of champagne sounds like a lovely idea," Lala said.

Lala sipped her champagne and stared out the window at the sun-drenched tarmac.

"Start spreading the news, I'm leaving today," she silently crooned.

Lala tried to flip through a gossip magazine, but most of the pictures were of celebrities frolicking in Los Angeles, so she slammed the pages shut.

Lala placed her glass on her tray table. She put her face in her hands and sighed.

"These little town blues, are melting away; I'll make a brand new start of it, in old New York," she very quietly sang into her palms.

Lala shook her head and sighed again. As she stayed in that slightly sinking forward position, she began to feel someone's eyes on her. Lala looked across the aisle. The window seat opposite hers was occupied by a handsome older man with a very kind and charming smile. Had she been feeling even a little less broken-be-yond-repair, she could have imagined spending the entire conti-nent-spanning flight flirting outrageously with him. The best she could muster at that moment was a weak smile in return.

"If we can make it there, we're gonna make it anywhere," the gentleman said. "I can't carry a tune, so I'll spare you."

"That song is about coming to New York. Not about leaving," Lala sighed.

"I know," the gentleman said. "Are you alright, my dear?"

"I'm fine. Really. Doin' great. Off on a new adventure. Califor-nia, here I come."

# CALIFORNIA, HERE SHE IS

Lala grabbed the tiny, clear plastic sword out of her very dirty vodka martini and used her tongue to slide all three olives off and into her mouth.

"I started crying very loudly just as the plane was crossing the Rockies. Very loudly. Needless to say, I was cut off from that point on. Which was a shame because they serve very lovely champagne in first class. Very lovely."

The two people next to her and the bartender at the small, cozy bar at LAX were looking at Lala with a mixture of empathy and great relief that their lives weren't as stinky as Lala's had been recently.

"Yeah, it's funny now, but trust me, it wasn't then. The way I'm describing it is that I've had a demi-nervous breakdown. I'm not sure if that's technically true. I'm not even really sure what I mean when I say that. But that's what I'm saying. My whole shtick from this moment forward is, unless I'm havin' fun, I'm not gonna do it. Because life is too barfing short."

"Good plan," the bartender said. "Another round?"

"Omigoodness, yes, please, maybe with—" Lala's cell phone rang.

"Yuh huh? They are? They have! I'll be right there!"

Lala searched her purse for her credit card.

"My babies have landed! I'm going to need to settle up. Please put their drinks on my tab. You're a love, thank you."

The bartender took her card and the two other customers began to demur.

"Hush, please," Lala said. "You think I don't appreciate how nice it was of you both to listen to the soused ravings of a complete stranger?"

Lala signed the credit card receipt with a flourish.

"That is a ridiculously high tip," the bartender said.

"Because you are ridiculously cute. And you have no idea how ridiculously much people will pay to live in Manhattan. I'm feeling oddly loaded at the moment, and I have always felt that loaded people should share the wealth. Hey! Loaded means rich, and it also means drunk! Okay, don't anyone ever again try to tell me we live in a random universe."

Lala ran past three other terminals to get to the one that was home to the Los Angeles headquarters of Precious Pets on Planes. She paced in front of their office until an attendant brought Petunia, Yootza, and Chester out.

"Ohhhhh," Lala said. She sank to the ground in front of the dogs and hugged them until the hugs morphed into her basically lying on top of the three hounds.

"They look so happy," Lala whispered. She gazed up at the attendant, who was smiling. "Thank you. Thank you so much for taking such good care of my babies."

"It's a pleasure, ma'am," the young man said. "They're really nice dogs."

"Did you hear that?" Lala cooed. "The nice man likes you! You're popular!"

Lala skipped out of the terminal clutching their leashes with her carry-on bag slung over her shoulder. And almost immediately smacked directly into Tom Hanks.

The icon's icon calmly caught Lala by the shoulders so that the force of their impact wouldn't send her falling backward on her ass.

"Gotcha," he said.

"Omigosh, I'm so sorry."

"No harm done." Tom leaned over to pet the dogs. "Nice pups you got there."

Lala watched him walk away, paying special attention to what was, she noted, an exceptionally firm tuchus.

"Did you see that?" she asked Petunia, Yootza, and Chester. "Wow. I guess I forgot there are some things about LA that are kinda cool."

Lala immediately felt disloyal.

"Not that one can't bump into a major superstar in New York. Often. Regularly. Tom Hanks. Big deal. There are a dozen Tom Hankses on any block in Manhattan. I could also bump into the real Tom Hanks in Manhattan. If he were there. Visiting or working. Or something."

Lala shielded her eyes against the glare and scanned the horizon.

"Jesus, it is bright here. Okay, babies, let's find our ride and get this new home, new beginning shit over with."

*Is that Salman Rushdie?* Lala thought.

She had just exited the car in Manhattan Beach a half block away from her aunt's house. Lala crept up to the fence that surrounded the lovely Spanish fourplex and whisperingly admonished her dogs to stay quiet.

"I want to surprise Aunt Geraldine. So don't make any noise, 'kay?"

Lala peeked over the white stucco and wrought iron fence and glimpsed Geraldine just as her aunt was in the process of hugging a man who looked very much like the celebrated author.

"So, Salman, how's that nasty *fatwa*?" Lala heard Geraldine ask.

Geraldine pronounced the man's name like the fish.

Before Mr. Rushdie could answer, Geraldine glimpsed Lala's head poking over the fence. She came barreling out of the gate.

"You're here!"

"I saw Tom Hanks at LAX!" Lala said. Lala and Geraldine danced around in a hug that resembled a freestyle form of competitive clog dancing. "I collided with Tom Hanks! He put his hands on my shoulders! He likes my dogs!"

Geraldine was not Lala's aunt by birth or by marriage, but rather by friendship. Geraldine and her husband, Hugh, were close friends of Lala's parents for decades. They never had children. Geraldine and Hugh loved to fuss over their niece and also over her best friend, Brenda, who was rapidly absorbed into the greater family unit after she met Lala in school.

Hugh had passed away almost three years ago. Geraldine would neither confirm nor deny the rumor that went around their circle that he had died peacefully in his sleep while they were having sex.

"I miss him like crazy," she often said. "But if you gotta go, which you gotta, I think he made a very nice exit. We should all be so lucky."

Geraldine was of an aggressively indeterminate age. She looked great. Her statuesque frame remained lithe and fit, and her hair was a closely cropped shade of luminous white. Though her face was covered with wrinkles, Geraldine had ice-blue eyes that conveyed more than enough wicked liveliness to erase the impact of the crow's feet surrounding them.

Lala and Geraldine released each other, and Geraldine immediately swooped down on the dogs.

"The babies are here!" she crowed. "This is the new one! I like the new one! A greyhound! Nice!"

Salman Rushdie had exited the gate as well and was standing next to them. Geraldine stood and swept her arm in his direction. She whispered to Lala.

"Don't tell anyone he's here. He goes by the name Thomas. As far as we're concerned, his name is Thomas."

"Of course," Lala whispered. She offered her hand. "Lala Pettibone."

"I've heard so much about you," Salman said. He took her hand and kissed it quite charmingly. "It's a pleasure to finally meet you."

When he spoke, his accent was clearly West Coast by way of a long stint in Maine or maybe New Hampshire. Lala didn't know what the hell was going on.

A decoy, she thought?

"I'll take the dogs inside," Geraldine announced. She marched through the gate with Petunia, Yootza, and Chester behind her.

Lala and Salman followed them in. Lala whispered to him.

"You're not Salman Rushdie, are you?"

"No," he whispered back. "I'm Thomas Gallagher. I keep telling Geraldine, but I think she thinks I'm just saying it to ensure her safety."

"The resemblance is amazing," Lala said. "Except for the full head of wavy blonde hair and no beard and no glasses."

"Yeah. Geraldine thinks it's part of the disguise. I think she likes the intrigue."

"I'm not surprised," Lala said.

"Come up here," Geraldine yelled from the balcony surrounding the second floor of her home. "I'm putting you in this apartment right above mine!"

Lala and Thomas walked up a short flight of beautifully tiled steps and followed Geraldine through the open front door. The dogs had already gotten themselves deliciously settled in the three large doggie beds that occupied a fair amount of the living room floor.

Lala let her carry-on bag drop to the floor in the entryway of the apartment. All around her were stucco walls and arched doorways and clean, cozy furniture and rugs covering tiled floors. The walls had perfectly placed, bold paintings. The room smelled vaguely and welcomingly of fresh-baked rolls.

"Can you believe they bottle that bread odor thing?" Geraldine asked. "And it doesn't even feel fake or anything. Is life amazing or what?"

"Omigod, this is so gorgeous," Lala whispered, her voice shaking. "You are spoiling all of us."

"Of course I'm spoiling you all because I love you, and I love the dogs and don't cry."

"I swear, Aunt Geraldine, I will make this up to you. You will never be alone. I promise. I'll always take care of you. I promise I'll—"

"That's nice, but let's not start crying because this is a happy day, and, knowing me, I start with happy tears, and then I get crazy and suddenly I'm sobbing. And I know you're the same way, so here's what we do. You go take a little nap because you've been traveling all day, and then we go shopping for some clothes, and then you and I and Thomas, because that's his name as far as we're concerned, and the lovely young couple who live below him all go into town and go crazy with fun. Okay?"

"You want to go clothes shopping first?" Lala asked.

"I like the all black, darling," Geraldine said. "Head to toe black? It's very New York, it's very dramatic, it's very sexy. I would just like you to alternate it with something that's got a little more pop. You know, something a little less 'I'm a character in a Chekhov play who's always yapping about being in mourning for life.' Which you never have been even when Terrence died, God rest, and you never will be in mourning for your life if I have anything to say about it, which I do because I love you like my own daughter, which as far as I'm concerned, now that your wonderful mom is gone, God rest, you are."

Geraldine gave Lala another big hug, then held her at arm's length to take in her niece with an eye that was equal parts admiring and assessing.

"And cleavage. More cleavage as we get older. I take my cues exclusively from Oprah and Dame Helen Mirren now. And you should be doing the same."

"Omigod," Lala yelped. "They have 'Yesterday When I Was Young!' In the original French!"

Lala, and what she had been referring to as her Fabulous New Entourage since the evening began, had recently entered a bar in downtown Manhattan Beach that was having Karaoke Night.

"Karaoke is a terrible idea," Geraldine fretted when Lala started pulling her toward the entrance of the bar.

Once inside, Geraldine whispered to Stephanie who, along with her husband Chuck, lived in the final apartment that made up the fourplex.

"Lala has a terrible singing voice," Geraldine confided.

"I heard that!" Lala yelled, not looking up as she scanned the thick notebook that catalogued the songs available to be belted to a captive audience.

"I say that with love," Geraldine added. "And with deep concern for your public humiliation."

"I must have very good hearing," Lala said. "Because I can hear people when they whisper, but apparently no one can hear me when I whisper. God or the universe can. I think."

Lala scribbled the title to the Aznavour classic on a slip of paper and handed it to the chubby young man who was on a break from running the karaoke machine. The young man's lack of any facial expression of any kind gave new depth to the concept of a poker face. Thankfully, Lala was grinning enough for both of them, so his seeming absence of excitement about the prospect of hearing her share a *chanson* didn't squash Lala's joy.

Lala joined Geraldine, Stephanie, Chuck, and Thomas at the bar. Stephanie and Chuck, Lala had established the moment she met them, were definitely young enough to be her children. They were both compact and pale and shared the fashion esthetic of dedicated followers of Chairman Mao. They were newlyweds, and they were constantly holding hands, as Lala had discovered earlier that evening.

*I remember when Terrence and I had to be in constant physical contact with each other,* Lala thought. *God, do I miss him. Also, I need to have sex again. Soon.*

Stephanie and Chuck were recent graduates of veterinary school. Lala immediately loved them and was immediately determined to adopt them and raise them as her own.

"My parents are both still alive," Stephanie responded to Lala's query about her and Chuck's general familial availability.

"Ditto," Chuck said. "Sorry about that."

"No, no, I'm happy," Lala said. "They should only live a long and joyous life, all four of them. Then it's settled. I'll be your aunt. And you'll take care of me when I get old."

"Sounds perfect," Chuck said.

"Yup," Stephanie agreed.

At the bar in the karaoke joint, Stephanie handed Lala a Happy Hour menu.

"They have Happy Hour until midnight," Stephanie said.

"Wow," Lala said, scanning the drink offerings. "This is my new favorite hangout."

Lala looked around at the large, cozy booths, the gleaming wood floors, and the flattering lighting.

"But for the large, cozy booths, the gleaming wood floors, and the flattering lighting, this place reminds me of one of my favorite bars at school. My favorite bar at school was not clean. Or charming. And the lighting was for shit. I mean, a bare overhead bulb was forgiving by comparison, but I didn't care back then because I was only just out of my teens. We didn't have karaoke back then. I only drank beer back then. Or grain alcohol punch. Quite possibly the worst hangover in the world from that swill, but it sure can make a frat party more palatable."

"Don't drink more, please," Geraldine begged.

"What are you talking about?"

"If you drink more, you'll sing. I just know it. Salman, I'm sorry, Thomas, tell her not to drink more."

Lala closed the menu.

"I haven't had a Long Island Iced Tea in decades," Lala said. She retrieved a credit card from her cleavage.

Lala was wearing a shirt in a vivid shade of evergreen that had patterns of lighter green waves weaved throughout. The fabric hugged her breasts and then cascaded over the waist of her new, tight black jeans.

"Please don't drink more," Geraldine said. "And by the way, that top looks fabulous on you."

"Thanks. And who knew not wearing all black could feel so sexy? Where's the bartender?"

"Is that Doctor McLellan?" Stephanie said.

Chuck turned in the direction Stephanie was looking, and so did the rest of the gang. Lala watched as a man in his early fifties approached the bar. He was smiling at Stephanie and Chuck. The man was tall and fit, and he had wavy salt-and-pepper hair that was unfortunately cut in what looked like a misguided attempt to bring back the mullet.

*Oh, hellooooo,* Lala thought. *Very cute. The 'do not withstanding.*

"He's too young for me," Geraldine whispered to Lala, "so I'm giving you carte blanche. What is with that hair?"

"Thank yoooooou," Lala whispered back.

"Hey," the man said.

"Doctor McLellan! You guys, this is Doctor McLellan. We met him at this veterinary conference last weekend, and he's amazing," Stephanie gushed.

"Amazing," Chuck echoed. "You haven't seen anyone calm a terrified stray cat like Doctor McLellan."

*Am I hearing this correctly?* Lala thought. *This gorgeous man is a veterinarian? A veterinarian with special powers? I bet I've got that shit-eating grin all over my face again. Damn.*

"Am I blushing?" Doctor McLellan asked.

It took Lala a few moments before she realized that everyone was staring at her. Which lead her to the startled conclusion that Doctor Devastatingly Handsome had addressed his question to her.

*Is he flirting with me?* she thought.

"Yes, you are," Lala said. "And it's a very good look for you."

*Am I flirting with him?* Lala thought.

"Will you join us, Doctor McLellan?" Stephanie said. "Our friends are very nice. This is our landlady and friend, Geraldine, and this is our neighbor and friend Thomas, and this is Lala, our new neighbor and friend."

"Please, would you join us, Doctor McLellan?" Chuck said.

*Stop stealing my lines, kids,* Lala thought.

"I will if you call me David. Let's grab a table."

"Thomas," Lala hissed. They were all following David to an empty booth across the room. Lala clutched Thomas's sleeve and stretched upward to bring her lips to his ear.

"I am awash in contradictory sensations," Lala continued in an urgent whisper. "He's not wearing a wedding ring, but that doesn't mean anything for sure, right? I swear, terror and lust are staging an epic battle in my psyche even as I appear to be calmly sashaying over to the booth to grab the seat next to Doctor David McLellan just in case maybe he's not married. So if I pass out at any point from the stress, if I fall face forward onto the table, promise you'll throw a glass of water on my head to revive me? Promise? Because I don't want to miss a moment of this evening. Unless he's married. In which case I plan to drink myself into an epic stupor. Promise you won't wake me up if he's married?"

"I promise," Thomas said. "Your tits look great, by the way."

"Omigod, I love you so much," Lala said. "How did you know that was exactly what I needed to hear right now?"

Lala released Thomas's sleeve and jogged over to the booth, sliding in not a moment too soon to wedge herself between David and the awestruck phalanx that Stephanie and Chuck had become.

"So, David," Lala said, "you live in Manhattan Beach?"

"No, I live in Manhattan," David said. "The real one."

The seat of Lala's pants skidded to a halt in its trajectory over the glossy black vinyl.

"What? Where in Manhattan?"

"The West Village," David said.

*Mother of GOD,* Lala shrieked to herself, *why does the universe torment me thus?*

"I do too! I mean, not right now, but I do, I'm just living here . . . in Manhattan Beach . . . for now. For now, I'm here. But I live in the Bancroft."

"Love that building," David said. "I used to live right near there in the Connaught."

"I love the Connaught."

"So does my ex-wife. So now I'm on Bank Street."

*Ex-wife,* Lala thought. *Things are lookin' up. I can't barfing believe we're neighbors in Manhattan, and I'm stuck in this shithole of a gorgeous beach town. Barf.*

A waiter came over to their table.

"How does everybody feel about champagne?" David asked.

"Cool," Stephanie said.

"So cool," Chuck said. "Wow."

"I think we'll need two bottles to start. Veuve Cliquot, please," David instructed the waiter.

*I think I'm having an orgasm,* Lala thought.

The waiter and a colleague appeared bearing tall ice buckets on thin legs. They popped their respective bottles simultaneously and poured out six glasses.

"Thank you," David said. He raised his glass. "If it's not too self-centered, I'd like to toast to adventure. In my case, to the sailing trip I'm starting with my sons tomorrow."

*Huh?* Lala thought.

"It's so cool," Stephanie said. "Doctor McLellan . . . Doctor David . . . McLellan . . . David told us about it at lunch at the conference. He's going to be sailing around the world for like . . . I don't know . . . months."

"So cool," Chuck said.

They all clinked glasses, and Lala drank her champagne in a daze that she hoped might prove to be permanent.

*Oy*, Lala thought. *Oy vey. Is mir. There goes my bicoastal romance.*

Lala reached over and grabbed one of the bottles. David just as quickly took it out of her hand.

"Please, allow me," he said. Her glass was instantly full again. And then it was instantly empty again.

*Oh, well, I have been meaning to try to live exclusively in the moment*, Lala thought. *I guess. What the hell, why not start now?*

The loudspeaker suddenly crackled and the impassive karaoke master's voice enveloped the room.

"Lala Pettibone, you're up."

"Ohhh no," Geraldine gasped. "Lala, don't . . ."

Geraldine was speaking to Lala's rapidly disappearing posterior. Lala leaped onto the small karaoke stage and grabbed the mic. Geraldine put her head in her hands.

"Ohhh, no."

The beautiful opening notes drifted out of the karaoke machine. David sat up straighter.

"In French?" he yelled over the music to Lala. "Please tell me it's the original?"

"Oh, *bien sûr, mon cher*," Lala cooed back. Or as much as one can coo when speaking at that volume.

"Please, God," Geraldine whispered into her hands, "make this nightmare stop. Give that poor girl a break. He'll never schtupp her if he hears her sing."

Geraldine's head snapped up as she felt the seat of the booth bouncing. David shooed Stephanie and Chuck out into the aisle so he could bound up to the karaoke stage.

David grabbed a second mic and the lyrics appeared before them on the screen. He was the first to sing, but Lala was right on top of him.

Geraldine listened to the singers. Her brow furrowed.

"Something's wrong," Geraldine whispered.

"They sound good," Stephanie said.

"He's so cool," Chuck said.

Geraldine hazarded a look at the crowd. Everyone seemed to not be angry or upset or in physical pain. They seemed to be pleased.

Geraldine looked at the stage and saw Lala and David with their arms around each other's waists as they sang with their mics held close. Their eyes stayed locked on the karaoke screen.

Geraldine looked over at Thomas, who was smiling and nodding his head along with the music.

"Salman, have I gone insane? Am I aurally hallucinating? Is she singing in perfect thirds?"

"Yeah," Thomas said. "Lala can really harmonize."

🍷

It was very tight in the cab. Stephanie was sitting on Chuck's lap in the passenger seat, and the remaining four in the celebratory group were stuffed into the backseat like so many clowns in a tiny circus car.

The applause following Lala's duet with David demanded that they follow their debut performance with encores consisting of "Mack the Knife" in the original German and "Love Me with All of Your Heart" in the original Spanish.

Lala had sung the encores phonetically and had acquitted herself quite well.

David, she was further aroused to discover, was multilingual, being fluent in French, German, Spanish, and Russian, in addition to speaking English quite beautifully.

He also spoke conversational Italian.

Upon discovering this, Lala excused herself for a moment and ran off the stage to deliver an urgent, hushed message to Thomas.

"I'm probably going to faint soon. In a good way. Have that glass of water at the ready."

And now she was in the backseat of the cab between David and Geraldine, and she was managing to resist the clawing temptation to recreate the beginning of so many sex-a-thons back in college by lifting her new shirt and flashing her boobs at this animal doctor of her dreams.

"Why didn't you ever tell me that you can sing in perfect thirds?" Geraldine demanded.

"I don't know what that means," Lala said. "Seriously, how cool is it that you can get hammered in Manhattan Beach because you can get a ride home in a cab or if you have an app on your phone. And what they do not have here is blue laws so you can buy liquor at practically any hour of the day or night. This place is so cool!"

"I nearly had a heart attack back there from anxiety," Geraldine said. "Can't you hear that you're harmonizing?"

"Ummmm, I was singing the song and . . . Wasn't I singing the same notes as David?"

"No, it's called harmonizing," Geraldine huffed. "I wish I had known you could do that, so I wouldn't have had to worry about you so much."

Lala gave a tight squeeze to the bottle of Veuve Cliquot David had only recently exploded out of the cab to purchase at a stop on the way home.

"Okay, well, ummm, now we all know, so that's good. David, did you also know that the weather's great here? David, David, David, David, David, David, don't you love Southern California?"

"I do," David said. "Try not to shake that bottle so much, okay?"

The cab pulled up to the fourplex, and David handed the driver a hundred-dollar bill.

"You've been great," he said. "Thanks for your patience."

Everyone spilled out onto the sidewalk. Stephanie and Chuck started to dance on their tiptoes with excitement.

"David, want to come to our apartment and meet our cats?"

"Absolutely," David said. "I will very much look forward to doing that next time I'm in town."

David grabbed Lala's hand and used his free hand to shake Thomas's hand and then Chuck's hand, and then used it to hug first Geraldine and then Stephanie.

"Thank you all very much for a great evening."

Stephanie and Chuck stood between David and Lala and the stairs leading to Lala's apartment. Lala noted that they really didn't seem to be doing it maliciously, which made her not hate them quite as much as she wanted to.

*Awww,* Lala thought. *I remember having a crush on one of my professors at school. Several professors, actually. And not all of them men. That is so cute that those two are so in awe of David. Take a number, kids, and get in line. And get out of my way.*

"Yeah it's been great! Hey, maybe everyone can come over to our place, and I'll make tea, and we can talk," Stephanie said. Lala gave Stephanie and Chuck each a big smooch on the cheek as she shoved herself and David past them and up the stairs.

"Kids, you are adorable, and we're gonna go get naked now. Right now. 'Kay? This was great! Let's do it again soon!"

Lala held the champagne under her left armpit as she searched through her purse for her keys.

"Gimme that," David said. He grabbed the bottle. "This is going to need to settle. It probably shouldn't be opened for a few weeks."

Lala found her keys and tried to get the correct one in the lock right-side-up.

"Oh, come on, it can't be this complicated," she huffed.

After several false starts Lala got the door opened, and they were greeted by a trio of very enthusiastic dogs.

"Look at these three," David said. He sat on the floor and let the hounds surround him with their energetic welcome.

"*Oy,* nooooo, they have to be walked!" Lala said.

She grabbed the three leashes off a hook by the front door and lectured her precious dogs as she attached the leashes to their collars, complete with wagging finger and grave voice.

"No sniffing! No being hounds! Pee, poo, and then we're right back here, got it?"

Lala and David rushed down the stairs and jogged through the circle of Geraldine, Thomas, Stephanie, and Chuck, who had seated themselves in the comfortable patio furniture to chat and enjoy the still pleasantly warm night.

Out on the sidewalk, Lala and David guided the dogs to a large patch of grass.

"I am not kidding," Lala said. "Do whatever you have to do. Right now."

"They're very handsome dogs," David said. "Have you had them all their lives?"

"No, no," Lala said. She tapped her foot impatiently and glared at Petunia, Yootza, and Chester. "I adopt senior animals. Not many people want older dogs. Like I have to tell you that. I got them all at Bide-a-Wee. I volunteer . . . ed . . . there. Past tense. Because for now I'm here."

David took a poop bag from the roll that was cradled in a little pouch attached to Yootza's leash. He bent down and scooped.

*You are so perfect,* Lala thought.

"The more I hear about you," David said, looking up at Lala as he patted Yootza's head, "the more perfect you seem."

When Lala would remember that long, but not long enough, night with David—and she would remember it often—she would reflect on all the moments as though she were looking through a beloved photo album. With herself, sitting next to herself on the couch. While she and herself drank a bottle of wine together and ate a lot of expensive chocolate truffles together or maybe a big sack of popped sour cream and onion potato chips if they were craving something salty. The dogs—all the dogs over the years— would sit on the couch with Lala and herself and would snooze through all the giggling and reminiscing.

"Oh, I love this photo," Lala would say.

"Me too," she would nod back to herself.

"I had just woken up with David's arms tightly around me and his fabulous bodingus wedged most delightfully against my tuchus, and the most amazing thought started to formulate in my mind, and so I very gingerly wriggled myself out of his grasp so I could reach down and slide open the drawer under my platform bed and grab the bottle I had—with a hopefulness that certainly did not mesh with my life experience of the past few years—placed there when I unpacked my travel cosmetics case. And, as I looked at the seemingly undisturbed bottle, I woke David, and when he got over his annoyance at being woken up after having slept maybe an hour, I asked him, 'Am I insane or did we not even touch this bottle of moisture enhancing Silk-E personal lubricant which intensifies comfort and intimacy with Vitamin E and soothing aloe by the number-one doctor-recommended brand?' and he said, 'No, you're not insane, because we didn't use it because we didn't need it,' and then I said, 'Wow,' and then we fucked again."

And then Lala would turn the page and see a different photo, one that made her wince.

"Ohhh, this is the part where I thought I truly screwed it up," Lala would say, pointing to a photo of her in the living room blithely and naively grinning as she put a Rick Astley CD on the player.

"Look at me go," she would say to herself. Herself would take a big honkin' gulp of wine because she knew all too well what was coming. "I had been lulled into a false sense of security by having just played a wicked cool selection of Steely Dan songs including 'Everyone's Gone to the Movies,' and, of course, David is looking at me like I'm wicked cool because I am wicked cool, and then I remember how much I love Rick Astley, and I put on his greatest hits, and David looks at me like I'm the biggest dork in the known and/or unexplored universe. And as soon as I see David's expression, all I can think is, shoot, did I screw up too soon? Is this a transgression that might have been forgiven after we were living together for seven months but will now totally torpedo our relationship because I did it on the first night?"

And then Lala would turn the page and smile at the photo of her sitting in the breakfast nook with David, both of them wearing nothing but cookie dough ice cream mustaches as they wolfed directly from a large container of Ben & Jerry's. The photo showed walls still wet with champagne and the rest of the Veuve Cliquot being passed between the two of them for gulps directly from the bottle.

"We thought the champagne might have settled down by then, but no," Lala would say. "David was so easy to talk to. Even in French. I don't know that I was making sense necessarily because I was still intoxicated, but I do always marvel at how much easier it is to speak a foreign language when you're plastered. David complimented me on my accent, and I told him I used to be an actress, which I could hardly say with a straight face because, as you know, I had no talent. But, okay, as I told David, that's maybe not entirely true. Every now and then, with that comedy group I was in years ago in New York, I wrote a sketch or someone else wrote a sketch, and the role was just so easy for me and the audience cracked up. But there was no rhyme or reason to it. And I was the laziest actress on God's earth."

"You really were," Lala's self would agree with her. "Somnambulistically lazy. Epically lazy."

"And when I was bad, I was very bad. I've seen videotape from some of our shows."

"Yeah, I've seen those. Yikes. Remember how you used to start answering a question before the other actor had finished asking it? Wow, was that lousy acting, or what?"

"Yikes. Stinky lousy. Look at this photo! We're watching *Casablanca*!"

And then Lala and herself would sigh deeply and wistfully.

"And after *Casablanca*, David suggested we watch one of his favorite old movies, *Random Harvest* with Greer Garson and Ronald Coleman, and asked if I had ever heard of it. And I nearly had a stroke because that's the movie, as you know, that Terrence and I would watch every single Valentine's Day because it's so lushly and painfully and unabashedly romantic, and so David and I watched that, and we made out a lot during both screenings, and it was great. And then the dogs started acting up again because they had to go out, and I nearly smacked them. Yikes, look at the expression on Aunt Geraldine's face! It was barely past dawn. Who knew she wore that kind of outfit to bed?"

Lala's self would lean forward and peer at the photo of Geraldine standing in her doorway in a sleek neon blue jogging suit and would crack up.

"She was pissed!" Lala's self would say to Lala. "And rightly so."

"Oh, yeah. I showed up at her doorstep after walking David to his cab, so he could catch his flight out of LAX with not one moment to spare, and I'm whining and mewling about how tragic my life is, and Aunt Geraldine looked at me with more contempt than she had ever looked at me before or has ever looked at me since, thank goodness. And who can blame her?"

"No one can blame her."

"I had it comin'."

"You certainly did."

"God love her, Aunt Geraldine read me the riot act. Which was apparently exactly what I needed that morning. I guess you could say, though of course I had no idea at the time, that that morning was when Act Two of my Act Two officially began to begin."

# Laugh Allowed

"Stop it," Geraldine said. "Get in here. Stop whimpering and do not make me regret offering you refuge."

"I shall swath myself in cotton from head to foot," Lala declared tearfully. She stood in the doorway and twitched, and Geraldine had to grab her and drag her inside. "I will never show my skin again. I will never be naked again, in any context whatsoever. I swear, I had you pegged for sexy nightwear."

"I don't wear this when I have male guests," Geraldine huffed.

She marched Lala into the kitchen and sat her down in the breakfast nook. Then Geraldine opened a cupboard and pulled out a large steel bowl.

"I'm making pancakes. And we're having mimosas."

"Omigod, that's a great idea," Lala said. She lunged for the refrigerator and thrust the door open. "I'll be the bartender. You're out of orange juice? I don't see any in here. We don't need it."

Lala sat in the nook drinking while Geraldine mixed and flipped.

"I truly wish I hadn't done any of that last night. I had such a great time with David. Gérard? We never had sex. Which in hindsight I see is a good thing. So I was thinking David will help me stop thinking about Gérard, and then it turns out David is delightful, and now I'm already mooning for David. I don't know, maybe there's still hope. Maybe David's horrible. Maybe I'll find out he's wanted in seventeen states for deceiving widows out of their money. What if he dies on that sailing trip? What if I never see him again? I've gotten so good at feeling sad. How will I ever not feel alone at the rate I'm going?"

Geraldine placed two plates full of fluffy silver dollar pancakes on the table and sat down opposite Lala.

"These are gorgeous," Lala said. She grabbed a fistful and shoved them in her mouth. "Forgive my manners. I'm stuffing down pain with food."

"Listen to me," Geraldine said. "You are done complaining. Do you understand me?"

"Yes, ma'am," Lala said. "God, these are delicious. You should open up a little breakfast café. In your courtyard."

"Let's stay on point, shall we? Do not make me show you news footage of people who are really suffering. Do you understand?"

"I do. You're absolutely right. If I could argue with you, I would. But I can't. I know when I'm being a pill."

"Would it be really nice if David lived here and you two love-birds could maybe see if this one-night-stand had any substance and you could maybe start your lives together?" Geraldine asked.

"Yup," Lala said.

"Yes, it would. Would it be really nice if no one in the world were ever hungry or poor or frightened again?"

"Yup," Lala said.

"Would it be really nice if no one were ever mean to animals, any animals, ever again?"

"Very nice," Lala said.

"Indeed. So what do we do in the meantime? We do our best. And we count our blessings. Do you understand me?"

"I do," Lala said.

"Good. Do not make me fetch a legal pad and stand over you with a ruler while you write a list of all the many things for which you should be grateful."

"Actually, by a not entirely surprising coincidence, I was doing exactly that right now in my head. Seriously. I'm not making that up. And it's a long list."

"Of course it is," Geraldine said.

Lala stood and lifted her plate and glass.

"Here, lemme clean up," she said.

"Sit," Geraldine ordered. "I'm not finished with you."

Lala sat.

"Uh oh," she said.

"I read your screenplay."

"Ohhhh nooooo!" Lala yelled. "Aunt Geraldine, unless you loved it, I'm definitely in no shape to hear you cut it to shreds today, so maybe we should wait for a few decades until I'm stronger and we can—"

"I loved it," Geraldine said.

"What?" Lala whispered. "But it's got one-dimensional characters and a cheesy—"

"This is not trigonometry," Geraldine said. "This is all completely subjective. You know that. Don't you? I've read reviews of *A Map Without Latitude*. Some people hate that book."

"Impossible," Lala gasped. "That book is genius."

"Honey, you think it's brilliant, and other people eviscerate it. Okay? I rest my case. There are no absolutes in creative work. Except for Jeffrey Koons. I swear, no one can convince me that he's not kidding with all that huge acrylic crap he creates. I happened to think your screenplay was entirely compelling. I was very involved in the story. I couldn't put it down."

"Wow," Lala said. "Is there more champagne? I didn't see any in the fridge. Do you have any hidden elsewhere in the house? We could put it in the freezer, and it would be ready to drink in about fifteen minutes. Or if not, I could run out and get a chilled bottle."

"Just do me one favor."

"Uh oh," Lala said.

"Please rewrite the damn thing as a comedic novel. You need lots of people to get on board, and you need lots of people to agree to give you money before you can get a movie made, am I right?"

"Yes, of course, but—"

"But today, you can publish your novel yourself, right away, am I right?"

"Yes, but . . . a comedic novel?" Lala said. "The story is so sad and tragic."

"Think Kingsley Amis. Think *Lucky Jim*," Geraldine said.

"I love that book! I laughed aloud at that book!"

"I know. I did as well. Because it's delightful. So please reread *Lucky Jim*, and please be inspired by it, and then please make your story laugh-aloud hilarious. Because, as much as I love the characters and their journey, at several points in the screenplay you're bordering on—okay, don't get upset—you're bordering on bathos."

Lala threw her head back. Geraldine thought she heard cartilage cracking somewhere in her niece's body.

"Bathos? I was going for pathos. Damn it!"

"The title's funny," Geraldine said. "So make the damn book funny. Now, clear this table and go upstairs and do your best. With everything. Because you know what today is, right?"

"I do?"

"Today is the first day of the rest of your life."

"Oh, that," Lala said. She nodded. "That's true. If I could argue the point, I would. But any way you look at it, today is indeed that."

Lala felt a bit unsteady on her feet when she exited Geraldine's apartment and walked up the stairs to her place. She had been hit with so many intense experiences since she met David less than twenty-four hours earlier. Plus, she had been drinking quite a bit of undiluted champagne since she got to Geraldine's house because there had, in fact, been no orange juice in the refrigerator, leaving Lala to wonder why Geraldine had mentioned the word "mimosas" in the first place—not that she cared because she loved champagne just by itself.

But the air was already fresh and warm by the seaside in Manhattan Beach, and the sky was such a lovely shade of bright blue, and, if there were any clouds on the horizon, Lala certainly couldn't see them.

*Fuck it*, Lala thought. *Why not seize the moments and do the best I can with them?*

Lala thrust her front door open. Her beasts were draped over the couches and were snoring and did not stir when she entered. Lala manifested a considerable snit as soon as she saw this.

*Oh, sure,* she thought. *Now you're passed out. But last night, when I wanted to bonk David some more? Then you're wide-awake and in desperate need of being walked.*

Lala scurried over and tickled her dogs between their toes, which brought all of them to slow, snuffling, old-dog consciousness.

"Okay, puppy dogs! Up and out! It is a gorgeous day, and we are not going to miss one more minute of it!"

"I think we might walk as far as downtown and see if there's a pet store that has sunglasses for dogs, shall we?" Lala asked her three hounds, who were all methodically sniffing the sidewalks as Lala tried, without success, to keep them at a little bit of a brisk pace. "Look how lovely this neighborhood is. Look how bright the sun is. At least look up once every five minutes and get your noses off the ground and notice how pleasant this day is, for Chrissake."

The troupe passed houses with small yards in a wonderful smorgasbord of styles. Some were classic California Mission, others looked like they belonged in the Cotswolds. Still others could have been transported to Charleston without a hammer swing's worth of renovation.

The fences surrounding the properties were also charmingly varied. Brick stood next to white picket which seemed to coexist quite peaceably with the adjacent stucco wall that was having a close relationship with a barrier of hedges on the other side.

Many of the homes had dogs that barked at Lala and her brood through windows or that rushed out an open front door to greet or confront the newcomers.

"It kind of kills me to say this," Lala confessed, "but it's nice here. Nice. Lots of dogs. Cute, cute, cute, cute, cute homes. I can smell the ocean. I'm kinda having a good time. Here. In California. Without the man whom I just recently spent hours *schtupping*, and whom I would really love to schtupp again tonight after a long, delicious dinner downtown at some charming restaurant that would then become 'our place' and the staff would all know us and adore us because we always leave a huge tip, and the owner would send over bottles of wine and stuff. I'm having a good time right now, right this moment. I'm not fretting. I don't know what's wrong with me."

Lala sat down on the curb and started crying.

"I don't know," Lala sniffed. She wiped her nose on the back of her hand. "I could be entirely wrong about this. My instincts right now could be as off as my gaydar was in the '80s. David could be a lunatic, a thief, a Republican. It's just that he was so sweet to me, and I think he might be a great guy. You guys never met Terrence. You would have loved him. And he would have loved you. Terrence was a great guy. Uh oh. Uh oh. Pathos-potentially-bordering-on-bathos alert."

Lala patted Yootza, Petunia, and Chester, then she abruptly stood and started walking again at an accelerated pace. Her dogs were startled by the steady pull on their leashes to discourage the nonstop sniffing that was their birthright.

"Let's get to town, people," Lala said. "We've got a ton of stuff to accomplish today. Our new life beckons."

By the time they were headed back to Geraldine's place more than five hours later, Lala had joined Geraldine's gym, signed up to volunteer at the Dogs of Love private animal rescue shelter run by a close friend of Geraldine's, and flirted shamelessly with the adorable waiter at Geraldine's favorite downtown restaurant that had an outdoor patio where "pooches were most enthusiastically welcome."

"Where would we be without Auntie Geraldine, huh?"

Lala gazed down at her dogs, who were marching at a pace that at first surprised her but then made sense when Lala remembered that they knew dinner was waiting for them at home. The pack looked quite jaunty, with all three sporting their new wraparound, high-UVA-protection doggie sunglasses to protect their eyes from the almost constant Southern California glare.

"I don't know how I'm going to make this up to Auntie Geraldine," Lala continued. "As God is my witness, I will care for her in her dotage, such as it will be because I bet she'll be a pistol right up to the end, and even that won't be enough to make up for her saving my life. What the fuck is that?"

Yootza, Petunia, and Chester were completely thrown off their stride when Lala suddenly started racing down the street, and they had to gallop to keep up. And they were even more confused when she just as suddenly stopped and began walking very slowly. But then their hound noses kicked in, and they saw what Lala was moving toward.

Up ahead, an especially huge Great Dane was barreling at them with his leash flying in his wake. And behind the dog was a man in an electric wheelchair, giving chase at what was probably the fastest speed the wheelchair could achieve. "Benedict!" the man shouted. "Benedict, come back, please!"

"Okay," Lala had enough time to whisper to her dogs. "Let's not scare Benedict away, okay? Calm energy. Calm."

Just as that last word calmly and quietly escaped her lips, Benedict caught sight of the group and altered his course to intercept them. Yootza growled protectively.

"No growling," Lala whispered. "Everything is fine."

But Yootza was having none of it. He reared up on his stubby hind legs and bared his teeth at the charging monster.

At which point the charging monster skidded to a halt in front of them, rolled over on his back, and, with his tail wagging, assumed the doggie Esperanto stance for "I submit to your superior status, Mighty One."

Yootza was as surprised as Lala. He got back down on all fours and, with a look that indicated he was still on alert for a possible deadly trap being set up by the quivering harlequin pony, sniffed Benedict's butt.

"Just know that I will not be lulled into a false sense of security by your admittedly very engaging and believable performance," Yootza's attitude seemed to say.

The man in the wheelchair came puttering up next to them.

"Wow, your dog is a sweetie pie," Lala said. Lala rubbed the dog's vast belly. "What a gentle giant. I love that phrase. Gentle giant. I love that. I love gentle giants."

"Thank you," the man said, his voice quavering. He grabbed Benedict's leash, but let the dog stay on the ground on his back, where the Great Dane seemed quite happy to be sniffed and rubbed and licked.

Lala stopped rubbing and stood up. She offered her hand to the man. As she did, she noted that he was a big man with his left leg in a cast, from thigh to toes. The man was, by Lala's estimation, a few years older than her Aunt Geraldine. He had a welcoming face, despite his lack of any lips to speak of, and one that was made all the more appealing by his clear agitation at having nearly lost his precious dog.

The man was, by any objective standards, very attractive. Lala smiled at him.

*Hello,* she thought. *Is it possible that fate has brought me a way to pay back Auntie Geraldine much sooner than I hoped?*

"Did your wife decorate the house? It's lovely."

"She did. Just before she passed away last year," Monty Miller said.

*God, I'm a horrible person,* Lala thought. *I ask this poor man a leading question just to find out if he's single.*

"I'm so sorry," Lala said.

She took a big bite of a large, fluffy, buttered biscuit. They were sitting in the living room of Monty's home. The house was quite spacious, but had the cute feeling of a public television set for a broadcast of one of Grimms' Fairy Tales.

Lala sat in a puffy armchair, and Monty had his broken leg elevated on a recliner. Between them, all four dogs were asleep on a futon that Lala had unfolded when everyone made as though to leap up on it.

"Wait! Wait, wait, wait!" she had demanded. "It will never accommodate you all like that."

Lala refilled Monty's teacup and then refilled her own. They gazed over at their sleeping dogs.

"Perfect fit," Lala said. Monty smiled at her.

"Are you married, my dear?"

"Widowed."

Lala saw Monty blanch.

"I'm so sorry," he said.

"Thank you, Monty. It's no fun, huh?"

"No fun at all."

"Did you and your wife always live in Manhattan Beach?"

"No, no, we lived in the other Manhattan. The one in New York. My daughter moved us out here when Trudy got sick."

"You lived in Manhattan?" Lala yipped. "So did I! The West Village."

"Oh, I always wanted to live there. We planned to move there one day. We were on the Upper East Side."

"I'm so sorry," Lala said. "I'm kidding, I'm kidding, forgive me."

"Nothing to forgive," Monty said. "I'm in agreement. It was fun before gentrification when we moved there after graduate school. But I could only put up with so many precocious youngsters being smiled at with parental smugness while the well-dressed little tykes ran to the curb and barked 'Taxi!' with that truly nausea-inducing air of self-conscious superiority that they all seem to affect."

"Monty, I adore you," Lala said. "Hey, I think it's getting close to cocktail hour. Don't get up, just tell me where you keep the booze."

Two hours later, Lala was cheerfully walking the comfortable distance from Monty's house to Geraldine's.

"You know what I must not do, right?" she asked her dogs. "I must not get ahead of myself. I mustn't get crazy and have that frantic energy that I so often do and then scare them both away from each other and screw this up entirely."

Lala undid the latch on the gate and the dogs calmly walked through to the courtyard with her. They felt no need to bolt up the stairs to their home because Monty had already given them all dinner along with Benedict.

"Okay, everyone," Lala said. "Cool is the word. Cool."

Lala rapped on Geraldine's front door. Geraldine opened it with a full martini glass in her hand.

"Lovely timing," Geraldine said.

Lala felt her jaw twitching ever so slightly as she crossed Geraldine's threshold.

*Don't do it*, she thought. *Do not do it.*

Lala walked very, very, very slowly across the tile floor of the entryway.

"I just mixed a fresh pitcher," Geraldine said.

*Don't do it,* Lala thought. *Do not do it.*

Lala spun around on her heels and let loose a deep, loud, triumphant cackle at her adopted aunt.

"And I just met your next husband! Shit! I did not mean to say that out loud!"

That evening, Lala must have enjoined Geraldine dozens of times to "please, please, please, please forget what I said."

"I am serious," Lala repeated. "I am instructing the jury to ignore the witness's outburst. The witness is a jackass."

Geraldine assured Lala that forgetting was out of the question, so they might as well make the best of it, whatever form that might take.

"We'll revisit tales of my new husband another evening soon, yes?"

"Good idea," Lala said. "We'll shelve it for now, and then maybe I'll calm down in a day or two and not ruin it all by talking about it like I'm on crack."

After Geraldine made a huge, mouth-wateringly salty salad of chopped tomatoes and onions, both from her garden, Lala left her adopted aunt's apartment to "go upstairs and start writing because I feel sure that if not all writers, then certainly at least Hemingway, would agree that when you're potted is an excellent time to start a massive reworking of a project."

Once back in her place, Lala ripped off her clothes and tossed them on the bed. She changed into cotton drawstring pants and a sweatshirt top and covered her feet with thick cotton socks. Then she fussed with the sparse items on her very neat and uncluttered desk. And then she carefully took all of her discarded clothes off the bed and hung up those that needed to be hung up in the closet and folded those that needed to be folded and put them in a drawer because the clutter was driving her crazy.

Yootza was on Lala's lap the instant she sat down at her chair. Petunia and Chester sat beside her and glared at their brother.

Jealousy hung heavily in the air.

"Mama's sorry, darlings," Lala said. She picked up Yootza, who growled at the disturbance and who was then swatted so tenderly on his nose as a correction that no canine could have interpreted the motion as anything but loving praise from an overly indulgent guardian, and went to get Petunia's and Chester's beds from the other side of the room. She positioned the beds, one on either side of her chair, and sat down with Yootza, who settled back on her lap.

Yootza looked down at his siblings, who had curled themselves into tight balls in their beds and were glaring up at him.

"Mama loves me more than you," Yootza's smug little face seemed to say. "You fat-ass losers."

"Ohhh, babies," Lala said, looking down from left to right at her larger dogs. "*Maman est désolée.* If you were three Chihuahuas, I might be able to fit you all on my lap right now. I'm afraid that life is not always fair. Being bigger has certain advantages. As well as certain disadvantages. As does being smaller. Trust me on that. I can't see substantial portions of the world unless I stand on a stepladder. Which is quite impractical when one is walking down the street. Oh my goodness, I seem to have lost my focus already."

Lala lifted the cover of her laptop. The screen glowed to life before her.

With some hesitation, and also a vague, almost unnoticeable stirring of excitement, she copied the Word document entitled "Dressed.Lady.Script" and named the new version "Dressed.Lady. Novel." Then she moved the arrow on the screen to the new document and pounded her index finger on the mouse.

Lala stared at the words in front of her. She thought she might be hearing faint, throaty voices . . . voices from the words on the screen that had come to life as malevolent cartoon personas to berate her.

"Ohhh, look at the writer. She's a writer. Go on, Writer, write something. Whatcha waitin' for, Writer? Show us whatcha got . . . Hey, I don't hear any typing . . . Anybody hear any typing?"

*There's nothing to be nervous about,* Lala said to herself. *Just ignore them. Have fun. Have. Fun. Don't do it if it's not fun. Operative word for the day. F-U-N. Operative word for from now on.*

"Get stuffed, voices of resistance and terror in my own head!"

In a sudden frenzy of activity, one that startled sleeping Yootza and made the spoiled little bastard growl again, Lala swooped forward and dramatically tapped her fingers on the keyboard.

On the screen the words "FADE IN" were replaced with the words "CHAPTER ONE."

Lala stared at the new letters. For several minutes. Until they all began to float around.

"Okey-doke," Lala said. "That's enough for the first session. Don't want to burn out from the get-go."

Lala dragged the arrow up to "File," found "Save As," whacked her index finger on the mouse, and closed out of the document after indicating that the genie inside the laptop should replace the already existing work with the revised version.

Lala very carefully stood. She cradled Yootza in her left arm and worked with her right hand to unleash her laptop from its wired confines, so she could take it with her to the couch in the living room.

She padded out of the bedroom. Petunia and Chester did not bother to wake up and follow her.

Lala slowly lowered herself onto the sofa. Yootza grumbled in his sleep. She placed him next to her, so she could balance the computer on a pillow on her lap.

Lala logged on to her e-mail and typed a new communication to her best friend.

The subject line read, "I HAD SEX."

Lala grabbed the remote and turned on the TV before she continued to the body of the missive.

Lala believed just because e-mails were electronic, that didn't mean they shouldn't be written with the same lack of ridiculous abbreviations and bizarre-but-now-commonplace symbols that were absent from the handwritten communications that had been deemed worthy of preservation in a volume of correspondence between a turn-of-the-last-century-before-this-one author and his closest friend.

"Hi, Brenda," she typed. "I apologize for shouting, but I HAD SEX. With a great guy and then he left the next day to go on a four-month sailing trip around the world with his adult sons. Fuck me, can you believe that shit?"

"Hmmm," Lala mused. "I'm thinking 'Fuck me' didn't show up much in the collected letters of Ralph Waldo Emerson."

Out of the corner of her eye, Lala saw a wonderfully familiar face on the TV screen.

"Omigod, Yootza," Lala yipped.

She lifted the sleeping dachshund and wiggled his stubby right front paw at the screen. Because it always cracked her up to make it look like the little guy was waving at something. And the more unlikely the object of his greeting, the better.

"Look," Lala giggled. "Our favorite movie is on again!"

Lala quickly returned to her e-mail to Brenda.

"Gotta run. *Casablanca* is on again. I watched it with that great guy I just told you about. After WE HAD SEX. I'll call you tomorrow to tell you more about that great guy. With whom I HAD SEX."

Lala hit "Send."

"I can't believe I just typed 'Gotta.' I must be really drunk. 'Got to run' looks weird, though. Fussy. Nineteenth century. What's a wordsmith to do in this modern era? How to balance colloquial and correct is the bedeviling issue of our time. *Oy vey.*"

Lala placed the laptop on the coffee table. She swung her legs up so that she and Yootza were lying flat on the couch. She had her head propped up on the pillow that had, up until a moment before, supported the laptop. Yootza was completely horizontal on her chest and tummy.

Lala watched as Paul Henreid marched up to the house band at Rick's Café Américain and demanded they "Play 'La Marseillaise'! Play it!" because the Nazis who were occupying *Casablanca* had started singing "Die Wacht am Rhein" in the café, and Paul was not about to stand for that, and of course all the band members had to wordlessly look over at Humphrey Bogart for permission to play the French national anthem because he's their boss, and there are Nazis in the café, and, of course, Humphrey wordlessly nods his permission because that's the kind of guy he is, and so the band starts playing, and everyone in the café stands up and sings the French national anthem and their voices drown out the Nazis, and the Nazis give up the fight. For now. And ultimately the Nazis lose the fight. Because of people like Rick and Ilsa and Viktor and even Claude Rains as Captain Louis Renault, who seems self-serving but is actually quite a hero himself.

"My GOD is this movie great," Lala gasped.

She swung herself back to a sitting position. Yootza rolled off her and onto the sofa, woke up and started snapping and snarling at the air around him until his rage spent itself. Then he turned in a circle several times and fell asleep again almost immediately.

Lala grabbed her laptop and conjured a blank document onto the screen. She typed with lust-filled urgency. And with a desire to remember her thoughts before they evaporated from her increasingly challenged mind.

"David, David, David, David, David . . . *Casablanca* is on again, and I wish you were still here so we could watch it again together and then HAVE SEX again together. Is there a moment in all of cinema more stirring than when Viktor Laszlo orders the band to 'Play "La Marseillaise"! Play it!'? Oh, I think not. And I think no one will have the cheek, the gall, the misguided foolishness to argue otherwise with me—because if they were to argue with me, then they would have to listen to a diatribe in response that only consisted of the words 'Are you out of your mind? You're out of your fucking mind, right? What, you're fucking crazy, or what?' repeated over and over again on an endless loop and how tiresome would that be? Bathos alert, David . . . I miss you already . . . Wow, that came out of (Note to self: consider replacing with 'outta') nowhere, huh? But it's true, and it apparently had to come out . . . because I seem to be powerless to stop the truth from revealing itself . . . and I have a feeling you're asking yourself right now, what's with all the ellipses, huh? God, are we in tune with each other, or what?"

# GREEN-EYED MONSTERS

The following weekend started with yet another gorgeous, sunny day. Lala had finally persuaded Geraldine to just check out Lala's new friend with the broken leg. It took some doing, as Geraldine had almost immediately abandoned the reasoned approach to the idea that she expressed when Lala first blurted it.

"I'm not in the mood," Geraldine said. "I don't feel like welcoming any major changes into my life right now."

"Oh, come on, it's no big deal," Lala responded. "There's no obligation. We'll just go over and see what you think, yeah? For fun. Just for the fun of it."

Geraldine was cradling Yootza in her arms like a baby as they walked toward Monty's house on the excuse that they were out walking the dogs—which was true because, of course, the dogs had to be walked often—and they had just happened to find themselves in front of Monty's house, no big deal—which, given the amount of coaxing and maneuvering it took to get Geraldine on the road, was aggressive bullshit. And especially so, given how long it took them to get dressed before they left. Multiple outfits were created and discarded before the two women emerged in studied, casual chic. They both were now in cute, comfortably tight jeans, sneakers that were meant for strolling and not for working out, and lush, warm, cotton sweaters. As much as they might justifiably be accused of looking like a mother/daughter ad for the Gap, the effect was working, and they knew it.

For some reason, shortly after they started out, Yootza sat down on the side of the road and refused to walk another step. So now Geraldine was carrying the stubborn, little pill.

"Why is this gentleman my next husband?" Geraldine asked. "I'm asking because I'm curious. Not because I'm necessarily even interested in having a next husband."

"Because he is," Lala said. She had Petunia and Chester on joined leashes around her waist, and she was swinging her arms in exaggerated optimism and encouragement as they walked. "Splendid day, eh? Splendid! A magical day! A day for magic."

"Why isn't he *your* next husband? Because I'm wondering where you got the idea that I want to get married again?"

"Fine," Lala huffed. "So he's your next boyfriend. Paramour. Hunka hunka burnin' love. Name your label."

"Why isn't he *your* next boyfriend, paramour, hunka—"

"Chester, please stop pulling. Mama's going to topple over face first. Is that your goal?"

Lala turned to Geraldine and stuck her tongue out at her and did a long, trilling raspberry in Geraldine's direction. "Because he's yours. He just is. He's not mine. Trust me, I wouldn't be sharing him if he were."

They walked in mutually stiff-backed, mutually semi-irritated silence for a minute or two until, out of the corner of her eye, Lala saw Geraldine suddenly smile broadly and wondered what the hell that was all about.

"Have you heard from David?"

Lala pursed her lips. Geraldine noticed this out of the corner of her eye and worried about what the hell that was meant to indicate.

"We agreed not to contact each other."

"Oh, for heaven's sake, why?"

"He's on the ocean. I'm by the ocean. At this point probably not even the same ocean. I don't want to like him any more than I already do."

"And from you I'm taking advice on romance," Geraldine said.

Lala nodded her head in the direction of a house just a few yards down the street from where they were.

"There he is. The one with the broken leg and the wheelchair. You can't miss him."

Geraldine narrowed her eyes to improve her focus.

"Cute," she said. "I think maybe very cute. I think maybe I like."

"But don't take any romantic advice from me," Lala said. "What do I know?"

A tall, brunette, imposing woman exited Monty's house carrying a blanket. She placed the blanket on Monty's legs. The woman was maybe in her late thirties, and she was very attractive, in a slightly rigid way.

Lala and Geraldine stopped walking.

*Merde*, Lala thought. *Monty's got a girlfriend.*

"Oh, for heaven's sake," Geraldine whispered fiercely. "He's got a girlfriend."

She spun on her heels, but Lala grabbed Geraldine's arm before she could complete her trajectory in the opposite direction.

"No, no, no, I bet that's his nurse," Lala said.

"Oh, look at the nice timing," the two women heard Monty cheerfully call in their direction. "Lala, I want you and your beautiful companion to meet my daughter."

*Better still!* Lala thought. *I hope I don't burst into maudlin tears of grateful relief. Must not do that. Must not burst into maudlin tears of grateful relief.*

"Hi! We just happened to be walking in your neighborhood! Walking the dogs! In your neighborhood. And you're outside in your yard. While we're walking by your house. Fun coincidence, huh?"

❦

Monty's daughter, Helene, was a wonderful hostess. She whipped up a delicious vegetarian lunch for their guests. During which Benedict the Great Dane stayed under the table and kept trying to park his snout on Lala's crotch. And after which, having been fed enough treats to actually satiate their hound appetites for a brief period, her three dogs lay together on their backs on the plush rug nearby, with their legs flopping open to expose their bellies as they all grunted and snorted in their sleep. Upon seeing this, Benedict finally removed his snout and went over to join his new friends. He put his big head on Petunia's tummy and sighed heavily. This did not wake up the beagle, though apparently Petunia did have a terrifying nightmare shortly after the large cranium settled on her gut, judging by the amount of twitching and whimpering that was going on.

During lunch, it was revealed that Helene was a published author. And a member of the acting company at a small but very prestigious theatre in Burbank.

*I want to go home,* Lala thought. *To New York. Now.*

Geraldine had instantly recognized that Helene's life would be upsetting to Lala. She gave Lala a comforting smile as Helene waxed rhapsodic about the joys of book tours, where apparently even the frustrations were actually answered prayers dusted in gold.

"Yes, it was well after midnight, and I hadn't eaten anything all evening, but that's what happens in a small town when the local bookstore is filled with fans. You can't get away. You just can't. You owe it to your public to chat, to answer questions, to inspire future authors. And it's more than owing. It's a joy. A joy. You just have to trust that there's a Denny's somewhere in the county that's serving eggs and hash browns at 2:00 a.m. And usually there is."

Lala was grateful when Geraldine discreetly reached over and gave her hand a comforting squeeze during Helene's monologue. But now they were all comfortably settled in the living room playing Trivial Pursuit, and Lala was starting to feel mightily jealous about the clear gaze of admiration and affection that Geraldine was already showing the warm and gracious young woman.

*Hello, everyone,* Lala thought. *Just call me Cinderelly before the ball.*

Monty had just asked his daughter a history question.

*I know this,* Lala thought. *It's Molo—*

"Vyacheslav Molotov," Helene said.

*Damn, she's smart,* Lala thought. *And throwing in the first name. Like we wouldn't have accepted the answer without that. I knew it was Vyacheslav. I wonder if she knows what Lenin's real name is.*

"I don't mean to be pompous," Helene said, smiling charmingly. "It's just that I had a Soviet History professor at college who placed great emphasis on the details. So it seems I will never forget that Lenin's real name is—"

"Vladimir Illyich Ulyanov," Lala said.

Helene's face lit up with the foreshadowing of recognition and maybe a new best friend on the horizon.

"And Trotsky?" she said.

"Lev Bronstein," Lala said.

"Do not tell me you had Pierce Parker."

"I did," Lala said.

"Do not tell me you went to Wesleyan."

"I did," Lala said.

"Were we in his class together?" Helene asked.

*Okay, I don't even care if she's blowing smoke up my tuchus,* Lala thought. *Now I can't even hate her because she's being so nice. I hate when that happens.*

"Oh, stop," Lala said. "I've got to be close to ten years older than you."

"You certainly don't look it," Helene said.

*Ohh, jeez,* Lala thought. *Helene's little finger? Allow me to introduce myself. My name is Lala, and I just got wrapped around you. Nice fit, huh?*

🍷

Monty kissed Geraldine's and Lala's hands as they all said goodbye. Lala could see how beguiled Geraldine was by him.

Before they left, Geraldine bragged to Monty and Helene about what a wonderful writer her niece was and about how she was working on a novel. Lala winced at the proud sounds her aunt was making, and, against all odds, successfully prevented herself from smothering Geraldine with an embroidered pillow to make her stop. And then Helene clapped her hands with delight and said that Lala absolutely had to come read some of her work at a charity event Helene was hosting for a local literacy program next week, and Lala said she would be delighted, and Monty asked Geraldine to be his date for the evening. And Lala wanted to stab herself repeatedly in the heart with one of the antique rapiers that Monty had in a display case in the living room.

*Well,* Lala thought as the whole fiasco was unfolding, *at least neither Helene nor Monty has asked me if I am in fact a published or produced writer. Because then I would have to say yes, twice. In* The New Yorker. *Back when Tammany Hall still reigned with an iron fist over Gotham politics.*

They walked home in silence with Lala frowning.

"Well, my dearest niece," Geraldine said after a few blocks. She was once again carrying Yootza like an infant because he had resolutely refused to walk another step after they got maybe a hundred feet from Monty's house. Clearly, this being carted around everywhere had become a happy habit in the little dictator's mind. "You are as brilliant an observer of the human condition as you are beautiful and caring and—"

"Yeah, yeah," Lala snorted. "I know exactly what you're doing. At this point, you'd probably bonk Monty just to make me feel better about myself."

"Yes," Geraldine agreed, "I probably would. Because you are very precious to me, and I recognize that you're maybe feeling a bit low right now. Fortunately, though, I would actually like to bonk Monty at some point, so you really are a very insightful matchmaker."

"Thanks," Lala said.

They walked along a bit in silence. Until Lala heaved a gust of a sigh.

"It's worse that we went to the same college," Lala said.

"I understand," Geraldine said.

"Whether that's reasonable or rational or not. It just is. And she's nice, which drives me crazy."

"I think it was lovely that she invited you to read at the charity event," Geraldine said. "Clearly she thinks of you as a peer."

"That's just because she doesn't know what a failure I am," Lala said.

Geraldine stopped walking. Her tone became very stern.

"I don't think any of the animals you have helped would agree with that assessment."

Lala, who had continued walking and had indeed picked up the pace considerably while Geraldine stood firmly in her indignant tracks, yelled back over her shoulder.

"Not fair! How am I supposed to wallow in self-pity when you say shit like that to me?"

Geraldine scrambled to catch up with Lala and Petunia and Chester. Yootza bobbled up and down as she ran, and his little head smacked against Geraldine's right breast, and he growled because Geraldine was disturbing his princely repose.

"Look, Helene's life is not a reflection on your life, okay?" Geraldine puffed. "Do not go down that path. That way lies madness."

"You're tellin' me," Lala said. "We are never seeing Helene again. Not ever. And we're not going to see Monty again either. Never ever. I'm sorry, but this has got to be my final word on the subject. Case closed. End of discussion."

🍷

"Why did you invite everyone?"

Lala smiled at her aunt even as her words to Geraldine were uttered through her teeth with intensity intended to convey a verbal slap. Lala returned a wave to Helene, who had flapped her hand across the room to Lala with a welcoming nod, followed by a raised index finger to indicate that she would be over soon to chat with Lala and Geraldine.

Lala surveyed the large central room of The Remarkable Bookshop in downtown Manhattan Beach. The family-owned emporium had been there for almost fifty years and was one of the last independent bookstores in the area. Or the state. Or the country. Or the Milky Way galaxy.

Geraldine grabbed two full champagne flutes from the bar right next to them and winked at the cute bartender. She handed one of the glasses to Lala.

"I invited our neighbors because they are our friends and because they like you, and I'm proud of your good heart. I'm proud of your tenacity. Don't be so cranky."

"If I'm cranky, it's because I haven't slept in a week worrying about this damn reading," Lala said. "You know how lazy I am. You know I write in fits and starts."

"I stopped by to check on you last night." Geraldine swooped in to dip a snow pea into a vat of ranch dressing. "Because I hadn't seen you all day. You were sound asleep in front of *Say Yes to the Dress*. You were drooling on Yootza's little forehead."

"Okay, but I was working in front of the TV because I write in fits and starts because I can't focus on anything for very long, and I probably was taking a short break from all the fabulousness on that show."

Geraldine saw one of their neighbors walking in their direction. She leaned in to whisper to Lala.

"Did you know they lifted the *fatwa* against Salman? Sort of. It's a long story. Salman told me. He still wants us to call him Thomas. I guess you can never be too careful."

Thomas was balancing five glasses of champagne on a disposable plate that was, thankfully, plastic and not paper.

"Oh, you've already got drinks," Thomas said.

Lala sucked down all the champagne in her glass and slammed the empty vessel on the top of the bar.

"Not anymore," she said and grabbed one of the glasses off the plate. In an instant, Thomas's carefully planned balance was thrown off, and it was only the quick acting of Geraldine and Thomas that saved the evening from complete disaster. Lala surveyed their handiwork admiringly.

"Wow, you two work really well together. Someone should write a screenplay about you. Kind of buddy flick meets . . . meets . . . I don't know what. Dame Helen Mirren could play you, Aunt Geraldine. And . . . umm . . . someone who looks a lot like Salman Rushdie could—"

"Shhh," Geraldine hissed. She glanced around nervously to see if anyone with ties to any *ayatollah* had heard Lala.

"Yeah. Oops. Sorry."

Their other neighbors, Stephanie and Chuck, came over carrying stacks of books and grinning dementedly.

"You can buy these here!" Stephanie trilled.

"They've got books that you can buy and take with you right away!" Chuck said.

Lala looked at the two young veterinarians and wrinkled her nose with her mouth open in the universal facial contortion conveying, "What the fuck are you talking about?"

"It's a bookstore," Lala said.

"Yeah, isn't that cool!" Stephanie said. "Amazon better watch out. This kind of convenience could catch on fast."

"Hey, Lala, have you heard from Doctor David?" Chuck asked.

*Oh barf,* Lala thought.

"He is so cool," Stephanie said. "What a great guy."

"Okay," Geraldine said. She put her hand on Stephanie's elbow and gently started to steer her away from Lala. "How about if Thomas and I take you two adorable kids over to the cashier, and we'll show you how to pay for these books in person? It's a little tricky at first, but I know you'll get the hang of it. Lala, you go ahead and get ready for your reading."

Lala watched the four of them depart. And then she hustled to the ladies' room, where she started twitching and hyperventilating until both her exposed and covered skin had a sheath of sweat on it, and where Helene found her dabbing under her armpits with a wad of toilet paper.

"Hi there!" Helene said, floating through the door. Helene's entrance almost seemed to transform the standard-issue, but very clean store bathroom, into a powder room Lala might have expected to find at one of New York City's most absurdly expensive hotels.

"Hi!" Lala said.

*God, she's got style,* Lala thought. *There's just something about her. Why do I so often find myself in the company of women about whom there is just something?*

Lala didn't turn around. She just stared at Helene's reflection in the mirror. Helene started to wash her hands.

Helene was wearing a pair of black pants with very thin, pale pink stripes and a matching jacket with short sleeves. The jacket was buttoned, and she didn't have a shirt on underneath. Her hair was up in a casual French twist. She looked gorgeous.

"Isn't this fun?" Helene said. "I'm so grateful that you could join us. I love your dress."

Lala did indeed have on a lovely new wraparound dress in a rich, blue shade that her aunt had picked out for her. Geraldine had insisted that she wear it with her new high, black boots after Lala came knocking on Geraldine's door an hour before they were supposed to leave for the reading, shrilly announcing, "I'm not going to the damn reading because I look like shit in every damn thing I have, and I don't need more humiliation in my life, thank you very much."

"Thanks," Lala said. She handed Helene a paper towel. "Helene, you look fabulous. You really do."

Helene gave Lala a quick kiss on the cheek and put her arm around Lala's shoulder. The two women made their way out the door.

"Come on, pal," Helene said. "Let's go glory in the written word."

♆

Lala guessed there were over a hundred chairs set up around the podium where the readers would be sharing their work. All of the chairs were occupied.

*I'm going to barf,* Lala thought.

Geraldine blew Lala a kiss from the front row. Monty, who had, since the last time they saw him, exchanged his leg cast for a much more relaxed but still substantial brace with thick straps of Velcro wrapped all up and down, was sitting next to Geraldine grinning like a pauper who had just won a Powerball lottery with the highest payoff in the history of legalized gambling.

Geraldine and Monty each gave Lala a big thumbs up. When they saw that they had made exactly the same encouraging gesture at precisely the same moment, they collapsed together in a fit of giggles.

*Sheesh,* Lala thought. *Look at those two. How cute are they? Seriously.*

After making a pitch for the literacy program that was as heartfelt as it was rote, Helene read from the first chapter of her soon-to-be-released book.

Lala had never read any of Helene's work before. She was miffed to find that Helene's writing was very good. Very, very good.

*The only thing that is saving my sanity,* Lala thought, *is that she writes mysteries and that's not my genre at all, nor do I ever want it to be. So I guess my raging jealousy has been momentarily subdued.*

Three other writers read before Helene called Lala to the podium. Lala found the work of two of them to be delightful and the work of the third to be insufferable. Several times as the young man was reading, Lala had to stop herself from groaning aloud.

"In the morn, in the dark, there are echoes of my time with Miriyan that whisper until I beg madness to overpower me."

*Jesus,* Lala thought. *What is he? In junior high? Where does he come up with this crap?*

The young man tossed his hair back and gave a soulful look to the audience before he continued.

"But then this morn, my comrade, Rothal of the Unicorn Leagues, reminds me that on this day we fight the united armies of Strobl and Lulilaerd. This day, we fight the darkness. This day, we fight for the good. This day . . ."

And here he paused.

*Seriously, shoot me now,* Lala thought.

"We fight for our lives."

The young man slammed his book shut. He stepped to the side of the podium, stood in full view of the audience, paused again, and then took a sweeping bow that brought his forehead in danger of colliding with the floor and that would have made the curtain calls of Sarah Bernhardt look folksy.

Helene led the enthusiastic applause as she approached the podium. Lala watched a row of young ladies that must have represented the cream of every cheerleading squad within a fifty-mile radius stand and wave their arms about like madwomen as they shouted, "Whoo, whoo, whoo!"

Helene gave the young man a hug. The young man blushed even as he lingered with his cheek hovering over Helene's bosom until Helene had to gently push him away.

"What a lovely reading," Helene said. "Thank you, d'Artagnan."

*Seriously, that's his first name,* Lala thought. *You are fucking kidding me. His parents have some damn nerve.*

"And now, please welcome Lala Pettibone."

Helene turned to her friend and made a cute, little beckoning "get-on-up-here-you-adorable-sassy-older-new-gal-pal-o'-mine" wave.

*And now, please don't let me trip,* Lala thought.

Lala stood. She walked to the podium. She placed the notebook that contained her carefully proofread work on the stand and opened it. And that moment of opening her notebook was the first moment in which she realized that everyone else who had read had been reading not from notebooks that they had created themselves, but from copies of their books. Copies of their published books. Copies of their writing that had been deemed desirable for publication. By an outside arbiter of some sort.

*Fuck me,* Lala thought.

Lala looked down at the words that were doing aquarobics and playing water volleyball and executing cannonballs off the high tower in front of her.

She debated whether running screaming out of that charming independent bookstore might feel defiant and liberating and brave and deliciously self-indulgent.

She glanced up at the audience and smiled.

*Fuck it,* she thought.

The first word she read was "The."

It came out sounding like the bleating of a severely congested sheep.

Lala cleared her throat.

"The Soused Cinéaste," she read.

Several people in the audience chuckled.

Lala froze.

*I fucked up, she thought. Are they making fun of me? Did I fuck up already?*

She took a deep breath. And then, without any conscious decision to unleash the fury, she let the floodgates open.

"Reflections on the world of film at thirty-seven thousand feet. Flying cross-country after having knocked back several glasses of quite lovely champagne. And may I pause to send my kudos to Sir Richard Branson and any other airline magnates who understand and appreciate and act on the public's desire to have their own damn private screen on the seat in front of them so that they can relish their own damn private selection of entertainment. Because, let me tell you, *in bubbly veritas,* and for my money, anything that can help make the time pass in any way is genius when you're stuck in a space that small with that many strangers for that long with no hope of escape. And didn't that just sound like a description of a maximum-security prison? Or Hell?"

An appreciative laugh rippled through the crowd. Lala paused and smiled nervously at everyone.

*Wait a minute,* she thought, surveying the warm, encouraging faces with her glazed stare, *I think I remember that sound. Was it . . . wait . . . when I was in that comedy group . . . on those rare occasions when I was actually any good . . . I think the audience would make that sound.*

Lala bobbed her head and grinned at everyone.

Geraldine looked at Lala with sudden and expanding concern.

"Are you okay?" Geraldine mouthed silently at her niece, with exaggerated clarity so that the movements of her mouth would be interpretable as words.

Geraldine also added a few gestures to up the odds of Lala understanding what she was getting at.

The gesture for "okay" was a broad smile and an insouciant sideways nod of her head. Accompanied by a wink.

Lala winked back at her and gave her the universal symbol for okay—tips of the thumb and forefinger of the right hand together in a circle with the other three fingers standing jauntily. At which point Geraldine slapped her forehead because she had apparently forgotten that of course that was the way she should have conveyed that word.

"Cool," Lala said. "Cool. So."

She went back to her pages.

"OMIGOD, there's a channel called 'Blockbuster Classics.' OMIGOD. Look at the offerings. *Thor*. I've already seen it, and I can't wait to see it again because it is genius. And did you know that the character of Thor is played by a hologram? Because NO MERE HUMAN can be that gorgeous and perfect.

"And may I pause to add that my dream *ménage à trois* consists of myself—which I suppose should go without saying, but I want to say it anyway so there's no misunderstanding should the opportunity ever arise—consists of myself, the God of Thunder, mighty Thor, and Loki, Lord of the Underworld.

"People, look at these blockbuster classics offerings! *Pirates of the Caribbean, On Stranger Tides*? I don't give a shit what the critics said. Vicious bastards. They eviscerated that movie, and they did it because they're jealous they didn't make that movie. It is genius. It has got Johnny Depp. Who needs anything else? I mean anything else . . . plot, characters, dialogue, when you've got Johnny Depp? The man is a movie star. The man is a genius.

"*Green Lantern*? It is a brilliant damn movie, okay? We've got Ryan Reynolds's star turn as a cocky pilot selected to put on a glowing green body suit by a bunch of creatures of all shapes and sizes and configurations wearing glowing green body suits, so they can team up to defend everything in the universe from this huge, ugly, bizarre mass that kind of has a face and that gets more and more powerful by feeding off the terror it inspires. And if that's not a metaphor for my college years, then I don't know what is. We've got good. We've got evil. We've got sex; we've got survival; we've got transformation. We've got a sequel coming. And then probably a prequel.

"And let me, once again, veer off topic for a moment to add that a *ménage à trois* with Johnny Depp and Ryan Reynolds wouldn't be such a bad thing to suffer through either, huh?

"We're hammered, and our cups are runneth'ing over with wine and love and entertainment at thirty-seven thousand feet.

"Hey, look at this! Other channels! With other themes! 'Lighter Fare.' Is that a name for a genre, or what?

"A teen romcom with that girl on TV who's dating that singer guy whose name I can't remember because I'm too hammered, and she's poor, and she's saved up enough to go to Paris with her friends, but then she ends up in Monte Carlo being mistaken for a duchess or countess or some fabulous shit like, that and they all end up in gorgeous ball gowns at the charity event of the decade dry humping a slew of lesser European royalty, and, Omigod, I just realized, it's like *The Prince and the Pauper*, kind of, in a way!"

Lala slammed her hand down on the podium.

"This movie is genius! Yes! Yes, I will have another glass of quite lovely champagne, you delicious air host, you! OMIGOD! *Transformers*, Episode I-Don't-Know-Which-But-What-Does-It-Matter! This is the one that got the People's Choice Award, right? No? Well, then I suspect it was robbed. And I'm going to watch the entire film right now to see if my instincts are correct. Twice. Yeah, maybe two times in a row. Because you can do that on a plane. What? We're flying over the Great Salt Lake? NO! It's too soon! We'll be landing in LAX shortly? NO! This flight was only a minute long. Because time has no meaning anymore because I've been transported to Magic Land! Because I'm in a plane, and I'm hammered, and I'm watching mooooovieeeees!"

Lala paused. The audience looked at her, unsure if she was done. Lala closed her notebook. And the audience applauded.

Lala's aunt and her aunt's date and her neighbors applauded. Helene and the other readers applauded. The cheerleaders applauded. Everyone applauded.

Lala clutched her notebook to her chest.

*If I were to, I don't know, pass out and die from an aneurysm at this very moment,* she thought, *with this image and this feeling and this experience as my last image and feeling and experience on this Earth, that would not necessarily be the worst way to go. Not by a flippin' long shot.*

🍷

*Okay, I'm definitely glad I didn't pass out and die right after my reading,* Lala thought. *Because they are serving a very nice white wine at this shindig.*

An older gentleman standing a few groups away from Lala caught her eye with a wave. He smiled and raised his hands in her direction to send a round of applause her way. Lala smiled and waved back, and debated running over and kissing the older gentleman full on the lips.

*And the adoration*, Lala thought. *The adoration, which is admittedly closer to some degree of validation than actual adoration, but I'm going to go ahead and up it more than a few notches in my mind. That and the white wine. Are definitely making me glad that I'm still alive. I'm alive! Still!*

These musings were putting yet another shit-eating grin on Lala's puss. She was standing alone near the bar after having returned from the ladies' room. It was the first time she was by herself since the readings ended.

Geraldine and Monty and Stephanie and Chuck and Thomas had grabbed Lala right away when she walked off the stage and showered her with their enthusiasm.

"You were delightful, my dear," Monty said.

"I'm so proud of you," Geraldine said.

She grabbed Lala in a hug and whispered in her ear, "Jesus, I nearly plotzed when it looked like you were about to go helter skelter at the beginning."

"'The Soused Cinéaste,'" Thomas said. "Great title."

"Too bad Doctor David wasn't here tonight! Bet he would have really laughed at your stuff!" Stephanie exulted. "He's so much fun."

Chuck nodded his head as his wife spoke.

"Wish Doctor David could have been here. That would've been really great."

Lala couldn't suppress a full-head twitch, but she was relieved to find that no one seemed to notice.

Nearly everyone who had been at the reading was staying for the party, and quite a few of the audience members stopped by Lala's circle to tell her how much they had enjoyed her work.

As she was standing at the bar alone, gathering her overwhelmingly happy thoughts, the cheerleading squad passed by Lala. The girls were moving as though they were one ecstatic, ungainly mammal on tiptoes rushing to thrust themselves into the orbit that was d'Artagnan and his brilliance. Then, quite suddenly, one of the cheerleaders extricated herself from the collective and ran up to Lala.

"Ma'am?"

Lala looked to her left and to her right and behind herself.

*I think she means me,* Lala thought.

"Mmmm?"

"I just wanted to tell you that I thought what you wrote was great!"

"Oh, thank you so much," Lala said.

Lala paused, feeling instinctively that she should add something else. Feeling that, somehow, she hadn't said enough to the cheerful and genuine young lady.

"Thank you, dear."

The cheerleader nodded and happily patted Lala's shoulder and skipped back to rejoin the acrobatic plasma life force.

*Ohhh, fine,* Lala thought. *Ma'am. One of the most fun nights of my life, and all of a sudden I'm matronly. Swell. And I'm using the word 'dear.' To speak to a young person. Because I'm suddenly so damn matronly.*

Lala watched the cheerleaders surround d'Artagnan in a clear attempt to absorb him into their pulsating energy field.

Lala's focus fixed on the Man of the Evening himself. The zygote scrivener was preening more than a peacock in mating season.

*Look at all that youth,* Lala thought. *God, I feel ancient.*

"I could be their . . . Sheesh, I could be their grandmother," she whispered to herself.

"Well, maybe, but those would have been some very early pregnancies because you certainly don't look it."

Lala spun around toward the masculine voice, and in spinning, wedged her nose smack into the grain of a soft wool suit covering a firm set of pectoral muscles.

She pushed herself back on her heels and looked up. Smiling down at her was a man with shoulder-length black hair.

*Notre Majesté Louis Quatorze?* she thought.

The man nodded toward the d'Artagnan vortex.

"Is that an amorphous gaggle of youth, or is that an amorphous gaggle of youth?"

Lala turned her gaze back to the kids.

"Listen, stop me right away if you're hopelessly enamored, and I'm just a bitter old coot," the man continued, "but what that young pup read? Was that for shit, or what?"

"Ohhh, yeah," Lala said.

"He's got a four-book deal, and they're filming that crap we heard tonight in New Zealand right now."

"Sheesh," Lala said.

"You know what I liked about your piece? You focused on a woman's reaction to movies as a woman. A specific woman with a hefty libido who speaks from her particulars to many other women, regardless of their circumstances."

Lala looked at the man to see if he was pulling her leg. Apparently, he wasn't.

"Yeah. I guess I react to everything as a woman . . . with . . . ummm . . . my specific libido and stuff."

Lala twisted her lips and wrinkled her nose.

"You made that libido comment because of my age?"

"It's an appreciative comment," the man said. "A very appreciative one. Made from my particular circumstances. Which, I guess, is the prism through which I view most everything. As it happens, I was married for over twenty years. For the last few of those, my wife lost her libido, so—"

"Well, you know, there are a lot of factors quite beyond our control, and so I don't think it's fair for you to put the onus on her if –"

"For me. I'm sorry, I didn't express that clearly. It wasn't lost. She found it just fine. With her business partner."

"Ohhh, sorry," Lala said. "I get strident sometimes. Please excuse me."

The man took a silver card case out of the pocket of his jacket and handed a business card to Lala.

Lala read, "James Lancaster."

*Nice name,* Lala thought.

Lala read, "President, Lancaster E-Publishing."

*Holy shiiiiit!* Lala thought.

"I'd love to read some more of your stuff," James Lancaster said.

*I'm gonna barf,* Lala thought.

"Ummm . . . yeah . . . great . . . that would be great. So you live here in town, yes? I mean, there's no urgency, right? I can get it to you sometime . . . very soon . . . ish?"

# Fever-ish

"Oh, for the love of God, honey, do not buy that dress. Trust me, you do not want to look like that on your wedding day."

The warm, reassuring lights of impending dawn were just starting to rise outside the many windows in Lala's living room. She was stretched out on the sofa, precariously balancing her laptop just below her chin. The cord connecting the computer with its power source wove around and over valleys and mountains of warm, unconscious dogs. The amount of cozy fleece on the couch in the form of drawstring pants and a crewneck shirt and infinite blankies was epic.

Yootza was positioned directly below the laptop and was functioning as a semi-smooth surface for the device. He had his little body draped out long on Lala's stomach, and his head was wedged between her breasts, where his mouth, surrounded by graying fur, was engaging in molasses-paced exhalations and inhalations that were punctuated by a whistling sound and occasionally interrupted by the staccato whimpering of a very lively dream.

Lala lifted the laptop slightly and looked at her dachshund.

"I confess I'm no natural fashion maven," she admitted to Yootza. "But even I know she does not want to look like that on her wedding day."

Lala had once again been trying to transform her screenplay of *Dressed Like a Lady, Drinks Like a Pig* into a comedic novel. She had begun the effort close to seven hours earlier, after she had come back from a delicious, relaxing dinner with Aunt Geraldine at a wonderful French restaurant that was within walking distance. They had shared a bottle of expensive red wine that was half-off because every Tuesday all the bottles of wine were discounted.

On that particular Tuesday, two of the letters on the tricolor neon sign above the entrance to the restaurant were out, so that Le Petit Bistro read as Le tit Bistro.

Lala's flirtatious French with the adorable young waiter, who had grown up near San Diego and did not speak a word of the language of the Gauls, had become more fluent and more panting with each glass of Châteauneuf-du-Pape.

"What is his name?" Lala slurred at her aunt. She scanned the crowded bar area to see if she could catch sight of her muscular conveyor of things vegetarian and things fermented. "Is he adorable or what? What did he tell us his name is? Is it Jean Luc? Thierry? Valery?"

"I think he said it's Steve," Geraldine said.

"Jean Luc!" Lala brayed when she saw Steve emerge from the kitchen. "*Je dois parler avec toi!*"

"Lala," Geraldine hissed, "it's not really the decibels that are making your voice carry quite so obnoxiously, it's the timbre. Tone down the timbre. Now."

Lala ignored Geraldine as she gazed up at Steve and smiled.

"You are one long *verre d'eau*, aren't you? You don't mind if I use the familiar form of 'you' when we *parler*, do you?"

"No, ma'am, I sure don't," Steve said. He cheerfully handed them each a small menu. "Did you ladies save room for dessert?"

Geraldine snatched the menu out of Lala's hands and gave both back to Steve without opening her own.

"My niece will have two servings of your brioche bread pudding. As a sponge."

Steve nodded and smiled and headed back to the kitchen to put in their order.

"'Ma'am?'" Lala said. "'Ma'am' he calls me?"

In addition to the absorbing powers of the two large helpings of doughy, vanilla-ganache-covered dessert that Lala had effortlessly devoured, the crisp evening air of the quick walk that Lala took with the dogs right after she got home had also helped to clear her head a little.

But Lala was still a bit potted by the time they got back and by the time she had prepared and served the day's final meal for her precious hounds and by the time she got into her loungewear and by the time they had all piled onto the couch, but—unlike the wonderfully liberating effects the alcohol had had vis-à-vis Lala's ability to speak French more fluidly because she was too drunk to give a damn if she used the present regular tense when the subjunctive was in fact required—having a buzz on had not much helped elevate her writing skills.

Nor had James Lancaster's assurance the evening of the reading that Lala could get her "stuff" to him whenever suited her best helped ease Lala's anxiety.

After slightly less than an hour of fitful work, which had consisted chiefly of the actual writing of anything being interrupted by frequent trips to the bathroom and the kitchen and frequent grabbings of the remote to turn the sound back on "just for a few seconds so I can catch my favorite scene in *Now, Voyager* of which, as you know, there are many," as she had explained to the dogs—who were, at best, uninterested in Lala's excuses, and, at worst, contemptuous of her lack of discipline, if their sleeping through everything she said or did was any indication. Lala decided to stop using her screenplay as an outline and just write whatever came into her mind while she kept the general goals of the story in view.

This new plan of attack had resulted, after four hours of actual time and maybe an hour and a half of actual work, in five pages of prose that Lala, after rereading her night's work twice, had decided to file under "unspeakable crap, but there may be some hope for it not to suck quite so bad if I rewrite the living shit out of it at some point in the future, and isn't that why Baby Jesus calls them 'first drafts' in the first place?"

And now the sun was nearly up, and Lala had been spending the past two hours watching all the episodes of *Say Yes to the*

*Dress* that she had stored up "for a rainy day or sometime when I'm trying to write."

As she watched, Lala typed.

> Dear David, this is another chapter in my bizarre kind of a diary but kind of not a diary and really more of a long, rambling letter to you that has multiple chapters or something, I don't know. I wonder where you are. I wish I hadn't insisted that you not contact me. No, wait. Pretend you didn't hear that. The jury is instructed to disregard that outburst. If I may suggest, why don't you write to Chuck and Stephanie? They would absolutely love to hear from you. And then they could tell me all about your adventures. So, tonight's episode of 'The Soused Cinéaste,' which has also become, at least in my crazed mind, a paean of sorts to you, though the official line is I'm doing it as a writing exercise, will be an exploration of two of my favorite reality TV shows, also known as the only reality TV shows I watch, I swear to God, other than *The Bachelor* and *The Bachelorette*. But those don't count because, at the beginning of every new season, I swear I'm not going to get sucked into the madness again, and every new season I do. I tune in to the first fifteen minutes of the first episode, and I get caught up in the lunacy. Because, inevitably, someone comes out of one of the limousines that deliver the contestants to the eagerly waiting world, and I instantly want to clean their clock, and so then I have to continue to tune-in to find out if anyone does, in fact, actually clean their clock during the course of the season.
>
> Don't you hate when people say or write 'a couple things' instead of 'a couple of things'?
>
> I know language evolves, but I really wish it didn't. For me, 'language evolves' is just another way of

saying, 'What used to be wrong is now going to be right because we're too lazy to make the effort to maintain standards.'

Also, as an aside, I've been thinking about writing a series of fake interviews with famous people, alive and dead. With the alive ones, I would write in big letters in whatever venue they appeared that it was a FAKE interview, and that I never actually met the famous person, I was just MAKING THIS SHIT UP to maybe amuse one or two readers, which I trust would protect me from being sued. Fingers crossed.

Okay, so back to *Say Yes to the Dress* and *Tabatha's Salon Takeover*. I don't imagine you watch either of them. Seriously, what are the odds? And, to be frank, if you did watch either of them as faithfully as I do, I'd be forced to question your sexual orientation, our epic night of screwing notwithstanding. The dress show is about brides-to-be making a pilgrimage to the Mecca of Bridal Salons—Kleinfeld's in Brooklyn. Had I known about that place back then, I would have bought my wedding dress there instead of wearing a cotton dress I picked up at a boutique on Lexington Avenue that made me look like Little Bo Peep. I've got the photos to prove it. The salon show is about a formidable British hairstylist who rescues American salons that are in trouble because either the owners or the staff, or quite often both, currently suck at what they do. And you know why I find these shows so mesmerizing? Because they're both about transformation . . . about becoming something more . . . something happier, something cleverer, something better dressed than you were before the magicians showed up.

Lala continued writing about the shows until she reached the end of what she wanted to say about them. The result was thirty-seven double-spaced pages of text.

"That is going to require some major deleting," Lala said. Her stomach had been growling for the last hour, and she marveled that her dogs were still asleep, proving they clearly weren't feeling any hunger pangs yet.

Lala exited the apartment in search of breakfast. She held a leash in each hand. One was attached to Petunia's collar, the other to Chester's. And strapped to Lala's chest, facing outward and nestled snugly and smugly in a baby papoose, was Yootza.

The little dachshund surveyed the landscape from his high vantage point, as they all walked toward Lala's favorite beachside café, like he owned the universe and every other living creature was renting space from him, and he was starting to reconsider the terms of the lease as maybe not having been entirely biased enough to his advantage.

As Lala had recently explained to Geraldine, "The spoiled little bastard isn't willing to walk anywhere anymore unless he decides that he wants to walk, which is generally only something he does around four o'clock in the morning just when I've finally managed to fall asleep, and which, apparently, is the optimal time for the spoiled little bastard to drag me along outside in the dark like he's running in a fucking marathon."

Lala stood outside the café studying the sandwich board that was hawking the morning specials. As she debated between going in the sweet direction via pancakes or taking the savory route by way of eggs and hash browns or being horrifyingly gluttonous and having both, her mind started to wander and obsess. Aloud.

"So you live here? What a stupid comment that was. I mean, how much did I age myself? Like I had somehow forgotten because I'm too doddering and old-fashioned to remember that you can e-mail stuff to anyone anywhere in the world because this isn't the 1980s. Barf. James Lancaster must think I'm such an untalented old crone—OMIGOD look at you! GOD, how did you sneak up on me so quietly. Are you a spy?"

James Lancaster stood next to Lala with a baby carriage, one that must have been oiled daily, judging by how silently it had traveled.

"Please tell me you didn't hear what I was just saying. Even if you did, please lie to me."

"I heard you mumbling, but, and I swear I'm telling the truth here, I couldn't understand a word. Not one word. To be frank, and I'm being frank so you will believe that I'm not lying about not hearing you, you actually sounded rather demented."

"Oh. Okay. Good. Thank you."

Lala rubbed Yootza's head with her knuckles as she took in the existence of the stealth buggy that apparently belonged to James.

"You have a baby?" Lala asked. She peered through the tightly-woven, dark netting that covered the front of the baby carriage, but all she could see inside was a mound of pink blankets. "Is that your daughter?"

James unzipped the netting and moved it to the side. He pulled back some of the blankets. Lala saw the head of a cocker spaniel poking out from beneath all the quilting. The dog was asleep and had probably been old when the original Rin Tin Tin was young.

"Yes," James said. "That's my little girl, Ruby."

After considering the sandwich board from their table outside on the patio, James said he didn't want to have to choose between sugar and salt and, if Lala was of the same mind, would she split an order of pancakes with him so they could also order maybe omelets and eat, essentially, way too much?

Yootza kept reaching his little neck over the top of the papoose and whimpering piteously in the direction of Ruby and her carriage.

"I think he wants to visit with her," James said.

"Would that be okay?" Lala asked.

"I think it would be great."

James very gently extracted Yootza and, in so doing, momentarily brushed his right hand against Lala's left boob. Neither of them acknowledged this by look or by word, both apparently and immediately having decided that the extra fabric of the papoose that separated flesh from flesh as an additional layer to the cloth of Lala's shirt had, for all intents and purposes, rendered the encounter at best nonexistent, and at worst nonsexual.

James put Yootza in the carrier next to Ruby. Ruby didn't wake up. Yootza snuggled next to her and passed out.

"The slumber party is on," James said. "I think the grownups should have a few mimosas to unwind while the kids are napping, don't you?"

*I think I love you,* Lala thought.

"I do some of my best writing when I'm slightly potted," Lala said.

"What a coincidence. I do some of my best editing when I'm half in the bag."

The mimosas were overwhelmingly champagne with really just enough fresh-squeezed orange juice to make them seem like a brunch beverage rather than an out-and-out Happy Hour libation.

"And that's the way I like my mimosas," Lala said. "In name only. P.S., these are the best pancakes I have ever had. That is not hyperbole. The honor was previously held by a little coffee shop in Montauk."

"Not LaSalle's Breakfast Bungalow?"

"Yes," she gasped. "LaSalle's."

"Cut it out," James said. "We went there all the time when I was growing up. Incredible pancakes, and, yes, these are even better."

"Where did you grow up?"

"In Connecticut. We went to Montauk every summer."

"Cut it out," Lala said. "I went to college in Connecticut."

"Yale?"

"Wesleyan."

"Cool. I went to Yale."

"You went to Yale? When were you there? Did I sleep with you? I didn't recognize your name when we met, but I definitely thought you were very cute, and maybe I can make the excuse that that's the champagne talking right now. Are you operating under a *nom de plume*? A *nom de guerre*? Are you in the witness protection program?"

"I would definitely remember sleeping with you. So I'm going to have to say, sadly, I don't think we have."

They discussed their favorite everythings over a second round of mimosas and bread pudding for dessert.

"This is the best bread pudding I have ever had," Lala said. "The honor was previously held by the Cornelia Street Café. In the—"

"West Village," James finished. "Best bread pudding on the East Coast. Second only in the world to this bread pudding."

"I had some lovely bread pudding the other night. I'm putting that one in third place."

"Don't change the subject. How can you say you prefer *Now, Voyager* to *Jezebel*? Bette is sublime in *Jezebel*."

"Agreed. But *Now, Voyager* is my favorite. Maybe because she transforms a tiny bit more in *Now, Voyager*."

"It's brilliant. No argument there."

"Please tell me you're a liberal Democrat. Please tell me you love *The Count of Monte Cristo*. Please tell me that if you could travel back in time, you would clean The Eagles' clock before they had the chance to write 'Hotel California,' because I swear, if I ever hear that song again, it'll be too soon."

"Duh. Duh. And duh," James said.

"Did you live in New York?" Lala asked.

"I've visited. I moved here as soon as I finished grad school."

"Why?" Lala asked.

"The weather, of course."

"Well, okay. But . . . really?"

"Yeah."

"Weather shmeather. There's nothing like New York," Lala said. "I moved there the second I graduated. Nothing could keep me away from Manhattan."

"So why did you move here?"

"Ohhh, it is a sordid story," Lala said. "Ummm . . . Well, my co-op had a huge assessment levied on it in a blink, and so I borrowed forty thousand dollars from my best friend who is very rich, and I moved here so I could rent out my cozy, adorable West Village one-bedroom as a vacation rental. You know tourists will pay insane amounts to stay in the West Village. I'm on track to pay my best friend back in just under eight months. Which is two months longer than the time between my late husband's diagnosis of stage-four stomach cancer and his death ten years ago. Wow, I must feel very comfortable with you, or I must be very drunk."

James was in the process of motioning the waitress over to order another round of mimosas when Lala blurted her life story to him. The waitress arrived just as the gravity of Lala's glibly delivered revelation was sinking in.

"One sec," James said before the waitress could speak. "Could you come back in a few minutes, please?"

"With two more mimosas, please," Lala said.

James got up and unzipped the cover of Ruby's carriage. He very carefully picked up the still sleeping dog and very gently placed her on Lala's lap. Then he picked up Yootza, who also didn't wake up, and cradled him in his lap.

Lala's arms melted around the dear, fragile old dog she held. She buried her face in the lush, wavy fur around Ruby's neck.

"Wow," Lala said. "Your girl does not smell like an old dog. I don't know what your secret is. I can't get my beagle to be sweet-smelling for longer than half a day after her bath. I'm sorry, Petunia, but I'd be lying if I said otherwise."

"Sometimes you just need to hug a dog," James said. "I know that sounds like an e-card, but I think it's true."

*And I think I love you,* Lala thought.

"I am so sorry about your husband," James said. "And you're picking up the check. Jesus. A vacation rental in the Village. Jesus, what are you raking in? Two grand a week?"

"Try three, Big Guy," Lala said.

Their next round of mimosas arrived, and, as they drank them, they sat in relative silence compared to how much they had been talking before Lala revealed that she was widowed. Their respective dogs stayed on their respective laps while the two bigger hounds slept in the sun on blankets from Ruby's stroller and woke occasionally to slurp water from a big bowl provided by the café.

Lala rested her champagne glass on Ruby's head between sips.

"Her skull is a perfect coaster," Lala said.

"I know," James agreed. "It's unusually flat. One of the many things I love about her."

Lala was surprised to note that she felt very at ease not talking much in James's company.

*Seriously, how often do I not feel compelled to chatter?* she thought. *I must be very, very, very comfortable around him. And I'm sexually attracted to him, and he's smart, and he has an old dog. All my bitching about the downs in my life up to this point aside, I have to say a big, fat thank you, universe, for introducing me to two perfect men since I set up camp here in the Beach that wants to be Manhattan. I'm not even feeling bitter that one of them left town right after we fucked. Because that would be greedy with Mr. James Adorable Publisher sitting right across from me, wouldn't it? It's like Jackson Platt said, you can't expect to—*

"Are you doing an inner monologue?" James asked.

Lala lifted her nose out of Ruby's fur and saw James smiling at her as he stuck two fingers in the air to get the waitress's attention and then mouthed, "Another round," as he twirled his index finger in a circle over their empty glasses.

"Yes, I am in fact going over my entire life in a matter of seconds to myself. And then just now I was thinking about a moment in *A Map Without Latitude* when—"

"Omigod, is that book crap, or what? I met Jackson Platt at a symposium last year, and he is the biggest tool. Why are you staring at me like that?"

"I'm reflecting on how relieved I am that you're not perfect, because I had up until just now been thinking that you might be, and now I know what a can of worms that is. *A Map Without Latitude* is my favorite contemporary novel. Jackson Platt is a genius."

"Check, please," James yelled in the direction of the entrance to the café. "Well, I guess I could be generous and say that literature is not plane Euclidean geometry, so there are no absolute right and wrong answers, but I prefer to just point out that I'm not the only not-perfect person at this table."

The bill came with their final mimosas of the day, and James pulled out his credit card and handed it to the waitress before Lala could shift Ruby on her lap so she could reach for her wallet.

"No, no, let me—"

"I was kidding about you paying," James said. "Jesus, I thought that was obvious. Your husband died, for fuck's sake. What kind of a schmo would I be if I didn't pick up the check?"

They were in no hurry to finish their drinks and leave. They sat together for another hour, again not saying much other than the staccato, punctuated ribbing of each other that they had fallen into with synchronized ease.

"*A Map Without Latitude*," James chuckled.

"Shut up," Lala said. She smiled at James and playfully swatted him on the shoulder, and then leaned over and put her head on that shoulder for a fraction of a moment, and then immediately jerked it up again and made herself dizzy.

"Oof. That was not a good idea."

"Jackson Platt," James snorted.

"Seriously, shut up."

"God, your taste is for shit. I can't wait to read your other stuff. Does it suck like Jackson Platt's stuff sucks? How come I enjoyed your piece at the reading so much when you have such shitty taste?"

"I love that 'how come' means 'why' in English, don't you? It doesn't in French. I don't think. *Comment venir*? No, that can't mean anything."

"We have a great language," James agreed. He stood up, cradled Yootza under his arm, and helped Lala get up out of her chair with his free hand. "Come on, let me walk you home."

Yootza and Ruby happily shared the baby carriage for the journey back. Petunia and Chester trotted next to the vehicle, their energy restored by an entire afternoon of hibernation.

Lala gripped one half of the handle to the carriage while James worked on keeping the movement of the group from swerving all over the place by steering with his right hand on the other half of the handle with his left arm firmly around Lala's waist.

"I love your website," Lala giggled. "I looked at it right away when I got home after the reading where I met you, and you gave me your card. I am focusing on the details and the specificity of the language I am choosing in order to counterbalance how muddled I am feeling right now."

"Of course," James said. "I understand. You drank as much as I did, and I'm what? Twice your size? Mind the ditch."

"I love your Bentley's Miscellany section! That's the Victorian magazine that serialized *Oliver Twist*!"

"Yes, I know. Though technically the actual inspiration for choosing that name was my childhood dog, Bentley von Schnauzer. Are you okay? You look very pale."

"Ummm, I think I might have to barf."

"Nope. Not now. We'll save that for when we get to your place and get you in the bathroom, right?"

"Ummm . . ."

"Take your mind off it," James ordered. "Tell me what you love most about writing."

"The words," Lala answered without having to debate. "I love words. There are infinite possible combinations of them, and they have infinite potential to do anything. Delight. Enrage. Sadden. Inspire. Educate. Divert. Unite. You know how to say grapefruit in French? *Pamplemousse*. Is that a fun word, or what? And their word for tire, the noun, not the verb, is *pneu*. And I love that they pronounce the 'p' when they say their word for tire, the noun, in French. Language. Is language swell, or what? And what is language? It's words! Words! And stuff! I can see my house from here. Two streets down. The pretty fourplex. Can you see it? I am definitely not gonna make it there before I have to barf."

"Don't think about it," James said. "Tell me what most vexes you about being a writer."

"Ohhh, that's easy too. I have the attention span of a hummingbird. And I don't know if I'm maybe falsely accusing hummingbirds of being as flighty as I am. It just seems like they might be because they move so fast. I used to see a lot of them when I was growing up in Santa Monica. I used to believe that they bring good luck."

Lala suddenly stopped.

"Are you going to puke?" James asked.

"Actually, I think the tidal wave of nausea may have passed, and five seconds ago I would not have predicted that could be possible. We should buy lottery tickets. I just now realized that Southern

California has hummingbirds, but I don't think New York, New York does. I never saw one there. The Bronx Zoo notwithstanding. Wow, there is actually something that I prefer about Los Angeles County. Wow, miracles actually happen."

"Hang on," James said. "We may have had sex in college. I'm having major déjà vu here. With much better weather this time around, of course. An attractive and very chatty Wesleyan student who was about to puke. We didn't screw that night because she smelled of vomit, but we did have a delicious weekend extravaganza a few days subsequent to her nausea battle. Could have been you, no?"

"God, wasn't slutty college sex fabulous?" Lala asked rhetorically.

"So, you were saying. Hummingbirds. Attention span."

They had reached the gate to the fourplex. Chuck and Stephanie were just at the door to their apartment, about to let themselves back into their home, as Lala and James and the dogs swarmed into the courtyard.

Lala noticed a very suspicious and surprisingly cold look from both the young people before they each gave her a grudging wave and rushed to get the key into the lock so they could slam their front door shut behind them.

*Hello?* Lala thought.

"Yup," she said to James. "It's my biggest stumbling block in terms of anything. I'm tremendously lazy and unfocused, and I so rarely do the things I should to be as creative as I want to be. Or as successful. It takes me forever to finish a project. Years pass. And suddenly I'm in my forties. Sheesh."

James lifted Yootza out of Ruby's carriage and carefully placed the dachshund back in his papoose. When his left hand once again grazed Lala's right boob, Lala felt fairly certain that it had done so on purpose.

"Take two aspirin," James said.

"Of course. And drink a large glass of water."

"Exactly. Then take a nap."

"Yup."

"And when you wake up, think about the advice I'm about to

give you. I doubt this is advice I would give to a young writer. And that's to your advantage and to the young writer's detriment to a great extent, so do not be insulted that I'm making that distinction."

"Okay," Lala said. "I won't be. I think."

"You've got a co-op in the West Village that you're renting out. You're incredibly lucky. You don't have to struggle for money as Hemingway and a million other writers have had to and will continue to have to."

Lala looked at James with more intensity than her mimosa-soaked brain should have made possible.

*He's right*, she thought. *I am incredibly lucky.*

"God willing, you've got more than a few good decades left to your life, right?" James said. "But you also know that you might not because your husband died young, right? So you know each day is a gift. Really, it is."

"It is," Lala said.

"So my advice to you is have fun and write whatever you want, whenever you want. Really, write what you love to write. And then send it to me. It might be for shit. Or it might not. If it's for shit, at least you'll have had fun writing it. And your bills will still be paid by that co-op in the West Village. Man, if I were you, especially if my beloved spouse had died instead of leaving me for someone else, and, if I had what amounts to dynamite economic freedom, I would not do one damn thing unless I wanted to. Not one."

Lala was asleep on the couch with the TV on when she was awakened by a gentle but insistent tapping on her front door.

*Maybe this should be the starting point for putting James's excellent advice to good use, and I shouldn't force myself to get up because I really don't want to?* Lala thought.

"Lala?" a female voice outside her door said.

"Are you alone? We don't want to intrude," a male voice said.

*What the fuck?* Lala thought. *Now my curiosity is piqued, damn it.*

She sat up. Yootza, who had been curled up next to Lala behind her bent legs in the small quadrangle that was created by Lala sleeping on her side with her face mashed into a pillow and a sizable portion of drool on the cloth beneath her face, rolled over onto his back and continued to sleep. Petunia and Chester, also not tremendously good watchdogs, did not stir from their repose on their beds on the floor next to the coffee table.

The moment before Lala flung the door open, she glanced down at her body.

*Oh, okay,* she thought. *I'm not naked.*

Chuck and Stephanie were standing at her door. Stephanie was holding a large platter of cookies covered with clear plastic wrap.

"I baked these, and I thought you might like some?" Stephanie said.

Lala grabbed the platter, tore off the wrap, and seized a chocolate chip cookie. Then she didn't so much eat the cookie as swallow it whole. She did the same thing to another cookie before she jerked her head toward the interior of her home and spoke through the third cookie, which she had decided to chew.

"Wanna come inside? I think I've got milk in the fridge. I think. These cookies are amazing."

"We'd love to stay and chat, but we've got to get to the clinic," Chuck said.

"Just wanted to stop by to say hello," Stephanie added.

"Well, that's very sweet," Lala said. "Thank you very much for the wonderful cookies."

Lala expected that the next thing that she would do would be to close the door on their departing figures. But, because their figures made no move to depart, Lala stood there clutching the platter of treats and wondering if eating so many of them so quickly had been a good idea.

At last, Stephanie spoke.

"So how've you been? Must be lonely without Doctor David here, you know? Long-distance relationships can be really difficult, you know? We know, because we had a long-distance relationship when we were undergraduates, and it was really tough, you know?"

*What the fuck?* Lala thought.

She twisted her face into an inquisitive frown and stared at the two young people. They gazed back at her with wide-eyed innocence that was fierce in its earnestness.

*Wait*, Lala thought. *No, come on, seriously. How cute are these two?*

"Wait," Lala said. "No, come on, seriously. How cute are you two? That person you saw me with is a potential publisher for the stuff that I'm not yet able to write with any consistency. Now, please understand that I think it's very sweet of you to worry about David's interests being protected, and I did mentally put 'David's interests' in quotation marks, but David's not in town. You do realize that, don't you? If he were, this conversation might make a tiny bit of sense. But I do love you both for your naïve, protective hearts. Now get yourselves to your clinic and go save some animals' lives before I throw up all over you. I definitely shouldn't have eaten that many delicious cookies without breathing between bites. 'Bites' in quotation marks."

Lala shut her front door without waiting for the crazy, adorable youngsters to move. For all she knew, they would be standing out there for hours. She just couldn't focus on that right now.

"Well, I'm awake now," Lala announced to her sleeping babies. "So maybe I feel like writing now? Maybe? Who knows? Let's find out, shall we?"

Lala went into her bedroom and unplugged her laptop. Back in the living room, she plugged it into another outlet and sat down next to Yootza.

"Look," she cheered. "It's another episode of *Tabatha's Salon Takeover*! I think I've only seen this one maybe two or three times! Cool!"

Lala flipped open her laptop and accessed a new Word document by clicking on all the correct links. A vast expanse of empty, pristine white appeared on her screen.

*Yikes*, Lala thought.

"Shall we start writing that column idea we've been toying with?" Lala asked her snoring hounds. "And when I say 'we' of course I mean 'I' since I don't imagine you guys toy with much other than thoughts of kibble past, present, and future. That's not a criticism."

Lala typed the words, "Lala Pettibone, Journalist to the Stars."

"I've had this opening in my head for a while," she told Petunia and Chester and Yootza. "I think I've almost got it memorized."

Lala read aloud as she typed.

"The Cole Porter who opened the door to his palatial house on the rue Monsieur near Les Invalides was not the Cole Porter who would soon burst onto the international musical scene as a master of exquisitely crafted lyrics of surpassing wit and intelligence. The Cole Porter standing before me on a frigid, clear day in Paris was just another artist with terror in his heart, and a pen and pad in his hands. He shoved his pen sideways into his mouth and stuck the pad under his armpit so he could dramatically run his fingers through his hair and then clasp them together under my startled nose in the universal gesture of supplication. 'Please tell me you can think of a word that rhymes with "bellicose." Please. For the love of all that is sacred and profane, what rhymes with "bellicose"? I mean, besides "verbose," of course. And "sucrose." And "lactose." And . . . Hey, I think I just solved my own problem. Come on in. Can I get you an *aperitif*?'"

After several hours and many flipped premium cable channels, Lala had a first draft that she didn't regard as entirely awful. She picked up Yootza and kissed his grey little snout. He didn't open his eyes.

"You know what I like about relatively short pieces?" she asked him. "They're relatively short. Like you, you cute, little nugget of cranky! And like me."

When Lala saw her aunt the next day, she didn't mention anything about James other than that she had bumped into him.

First Lala read her piece about interviewing Cole Porter aloud to Geraldine. She had revisited the piece again later the night before, after going out to get a big serving of twirled French Vanilla and Oreo Cookie frozen yogurt with huge servings of cookie dough chunks and cute, tiny, little chocolate caramel cups as toppings.

"How can they make these little thingies so cute and small?" she wondered aloud as she heaped spoonful upon spoonful into her extra large cup of yogurt. "It's like they're candies in Lilliput. So damn cute!"

The interview piece had ended up being much longer than Lala originally envisioned it. She had kept on writing until she didn't feel like writing any longer. Geraldine listened to Lala's reading with clear enjoyment and laughed at all the places where Lala had hoped she would laugh. When Lala was done, Geraldine applauded.

"Lovely. I really enjoyed that. I think it should be a series."

"I was thinking that too!" Lala crowed. "I thought maybe I could—"

"Excellent. That's settled. So? James?"

"He is a nice man. Very cute."

"Did you fuck him?" Geraldine asked. "I always feel so young and hip and wicked when I talk like that."

"He's very nice. I'm not going to presume to speak for both of us, but I got the impression that we were both holding back. Yes, we did kiss at the door. With tongues. But in our defense, we had been drinking all afternoon. I think we both think it might be best to just stay friends. I have no actual idea why we think that would be best or, in fact, what I'm even talking about."

"So you didn't fuck him?" Geraldine asked. "Why haven't you fucked him yet? I am so wicked and sassy and youthful with that kind of mouth on me, don't you think?"

"Excuse me," Lala said, "but last time I fucked someone, he left town. He fled. He put himself in exile. He banished himself."

"That wasn't a cause and effect. If I've got this right, he had that trip planned before you fucked him, am I right? Is it just me, or do you never fuck people who live in the same time zone as you? I like that word, fuck! I do! I think it's evocative, don't you?"

"Okay," Lala said, "so while we're on the subject of your new favorite word, did you fuck Monty?"

"Oh yes," Geraldine said. "Repeatedly. Often."

Lala did a visible double-take.

"Why did you do a double-take?" Geraldine asked. "I don't think I've said anything outlandish, have I?"

"I . . . I don't know why, but I just wasn't expecting that answer. I was expecting to shock you out of your weirdness by, you know, turning the tables back on you."

"You might give me more credit," Geraldine huffed.

"I'm sorry. It's just . . . isn't his leg still broken?"

"It's healing nicely. I do have to do most of the athletics so far, but Monty has promised to more than make it up to me when he's completely back in form."

# EVERY CLOUD HAS WHAT?

Monty's daughter Helene came down from Beverly Hills at least once a week to check on her dad. Almost every time she was in Manhattan Beach, she made a plan to see Lala. Often, Helene and Lala would have lunch with Geraldine and Monty, and afterward the two "youngsters," as Monty affectionately called them, would go to a brand new bar downtown that looked like it belonged in Paris's First Arrondisement, where Helene would order them bellinis with just a whisper of *pêche* in French that was perfect in accent and syntax.

*Damn*, Lala would think as she sat at the bar during their Happy Hour soirée watching the handsome, young French bartender drown in the inexorable pull of Helene's confident, faux-Gallic tide. *She's kind of annoyingly good at everything and kind of irresistibly fabulous to be around at the same time.*

After Lala returned home, Geraldine would hear her footsteps on the ceiling and would rush upstairs for a blow-by-blow.

"I've been fucking Monty since we left lunch," Geraldine announced when Lala opened her apartment door.

"Yikes," Lala said.

"Indeed. So? How was Happy Hour?"

"Fab-u-lous. Helene is really something. She is fab-u-lous."

"Just be careful," Geraldine said. "I'm not entirely sure she's as benignly perfect as you seem to think she is."

"Stop being so negative. Maybe you're just jealous because Helene and I are such good buddies already."

Lala didn't have much to offer besides those platitudes because she knew she was indeed in the early stages of a love affair powered by that heady feeling when someone cool and more successful than you are seems to like you and seems to think you've got talent. She approached her feelings about Helene with a level of awareness that might have earned professional and audience kudos on afternoon TV.

"I'm not jealous," Geraldine responded. "I'm just curious as to why you're so taken with her."

"I think of it as a girl-crush, but I don't know why I'm adding 'girl.' Maybe to disavow a sexual element. Which, by the way, I'm not entirely sure is not there. I mean, probably not, but, hey."

Years later, Lala would be convinced that Helene must have known how vulnerable and overly excitable Lala was back then.

"Oh, Girlfriend loved having a new acolyte. And she'd be the first to admit that," Lala would chuckle with abiding affection, but only after several snifters of expensive brandy, which would become Lala's aperitif of choice when she entered her seventies. "She played me. Like a virtuoso, she plucked my strings. Tickled my ivories. Slapped my bass. You get where I'm going with this."

Monty had gotten tickets for a local theater production of *Hairspray*. He and Geraldine were planning a romantic dinner before the show, and then Monty wanted to take Geraldine out for cocktails at a nearby hotel after the show to celebrate his having stepped up from wheelchair to crutches.

"And you know what that means," Geraldine winked at Lala.

"Yeah, I think I have some notion. So there's no need to say it aloud because I'm pretty sure we're thinking of the same general thing, so—"

"It means soon Monty and I can fuck standing up!"

"God, you get crazy when you've got a new boyfriend," Lala said.

"I know! I feel like a schoolgirl again. Like a nasty, dirty, little schoolgirl in love."

"Okay, enough," Lala said.

Lala assumed that Helene wouldn't be in Manhattan Beach that Saturday since her dad was covered for the entire evening. So she was mildly surprised to get an e-mail from Helene asking her to come to dinner at Monty's house for a special reason—she wanted ideas for her new novel.

Lala was mildly surprised and massively panicked.

"I'm not an idea person!" she wailed at her aunt.

"Is she paying you?" Geraldine asked.

"Of course not. What a silly question. I'm honored she asked me. This is what fellow writers do for each other. Or so I've heard. We get together, and we support each other by brainstorming ideas. Helene wouldn't have asked me to help her think of ideas for her new novel if she didn't respect me, right? I've got to come up with good suggestions. I want to be worthy of her respect."

"Really? Because then my next question has to be why you give a shit what Helene Miller thinks of you?"

"Were you always so negative?" Lala demanded. "And if the answer to that is yes, why were my parents friends with you for so many decades?"

❦

*Oy,* Lala thought. *Look how fabulous she looks. After cooking. If I had been cooking anything? Anything. Scrambled eggs even. I would look like a wreck.*

"You shouldn't have brought anything," Helene said. She ushered Lala through the door and admired the bottle of red wine Lala handed her.

"Stop. Like I'd come empty-handed. My mother would throw bolts of lightning down at me if I did that."

"Mine would, too," Helene said. "I mean, at me. If I did that. Not at you. Come sit down. We'll have some champagne with the appetizers and then open this delicious bottle with our dinner, and we can . . . Benedict, NO!"

Lala saw a huge blur of black and white lunging at her across the entryway, and, before her brain could analyze the frenzied input, she was on the floor, and the Great Dane was on top of her. His tongue was large enough to saturate her entire face via repeated swipes of his saliva-drenched affection.

Helene furiously yanked at Benedict's collar, to no effect at all.

"Bad boy! Bad! Get off her!"

"No, no, it's fine," Lala giggled. She cheerfully gasped for air. "I love dogs. It's great."

Lala rubbed the sides of Benedict's neck. She gradually was able to get herself up on her elbows. She covered Benedict's face and neck with hugs and kisses.

"Who's a good boy? Who is a good boy? Someone answer me right now."

"He loves you," Helene said. "He can't stand me."

"I'm sure that's not true. I'm sure he loves you."

Lala got herself to her feet. Benedict leaned his big head against her outer thigh, and Lala cradled his jowls in her hand.

"Nope," Helene said. "I'm not comfortable around dogs. I think the big oaf knows that."

"Well, yeah, he probably does."

"I just think pets are so messy," Helene said. "You want to go freshen up?"

When Lala came out of the downstairs guest bathroom—happy that Helene had suggested she pay it a visit because her image in the mirror had shown a woman who had just been hit by a runaway delivery truck ferrying beer gone sour—Helene was sitting on the sofa opening a bottle of champagne. Benedict was not to be found.

"I put the monster in an upstairs bedroom, so he won't bother us. Oh! There's that happy sound!"

The cork hit the ceiling, and Helene filled two glasses.

"Okay, so here's what I'm thinking. Let's get the work part of the evening out of the way before we get drunk, yes?"

Lala sat next to Helene. Helene clinked her glass against Lala's.

"To the beauty of words."

"Yeah," Lala said. "Yup. Uh huh."

*Why am I so nervous?* Lala thought. *Keep that champagne comin',*

*Helene.*

Helene placed her glass on the coffee table next to an array of appetizers that were arranged in a lovely pattern emphasizing the harmonious balance of their variety of colors and sizes and shapes.

*It all looks fucking gorgeous and delicious,* Lala thought. *If I served appetizers, they'd be guacamole in a bowl, salsa in a bowl, and a big bowl of chips. Which is actually quite delicious, when you think about it. God, why is Helene so fucking perfect? Please, let her have some sinister secret that she spills over dinner. Please.*

Helene took a laptop off the seat of the chair next to her. She lifted the screen and began typing.

"Okay, so I have my protag with . . ."

*My what?* Lala thought. *What, words are suddenly becoming too long for us? It's protagonist, cookie. Jesus!*

". . . the person the reader thinks up until now is my villain locked in the wine cellar of a mansion on Lake Como. They were married once, many years ago, when they were just kids."

*Wow, that sounds good,* Lala thought. *It's clever. I want to find out what happens next. Damn it. Damn her.*

"We've just learned that the person who has been stalking Brenda . . ."

*Ohh, that's nice of Helene,* Lala thought. *No. Wait. She doesn't know Brenda. So it can't be a conscious nod to my best friend. Never mind.*

". . . is not her ex-husband, Claudio, but in fact Claudio's second wife, the seemingly kind, but actually quite evil, Sophia. So what I would like us to brainstorm is what happens between Brenda and Claudio while they're in the basement, and how they get out."

*I am fucked,* Lala thought. *If I have any kind of an area of storytelling expertise, this is not it. I hate conflict. And I don't know how people get out of situations. God, I'm schvitzing.*

"Well, ummm, maybe . . . uhhhh . . . and I don't know . . . of course . . . what your . . . ummm . . . tone has been in the novel up to that point . . . and I'm . . . I'm . . . I'm . . . I'm . . . not a student or even really a fan of mysteries per se, sorry, but maybe, this would be the place to insert a little humor?"

Helene peered at her.

*Barf,* Lala thought. *She's looking at me like I just suggested a plot twist hinging on subterranean snail racing in Lombardy. Told in real time.*

"You know, get a little Hitchcockian. With maybe some elements of schmutz, too."

"Sure, let's explore that," Helene said.

"Because . . . because . . . because, if I were Brenda and I thought I might be about to die in a basement, I would definitely get drunk on all the wine down there, and I would find something, scratch that, someone to have sex with."

Helene typed and nodded.

"And maybe you could have Sophia watching them on hidden, closed-circuit TV or whatever the twenty-first century equivalent of that is."

"Okay," Helene said. She continued to type and bob her head.

Thinking on her ass, Lala scrunched into the cushions of the couch and, gulping champagne as she spoke, wove a story of two people who had been apart for years, and, in the course of a night that they thought would be their last on earth, told each other everything that had happened in their lives after they split up. And then fucked. Repeatedly.

"And then maybe, I don't know, maybe after they've been bonking each other, Sophia can go completely crazy because the protag . . . onist . . . has won because it's clear to Sophia that Claudio never stopped loving Brenda, and so Sophia speaks to them via intercom, or whatever the modern equivalent of that is, and she curses their love, and then she floods the wine cellar with a deluge of priceless Bordeaux, and Brenda and Claudio are trying to stay afloat and are clinging to each other as the exceptionally delicious red wine threatens to rise right up to the high ceiling of the cellar."

"That would be very cool," Helene said. She smacked and smacked the keys of her computer. Lala stood and began pacing the room. Several long moments of relative silence ensued as no additional words were spoken, and the only sound was the rhythmic thud of Helene's fingers on the laptop as she caught up with everything Lala had been saying to that point.

When she had gotten everything down and had tapped the "Save" key, Helene looked up at Lala with eager expectation. Lala stopped pacing.

"Yeah. No. As to how they're going to get out of the wine cellar, I don't have a fucking clue. I got nothin'. Maybe the local gendarmes, or whatever they call the police in Italy, bust open the door."

Helene shut her laptop and stood.

"No problem. I'll figure something out. You're good at this! I really appreciate your help. Come on, let's go stuff ourselves."

Dinner was delicious but, to Lala's great dismay, contained no revelations of hidden deeds from Helene's past. Just stories of a happy life that was only darkened when her parents decided to adopt "that drooling beast."

"Don't get me wrong, I'm glad Benedict makes my dad so happy, and I'm glad he's such good company for my dad, but yuck with the saliva and the shedding and the farting and all that old dog stuff that goes on."

Helene, Lala discovered, had never married, but had a long history as a serial monogamist. And it was apparently Helene who always did the breaking up.

"Gérard was lovely, but . . ."

*What?* Lala thought. *Okay, sure, what are the odds, but WHAT?*

"Was Gérard a publisher?"

"No, he was a racecar driver," Helene said.

*Oh. Okay. Wait! Do I know for sure that my Gérard never competed in the Grand Prix?*

"Short? Sexy? Irresistible?"

"Yes, sexy, yes, irresistible, but very tall. Could-have-been-a-basketball-player tall."

*Oh, okay,* Lala thought.

"He desperately wanted to marry me, but I had plateaued at that point in our relationship. It was time for me to move to the next level in my life. So I spent a year as a fundraiser-slash-hands-on-lay-person-assistant . . ."

*A what?* Lala thought.

". . . for Doctors Without Borders."

*Oy,* Lala thought. *Can't fault her for that. She is something, this gal.*

Helene insisted that Lala take some brownies home with her. At the door, Helene kept shoving a big plate covered with aluminum foil into Lala's hands, and Lala kept shoving it back.

"I can't! They're delicious, and I need to lose weight, so I can't. Thank you for a lovely evening. Keep your delicious darn brownies!"

"You look great. You don't need to lose weight. I can't thank you enough for helping me with my new manuscript. Oh, and listen, you're coming to my house in LA on the fifteenth. I'm having a book release party. And one of my favorite authors is going to be in town, so it's going to be a really great evening. He's an old friend from graduate school. I don't know if you've read *A Map Without Latitude?*"

❦

Lala was on the couch in her sweats with the plate of brownies balanced next to her laptop. The three dogs were staring at her from their various perches with agonized expressions.

"Of course you can't have any. It's chocolate. Not good for dogs. And you just had dinner. Like I'm one to talk. Christ, these are delicious."

*I am just not going to think about meeting Jackson Platt,* Lala thought. *I'm just not going to fantasize about him falling in love with me and marrying me and us being deliriously happy authors together with a big office in our gorgeous house with huge and fabulous desks next to each other where we create brilliant work and interrupt our days of dedicated wordsmithing only to bonk or go out for lunch. I'm not going to imagine all the wonderful trips we'll take together, when we're married, to book fairs in delightful locations. I'm not going to think about any of this, because if I do, I might freak out and spontaneously combust.*

Lala stared off into space. She fantasized about meeting Jackson Platt and marrying him and having epic sex with him. For all she knew, she might have been sitting that way, with her eyes nearly rolling back in her head, for hours. It was Petunia's mournful whining that brought her back to the immediate world.

*Okay,* Lala thought. *I am going to have to forbid myself from indulging in any of that obsessive thinking before our fateful, on-a-par-with-Zhivago-in-terms-of-sweeping-romance meeting. Because I seriously do not think the centers in my brain that govern lust can preside over this kind of pornography without short-circuiting the entire grid.*

Lala patted Petunia's head and turned on the TV.

"My evening with Helene has resulted in me being a strange mixture of inspired and depressed," Lala told the dogs. "Ahhh. I get it. So this is the ambivalence my therapist was yapping about for all those years. Shush, Petunia. You are not getting any brownies. End of discussion. I will eat them all myself, if I have to, just to shut you up."

Lala methodically put one brownie after another into her mouth in succession until the plate was empty. She then presented the plate to the dogs. The three hounds jostled each other to passionately inspect the crockery with their noses. The three sets of nostrils worked overtime, until it was clear to Petunia, Yootza, and Chester that not even a crumb remained. At which point all three sulked off. Not even Yootza remained on Lala's lap, so profound was their shared feeling of disappointment and betrayal.

"Never let it be said that I will not make myself physically sick to make a point," Lala declared to their retreating hindquarters.

Lala settled deeper into the couch.

"Well. Okay," she announced to the empty room. "Television's on. Low. In the background. Can't really hear it, but it's there in case the pressure of producing words makes me freak out. Because, damn it, Hemingway wrote in a café that must have been noisy and crowded for at least part of the day, so I think that my choice of workspace is certainly valid."

She suddenly turned and yelled in the direction of the hallway down which the dogs had just retreated.

"You guys, get back in here, so I'm not talking to myself and sounding crazy because I'm talking to no one!"

Lala opened her laptop and clicked on a Word file. MyNovelFromMyScriptWhoGivesAShitWhatHappensIAmHappyNow. doc opened and Lala stared at the resulting letters on the screen. The document was what she had renamed DressedLadyNovel.doc in the hope of starting each work session with a defiant giggle.

"I am both overwhelmed by the prospect of writing a novel and oddly champing at the bit to really get started on this thing. To go for broke. To give it my all. To . . . to . . . I'm fresh out of clichés."

Lala stared at the screen.

"Maybe I'll spend some time with the pieces of the story. Because pieces are shorter and so maybe they won't scare me as much as an entire novel. Pieces. Yeah. Pieces that connect. You know, pieces in a row. You know, like a series . . ."

She suddenly whipped her head back toward the hallway.

"You guys, I am not kidding! Get back in here and sit with Mama so Mama can talk to you so Mama doesn't start thinking she might be a crazy person!"

🍷

In the future, when she was feeling introspective or nostalgic or potted, Lala would observe that it's kind of amazing how, with a new friend, everything can go to shit in a heartbeat. Or in the course of one hellish evening.

"I was on a losing streak back then where the ides of any given month would screw up my life somethin' wicked," Lala would explain to one of the many young people in her older life that she had de facto adopted as her grandchildren. "Of course, much of the crap could be said to be my own fault, and, on several levels, it wasn't anything more than I deserved. To this day, I'm still amazed that Brenda forgave me. I don't know that I would have forgiven her if she had behaved like quite as much of a royal twat as I had. Of course, it probably helped that I didn't give Brenda all the gruesome details of what a lousy friend I was for that particular episode. Sweetheart, go and fix Grandma Lala another martooni, wouldja? Thanks, precious."

Just a few days after Helene invited Lala to her book signing party, Lala came home after the morning walk with the dogs and checked her e-mail. There were several e-mails from Brenda's account, all of them with subject lines in screaming capitals with aggressive and relentless punctuation.

OPEN THIS RIGHT AWAY!

ARE YOU AWAKE YET?!

WHY AREN'T YOU AWAKE YET?!

CALL ME AS SOON AS YOU WAKE UP!!!

I HATE THIS DAMN TIME DIFFERENCE BETWEEN THE COASTS!!!!!!!!!

*Omigod, is someone sick?* Lala thought. *Is someone dying?*

She frantically clicked on the first e-mail. In it, Brenda joyfully announced that she was going to join Frank on a trip west because he had to attend a conference in San Diego, and so she would be in Southern California for just one night, and she had searched all the spas in the area so she and Lala could have a Gals' Night of pampering while Frank talked about concrete and dry wall with his fellow construction moguls.

*Ohhhhh, WOW, this is wonderful!* Lala thought as she read. *It's going to be so great to see Brenda and . . .*

The phone rang. Lala had left the receiver in the cradle in the other room. She waited to hear who was calling before she ran to answer, so she could finish Brenda's first e-mail.

". . . so don't plan anything for the fifteenth, okay, because you and I are going to . . ." Lala read.

*Shit,* Lala thought.

There was a beep on the answering machine, and Brenda's loud and enthusiastic voice swept over the entire apartment.

"Are you awake? Why aren't you awake yet? Wake UP!"

*Shit,* Lala thought.

"Read my e-mails! And call me A.S.A.P. I can't wait to see you!"

*Seriously, shit,* Lala thought. *Okay, okay, okay, okay, think . . . I can't call her now . . . I can't. What the barf am I going to do about this?*

Lala stood.

"Right," she said. "I can't figure this out now. I cannot. Must go to gym. Must put in several hours volunteering at rescue group. Must take barge cruise down sunny river of distraction. Must."

When Lala returned home nearly eight hours later, having, in the interim, called Geraldine to ask her to please walk her puppies, it was still early enough in New York that if she e-mailed Brenda instead of calling her, Brenda would smell a big, fat, smelly rat.

*God, I am a horrible person,* Lala thought. *I can't not meet Jackson Platt. I just can't. Sheesh. I hate myself.*

Lala didn't bring her laptop with her to the couch when she sat down to watch all the episodes of *Tabatha's Salon Takeover* that she had recorded.

"Like I could write one word that wasn't selfish, self-serving crap designed to justify my selfish, self-serving plans," she explained to her dogs. "What do you want to bet that if I were to try writing anything, I would end up giving one of my characters a monologue about how she just had to blow off her best and most wonderful and kindest and most generous and caring friend to indulge in a fantasy that had existed since she first turned the first pages of *A Map Without Latitude*? Don't take that bet. Trust me. It's a sucker's bet."

When it was finally, almost midnight West Coast time, and Lala could reasonably maintain that she hadn't wanted to risk waking Brenda, Lala got her cell phone and her laptop and brought them over to the couch.

There were eight messages from Brenda on her phone.

*I'll listen to them tomorrow,* Lala thought.

There were five new e-mail messages waiting for her.

WTF?!

ARE YOU SLEEPING ALL DAMN DAY?!

I JUST CALLED GERALDINE, AND SHE SAID YOU'VE BEEN OUT ALL DAY! DAMN IT!

WELL, OF COURSE I'M GLAD YOU'RE NOT DEAD, BUT, JESUS!

WHY AREN'T YOU CHECKING YOUR VOICEMAIL?!? GODDAMN IT!!!!!!!

*I just have to do this,* Lala thought. *I just have to get this over with, and then I just have to figure out how to make amends and how to make this right and how to make up for being such a completely colossal lust whore . . . after Jackson Platt asks me to marry him. I hope Brenda will forgive me in time to be my matron of honor.*

Lala bunched up and then stretched her fingers and then interlaced them and stretched them away from her body palm-side outward with an overindulgence in exaggerated comic repetition that would have been more than welcome in any Saturday afternoon cartoon classic from her childhood. She placed her fingers—steeled for battle as they now were—on the keyboard of her laptop as though she were about to play a discordant symphony. And then she just as quickly removed her fingers.

*If I tell her the truth, she'll understand,* Lala thought. *She knows how much I love Jackson Platt.*

Lala got up and went into the kitchen and poured a glass of wine. She had to walk very slowly to avoid spilling as she returned to the couch, and even with her constantly focused effort, several large drops plopped over the sides and splatted on the floor because the liquid had been poured to within a whisper of the rim of the glass.

Lala sat down and spilled a fair amount of the wine on her chin as she took the first swig.

*What if she's hurt?* Lala thought. *She won't say she's hurt. But what if she's hurt? I think I might be hurt if she would rather see a complete stranger, albeit one she has had having sex with on her to-do list for years, rather than see me. I don't want to hurt my best friend's feelings. I can't risk that. I just can't.*

Lala placed the wine glass on the coffee table. Her fingers slowly approached the keyboard. She winced when they made contact with the plastic squares.

"Brenda, I love you," Lala typed, "and I'm so sorry I've been away from civilization since the moment I got up this morning and had to rush out of the house until just this very moment when I got back home, and I would call you right now if it weren't so late in NYC, damn this damn time difference! Ohh, sweetie, I am heartsick. Absolutely heartsick. I'm not going to be in town on the weekend of the fifteenth. I'm not even going to be in Southern

California. I have to go to . . ."

*To . . . to . . . to . . . to,* Lala thought. *Hell in a handbasket?*

". . . to Fresno . . ."

*Fresno?* Lala thought.

". . . to help some people who are affiliated with one of the rescue groups here transport a large number of dogs to a no-kill shelter in Phoenix."

*I am loathsome,* Lala thought. *This is how I use my admirable dedication to the welfare of animals to advance: my own base and nefarious goals. I should be pummeled senseless for being a lying sack of trollop.*

"Please, please, please forgive me. Listen, I am going to make this up to you. I'm going to fly you out to Vegas so we can go crazy together in Sin City and catch up over slot machines and buffets. Okay? As soon as possible, okay? I love you. Please forgive me."

Lala hit "Send" before she could change her mind. She slammed her laptop shut.

"Let's get drunk," she told Petunia and Yootza and Chester. "Because that's the only way Mama's going to get any sleep tonight. And believe me, you wish you could drink booze, because if you knew how hateful I am being right now, you'd need to get drunk to be willing to sleep here tonight. Trust me, if you knew what I just now did vis-à-vis Auntie Brenda, you would be running down the stairs and howling at Auntie Geraldine's door begging to be let in so you could live with her."

Y

It shouldn't have taken Lala as long to get dressed as it did.

"This outfit is even more fabulous than the last damn one I created!" Geraldine spat at Lala. "And the one before that and the one before that and the one before that. You are being absolutely ridiculous."

"I don't feel pretty!"

"You are pretty! Damn it!"

Lala looked over her shoulder to view herself from the back in the black pants and black shirt Geraldine had chosen for her. A chunky yet elegant necklace of green ceramic pieces sat at just the right place on Lala's collarbone. All eyes, Lala felt instinctively, would be drawn to her subtly peeking cleavage.

"Black on black," Geraldine said. "Not always. But sometimes it's just right. Especially when jewelry gives a fabulous burst of color."

"It's true. And I'm thinking that 'I have to be pretty in order to be valued' garbage is often reflexive, huh? What, we're hardwired to search for the symmetrical? To crave the comely? Call Helene. Please. Or ask Monty to please call Helene. Tell her I'm too sick to come to the phone to make my excuses."

"I swear, I am a blink away from slapping you," Geraldine whispered with terrifying calm. "Hard."

"I'm not cool!" Lala wailed. "I can't go to a party replete with cool people! And why am I torturing myself about that? What, are we hardwired to hanker after hip?"

Out of the corner of her eye, Lala thought, or perhaps just imagined, that she was seeing Geraldine wind up to take a resounding swing at her. She instinctively ducked out of the way.

"This is not just me whining and being crazy," Lala continued. "I am not cool. It's not that I tried out for cheerleading and didn't get picked. I couldn't do a cartwheel."

"Seriously?" Geraldine asked.

"I still can't do one. I don't even get how they're done. It makes no sense to me at all."

"Okay, that notwithstanding, let me ask you this. Would Terrence have loved you so much if you weren't cool?"

"Man, you play dirty," Lala said, smiling. "I did always feel cool around him. And you know what? I got hit on all the time when I was married."

"Confidence," Geraldine said. "Knowing that you're loved, so you've got that who-gives-a-shit attitude whether or not someone else loves me. It's sexy."

"Yup."

"So remember that you're loved, by quite a few of us who are here and several others who are on the other side. So go to this party tonight not giving a shit if anyone else loves you."

Lala gave Geraldine a big hug.

*Except Jackson Platt, of course,* Lala thought. *I'm sure Geraldine understands that Jackson Platt falling in love with me is an exception to that lovely advice. Probably don't need to mention it. It's understood, I'm sure.*

"I love this outfit, I love your patience, and I'm sorry I'm so weird. This has been a rough week, Auntie."

Geraldine nodded sympathetically without having the specific knowledge of why the week had been especially hard on Lala. Because Lala was too ashamed to tell her aunt that Brenda had a trip to Southern California planned, let alone to mention why Brenda had decided to not join Frank, after all, when he headed west.

Brenda had finally written back to Lala after leaving her hanging for two days. Two days during which Lala had spent nearly every waking minute deciding she was going to just book a reservation and get on a plane and fly to New York to come clean and beg forgiveness from her best friend.

The best spin Lala could put on Brenda's e-mail in response to hers, when she went over it endlessly with her dogs, was that it was "cordial and understanding, and I can tell she's really disappointed and maybe even hurt, but I think I might have a hope of making it up to her if I pay for an amazing, week-long bachelorette party for just the two of us in Vegas or maybe Paris when I get engaged to Jackson Platt. Fingers crossed. I can't think about it right now."

Geraldine sat Lala down in front of her mirror. It was a classic, old-style vanity, complete with ornate, etched scrollwork around the glass, a cushioned chair, and a whitewashed table with legs that curved out elegantly and ended in swirls at the base. Marie Antoinette, Lala had always imagined, might have felt right at home putting on her makeup there. Lala had had her eye on the whole set-up since she was a kid and had persuaded Geraldine to leave it to her in her will, even though Brenda and also Geraldine's actual nieces had clamored for it as well.

Geraldine opened her massive makeup case and began by sweeping a concealer stick underneath Lala's eyes.

"I so admire and am so envious of anyone who can pull off a visual aesthetic," Lala said. "And you make it look so damn easy."

"It must be genetic," Geraldine said. "Your dear mother, God rest, had none either. Her idea of decorating was to put the couch against the wall and call it a day."

"So true," Lala said. "And her idea of getting gussied up was lipstick and maybe a little blush. God love her, she still always looked great."

"And so do you," Geraldine said.

"Have I mentioned lately that you're the best aunt, adopted or otherwise, that a person could hope for?"

Lala had been facing away from the mirror so Geraldine could put the magic unguents on her face. With a final sweep of powder to seal and protect her artistry, Geraldine turned Lala's chair back to the looking glass.

Lala leaned forward and stared at herself.

*Best aunt ever,* Lala thought.

"Omigod, I look good. I swear, I do not know what I would do without you. I feel good. I feel positive. I feel optimistic. I am strong. I am invincible. I am woman. Yeah, hear me roar. Hey, you know what would make tonight perfect?"

"Don't start that again," Geraldine said.

"I don't understand why you and Monty aren't coming to the party tonight!" Lala wailed.

"Monty said he's been to a million of these for Helene."

*A million?* Lala thought.

"He said he really doesn't need to go to yet another."

"A million?" Lala gasped. "How successful is she?"

"Stop that. It's just a figure of speech."

"What the barf?" Lala said.

She was squinting at the twisting road and listening to the voice of the French woman she had programmed on the GPS of Geraldine's car to give her directions.

Lala had originally programmed the GPS to speak in the voice of a French man, but had immediately discovered that the sultry tones reminded her of The One Who Got Away.

"Gérard. Gérard. *Pourquoi tu ne m'aimes pas?*" Lala plaintively inquired when she pulled over almost immediately after leaving the environs of Manhattan Beach and pounded her index finger on the GPS to change the settings.

The trip to Beverly Hills from Manhattan Beach, with the GPS set to avoid highways, had taken only an hour, and Lala had allotted herself two, in case of emergencies. So she had a full sixty minutes to sit on a bench—one, she felt sure, fate was speaking to her through when it placed the bench in front of a bridal salon on Rodeo Drive—and enjoy a ridiculously overpriced iced tea while she imagined how she wanted to look at her wedding to Jackson Platt.

*Off-the-shoulder,* Lala thought. *That will be most flattering. Tea-length maybe. Jesus, is every damn wedding dress in the world strapless? We're not all brides in our twenties, thank you very much. I am clearly losing my mind sitting here on a balmy evening thinking about wedding dresses. But so what? I should definitely go for a fabric that drapes rather than clings. Maybe we'll get married in Paris. I bet those dresses in that store are exorbitant. I'll go to Kleinfeld's and get something off their sale rack. Maybe I'll be on* Say Yes to the Dress*! That would be wonderful. And I'll donate the difference in cost to charity. To an organization of my beloved's choosing. In honor of my beloved. As long as it's something that helps children or animals. Or advances the causes of the Democratic Party. I wish I'd gotten a muffin to go with my iced tea. Or maybe a scone.*

"*Allez tout droit. Je répète. Allez tout droit.*"

"*D'accord, Marianne,*" Lala muttered. "*Je vous ai comprise.*"

*Is that the address?* Lala thought, peering over the steering wheel. *Would you look at that place? It's a flippin' chateau. Oh, for the love of God, is that a valet service? I want to go home. To Greenwich Village. Now. Maybe I can drive there. On side streets. Actually, that might be fun. And then I could write a novel about it. Or maybe a short story. Maybe a series of short stories. Why is that valet grinning at me? Do I look weird?*

One of several valets standing at the ready in Helene's majestic circular driveway sprinted over to Lala's door and opened it for her.

*Please don't call me "ma'am,"* Lala silently begged the strapping lad. *Please. There's only so much I can take.*

"Good evening. How are you tonight?"

"I'm doing very well, thank you," Lala said.

*Is that a warm smile?* Lala thought. *A genuine, warm smile that I only just moments ago referred to quite derisively as a grin in my muddy mind? Am I that much of a cynical hag now?*

"How are you?" Lala asked the fine, young man.

"Doin' great," the young man said.

Lala gave him a big, warm, sincere smile and handed him the car keys.

"Thank you very much," she said. "I appreciate your help."

Lala stepped around the car and entered the wide double-doors of Helene's home. A two-story entryway rolled to the horizon before her. Lala felt almost assaulted by the lively yet subdued colors, the classic yet cozy furnishings, the air of vibrant tranquility.

*Shoot me,* Lala thought. *This is gorgeous. Please tell me she didn't decorate this place herself.*

At a table against a wall to her right, a young woman sat with a series of nametags spread before her in neat, alphabetical rows. The young woman smiled at Lala and gave her a welcoming wave.

*That's it,* Lala thought. *I am officially over myself. As of right now. I'm done being a grump. There are only so many warm, genuine smiles I can withstand.*

"Hi!" Lala said.

"Hello!" the young lady said. "Welcome! May I have your name, please?"

"Lala Pettibone."

"Great name!" the young lady said. "I noticed it when I was printing the nametags. It sounds so epic!"

"You think?" Lala said. "Thank you! I really appreciate that . . ."

Lala glanced at the young lady's nametag.

". . . Brenda! Ohhh, that's my best friend's name! What a lovely name!"

"Thank you!" Brenda said. "The party is straight through there in the atrium. Have fun tonight!"

"Thank you," Lala said. Lala walked down the hallway and

tried to figure out where to fasten her nametag.

*Oh, what the hell,* she thought. *I'm putting it right next to my tits. This is no time to be reticent. Where's the bar?*

Lala smiled the rest of the way, until she reached the end of the hall and found herself standing at the top of a small staircase leading to the atrium. The glass-enclosed expanse of the room glowed beneath a ceiling of sparkling white lights. Spread below Lala was a sea of people. Lala nervously scanned the group. Her best first assessment was that it was an attractive, successful, moving and shaking crowd.

*Shy,* Lala thought. *I'm feeling it. Here it comes. The Dreaded Shy. Must have an activity. Now.*

Lala grabbed the railing of the stairs for dear life and for dear dignity.

*If I fall as I descend,* Lala thought, *I will just stay there. In a heap. Until death overtakes me. Even if it's years from now. It's only a few steps, but, sheesh, they have been polished to within an inch of my life.*

"Lala!"

Lala looked around to find where Helene's voice was coming from. She saw her hostess gracefully weaving her way through people to get to her. Helene was wearing a sumptuous red, strapless cocktail dress that just grazed her knees.

*Sweet mother of God,* Lala thought. *She looks fabulous. And together we're wearing Wesleyan's colors. I feel dizzy. I want to go home.*

Helene gracefully gamboled up the steps and wrapped Lala in a hug.

*Oh, God, please don't let me fall on my ass,* Lala silently begged. *At any point. Ever. For the rest of my life. You owe me that much. I was widowed in my thirties.*

"I'm so glad you're here!" Helene said.

"You look gorgeous," Lala said.

"Stop it! You look gorgeous!"

"I love your home. It's gorgeous. Please tell me you didn't decorate it yourself."

"Oh, stop it," Helene said. "It was no big deal. I had fun doing it."

*Shoot me now,* Lala thought.

Helene linked her arm with Lala's and led her down the stairs.

*Whoa! Not so fast*, Lala thought. *These damn steps are like ice. What, you can't put a little rubber matting on these damn things?*

"We're wearing WesU colors!" Helene said. "Come on. Let's go to the bar and get you a drink."

*That is a genius-level idea*, Lala thought.

"Listen," she said. "I'm feeling a big ol' wave of shyness."

"Stop it. Everyone's going to love you."

"I need a job."

"What?"

"Let me help tend bar."

"But . . . but, you're my guest."

"Please. Think of me as a border collie. I need to work, or I'll just run around in circles and whimper and get that crazed look they get as if they're saying, 'Want me to herd something? Huh? 'Cause I'm ready if you do. Right now. Got any sheep? Huh?' I realize dog imagery is wasted on you. That's not a criticism."

"Well, sure, why not?" Helene said. "If you think that would make you enjoy the party more?"

"It definitely would," Lala said.

*Or, at a minimum*, she thought, *it might keep me from succumbing to this overriding impulse to fashion a cave out of cocktail napkins and hide inside it for all eternity.*

🍸

"Cute guy at three o'clock. Very."

*Jackson?* Lala thought. *Is it Jackson Platt? Where the hell is he?*

Lala peered toward where her colleague behind the bar, who was nodding in the direction of a noticeably attractive man at a distance to their right, was indicating.

*Damn it*, Lala thought. *That's not him. Where the hell is he? But that guy is very cute.*

Lala smiled at Ariel and nodded in agreement. Ariel was exactly half Lala's age. She was tall and sporty, and she was putting herself through the master's degree program in the Luskin School of Public Affairs at UCLA.

Lala had already established that Ariel was the youngest of four children and the only girl—she had grown up in Sacramento, was an Aries, a dedicated feminist and progressive Democrat, and she was planning to run for the California state senate as the first of her public offices, with an eye toward the governorship of the Golden State and maybe a run for the White House.

"Ariel," Lala said. "I am going to repeat this because it bears repeating. You are the daughter I never had. And if you don't let me run your election campaigns—all of them—I will be very hurt. Wow, I seem to be a natural at this parental guilt trip thing. That guy is very cute. P.S. you're already signed up to be one of the young people who takes care of me in my dotage. Just FYI."

Lala grabbed one of the many elegant pitchers that graced the ornate wooden bar. It seemed that among Helene's copious talents was a flair for mixology. For this special evening, Helene had created a signature cocktail that involved a fusion of champagne, vodka, the pulp from maybe a bazillion hand-squeezed oranges, and edible gold flakes. And at this point in the night's festivities, Lala was too cheerfully buzzed to say anything negative about Helene's overabundance of ability.

"Edible gold," Lala said to Ariel. "Seriously, who knew?"

Lala poured them both another goblet, and they sipped as they continued to scan the crowd. This was another unpredictable lull in the evening's distribution of libations. It was definitely feast or famine. At times the two lines to the two bartenders were long enough to prevent Lala from doing a tremendous amount of gabbing with each guest. And then there were the happy occasions when a guest or two would stay at the bar to chat with Lala and Ariel, and no one else would show up to interrupt them for a good five or ten minutes. All in all, Lala was thrilled with her plan to stick herself behind the bar. It gave her a chance to meet nearly everyone without having to conjure any transparent excuses to move from one group to the next.

"You're not driving home, are you?" Ariel asked.

"Nope. I'm probably going to have to sleep over. Not that I've checked with Helene yet to see if it's okay. But, sheesh, look at the size of this place. I could curl up in a bathtub in the east wing, and she'd never know I'm here. You?"

"My boyfriend is picking me up," Ariel said.

"Excellent! I'll look forward to meeting him. Is it serious? Huh? Yeah? Huh? Is he going to be the future son-in-law I never had?"

"You are such a nut," Ariel giggled.

Lala was just about to applaud Ariel for her keen insight when a strident male voice appeared out of nowhere, followed by the sound of cranky tapping of an index finger or possibly a ball peen hammer on the bar.

"Can I get a drink? Whatever Helene's dreamed up will have to do, I guess. Unless you've got any bourbon?"

Lala turned and found an ogre scowling at her. And she was horrified to discover that she might be in the process of recognizing him.

*Omigod,* Lala thought. *It can't be. What does his nametag say?*

"I'm so sorry, we don't have bourbon," Lala said.

"Jesus," Jackson Platt growled. "Okay. Just pour me some of that stuff."

Lala found herself about to say an elongated version of the word "please" aloud, as she might have to a surly kindergartner who had clearly not been taught any manners. Instead of speaking, she pursed her lips in a tight, contained frown. She picked up a pitcher and filled a large glass and handed it to her favorite contemporary author—who grabbed the glass and walked away from the bar without a word or even the most perfunctory gesture of acknowledgement.

"Yikes," Ariel said. "Dickhead alert."

"Wow," Lala whispered to her. "He doesn't look anything like he does on TV. On screen he comes across as an affable, cauliflower-nosed intellectual. Which can be very sexy in the right context. Up close, I'd be forced to say he's more got the air of a cheerless, ape-like creature. Which, I'm sorry to have to report, is rarely, if indeed ever, sexy. Jesus, you'd think it would kill him to crack a smile. And somebody must be doing a Cyrano thing with him whenever he's being interviewed because he is charming. I'm not kidding. Cute and funny and smart and engaging. What a dickhead. You know what else is really weird? In his case, the camera takes off ten pounds."

"Who is he?" Ariel asked.

"That's Jackson Platt," Lala said. She was trying very hard not to cry. She grabbed her glass and started gulping down signature cocktail in horrible gurgling little spasms. "He's an absolutely amazing—"

"Omigod," Ariel groaned, "he's the dickhead who wrote that piece of crap, *A Map Without Latitude*. I had to read that for a class, and it was torture. That man should be tried for war crimes. Crimes against humanity. Crimes against good taste and punctuation."

Lala gaped at Ariel. She felt the rhythm and sound of waves crashing in her ears.

"That . . . that . . . that . . . that stuff he does with exclamation points? It's intentional. He does that because he's trying to—"

Before Lala could give in to her itching desire to start thumping sweet and guileless young Ariel about the head and shoulders as a physical gesture of emphasis to lend support to her literary hero's calculatedly abundant use of, arguably, that most enthusiastic, if not most subtle, mark of punctuation, Helene's voice reverberated over and through and all around the room on a sound system that the engineers at Madison Square Garden might have considered boorish.

"Hellooooo, my dear friends!" Helene's voice boomed.

"Ahhhhhhh!" Lala wailed in terror. Her grip on her substantially full goblet was instantly a thing of the past. The glass dropped to the floor, sending liquor and gold flakes out in a wide radius that had an air of Mardi Gras about it.

Every pair of eyes in the place turned toward the bar. Lala looked back at everyone, her placid expression a dazed cipher.

*What the fuck are you looking at?* Lala silently demanded.

"Uh oh," Helene proclaimed cheerfully through the microphone. She was standing on the top step of yet another coy, short little staircase, this one leading to the pool and tennis courts. "I think we might have to cut off my dear friend over there after a few more drinks!"

*Ha ha*, Lala silently sneered. *You are a crackup, Helene. Where's a clean glass?*

"Are you okay?" Lala whispered to Ariel. "Did you get soaked? How did that glass not break?"

"I'm fine. I know; that's so weird. Is it plastic?"

"That is very weird plastic," Lala said. "I'd like to know just what the hell our hostess is up to. By rights, you and I should be impaled by shards of glass at this point."

"I just wanted to take a few minutes to thank you all for coming tonight to celebrate the release of the next book in my European Murder Capitals series," Helene boomed. "Thank you so much for sharing my joy with me. I love to write. I've never wanted to be anything except a writer."

Lala listened from beneath the bar, where she was crouching on her heels.

*If there is not another clean glass back here, I swear I will start drinking directly from one of these pitchers,* Lala thought.

"So please be sure to take your gift copy of *Copenhagen Pardons No One,* and please be sure to let me sign it for you before you leave tonight. Okay, just one more thing and then we'll go back to celebrating."

*Seriously,* Lala thought, *which one of these labyrinthine cabinets has fresh glasses?*

"I just wanted to bring up my wonderful agent, Kelly Franklin Adams, so I can say a big public thank you to her for getting me a meeting next week at Paramount to talk about the film version of 'Paris for Homicide Lovers.'"

Lala froze. Then she very slowly put her fingertips down on the floor to steady herself.

*I think I may be having a stroke,* she thought. *Did I just hear that correctly, or did I just have a stroke and die and go straight to Hell? Am I in Hell right now?*

As the crowd applauded, Lala very slowly rose. She peeked over the top of the bar. Helene was hugging a frighteningly thin woman. Her short hair was slicked back. It might have been the blackest organic material Lala had ever encountered. Her hair seemed to suck the light in its vicinity into its infinite depth.

Helene and the woman hugged each other and then waved at

the crowd as though they had just been nominated by their political party for national office.

Yeah, I'm having a stroke, Lala silently concluded as she stared at the woman who had brutally rejected her screenplay on the Ides of March of that same year, a.k.a. two seconds ago if Lala's vivid agony was any indication.

"Thanks again, everyone!" Helene bellowed. "Wish me luck next week!"

Lala turned to Ariel.

"Is anyone looking at me?" she asked. "I don't trust my own powers of observation."

"Umm, no," Ariel said. "Pretty much everyone is heading over there to surround Helene and her agent. Are you okay?"

"I'm fine. You're a dear and wonderful young person."

Lala grabbed one of the pitchers and drank directly from it.

*Awww, JESUS!* Lala thought. *It didn't occur to me to check who Helene's agent is? It didn't occur to me to make sure it's not Kelly Franklin Adams? Stay cool. Yes, I am drowning in a Noah's Ark-level flood of angst right now vis-à-vis how successful Helene is and what an abject failure I am. Yes, I am feeling a tsunami of disappointment crash over me right now because the literary man of my dreams appears to be a major tool, but I am not going to have a public meltdown the way I did last time my hopes were submerged in a roiling cauldron of watered agony. And, yes, I have zero idea what's up with all the liquid imagery.*

Lala grabbed Ariel's wrist and urgently whispered to her.

"Ariel, I need to get out of here and I definitely shouldn't be driving, so can I impose on you to help me figure out how in the living hell to work that app thing, so I can get a ride out of this god-forsaken burg? I mean, in New York, you go to the curb, you stick your hand up in the air and boom, you're in a cab. Awww, JESUS!"

Lala saw Helene and Kelly Franklin Adams and Jackson Platt making a bee-line for the bar.

*A trifecta of tsuris hurtling toward me,* Lala thought. *Great. What's next? Leprosy?*

"Hi!" Lala said. "Lovely speech, Helene. I'm so excited about Paramount! Listen, I hate to drink and run, but I've got to—"

"Lala!" Helene began.

*NO!* Lala silently screamed. *Don't tell Kelly Franklin Adams my name! Damn it, why don't I have a normal name? Why do I not have an average, forgettable name? DO NOT tell her my last name! Hey, is Jackson Platt looking at my tits?*

"I wanted to make sure to introduce the fellow Wesleyan grads," Helene continued.

Don't say my last name, Lala silently pleaded.

"Kelly Franklin Adams, this is my new and very dear friend, Lala Pettibone."

*Barf,* Lala thought. *There was a definite spark of recognition in her eyes. She knows she knows me, and she maybe even knows how she knows me. Barf.*

"Hello," Lala said. She extended her hand.

Upon seeing Lala's extended hand, Kelly Franklin Adams didn't so much take it in hers as allow Lala to lean closer and grab her hand so that Lala wasn't standing there with a free-floating hand looking like a hapless urchin.

"Nice to meet you," Kelly Franklin Adams said.

Kelly Franklin Adams's handshake had the warmth and enthusiasm and tactile commitment that Queen Elizabeth might have exhibited had an exceptionally unwashed commoner broken all rules of royal protocol and grabbed the hereditary monarch for a big, drooling hug at a ribbon-cutting ceremony.

"I thought she was one of the servers," Jackson Platt said to Helene. He turned to Ariel. "I need another glass. Can't remember where I put mine, and I'm desperate for another Gold Rush. Gold Rush. Yeah. Clever. I just came up with that. Helene, you should call your cocktail that."

Ariel gave Jackson a smile that—it was clear to Lala in a world where nothing was clear to her any longer—was a fence holding back a herd of unbroken mustangs of rebuke for the acclaimed author's surpassing rudeness.

*God, my Daughter-I-never-had is formidable,* Lala thought. *If Jackson were paying a drop of attention, he would see that she's about ready to kill him. Good for her. Tell him to jump up and kiss your ass, sweetie. What a jerk.*

"I'll just run to the kitchen to get a few fresh ones," Ariel said. She directed her next words to Lala. "I'll be right back."

Jackson scoffed at Ariel's retreating figure.

"Shoddy anticipation of guests' needs," Jackson said. "Don't hire this outfit again, Helene. So, Lala. Lala Pettibone. What an amusing name. It's got just enough overtones of the absurd to intrigue me."

*Shut up*, Lala thought.

"Where do I know that name?"

*Awww, JESUS!* Lala thought. *Did Kelly Franklin Adams give him my script to read? Did they mock it together? Does the entire world know how much I suck as a writer?*

Jackson snapped his fingers and pointed to Helene.

"Your dad is dating her aunt."

"Yes, he is," Helene said. "That's how I was lucky enough to meet dear Lala!"

Jackson winked at Lala.

*What?* Lala thought. *Why are you winking at me?*

"Salman Rushdie, yeah?" Jackson said. He bobbed his head with a knowing, conspiratorial grin and winked at Lala again. "Priceless. You can't write stuff like that. No one would believe it."

*Oh, that's why*, Lala thought. *You're winking at me because you're a massive dickhead.*

"Helene, we need to go talk to your editor," Kelly Franklin Adams said.

"More on this later, dear ones. Would you excuse us? Jackson, flirt with Lala."

"With pleasure," Jackson oozed.

Lala winced as Helene and Kelly Franklin Adams strode away. She felt Jackson's hot, leering gaze on her and reluctantly rolled her eyes in his direction.

"So. Lala Pettibone. I think it's about time we blew this shit stand, yeah? Where are you taking me for a nightcap?"

🍷

Lala was happily engulfed in a white bathrobe that felt

like a rich, thick cloud. She was in a California King bed with 800-thread-count sheets. She had created a sloping wall of pillows against the headboard of the bed to prop herself up in a semiprone position. Room service had knocked on her door an hour earlier and brought in a cart covered with two servings of french fries and chocolate molten lava cake with vanilla ice cream for dessert. The TV was on to *Say Yes to the Dress*, and Lala was on the phone with Geraldine.

"I swear, I became Blanche DuBois tonight. The Daughter-I-never-had, so that makes her the grandniece-you-never-had, was very skillful at getting me out of the house without making it at all obvious that I basically couldn't walk without weaving. Not so much because of the alcohol as because of the impotent rage I was choking on. And I owe Ariel my freedom because she also prevented me from committing homicide against a certain unctuous author before I left.

"Maybe Helene can use tonight's murder-mystery-plot-that-almost-happened for her American Killing Capitals series, which I assume she's feverishly working on right now because Paramount and Sony and the Weinsteins are in a bidding war for her work.

"Ariel basically grabbed me by both elbows and glided me over the wood floors, which were, by the way, dangerously polished. I'm surprised someone, and by someone I mean me, didn't break a hip. Thank God Ariel is very sporty, because between the booze and the bile, I could not have been easy to maneuver.

"Then the adorable young valet drove me over to the hotel in my car while another adorable young valet followed us in his car so the two of them could head back to Helene's house after they deposited me in the lobby of the hotel and stayed long enough to make sure there was a vacancy.

"I think you can imagine how much resolve and conviction it took for me not to invite the two of them up for a *ménage à trois*. Seriously. But for the kindness of strangers, and my own last shreds of dignity, who knows what I would be doing right now. And with whom. And how many times.

"Damn it, they really were both quite sexy. I should have gotten one of their cell phone numbers. Maybe I can get the concierge here to send someone over to Helene's house to get one of their cell phone numbers.

"You want to know something hilarious that happened? One of the bellboys, who was adorable, by the way, escorted me to my bungalow. This place is amazing. They have bungalows, and it's so cute. So, as we're exiting the lobby, I walk right into a bee. Or it dive-bombed me, I don't know. The bee just smacked right into my face. My left cheek just below my eye, specifically. It didn't sting me. It just whacked into my face and then flew right away. I was absolutely terrified for a moment, and then I started laughing because it was so bizarre, and then, of course, my laughter segued right into me sobbing all the way down this exquisite garden path next to the unbelievably posh pool to my adorable bungalow.

"Have you got me on speakerphone? Please tell me you've been accomplishing things while I've been raving. I can't believe how much of your time I'm taking up. Shouldn't you and Monty be bonking each other right now?"

"Monty can wait," Geraldine said. "And I do not have you on speakerphone. I am listening to your every word. I did blank out for a few seconds during the part about the bee. I am not doing anything else while I am listening to you. Because I love you, and you are very important to me."

Lala grabbed a cloth napkin off the room service cart that she had wedged right next to the bed to keep her need for movement to an absolute minimum. She frantically dabbed her eyes.

"Ohhh, Auntie Geraldine," she gasped. "Please don't be so kind to me. If I start crying again, I'll probably explode or something. Or my face will get beet red once too often, and it will stay that way for the rest of my life. I'll have to wear kabuki makeup all the time just to look even vaguely normal."

"Listen, you go ahead and cry if you have to," Geraldine said. "You relax and do whatever feels comforting and soothing tonight. Except have sex with two young and adorable valets, or any number whatsoever of nearby and thus easily accessible bellhops."

"Are you sure?" Lala whimpered. "Maybe that would actually be just the thing I need to take my mind off—"

"Absolutely not," Geraldine said. "And tomorrow you come

home, and we'll start on Act Two of your life, okay?"

# A SILVER LINING

Before she went anywhere near the fourplex, before she showed up at Geraldine's door to collect her dogs from their spontaneous slumber party with their great-auntie, Lala pulled Geraldine's car into the driveway of Monty's home.

Monty opened the door and when he saw that it was Lala standing there, he moved toward her with welcoming arms outstretched. Lala brushed past him into the house. Her self-righteous forward momentum was immediately halted by Benedict, who sailed through the air and tackled her to the ground with his Great Dane adoration.

"Ufff," Lala grunted.

"Benedict!" Monty barked. "Bad boy!"

Lala spoke and giggled between the slurpy Benedict kisses that covered her face.

"It's okay, it's okay, I love it," she said. "Now, Monty, listen, I came right over here as soon as I got back to town."

Lala grabbed Benedict around his waist and rolled the massive beast over with her as she turned on her side. Benedict cheerfully complied. It seemed he thought they were now wrestling and wouldn't that be wonderfully fun? In an instant, he was on his back, and Lala was rubbing his tummy, and she managed to get up on her feet without Benedict tackling her again.

Monty eased into his recliner and Benedict jumped up on the couch.

"Come sit next to us, dear girl," Monty said. "I can't stay on my feet too long."

"Of course not," Lala said. "How's your leg?"

"Much better. Not quite there yet, but almost."

Lala sat on the couch to Benedict's right so she could also be next to Monty's chair. Monty took Lala's hand and kissed it.

"Are you okay?" he asked. "Geraldine said you had a rough night. I'm so sorry, my dear."

"I'm fine. Thank you for asking. Please don't worry about me. Now, Monty, listen, forgive me for being brusque, but you better not be dicking around with my aunt. I swear to God, if you are not taking her seriously, if she is just some kind of sunset-years sex toy for you, if you hurt her feelings in any way, and let me repeat that, in any way at all, I will break your other leg. I won't do it myself. But I bet I could find someone who would do it for me. If I pay them. Which I will. Happily."

Monty nodded his head as he listened to Lala. When she stopped speaking, he gave it a few seconds to make sure she was done before he said anything.

"My daughter has many good qualities. But sometimes she can be self-absorbed. And sometimes that leads her to lack grace."

*Great,* Lala thought. *Like I can continue to harbor a grudge against her for that. Pot? I'm kettle, and I guess I'll have to stop calling you black right about now.*

"What did she say last night?" Monty asked.

"It was her friend. An author. An unctuous author. He apparently had heard about Salman Rushdie. He spoke very derisively about my aunt. I wanted to clean his clock."

"I wish you had," Monty said.

"Yes, in retrospect I'm sorry I didn't. I like you, Monty, but if you've been making fun of my aunt behind her back, I am not kidding about breaking your leg."

"Helene was here once when Gerry mentioned your neighbor being under a *fatwa*. I would never mock your aunt. I take her very seriously. I'm going to ask her to marry me."

"WHAT?"

Lala covered her face with her hands and burst into tears. Monty moved to come over to comfort her, and Benedict nudged her elbow with his huge, concerned snout.

"Don't get up! It's okay! I'm so happy!" she wailed. "My God, is it amazing how much a person can cry, or what? Seriously, if I'm any indication, tears are a perpetually replenishing natural resource. We should use them for power plants and cars and stuff. Monty, I'm so happy for you both! Listen, when are you gonna ask her? Because it better be soon, or else you should not have told me about it, even if I was going to have your leg broken, because if you don't ask her by . . . tomorrow at the latest, I will blurt it out to her. Because I'm a blurter. So you can kiss your romantic element of surprise goodbye. I'm sorry, but that's just the way I'm built."

"Okay, I'll ask her tomorrow," Monty said. "Let's have some tea to celebrate."

"Great idea. I'll go make it."

"Thank you, darling. I think there are some shortbreads in the cabinet. From that cute place downtown with all the homemade stuff."

"I love those," Lala sniffled. "I'll go make the tea."

"Great idea, darling. And you'll stop crying, okay, honey? Because I think Benedict is about to break the door down and run out to get help."

Lala stood up from the couch. She wiped her nose on her sleeve and padded toward the kitchen. She called back to them as she left the room.

"Oh, yes, Lassie. Lala has indeed fallen down the well. But as God is Lala's witness, she is going to claw her way out even if she dies trying."

There was an unopened package of those exquisite short-breads in Monty's kitchen cabinet. Lala grabbed it to her chest and hugged it tight and prayed that it was even a tiny sign that her luck was turning around.

Lala looked up at the ceiling and whispered, "In the right direction, I mean. In case that wasn't clear."

Y

"Are you sure you don't want another one?" Lala asked Monty. She poured him a fresh cup of tea. "You've barely had any of the shortbreads. They're so marvelously dense. They're as marvelously dense as the first guy I dated as a freshman in college. Conrad Gettinger. He was brilliant. But dense. Walked around in a fog all the time. You had to spell things out for him. Any subtlety at all in your communication and he would give you the blank stare. But, amazingly enough given that fact, he was a natural superstar in the sack. Come on, have another shortbread before I eat them all."

"You enjoy them. I do not know how you can eat so much and still stay so trim."

"Anxiety," Lala explained. "Anxiety and exercise. You can't beat that combo. I worry the calories away."

Monty pointed to the wet bar.

"Go grab the brandy, please, hon," he said.

"Jesus, I thought you would never ask."

"What? You had to wait for an invitation? You're not at home here?"

"Yeah, you're right, Uncle Monty," Lala giggled. "That's the last damn time I stand on ceremony."

Lala climbed over Benedict, who had been using her feet as a pillow for the last hour, and ran over to search the bottles on top of the bar. When she found the right one, she seized it, trotted back to the sofa, and poured a stiff shot into each delicate china teacup.

"Atta girl," Monty said. "So, now you tell me what Helene did last night to upset you."

"It's not her. It's not her fault. It's me. It's me; I'm insane. But not for long. I've got a plan."

"Good for you. What did she say last night? Was it about Paramount? Was she crowing about her meeting? I can understand how that's not easy to hear."

"Yeah, but, I mean, I can't blame her," Lala said. "Though I did wear her out in my mind in the car ride to the hotel. I had some major *esprit d'escalier* goin' on. It was mostly inchoate grunts and snarls, but it got the job done."

"Good for you," Monty said.

"Yeah, but I mean, I don't have a right to hate her because she's successful. I mean, of course, I hate her for being so successful. But it's wrong, right?"

"Wrong, schmong," Monty said. "It's human. Every time a friend succeeds . . . I know you can finish that one for me."

"I die a little," Lala said, smiling. "Let's raise our brandy snifters masquerading as teacups in Gore Vidal's honor. I loved most of his politics most of the time, and I love him for making my bitter envy more socially acceptable and maybe even mainstream."

🍷

*Home again, home again,* Lala thought, *and with that big stupid grin I can't control. I'm going to have to start planning the bachelorette party A.S.A.P.*

Geraldine threw open the door to her apartment, grabbed her niece, hugged her tight, and started sniffing the air.

"You didn't drink and drive, did you? I will kill you if you did that!"

Lala planted a big kiss on Geraldine's forehead. She put her arm around her aunt and marched Geraldine into the living room, where her dogs were sleeping on a huge pile of blankets that had been lovingly and strategically placed in a large wash of warm sunlight.

"I went to see Monty, and we had tea with brandy. Lots of it. Not lots of tea. Lots of brandy. Your car is still in his driveway. I walked from there. Because I am hammered."

Lala ran across the wood floor and dove into the pile of hounds and blankets.

"Mama's home!" she crowed.

None of the dogs woke up.

"Why did you go see Monty before you came home?" Geraldine demanded.

*Ooops,* Lala thought.

"Forget I said that. You misunderstood me. Hey, come join us.

I've got tales out of school to tell."

Geraldine, still eyeing Lala suspiciously, sat down on the blankets. She grabbed Yootza and put him on her lap.

"Get this," Lala said, "Monty told me that one time Helene was flying to Paris on Air France, and she was using miles for the tickets, and she had enough for one first-class ticket but not two. Right? And she was traveling with her live-in boyfriend who was basically her common-law husband at that point, and, instead of using the points for two business-class tickets, she got herself a first-class seat and made him sit alone in business class. Can you believe it? It was supposed to be a romantic trip for them, and she started the *voyage d'amour* by having them sit apart for the twelve-hour flight because she absolutely had to be in first class. *Merde! Ça c'est une princesse!* But you know, God love her, no one's perfect."

"No. That's certainly true. No one is. But why didn't they just add cash to the miles so they could both sit in first class?"

Lala giggled.

"I don't know. That's not part of the story."

Lala leaned her head against Chester the greyhound's big belly. "Isn't life grand?"

"Why are you winking so often?" Geraldine demanded.

*Ooops,* Lala thought. *God, I feel like there's a nuclear bomb ticking inside my skull, and Goldfinger is cackling, and James Bond is nowhere to be found.*

"No particular reason," Lala said. "Maybe I've got dust in my eye. Maybe I'm just happy and my happiness is manifesting itself in a jovial but clichéd facial tic. Who can ever know why things happen?"

"Well, it is getting a bit annoying. You might want to put some drops in. But it's nice to see you smiling again. You're smiling quite a lot today, and it's lovely. I think it's a very good sign for this Act Two of yours, don't you?"

"Ohh, yes," Lala said. "Out with The Old. Take a hike, The Old, for you are banished. We're makin' room for The New. The Brand Spankin' New."

"Good for you." Geraldine stood and carried Yootza with her as she exited the room in the direction of the bathroom. "Let me get you some drops before I lose my mind with all that damn winking."

🍷

Lala was very pleasantly surprised by how straightforward a process it was to pay Ariel's graduate-school expenses. And now she was on the phone with Ariel, and she was getting a strong message of self-reflection in the course of the conversation.

*Wow,* Lala thought. *After just a few minutes, maybe not even a few, it is kind of annoying when someone cries so much. I have to try to remember that when I'm on my next jag.*

"This is a happy thing," Lala said. She managed to keep almost all of the irritation out of her voice. "Don't cry. This is good news."

"But how will I ever pay you back?" Ariel wailed.

*Wow,* Lala thought. *We must be related. We must be third cousins or something. I feel like I'm looking in an aural mirror.*

"It's not a loan," Lala said. "I'm paying your school expenses. All of them. Because I can."

"But how will I ever make this up to you?" Ariel howled.

"Make it up to me by going out into the world when you graduate and doing good. For those who need help. Human and animal. And, of course, by taking care of me in my dotage."

There was a brief moment of silence on the other end of the line.

"I thought you were kidding when you said that at the party."

"Absolutely not," Lala said. "I'll be taking care of my Auntie Geraldine, who is also childless, and you will carry on that tradition. But don't worry, I'm not talking about any of this happening any time soon. I intend to rage, rage, rage against the dying of the light for a good many years to come."

Lala was finally able to get off the phone with Ariel after assuring her for a full five minutes that there was no issue about interest rates and repayment schedules because this was a flat-out, simple-as-pie, what-are-you-not-understanding-about-the-word-gift gift for chrissake, and, after that, Lala spent the next full five minutes reminding Ariel that she was seriously not, for chrissake, kidding about expecting Ariel to mix her cocktails and get her prescriptions filled and order her Chinese food deliveries when she was too feeble to do those things for herself.

Lala cheerfully returned her attention to her laptop and pulled up a blank screen. Yootza was on her lap sleeping. She pulled him to her with her left hand and nestled him under her chin as she typed and moved the mouse with her right hand.

The words "Monthly Donations" appeared at the top of the screen, centered and in bold.

"Okay, okay, okay, let's think," Lala mused. "Any thoughts. Anyone?"

Her query was greeted with an expected chorus of snoring from her canine consultants. Lala smiled contentedly.

*I love having old animals,* she thought. *It's so peaceful. I haven't had to throw a Frisbee or a squeaky toy or really anything at all for . . . gosh, years. I like it this way.*

She began typing again and narrated as her right hand did the work for two.

"Well, certainly Bide-a-Wee. And KidSave. And of course Dogs of Love. And the Democrats. And I have to look up organizations that provide scholarships for poor kids. Gosh, this is fun!"

There was an energetic and distinctly cheerful rapping on Lala's front door.

"Here she comes!" Lala announced. She carried Yootza with her and kissed his little forehead as she sprinted to the door.

*Be cool,* Lala thought. *Be cool. Just. Be. Cool. For. Fuck's. Sake. Act surprised. Do not ruin this moment for her. Do. Not.*

"Hi, what a nice surprise. Come on in! What brings you here?"

Geraldine's face fell.

"You already know?"

"Yup. He told me when I got back. It wasn't his fault. I had threatened to break his other leg. It almost killed me not to tell you. At one point yesterday, around that time I was doing all that winking? I thought my head was going to explode. Please don't be disappointed. We can still celebrate! We must still celebrate! Where's the ring? For chrissake, show me the ring before my head explodes!"

With all the finesse and charm of a starlet of the 1950s who had just landed the millionaire leading man in a Technicolor extravaganza destined to be a camp classic, Geraldine coyly smiled and slowly raised her hand to her cheek with the palm facing inward. She wagged her fingers to make the diamond sparkle and Lala gasped.

"It's exquisite," Lala whispered. Her voice caught in her throat. *Do not cry!* She silently yelled at herself.

Geraldine and Lala hugged. Yootza, who was mashed between them, let out a grunt by way of a yip and then growled before he fell back asleep.

"You didn't blurt," Geraldine said. "You're evolving! Why are you still in your bathrobe?"

"I guess I'm getting a late start to my day."

"It's half past five," Geraldine said. "In the afternoon."

"Great! Happy Hour!"

Lala had enjoyed the past two weeks immensely. She had showered regularly, but she had rarely put on anything other than her bathrobe or her exercise clothes.

On the limited occasions when she left her apartment, it was to go to the gym or to volunteer at Dogs of Love. She didn't go shopping for anything. Her food was brought to her either by a grocery service or, more frequently, by delivery people from local restaurants. Her toiletries and over-the-counter drugs and paper goods were delivered by a very nice young man from the local branch of a national chain of drugstores. Lala wanted to flirt with him, but she forced herself not to.

When Lala did venture out into the world, she hid her identity under a large oatmeal-colored hat that she had ordered online. She scurried from the apartment to her aunt's car. She behaved like a celebrity being mercilessly stalked by the paparazzi. When she took the dogs out for their frequent walks in the neighborhood, she looked like a cotton-encased mummy.

At home, she slept only when she passed out from exhaustion, and always at odd, off-sync hours, as though she was suffering from ongoing jetlag. She spent nearly every conscious minute at home on her couch surrounded by hounds, writing. Writing whatever she wanted to write, be it another episode of "The Soused Cinéaste" or another chapter in the comedic novelization of her screenplay.

Lala had been enjoying looking at her story in a new light.

"I'm thinking of it as a coming-of-age novel," she explained to Yootza who, if his closed eyes and limp body snuggled deep within the folds of the couch were any indication, was not a rabid fan of her work. "A coming-of-age novel with a forty-year-old protagonist. Anyway, I'm having fun with it, so I think that's good, huh?"

In her writing, Lala returned again to thoughts of David. Her writing sessions almost always began with a message to him, all of which she kept in a folder on her laptop.

"Wonderful David, I must confess to you that I've been untrue in my heart. And in my imagination. In that I gave some serious time and energy to envisioning my wedding to a total douchebag. I had picked out the appetizers and had settled on two flavors for the wedding cake: white chocolate raspberry and snickerdoodle. I am not proud of myself. I hope you can forgive me. I write to you in this moment, David, as I write to you always, now, knowing that our love was doomed from the start. For you are at sea. And I am adrift."

Ψ

Geraldine had been buying her niece's excuses about why she couldn't go to dinner with Geraldine and Monty, or why she couldn't go for a walk on the beach, or why she couldn't come over to watch *Casablanca*. Until she stopped buying them.

"I thought it was very clear what I meant when I said Act Two! This is absolutely NOT what I had in mind when I said Act Two!"

"If I pour you a drink, will you stop yelling at me?" Lala asked. Geraldine interrupted her pacing of Lala's kitchen only long enough to glare at Lala.

"Why aren't you dressed? I mean, in real clothes? When was the last time you dressed in real clothes?"

Lala sighed heavily and opened a bottle of red wine.

"Well, you might as well know now. It was bound to come out at some point. I've decided I'm going to be a hermit. *Je suis une . . . hermite*, or however you say that in French. My philosophy has always been, might just as well go ahead and pronounce it with a French accent and see if that flies. Because sometimes it does. And if that's not a metaphor for life, I don't know what is."

"Gimme that," Geraldine barked. She grabbed a full wine glass out of Lala's hand and downed it. "You make me so mad sometimes."

"Well, even in your enraged state, I think you have to agree that I've got to start doing things differently in my life. Because clearly what I have been doing up to now has not been working."

Geraldine abruptly turned her back to Lala and snapped open a cabinet to stick her head in.

Lala called after her.

"Come on, you can't be so angry with me that we can't have a nice little chat about this."

"I need some snacks," Geraldine huffed.

"Oh, okay," Lala said. "That's a great idea. There's a ton of stuff. I just had another delivery this morning. I'll meet you in the living room."

She settled herself comfortably on the welcoming couch, the couch that had been her coziest and most steadfast friend in this new stage of her life. Lala nuzzled her hounds while she waited for Geraldine to join her. Geraldine entered bearing a tray heaped with chips and dips and broccoli florets. She slammed the tray on the table and then slammed herself down on the couch.

"When I said Act Two, what I had in mind was you just letting it all go and having adventures and not fretting so much . . ."

"Okay, well, in my own defense," Lala said, "that was more implied than specifically stated. So I don't think I can be blamed for the misunderstanding."

"I meant that you should just say 'what the hell,' and you should go out and stop worrying about what other people think or say or do and just have fun . . ."

"I am having fun. I've started my own little philanthropic organization. I make donations online. By way of a thank you for my life which is, by any reasonable standard, entirely blessed—a word I use not in any religious reference and a word I use despite the fact that I have no expectation of ever being kissed or schtupped or of approaching anything with unbridled, unabashed, unfettered—you see where I'm going with this—joy ever again."

Geraldine stopped slamming air-popped chips into the tub of organic, all-natural French onion dip and aggressively shoveling them into her mouth between surly gulps of her second glass of wine, which she had refilled herself because she was too ticked at Lala to ask her for anything.

"It's your good heart," Geraldine whispered. "It's your good heart that makes me love you and makes me want better things for you."

*Do not start crying,* Lala thought.

"Hey, if you start crying, then I will, and then what?" Lala said. "I'm fine. I'm getting a lot of writing done, and I'm really, really, really enjoying myself."

"I'm delighted you're enjoying yourself. Why can't you enjoy yourself and also go outside and be involved with people and meet someone nice and get married again, and maybe we could even make it a double wedding if you hurry up, and that's what I meant when I said Act Two. I don't know, for some reason I'm not feeling this red wine. Let's have champagne instead."

Geraldine sprinted toward the kitchen.

"I'm not letting new hope into my life," Lala said solemnly, or with as much solemnity as one can convey when one is shouting through a living room and down a hallway and into a kitchen to be heard.

*I should just get up and go talk to her in the kitchen,* Lala thought. *Fuck it, I'm too lazy.*

"I can't let myself be disappointed again. If, as you suggest, I go out on anything but the most furtive jaunts, I will indeed see people, and I'll most likely engage with them, as you recommend, and I'll maybe even meet new people, which you also seem to want me to do, and I'll start to get ideas about the future, and I can't do that. I can't let myself hope for anything again. I think I'm hurting my voice with all this shouting. Maybe permanently."

Geraldine came back brandishing a bottle of Veuve Cliquot, which she proceeded to open dramatically. The cork ricocheted off the ceiling and bounced off Petunia's tummy, which, amply cushioned by a layer of subcutaneous fat, absorbed the brunt of the assault without waking the beagle. Geraldine was ready for the overflow of the bubbly, which she gracefully gathered in one of two flutes, as she balanced everything on her way back to the couch.

"I'm sorry it took so long. I couldn't find the Veuve because you have that refrigerator packed so damn full."

"Life is amazing nowadays," Lala said, smiling. "I can go on this website and order anything. I just have to check off the boxes for what I want and then stuff is brought right to me, right away. Really, I think this is a positive step for me. I'm looking at myself as a twenty-first-century Salinger. A Garbo for the New Millennium. Except without the talent and the acclaim and the cheekbones that could cut glass."

Geraldine raised her champagne flute in a toast to her beloved niece.

"What are the last three words of *The Count of Monte Cristo*?" she barked.

"Shut up," Lala said. "I knew you were going to bring up the one thing that renders my new philosophy of life to be essentially full of crap."

"What are they?" Geraldine demanded.

"Wait and hope! Wait and hope! Okay? The last three words of *The Count of Monte Cristo* are the Count exhorting his young charges that all of life's wisdom can be summed up in three words. Fucking wait and fucking hope! Okay? Are you happy now?"

Geraldine gave her niece a smug little smirk of self-righteous satisfaction.

"Well, I'm happier," she drawled.

"I don't care what he wrote!" Lala yelled, smiling despite herself at her aunt because her aunt loved her, and her aunt refused to give up hope, and that was both heartbreaking and delightful. "And I don't know why I'm on the verge of giggling because, when you think about it, it's very sad that I'm choosing to live without thoughts of yearnings fulfilled and probably without any yearnings themselves for the rest of my life, however long or short that may be, but I am, nonetheless, thinking Edmund Dantes and Dumas, *père*, should both just jump up and kiss my *sans espoir* tuchus, and that is giving me a chuckle despite myself and despite everything else."

🍷

Lala hadn't heard from Helene since what she described with her mind's voice as "our break-up."

Lala was both relieved to not have to deal with Helene since that last night and sad and insulted that Helene had not contacted her since their split.

And then an e-mail from Helene arrived with the subject line, "Miss you!"

*Merde*, Lala thought.

Lala was grateful to be on the couch surrounded by hounds when she saw the e-mail. The warm and somewhat rank presence of the old beasts was always a soothing and protective influence. Despite the moat of fur, Lala did wince as though she were being swatted in the face when she finally forced herself to open Helene's e-mail.

"Listen," it began.

*Christ*, Lala thought, *I hate it when people write e-mails in that folksy, I'm-just-talkin'-to-ya, kind of style. What am I listening to? You're writing words. So what exactly is it that I'm listening to? Your writer's voice? Jesus.*

> Kelly told me all about it. Are you avoiding me because you feel ashamed? Look, it's not algebra. One man's meat, you know all the clichés. Let me read your script. I bet I'll love it. Rejection isn't easy, I know. I was rejected quite a few times when I started out. I remember a couple times when . . .

*Oh, God,* Lala thought. *It's a couple OF times. Jesus. Didn't they teach you anything at Wesleyan?*

Lala skimmed the paragraph about the couple things Helene remembered.

> Anyway, I'm writing to tell you that I got the Paramount deal and also to say that I'm sure one day the same kind of triumph will happen for you, so I want you to take heart that it can happen, big things can happen, and I want you to share in my joy, and I won't take no for an answer.

*Well, actually, yes, you will,* Lala thought. *Because, what? I say "no," and then you hit me and I'm forced to change my answer to "yes?" Nuh uh, babe.*

Lala read the details about the intimate, but not small, dinner party Helene was going to be throwing in Los Angeles the following week to celebrate her conquest of the movie kingdom. Then Lala slammed her laptop shut, picked up Yootza because he was the only dog she had who was small enough to seize, and turned up the volume on *Say Yes to the Dress* until the voices of the consultants and customers drowned out the voices in her head.

Lala remained still on the couch, staring at but not seeing the parade of strapless white dresses on the screen, hearing but not listening to the parade of brides' stories.

*Merde,* Lala finally thought when she started thinking again, an activity that was not entirely by choice and was not welcomed with complete enthusiasm. *Silence implies consent. Now I have to write back to her.*

Lala opened her laptop and brought up the blank page of a new Word document. She planned to write to Helene until she had nothing more left to write and, having been burned once too often before by a glitch in the ether of the Internet that made her lengthy e-mail and all its contents disappear when she hit "Send," Lala decided to write to Helene in a document that she knew how to save on her laptop, and that she could append to her e-mail to Helene as an attachment.

"Dear Helene," she typed.

*Mmm. Looks a bit cold,* Lala thought.

"Hi, Helene, thanks for your e-mail."

"Could I come across as more insincere?" Lala asked Petunia and Yootza and Chester. "Like I'm thanking her because I'm so freakin' happy I got her flippin' e-mail?"

"I'm very happy for your success. I really am. But, as you've noticed . . ."

Lala paused.

*It's not really a "But" situation,* Lala thought. *It's more of an "And" situation.*

She hit the delete key and then typed anew.

"And, as you've noticed, I'm in a bit of a skunky place in my own life."

*My own life,* Lala thought. *As opposed to my someone else's life. Christ, am I a lazy scribe or what?*

Lala typed and typed and typed her heart onto the screen, and, when she was done, the Word document encompassed four single-spaced pages.

Lala scanned her work. Lala reread her work. Lala laughed aloud at her work.

*Someone is taking someone's self far too seriously,* Lala thought.

Lala made a copy of the document just in case she had an aneurism and subsequently decided to embrace the overblown after all. She titled her new communication Lala.Gets.Over.Herself.But. Good.doc.

"Okay, let's take it down several notches, shall we?" Lala asked her beloved pets, whose responsive silence, she inferred, implied a great big "Guh head."

Lala deleted the part wherein she thanked Helene for her e-mail because it really was too insincere to stand, and then she reread the new first sentence of her missive about being happy for Helene's success.

"I'm not sure where this is coming from," Lala said, "but I think I'm actually genuinely happy for her. Seriously, I have no idea how that's possible, but I think I'm not kidding her or myself about that. Okay. Onward."

Lala once again reread all the paragraphs she had written, which, she had to admit, sounded a bit like the ravings of a madwoman, especially the part where she conveyed to Helene the truth of her sometimes-almost-impossible-to-suppress urge to delete all the files on her hard drive—everything she had ever written and every other piece of information her computer contained—which Lala likened to a despondent writer's version of that cutting-their-own-skin thing that she had read teenagers did in alarming numbers.

Lala held her index finger down on the delete key until nothing remained on the screen but the salutation and the good wishes. And then she began typing again.

> I really do wish I could go to your dinner party, but I just can't. I will be celebrating with you in spirit. In a spirit form of me that is stronger than the actual me is right now. I hope you understand.

🍷

"Open up, please, dear," Geraldine yelled from the other side of Lala's front door. "I know you're in there."

*Duh, Sherlock,* Lala thought. *I more or less never go anywhere, so, yeah, duh, I'm in here. Big fat A-plus on the deductive reasoning.*

Lala opened the door and greeted her aunt with a welcoming smile.

"Look who's with you!" she said.

Standing next to Geraldine and sporting a grin both sheepish and bemused, was their neighbor Thomas Gallagher, a.k.a. Salman Rushdie. Geraldine had her arm tightly entwined with Thomas's, and she plowed into Lala's apartment towing him closely.

"Salman, I'm sorry, Thomas, knows everything about you being a hermit and the rest of everything you're doing to your life, which is absolutely not what I had in mind when I said the Act Two of your life, except the part about the grassroots, de facto philanthropic organization, which I think is so lovely and kind that I get teary whenever I think about it. Don't even get me started right now."

Geraldine made dramatic air quotation marks with one of her arms still violently hooked through Thomas's, so that he was lifted slightly onto his tiptoes as she raised her four fingers to frame the ensuing proper noun.

"'Thomas' would like to talk to you about courage," Geraldine announced.

Geraldine released Thomas, and he wobbled slightly from unexpectedly being at large. He caught his footing and stood there as Geraldine smiled at him with wide-open, encouraging eyes and with her head bobbing nonstop.

"Go on, honey," Geraldine trilled. "Speak the truth. Tell her what it's really like."

*Cool*, Lala thought. *This oughta be good.*

"Well," Thomas began. And then he dissolved into a fit of giggles.

Geraldine's face was, instantly and without any previous training in the theatrical arts, a textbook example of how to show a changing range of emotions and make your audience believe you're genuinely experiencing each distinct and contrasting feeling. She looked perplexed. *What is Salman up to?* And then her twisted mouth and scrunched right eye of confusion seamlessly morphed into the raised chin and open mouth of comprehending skepticism. *I'm thinking Salman's up to something and maybe it's no good.* Finally, that stance became the semi-closed eyes and sucked-in upper lip of compassionate understanding.

"That's nervous energy," Geraldine whispered to Lala.

*Of course it is,* Lala thought. *God, this is great.*

She hugged her aunt and smiled at Thomas.

"You were saying?"

"It's . . . It's just that . . ." Thomas stammered.

"He had a *FATWA* on his keppie, for the love of God!" Geraldine screeched. "He went out with a *FATWA* on his KEPPIE, for the LOVE of GOD! And now that the *FATWA* has been removed or whatever you do to a *FATWA*—cancelled, rescinded, I don't know what they call it when the *fatwa* stops—he can look back and maybe agree that it was nuts of him to go anywhere with a *FATWA* hanging over him. But that's courage. Crazy courage."

Geraldine paused dramatically and puffed herself up. Lala and Thomas looked down at the floor and waited, trying desperately not to giggle.

"And you," Geraldine began, glaring down her nose at Lala who, thankfully for the sake of the effect, was much shorter than her aunt. "You have no excuse. No excuse for acting like a crazy person in cotton. None. Zip. Zero. Nada."

There was another dramatic pause. Lala and Thomas wondered if Geraldine had concluded her remarks. They made the mistake of lifting their eyes but not their heads at the same time and catching a glimpse of each other. They both, then, did a mediocre job of trying to cover up their giggle fits by pretending they were, in fact, coughing jags.

"Okay," Lala gasped. "Now that we've got that out of the way, I'm thinking a pitcher of bone-dry martinis is in order, no? And I've got the take-out menu from a fabulous new Chinese place. It is time to celebrate, people! Something. I don't know what. Life? We'll celebrate life. Courageous or hermitic or otherwise. *L'chaim*! Am I right or am I right? *L'chaim*!"

# OKAY, MAYBE NOT *EVERY* CLOUD

For the next two days, Geraldine joyously displayed her clear hope that the lecture she and Thomas had delivered would result in a positive change in Lala's behavior.

Geraldine left chirpy messages on Lala's phone outlining "all kinds of fun plans that I've got in mind for us now that you're not crazy anymore, and you'll be beginning the fabulous Act Two of your fabulous new life in earnest."

*Sheesh,* Lala thought. She was on the couch with her dogs and her laptop. Her new vice, *Undercover Boss,* was on the TV as Geraldine's ebullient voice competed with the dialogue between the CEO of a major department store chain, who had disguised himself as a temporary worker and was making a mess of his duties in the men's shoe department, and the earnest young sales clerk who was trying to help out this poor schlub who was actually his boss.

"I've seen this episode," Lala told Petunia and Yootza and Chester as Geraldine listed grand future activities that included a trip to the Napa wine country and a week in Peru on an ecological safari that she had just discovered on a website that promoted charity via tourism.

"You should see the pictures they've got!" Geraldine yelled into the phone. "The guys are adorable, and you know they care about wildlife, so you know you'll love them and what better way to find new romance than when you're engaging in activities that genuinely interest you? Are you there? You must be there. Why aren't you picking up?"

"Sheesh," Lala said. She picked up Yootza and made his little front paw wave at the television screen. "Anyway, so this episode is maybe my favorite one ever. The CEO learns so much about the people working in the stores. He lost his dad in a terrible car accident, and the young lady he's going to work with next in their Omaha store? She lost her dad recently, and she's working full-time to pay for college at night, full-time. So, at the end of the show, the company offers to pay for all her college expenses. So get ready for me to start bawling in approximately fifteen minutes."

"I think I'll come up and knock on your door so we can look at this wonderful website together," Lala heard Geraldine declare with conviction that foreshadowed immediate action on the threat. Lala grabbed the phone and hit "Talk."

"I'm asleep!" she yelled into the phone. "I'm taking a nap. I love you, and we'll make plans together tomorrow, okay. It'll be great! I'll see you tomorrow!"

At seven o'clock p.m. the next day, a day following an evening and a night and a morning and an entire afternoon during which Lala only left the couch to plod over to the bathroom or to heat up leftover food from previous deliveries, Lala heard Geraldine stomping up the stairs.

*Here we go,* Lala thought.

Geraldine pounded on Lala's front door and screamed so she could be heard through the wood and over the banging.

"We're going to Catalina this weekend! Do you understand me? End of discussion! We're going to have a fun Gals' Weekend in beautiful Catalina! We're going to dance and flirt and drink and gamble, and Monty understands that I'll be flirting only theoretically, and that is what we're doing, and, if you don't come with me, I will sign you up for a six-month charter membership to JDate, and I'm going to fill out your profile, and I'm going to set up coffee dates for you, and I am going to bring you to those coffee dates at gunpoint if I have to! Okay, maybe not gunpoint. Maybe I'll use one of those lovely antique rapiers Monty collects. Either way, you are not going to be a hermit! I will not allow it!"

Lala heard Geraldine pause to catch her breath and then turn and stomp back down the stairs.

*Uh oh*, Lala thought. She held Yootza under his furry little armpits and turned him to face her so she could go nose-to-nose with her beloved little hound.

"Uh oh," Lala said. "Mama's in trouble. Mama needs a plan."

After spending the rest of the evening and the night dozing on the couch between writing sessions, Lala woke the next morning with a terrible crick in her neck and a brand new chapter of her novel. She carried her laptop to the kitchen and reread her work while she waited for the ancient coffee, that had been sitting in the fancy coffeemaker Geraldine had given her as a housewarming gift, to reheat.

*I can't believe it*, Lala thought. *This kinda doesn't suck.*

Lala found her energy and her spirits rising as she continued to read. She even felt a stirring of hope and did her best to ignore it in the hope that it would go away.

"Wow," she called to the three hounds who were still asleep in the living room. "I don't think I think this sucks. And don't you all start thinking that the irony of me being willing to let hope into my heart again long enough to hope that that stirring of hope about my work and my future would leave me the hell alone is lost on me, because it's not."

Lala absentmindedly filled a mug and absentmindedly took a big gulp as she read.

"Mother of God!" she yelled. "Which one of you hound bastards put battery acid in the Krups?"

When Lala left the house to go to the gym, she still didn't have a plan of defense against Geraldine.

Her first stop, after changing in the locker room, was the treadmill. Her routine had always been to work her muscles with machines or free weights and then do some kind of aerobic activity, but on this day she decided to change things a bit.

*Because you need a change every now and then*, Lala thought. *Sometimes, you just need a change.*

Lala put her towel and her keys in one of the round cup holders on either side of the imposing treadmill. She punched in all the information for a long session that she would control manually rather than giving her workout over to a predesigned program. She placed her latest issue of *The New Yorker* on the little reading ledge that bordered the surface of the console and started her warm-up at a low setting on the incline and a comfortable pace on the speed.

*Maybe if I tell Geraldine about how I made a big change in my life today by being willing to submit to thoughts of hope, and, of course, I don't have to tell her the full context of me literally hoping against hope, she'll back off,* Lala thought, as she stared out the bank of floor-to-ceiling windows at the sunny street scene on view below the second floor of the gym.

Lala started to read an article about life in a village in Wales where the inhabitants speak English that is virtually indistinguishable from the way it was spoken in the Middle Ages. She upped the incline on the treadmill at regular intervals and alternated between running for a minute and walking quickly for a minute. She was starting to get that lovely feeling of invigoration and relaxation that exercise almost always brought her, when one of the club's many adorable young trainers escorted a client to the treadmill that was one removed from hers.

"Okay, Melanie, let's torch some calories," the trainer said.

*Ohhh,* Lala thought. *What a great idea. Torch calories. Torch. I like the sound of that. Torch. Was it always a verb and a noun? Who cares?*

Lala smiled and nodded at the trainer and the client. Then she hit the up arrow on the incline level for her treadmill until it reached the maximum reading of a bright red "15." The gears on the treadmill went into action, and in seconds Lala was jogging at an angle that approached the sheer face of a rock-climbing wall.

*Yeah!* Lala thought. *Yeah! Torchin' those calories! Take that, ass fat.*

Lala left the gym feeling more alive than she had in ages. Geraldine was gardening in the courtyard when she opened the front gate to the compound.

*Damn,* Lala thought. *Gotta go to Plan B. I have no Plan B. I don't really have a Plan A.*

"You went out!" Geraldine said. She stood and rushed toward Lala brandishing her gardening sheers like a weapon. "And you look happy!"

Lala swerved to avoid being stabbed and sprinted up the stairs.

"I sure am happy! Tell you what! I'll go take a shower and maybe have a little nap, and then we can go out for dinner and maybe go to our favorite karaoke bar."

As she fumbled for her keys and then thrust her door open, and just as quickly slammed it shut behind her, Lala heard Geraldine happily calling up to her.

"What a delightful idea! Shall I pick you up, or should we meet in the courtyard? Oh I guess either way it will be just delightful to finally . . ."

"Ha ha, sucka!" Lala whispered to Geraldine through her closed front door.

Lala triumphantly bolted the extra locks on her door that she had installed after she moved in over her aunt's protests that this was an exceptionally safe neighborhood, and, besides, there was also a lock on the gate to the courtyard so what the hell was she being so paranoid about? Which Lala countered by reminding Geraldine that she had lived in New York City for many years, and she just didn't know how to sleep without multiple locks, and also certainly not without one of those deliciously old-fashioned chain locks that just screamed Manhattan Island to Lala.

Lala got out of the set of sweats she had changed into for the ride home and took a long shower. She wrapped herself in her robe and snuck the dogs out through the back door that led from her kitchen to the alley next to the compound.

"Come on, let's go, let's go, pee, pee, poo, now, right now before Auntie Geraldine catches us."

None of her hounds were willing to be rushed, so nearly a full, fret-filled half hour had to be spent outside with their tracking noses to the ground, and Lala's eyes darting all around as she stood guard for any Geraldine sightings before she could urge everyone up the stairs and back into the apartment.

Back into the apartment where, four hours later, Lala was stretched out on the couch, asleep and oblivious to the world, when

Geraldine was back to pounding on her door.

"I am beginning to resemble a neighborhood character with all this pounding! Someone eccentric and odd and maybe even a little dangerous! Get out here like you said you would, so we can go out like you said we would!"

*Oy vey*, Lala thought.

She lifted her head and slipped her right arm out from beneath Yootza's curled up little body. Lala began to swing her legs off the couch. And screamed in agony.

"What the hell?" Geraldine yelled. "Lala? What's wrong? Lala!"

*Omigod*, Lala thought. *Who's got a voodoo doll of me? Brenda? Helene? Can I have offended them so deeply? Fuck me, does this hurt.*

Pain radiated up and around and through the left half of her body below her waist. She was afraid to breathe, and she was afraid to move. She froze there, leaning on her right leg with her left leg suspended a few inches off the couch.

"Lassie?" Lala bleated almost silently, terrified that the use of any muscles might bring on a fresh wave of torture, but still trying to distract herself from the terror with a steady stream of blather for no one's benefit but her own. "Lassie, I'm at the bottom of the well, and my leg is broken, girl. Run and get help, Lassie, before I pass out. Good girl, Lassie. Run, Lassie. Run like the wind, noble beast."

🍷

The gentle, compassionate, and quite young and attractive sports medicine doctor at the emergency room had nodded sympathetically and had said that maybe running on an incline that high wasn't a great idea for anyone older than a teenager, and it wasn't actually such a great idea for teenagers either.

Geraldine didn't say much to Lala while they were waiting in the crowded lobby of the emergency room. She accompanied Lala into the examining room and didn't say much in there either.

Geraldine held Lala gently by her elbows to keep Lala standing relatively upright while Dr. Pradha gently massaged Lala's left leg and asked where it hurt.

"Everywhere," Lala gasped. "It hurts all over. It hurts when you touch my leg. It hurts when you look at my leg. It hurts when you think about my leg."

"Let's have you lie down on the table," Dr. Pradha suggested. Lala winced the moment she heard his words and comprehended their meaning.

"Oh, please, God, no. Please let me stay motionless. Much like my dating life before I met my beloved husband. I am anticipating pain with every move."

Dr. Pradha established that Lala was not suffering from sciatica, a possibility she had suggested based on what was of course her nearly complete ignorance of what sciatica actually is, a possibility that had come only from "having read something about sciatica somewhere once, maybe it was in a magazine, maybe it was online, I'm not sure, but you never know, I mean, it could be, right? So I just thought I'd bring it up, just in case."

"It's not a nerves thing. It's because you ran like a crazy person on the treadmill," Geraldine had muttered testily when Lala advanced her theory.

Lala had noticed the edge in her aunt's voice, but quickly forgot about it when Dr. Pradha used the words "prescribe" and "Tylenol with codeine," and "Vicodin if that doesn't work" and "three refills on each" in the same sentence.

Now that she was in the passenger seat of Geraldine's car, with the first dose of painkiller starting to maybe have some effect, Lala noticed that Geraldine had not said a word to her since the orderly had helped Lala out of a wheelchair and into the Lexus.

*Hello?* Lala thought. *She's miffed at me?*

Lala nervously fiddled with one of her prescription bottles.

"Wow," Lala said, then giggled. "You're not supposed to drink alcoholic beverages while taking this medication. *Merde.* This is going to be a harder recovery than I thought."

The silence in the car was vicious in its rebuke.

*Merde,* Lala thought. *Why is she miffed at me?*

Lala's thoughts whirred obsessively in her head, and she tried not to blurt out the painful, plaintive question that was shrieking in her brain, the answer to which she desperately feared might be in the affirmative, until she could no longer stand not knowing and, without consciously deciding, decided it would be better to know the awful truth than to endure this soundless unknowing for one more instant.

"Auntie Geraldine, are you pissed off at—"

"Tell me the truth," Geraldine growled, her eyes on the road, her hands white-knuckled on the steering wheel, her jaw clenched. "Did you do that on purpose?"

*Did I do what on purpose?* Lala thought.

"What do you mean?" Lala said. "Did I intentionally make a joke about booze and narcotics? I'm sorry if I sounded glib, but I was just trying to lighten—"

"Did you purposely injure yourself?" Geraldine demanded. "So I couldn't nag you anymore about going outside? So you would have a pathetic excuse, a feeble justification, a sin-against-man-and-nature foundation for your nut-job, giving-up-on-life, squirrelly decision to become a hermit?"

*Wow,* Lala thought. *That is brilliant.*

"Did you?" Geraldine asked. This time, her tone sounded almost a little sad to Lala.

"No. Truly. Apparently I'm not nearly as devious or as clever as you are. Because that idea did not occur to me. Certainly not consciously."

*Wow,* Lala thought. *Did I? Did I subconsciously injure myself so she would be forced to shut her piehole about me starting my flipping sunshine-and-strawberries-and-double-dates-at-the-movies-with-her-and-Monty-and-my-fabulous-new-beau Act Two of my flipping life?*

"Gosh, I really don't think it did occur to me. But don't quote me on that."

"Okay, sweetie," Geraldine said. She nodded in Lala's direction and quickly patted Lala's shoulder. "I'm sorry I went there. It's just that I love you so much, and I want so much for you, and I do get more than a little frustrated and impatient when you seem to be sabotaging your own happiness."

"It's okay, Aunt Geraldine," Lala said. "I understand your only motivation is care. I appreciate it. Really, I do."

"I won't go there again," Geraldine promised.

*Wow,* Lala thought, *so now she really is going to have to shut her trap, isn't she? So that give-myself-a-debilitating-injury plan was, in fact, one superbly brilliant idea, wasn't it? God, I apparently had no concept of how clever I am. And how devious.*

"That was the worst idea I ever didn't subconsciously have! Ow! Ow! Damn it, owwww!"

Lala writhed on her couch, trying to absolutely no avail, to somehow find a position that might bring the level of pain in her leg down at least one or two notches.

"Damn it! It hurts to yell!" she yelled.

Lala's apartment was completely empty of fellow sentient beings. Yootza and Petunia and Chester were staying with their Auntie Geraldine for the foreseeable future, or until Lala got her hands on some chemical-warfare-grade morphine, whichever came first.

Despite every effort of stern rebuke and bleated pleading, Yootza could not be persuaded to refrain from jumping on his mama's lap. Lala had loudly and repeatedly compared the effect of the little beast's body landing with a thud on her injured leg to having to sit through a marathon performance, in a theater without stadium seating, of a non-union interpretive dance troupe, performing to recordings of the collected radio broadcasts of Rush Limbaugh, without benefit of the anesthetizing effects of buckets of popcorn and tubs of Diet Coke.

So now Lala was completely alone, and she was sounding completely unhinged as she ranted to no one but herself.

This had been happening on a regular basis since Lala had come home from the emergency room, and the full impact of what she had done to herself emerged. The painkillers brought some relief, but the relief was by no means enough to completely remove the pain. Lala slept fitfully, if at all. She had to lie on her right side, which had never been her first choice for sleep positions, with a pillow between her knees to cushion her left leg. Lala couldn't really get comfortable in bed, so she spent most of her time propped up on the couch with the TV on.

It hurt to get up off the couch. It hurt to shuffle down the hallway to the bathroom. It hurt to stand in the shower.

"I did this to myself!" Lala shouted to the barren space. "And you know what? I think I did it consciously. I just think I wasn't aware that I was consciously doing it."

Geraldine knocked on Lala's door.

"Can I do anything to help?" Geraldine asked.

"Can you shoot me?" Lala yelled at the door. "Ow!"

"No, I can't. I couldn't the first five thousand times you asked me that, and I can't now."

"I think that number is an exaggeration," Lala yelled.

"No, it's not. I'll bring you some dinner later."

"Thanks," Lala yelled. "Love you!"

During the third week of this *passionsspiele*—at a time when it seemed that every moment Lala felt that her leg might be getting a little better, that it just might be hurting a little bit less, and each of those moments were guaranteed to be followed by Lala somehow moving in some small direction that sent fresh waves of hell all up and down her side—Lala woke one morning, after what she would subsequently swear was a night during which she got "literally not one moment of rest, not one moment of respite from the nocturnal torture that seemed to have become my lot in life," and slowly shuffled her way to the bathroom. Lala looked in the mirror. And screamed.

Her skin, which she could have sworn was relatively pristine if a bit pasty the night before, had been attacked and invaded and subjugated.

"Wrinkles and acne?" she whispered bitterly, her voice breaking. "It's not fair. Damn you, Fate, it's not fair."

It wasn't so much the quantity as the quality, which was of the horror-movie level. A horror movie with a budget too low to allow for high quality makeup, so that the effects are so unrealistic and exaggerated as to lend the entire enterprise an air of the absurdly grotesque and amateur.

Lala stared at the three massive pimples, one on her forehead, one on her chin, and one directly next to her left nostril.

She put her head in her hands and burst into tears.

"My body is trying to tell me something," she sobbed. "My body is shouting at me. And my body is extremely strident. Also more than a little self-righteous."

She shuffled out of the bathroom and got herself over to the big bay window with an obstructed view of the ocean.

The day couldn't have been sunnier or lovelier.

The lovely, sunny day could not have held more rebuke.

*I love to walk,* Lala thought. *Even if I were a full-fledged, card-carrying hermit who never wanted to speak to another living soul except my beloved puppies ever again, I would still love to go for long walks in the fresh air and sunshine. And now I have rendered that impossible. First of all, because I have made it such that I can't walk. And, second of all, because my apparently extreme level of bile has resulted in my face becoming disfigured to the point where small children would run from me screaming, as from the Frankenstein monster. Or a Jehovah's Witness.*

Geraldine tried to use her key later that day to open Lala's door so she could bring the dogs in for a stringently supervised visit. Her entry was abruptly halted by the secured old-fashioned chain lock.

"Are you all right?" Geraldine shouted.

"I'm fine," Lala yelled wearily from the couch. "Ow! Hang on. Let me get over there so I don't have to yell. Hold on. Hang on. I'm swinging my legs off the couch. Damn it, that hurts! Okay. Here I come. You all might want to sit on one of the steps while you wait. This is going to take a bit."

Lala arrived at the door panting from the exertion. The dogs started barking and sticking their noses through the gap in the door.

"Ohhh, babies," Lala sighed. "This is not a good time."

"What are you talking about?" Geraldine demanded. "Why can't we come in?"

"Trust me, you don't want to. If you look at my face, you'll probably turn to stone. Or to a pillar of salt. Something biblical, trust me."

"What are you talking about?"

"Adult acne. Epic adult acne. You can't see me like this."

"Ohhh, sweetheart," Geraldine said. She paused. "I understand. Maybe I could come in and keep my eyes shut? Just so the dogs can see their mama? They really miss you."

"And I really miss them," Lala said, trying hard not to cry. "But, A, you would sneak a peek, I know you would."

"That's probably true," Geraldine confessed.

"Uh huh. And then you would be struck dumb or dead or who knows what. And, B, the puppies also might not recover from the sight of me. Animals are so trusting, so innocent, so guileless. How could I explain something this horrifying to them?"

Geraldine paused again.

"You've got me very curious."

"Yeah," Lala said. "I bet I have. Suffice it to say that I am not exaggerating the trauma. In fact, I'm probably underplaying it."

There was another pause.

*Here it comes,* Lala thought.

"You couldn't maybe snap a quick photo?" Geraldine said. "I promise we could erase it right after I look at it. I mean, I'm really curious here."

"Trust me, the camera would break. The lens would shatter into a million pieces. Trust me on this."

Looking back at this turning point in her life that she would come to view as a major crossroad, Lala could never quite remember when it was that her leg began to hurt less. Gradually she noticed that there were isolated moments—isolated, but distinct moments nonetheless—when readjusting her position on the couch or in bed actually produced some higher level of ease. She wasn't comfortable, but she was certainly less miserable. And then the time came—slowly, agonizingly slowly—when those moments of even the slightest relief were not instantly followed by a movement on her part that suddenly produced new and intense pain.

*Wow,* Lala was thinking more and more often, *I don't think it's as bad as it was. I think it's getting . . . What's the word I'm looking for?*

*I can't remember it . . . Begins with a "b"? . . . Wait . . . Yes, I think I
remember . . . It's getting better. Better! That's that lovely word. That's
my old friend. Better. Things are getting better!*

The progress with her skin clearing up was equally painstaking and tedious. But one morning she looked in her mirror—once again, as she had each morning for countless days, anticipating the sight of her face with a weary mixture of dread and resignation—and was initially skeptical and then warily delighted to find that the three mountainous colonies that had established themselves on her face had actually receded in size and shape and color and anger, to the point where a judicious application of spackle-quality concealer might actually make it possible for her to go among fellow humans and precious doggies again without being stoned and cast out of the village.

*Okay,* Lala thought. *This is it. Time to start over. Right now.
Before something else weird grows on my face.*

Lala took a shower, and she got herself dressed, and it still hurt to move her leg but nothing like it did before, and, after she blew her hair dry and spent nearly an hour making up her face, she began to feel something wash over her that she felt sure any objective observer might recognize as positive energy.

Lala noticed her aunt quickly suppress the physical manifestation of a feeling of shock and delight when she saw Lala emerge from her cave. Geraldine was gardening outside in the courtyard. She looked up when she heard Lala's front door open and then shut, and she let her eyes bulge and her eyebrows raise and her lips curl into a distorted grin for just a second before she slapped on a poker face and directed her focus back to her violets.

*God, how adorable is that?* Lala asked herself as she very, very, very carefully walked down the stairs.

"Hey, Lala," Geraldine said. Lala saw her aunt peering at her without trying to make it look like she was peering at her. "How are ya?"

*Ya,* Lala thought. *How are ya? Adorable.*

"So, what's new?" Geraldine asked. She was fussing over a package of loam to the point where the poor box of dirt would have been completely within its rights to scream, "Jesus, back offa me, wouldja?" before filing a restraining order. Lala could feel her aunt's psyche desperately trying to stop her aunt's body from rushing over to help Lala down the stairs.

"Get over here," Lala gasped. "I won't feel smothered, I promise."

Geraldine dropped her tools. She had one arm around Lala's shoulder and her other hand grasping Lala's hand before Lala could blink.

"Are you sure you should be out? Maybe it's too soon? Are you feeling okay? Do you need to sit down?"

"I feel better," Lala grunted. "Not great. Better. I have to get out of the house."

"Good," Geraldine said. "Good for you. Come sit outside for a few minutes and then we'll get you back upstairs, and you can rest."

Lala was now on ground level, and she continued to limp toward the door leading to the garages, even as Geraldine was determined to steer her to the outdoor dinette set under the big, colorful umbrella.

"I'm going to Dogs of Love," Lala said.

"Honey, it's too soon!" Geraldine practically screeched. "Go in a month or two! You've been donating to them. They'll understand if you can't actually be there helping out until the fall. Or maybe spring of next year!"

"Auntie Geraldine, sometimes you have to make your charitable work hands-on. Sometimes your soul requires that."

Geraldine ceased her gentle but constant and insistent tugging on Lala. Lala nearly toppled over in the direction in which she had been exerting a counter pull against Geraldine's determination. She would surely have ended up in a heap on the ground if Geraldine hadn't caught her in a big hug.

"It's your Act Two," she whispered to Lala. "I just know it is. The Act Two I have dreamed of for you is beginning right now. You want me to drive you?" She held her niece at arm's length and beamed at her. Until she remembered that thing she had been so curious about.

*Oh, no,* Lala thought. *Will it withstand this kind of laser scrutiny?*

"I can see what you meant," she said. "Those must have been

doozies. But, if I hadn't known about them, I'm not sure I would necessarily notice them now."

"Okay," Lala said. "Good enough for me."

Lala started to sway a little.

"You know what, I'm feeling a bit dizzy."

Geraldine all but hoisted Lala over her shoulder to get her to one of several cushioned gliding benches that adorned the festive courtyard. Lala felt steadier as soon as she sat down. She rested her head on Geraldine's shoulder and closed her eyes. The sun felt good on her skin. The fresh air felt good on her skin. Her left leg still hurt like the dickens. But not as much. Not nearly as much as it had.

"No one is more surprised or more grateful than I am to discover that, apparently, self-pity has a relatively short shelf life," Lala said. "Because if you had asked me at the beginning of this episode, I would have sworn that wallowing is infinite."

"I'm so relieved," Geraldine sighed. "I swear, I had no idea how to help you drag yourself out of that shit-filled sink hole you had sunk into."

"You're tellin' me," Lala said. "Can I borrow your car?"

"I'll drive you."

"No, no, stay. Garden. I've got it. I'll be using my right leg. My left leg can just sit there and keep its opinions to itself."

Geraldine helped ease Lala into the front seat of her car and stood there waving and blowing kisses as Lala adjusted the mirrors and snapped her seatbelt shut.

The second she got in the car, Lala realized she had made a terrible mistake.

*Motherfucker does this hurt!* Lala silently screamed. *Don't let on. Don't make her worry. GODDAMNIT OWWWWWWW!*

Lala gave a broad, cheerful wave to her aunt and triumphantly hoisted both her thumbs skyward. She rolled down the window and yelled to her aunt as she shifted into drive and coasted out of the alley behind the apartments.

"Yeah! Uh huh! Act Two! Rock ON!"

❧

"What's amazing, I think, is when you think you're utterly fucked and suddenly you kind of move a little, and it starts to feel like maybe your leg isn't actually being squeezed in a massive vise. I think the technical term for that is 'healing.'"

"I'm so glad you're feeling better. We've all missed seeing you here."

Lala was lying on her back in a large pen in the open reception area of Dogs of Love. One of the other volunteers, a charming high school school student named Andrew, had helped her down onto the carpet and had then put a pillow under Lala's head and also one under her left hip and left knee. Lala kept calling him her angel and kept telling him to call her Grandma, and kept assuring him that his place in Heaven was secure because of his kindness to a wounded lady.

Andrew was sitting cross-legged next to Lala. He had a very old terrier on his lap. Lala was surrounded by very old dogs, all of whom had fallen asleep right next to her.

"And this is my idea of what Heaven is like," Lala said. "Where your place is secure, by the way."

The week before, Lala had paid for all the dogs to be transferred off death row in several LA County shelters so they could live safely in the no-kill haven that was Dogs of Love. A good number of the dogs were already being fostered by local residents. Lala was paying all the expenses for their care.

Lala rubbed the snoring head of a dog that looked like what might have been the consequence of a Borzoi having an unprotected encounter with a Shar-Pei. The resulting mishmash of sagging skin, wispy and curly fur, and a reed-thin body topped by a huge, snub-nosed head, was more than Lala could stand. She had determined that Eunice, as she had named the trusting old girl, would be coming home with her and joining her pack.

Eunice sighed in her sleep and put her snout on Lala's tummy. Lala burst into tears.

"I want to help them all! All of them! Everywhere! I'm still on a lot of painkillers. OMIGOD, look who's here!"

The front door had opened shortly after the aqueducts in Lala's eyes did, and Lala's eyes saw, through lenses that resembled a car windshield with malfunctioning wipers in a cloudburst, the charming figure of publisher James Lancaster walk through the front door of Dogs of Love. Her instant recognition of him, along with her instant desire to make out with him again, were to no small degree ushered into existence by the fact that James was pushing the beautifully familiar carriage that Lala knew would be carrying his precious dog, Ruby.

Lala tried to get herself up off the floor. Andrew jumped to her aid. As did James, who parked the carriage and handily stepped over the collapsible chain walls of the pen with his long legs to grab the elbow opposite the one Andrew had seized. The two men easily lifted Lala to her feet and held her airborne while she winced and grunted.

"It's not bad. It's really not nearly as bad as it has been. Maybe I should sit on the couch for a few minutes."

Andrew undid the gate to the pen and, together with James, helped Lala over to the couch, where she collapsed onto her right side and smiled up at them both.

"Can I pet Ruby?"

"Yes," James assured her. "I'm sure she'd love to have you pet her in a few minutes. My God, are you pale. Is anything wrong? Are you sick?"

*Oh, God,* Lala thought. *I hope he can't see the craters on my face. I hope "pale" isn't a euphemism for "ghastly."*

"The sun is bad for you," Lala chirped, hoping to redirect the conversation. "Did you know that? It's bad for you."

"Some sun is okay. You look like one of the undead. No offense. I mean, don't get me wrong. It's sexy in that vampire mania kind of way."

*Oh,* Lala thought. *That's nice. He thinks I look sexy. Wow. I've been fearing my days of looking sexy might be over.*

Lala hoisted herself up off the couch and was shuffling toward Ruby's carriage before James or Andrew could utter a word of protest.

"Wait," James said. "Let me help you."

"I've got it, thanks, I'm fine," Lala said. She dragged her damaged leg behind her and James watched her tedious progress across the floor.

"What's wrong with your leg?" James asked.

"It's a long and not at all flattering story," Lala said. "Ohhhh, look at Ruby! Who's a beautiful girl? Who is? Ruby? Yes, Ruby is!"

Lala stuck her face in Ruby's carriage and loudly covered sleeping Ruby's tummy with kisses.

*James is perfect,* Lala thought. *He's perfect.*

"I might have guessed I'd see you here, James, you kind, caring, compassionate, hunka burnin' love," Lala cooed toward Ruby. "Because you're perfect. I'm on a lot of painkillers. Which is not by way of meaning to suggest that my assessment of you as perfect is inaccurate because it's drug-fueled. It's by way of pointing out that I'm saying things aloud that might be better left kept to myself."

Lala lifted her head from Ruby's domain and dramatically blew a big kiss toward the smiling James.

*He is so cute,* she thought.

"You are so cute," she said. "Have you met Andrew? He's my new grandson. Not that I'm old enough to have a grandson. Unless there were some very young pregnancies in two generations. Very young. Very. Hey, James, guess what?"

"What?" James said. "You need to sit down again? It's a good idea for you to sit down again? You're going to let us help you sit down again?"

"No, no," Lala giggled. "Those are all terrible guesses. I wanted to tell you that I've been inside my home all the time, writing. A lot. I'm having fun."

"That's great," James said.

"Hey, I met Jackson Platt. You were right. What a putz. I'm going to go back and read his masterpiece, and I hope and trust this time around I'll think it's for shit."

Lala enjoyed taking in James's smile in response to her *mea culpa*. It was an especially warm and gratified smile, and so, to her, it felt warm and gratifying to have elicited this response in James.

*Woof,* Lala thought. *You are making me purr, Big Guy, just to mix species references.*

Lala smiled and nodded back to James.

"I think I need to sit down," she said.

James and Andrew had Lala back on the couch in a second and then both of them sat down on either side of her, apparently ready to catch her if she should sway and crash.

*I am bookended by two devastatingly handsome men,* Lala thought. *One of is them way too young, so he's out of the picture on aesthetic and moral, if not legal grounds.*

Just as Lala felt herself about to lean her head on James's shoulder and declare, "I just love you, Big Hunka Burnin' Love Jamie, y'know?" the door to the shelter burst open and a gust of energy took over the room, in the person of a dazzling, gigantic blonde woman.

The woman was resplendent in jeans tucked into Wellingtons and a sweatshirt that was seductively too tight on her. Her long ringlets were piled atop her head. She brandished a shovel and a bucket with military confidence.

"Andrew, my darling!" the woman said in a voice that, though appealingly energetic, was far softer than her stature might suggest.

"Hi, Candace," Andrew said. He got up and gave her a big hug. "I don't think you've had a chance to meet Lala Pettibone?"

"Omigod," Candace gasped. She threw down her bucket and shovel and seized Lala, lifting her off the couch with far less exertion than James and Andrew as a team had been required to expend before. She hugged Lala and kissed her on either cheek, then she pointed to the dogs that were still happily sleeping in the pen.

"You did this. All of this. I love you. I'm not kidding."

Candace released Lala, and Andrew caught her before she fell backward. Candace then seized James's hand and pumped it vigorously.

"Candace Isaacs," she said. "Brand spankin' new Volunteer Coordinator at this fabulous place. Are you James? I saw you on our list for today."

"Yes," James said. "Great to meet you."

"Excellent! I'll be cleaning out the dog runs in the back. See you all again very soon. Can't thank you enough. Can't. Gonna keep on trying, though."

Candace grabbed her shovel and bucket and, with bouncing

steps, took her bright energy out of the room through a back door to the outside enclosures. Lala recognized how deflated the space suddenly felt.

*Wow,* she thought. *One word comes to mind. Dynamo.*

"I think I've exhausted myself," Lala said. "Time to go home."

James told Andrew that he could escort Lala to her car so Andrew could get back to giving the old timers in the pen more of the loving they deserved.

*God, how adorable is James?* Lala thought. *How dear and kind and caring? How fuckable?*

Lala told Andrew that her Auntie Geraldine would come to the shelter tomorrow to pick up Eunice, and then James admired Eunice, and Lala told Eunice that she would be meeting her new brothers and sister very soon. Andrew gave Lala a hug and called her Grandma, and Lala pointed out that she had meant to tell Andrew to call her Ridiculously Young Grandma.

James gently and carefully helped Lala out the front door. As they slowly walked toward Geraldine's Lexus, Lala imagined them doing the same thing together decades from now, both in their dotage and still as in love as ever. Except that she would be shuffling then because she was so old, not because her leg, though quite a bit better than it had been, still hurt so goddamn much.

Once the slow process of getting Lala into the driver's side was finally over, James reached the seatbelt across her and snapped it shut.

"James," Lala said, "in Percocet *veritas.* You are my hero."

James smiled and said, "Can I do anything else?"

*You can throw me on the backseat and ravage me,* Lala thought. *Well, I guess that might be a bit much for my leg. For now.*

"I can go shopping for you. Whatever you need."

"Thank you, that is so lovely. I think I've got it covered."

James shut the driver's side door and leaned on his elbows on the open window. He kissed Lala's forehead.

*Hey,* Lala thought, *maybe if I take enough painkillers, we can boink tonight. I think that could definitely work.*

"Look," James said, "just send me your stuff now. Okay? Whatever it is. Everything you've been writing. Why not take a leap of faith?"

Lala smiled at James with forced confidence.

*Oh my fucking God,* Lala thought. *Why not? Maybe because I'm terrified you'll hate it all?*

"That's a great idea! I'll do that as soon as I get home."

# IT'S ALWAYS DARKEST BEFORE WHEN?

Lala was sitting at the desk in her bedroom. Because she could. Because sitting didn't hurt too much any longer. Nor did lounging almost horizontal on the couch with her laptop balanced just below her chin. Nor did walking up or down the stairs to her home.

Almost a week had passed since her visit to Dogs of Love. Once Lala had started to feel better, the improvement increased exponentially. Lala was even beginning to envision a time in her life when she might be able to go back to the gym, and not just to haunt the smoothie shop in order to down Berry Banana Boosts and ogle comely trainers. She was actually coming close to realistically imagining herself working out again one day.

Things in Lala's life were starting to look to her like a genuine Act Two. One that didn't involve limping and Epsom salt baths and heating pads and lots of hallucinatory dreams brought on by all the narcotics.

Yootza was sleeping on top of a pillow on Lala's lap. Geraldine had returned Lala's beloved pets to her after Lala had assured her over and over and over and over again in English and then in halting, probably far too literally translated French, because "you don't seem to be understanding me when I speak in our native tongue, so let me see if the language of Moliere and DeGaulle will get the point across any more emphatically, for chrissake," that she was quite sure that she was healed enough to not be in danger of further injury from Yootza's exuberant love.

"Petunia and Chester and Eunice won't try to jump on you," Geraldine has said. "It's the Little Terror I'm worried about."

And so Lala had suggested that they explain everything to Yootza. Geraldine brought the dogs upstairs to Lala's place. Yootza was in his papoose. Petunia and Chester and Eunice came in, gave Lala lazy licks on her hands that were rubbing them all over their delicious old jowls, and then loped on over to their couches, where they climbed up onto the cushions and fell asleep as though nothing in their world had changed or ever would change, which clearly, as far as they were concerned, was a very good thing.

Yootza had been straining against the bonds of the papoose the moment he saw Lala. Lala rushed over to him and tried to put his tiny head entirely in her mouth. Yootza trilled with joy.

"Mama loves you, Mama loves you, Mama loves you, Mama loves you, Mama loves you sooooooo much! Now, listen to me, *Monsieur Le Petit Bastard*, no jumping on Mama for a while, okay? I'll pick you up when you want to sit on Mama's lap, okay?"

And since then, Yootza had been very cooperative. He always waited patiently for Lala to lift him onto the pillow situated on her lap to provide extra cushioning. Life, in what was seeming to be her Act Two, might have been sweet and comforting and optimistic had Lala not been forcing herself to spend the days since she saw James at the rescue group agonizing over what to do next and how she was going to do it. Until she had woken up that morning with the phrase, "Fuck it, let's go for broke," pounding in her head.

Lala had edited her magnum first draft of an e-mail to James down to one paragraph, which she was now reviewing, yet again.

"James, my dear," Lala read aloud.

*Too presumptuous?* she thought. *And too asexual? And too Merchant-Ivory? Fuck it, I gotta keep movin'. Movin'. No "g." No kiddin'.*

"Okay, clearly I was overly optimistic when I said as soon as I get home," Lala continued.

*I never know for sure what should and should not have quotation marks around it,* Lala thought. *Fuck it. Keep movin' where? Forward.*

"I've attached one of those zip file things because I've got a lot of stuff to send you. Because I've been inside a lot. Don't ask how long it took me to figure out how to create a zip file. Really, that more or less accounts for the entire delay in getting back to you."

*Oh, Christ,* Lala thought. *Here comes the closing. Sincerely? No. Xs and Os? No. Hug me, kiss me, throw me on the bed; I think my leg can take it now? No.*

Lala looked down at Yootza. Who had his head mashed into the pillow and was twitching his lip and snoring.

"You are no help at all," Lala said.

And then she very quickly typed, "*Mazel, mazel,*" and hit "Return," and then typed "Lala," and hit "Send," and then started to freak out.

"Okay, yes, yes, '*Mazel*' is probably safely in the Universal Lexicon, but I don't know if he's Jewish, and I don't know if he knows I'm a solid non-practicing Jew from solid non-practicing Jewish stock so maybe that sign-off will sound incredibly affected and, Omigod, what if he hates everything I sent?"

Lala slowly sank her head down on her desk until her forehead made gentle contact with the wood. She stayed there with her eyes shut, spastically panting her breath in and out, in an effort to shut off the voices in her head. Until she heard another voice calling, one that she recognized as the bottle of prosecco chilling in her refrigerator.

*Yum,* she thought. *With frozen raspberries floating in it. Yeah.*

Lala cradled Yootza and hugged him tight. He growled.

"Shut up," she cooed. "My leg doesn't hurt much, and I'm more or less off painkillers, so I can drink again. Hallelujah. The possibilities are limitless."

Lala cradled Yootza in one hand and her laptop in the other. She walked out of the bedroom toward a land where a champagne glass could and would be filled and bags of popped salt and pepper potato chips could and would be snarfed and websites about agencies that provide classy male strippers could and would be surfed and *Say Yes to the Dress* or *Tabatha's Salon Takeover* or *Undercover Boss* could and would play on TV in the background as mountains of festive research was done.

"We can't worry about James's reaction right now, Surly Little Man," Lala instructed Yootza. "We have got a bachelorette party to plan."

❦

"Brenda, Helene. Helene, Brenda."

This was not Lala's first potentially very awkward encounter of the day.

❦

Brenda's bachelorette gift to Geraldine was a limousine with a wet bar and a flat screen TV and a driver who was far too cute—when Lala saw him, she felt sure that Brenda had clicked on the button specifying "far too cute" (right below the button specifying "not cute at all so there won't be any worries about drunken misadventures en route") on the limousine company's website—to pick up the bachelorette party guests and drive them to Las Vegas.

Clark, the adorable young limousine driver, was tall and sculpted, and his gently red hair underneath his chauffeur's cap matched his lilting hint of an Irish accent.

Lala wondered if Clark might not also be a male stripper, and then marveled that one still had to add the word "male" to the word "stripper" and wondered if maybe she could just stop doing that in her own mind for chrissake, no matter what an unenlightened fourth estate and blogosphere were still doing.

Clark's first stop of the day had been at Geraldine's fourplex to pick up Lala and the bride-to-be. Stephanie had, of course, also been invited to the seventy-two-hour brouhaha in the desert, but she had to study night and day for a continuing education seminar she and Chuck were taking at USC to learn Mandarin so they could travel to China at least once a year to aid a global animal rights group in working to protect animals there.

"That's in addition to all the great *pro bono* work those two kids do all around the United States," Lala said in the limo. "Sheesh. I get tired just thinking about those two wonderful kids. I promised

Stephanie that you and I would make it our personal mission in Vegas to drink one cocktail for her per each cocktail we drink for ourselves. Hey, Clark, I'm gonna pop open a bottle of champagne. Just wanted to let you know so you don't get startled and swerve. And I think we should pull over on the way to Vegas so you can have a glass. Or two. We can always flag down a taxi for the rest of the trip."

"Excellent, Ms. Lala," Clark said.

Petunia, Yootza, Chester, and Eunice would be staying at Stephanie and Chuck's apartment while their mama and their auntie wreaked havoc on the sandy plains of Nevada. This made Lala very happy because "ya know, they're vets and stuff, in addition to being absolutely delightful."

Clark drove Geraldine and Lala to Beverly Hills. To pick up Helene. Which was one of the main reasons Lala had felt it was definitely not too early to start downing mimosas.

*Oy vey*, Lala thought. *I just can't take a lot of awkwardness this weekend. Freight trains of unspoken prickliness. Massive dunes of terse and pointed subtext. I just can't.*

"Any thoughts?" Lala asked Geraldine as the car smoothly cruised into Helene's driveway.

"Grace," Geraldine said. "Grace and alcohol. A surefire combination."

Lala saw Helene glide out of her front door wheeling a very large weekend bag.

*Geraldine's right,* Lala thought. *Grace.*

Lala jumped out of the limo and sprinted over to Helene to force a preemptive hug on her.

When Helene responded to Lala's almost frantically enthusiastic body language with what Lala perceived as equal relief, Lala felt a rush of gratitude. She was also cheered by the distinct aura of booze that surrounded Helene like an expensive Parisian perfume.

"I'm so glad you invited me," Helene said.

"Oh, stop it," Lala said. "Like I wasn't going to invite you."

*Okay, I did consider it for maybe three seconds,* Lala thought. *What am I, a freakin' saint? And that secret goes with me to my grave.*

Helene pulled Lala off to the side with an earnest tug on Lala's elbow.

"I have to share something with you," Helene whispered. "I have to apologize for being so self-absorbed sometimes."

"Listen, I am the last person you have to apologize to for that, because—"

"Lala, I have the floor," Helene said.

"Oops," Lala said.

"My dad reminded me of something, and it's made me take a look at myself, and I'm not entirely thrilled with what I see. He reminded me about my best friend in elementary school. Her family lived right next door to us. One day I was over at their house and Jill and I were playing and the phone rang, and she went to answer it, and she came back with a startled look on her face and said 'Oh, Helene, I forgot you were here. I just said I would go over to Becky's house to play.'"

"Yikes," Lala said.

"Yeah. So I went home and I cried, and I told my dad what had happened and he commented that that wasn't very nice of Jill, and I hadn't thought about it for years, and my dad reminded me of how sad and dismissed Jill's ostentatious popularity made me feel."

*Uh huh*, Lala thought. *I do of course understand that you're Popular Jill, and I'm Banished Helene in our version of this story. But go on.*

"My dad also ordered me not to screw everything up by being, and I quote, 'a total pill princess' to his new niece."

Lala smiled.

"Helene, this is a wonderful and very meaningful revelation all around, and I'm very grateful that you had the grace and courage to share it with me, but we're kind of in a hurry here, so I'm going to sum up my world view vis-à-vis us, if I may. I'm really glad you're coming to Vegas, and I'm really glad your dad is marrying my aunt."

"Ditto," Helene said.

*Booze*, Lala thought. *And grace. Surefire.*

They returned to the car and Helene gave Clark her weekend bag, and the two women feasted on the sight of him loading it into the trunk. Helene winked repeatedly at Lala, who nodded and winked back and mouthed, "I saw him first," which Helene couldn't make out so Lala had to whisper far too loudly, "I SAID, I saw him first."

Back in the limo, after Geraldine and Helene hugged and after Lala made a fresh mimosa for Helene and then refilled Geraldine's glass, as well as her own, and after many toasts were made, including one to eternal friendship and hot sex over forty in the same breath, Helene started fishing around in her voluminous handbag and pulled out four DVD cases.

"I brought porn!" she announced. "Good stuff. Three-act story structure. Character arcs. Unbelievably hot actors. Titillation without the groan factor."

"Wow," Lala said. "Helene, I have not given you enough credit. You are delish."

Despite the relatively short drive to LAX, Lala and Geraldine and Helene popped *Will You Still Fuck Me Tomorrow?* into the DVD player, reasoning that they could restart at the beginning when Brenda was in the car, and they were on their way to Vegas so that Brenda wouldn't have to miss "a beat, not one, hello, who is that gorgeous guy, I think I saw him in an evening of improv at the Groundlings a few years ago."

"Clark, things may get loud back here," Helene said.

"Excellent, Ms. Helene."

And now they were at the curb at LAX, and Brenda had just exited the arrivals terminal, and Lala's heart was in her throat.

"Brenda, Helene. Helene, Brenda."

Lala watched Brenda and Helene eye each other warily.

And then Lala watched big, genuine smiles spread over each of their faces, and she watched the two women hug each other in what she had no choice but to interpret as a genuinely warm hug, because there wasn't enough cynicism left in her to question their gracious sincerity.

"I'm so glad to meet you," Helene said.

"Me too. This is going to be so much fun."

*Wow,* Lala thought. *Tons of grace. And tons of booze on the horizon. Was I Joan of Arc in a previous life? Is this payback?*

"May I borrow Brenda for a quick moment?" Lala asked.

She pulled Brenda a few feet away from the limousine.

"Okay, a couple of things. I can't thank you enough for being so warm and gracious to Helene. I absolutely do not deserve you. You should be punching me right now for having been such a completely self-absorbed, godawful whorebag. Punching me. In the face. Repeatedly."

"Shut up," Brenda said. "If I had done the same thing, would you have forgiven me?"

"I swear, I would have. Just don't get too chummy with Helene, okay? You know how sensitive I am."

"Shut up," Brenda said.

Lala handed Brenda an envelope. Brenda opened it and pulled out a check. A big check. Big enough to be the final payment on the forty-thousand-dollar loan.

"It is lunacy what people will pay to live on the Island of Manhattan," Lala said. "I mean, crazy. Nutso. Ruth at the rental agency suggested a few cheap upgrades to my place, and now I'm charging a thousand dollars more a week. Because I can. Don't go blowing all that at the blackjack tables."

❦

"What are the odds that Auntie Anne's Pretzels serves cocktails?"

Clark had just dropped the ladies off at the Desert Hills Premium Outlets, an oasis of discount consumerism. Lala had leaned in the driver's side window and pushed her boobs together with her biceps, handed two crackling crisp one hundred dollar bills to their driver, flashed him a knowing grin, and told him to go somewhere and get himself a nice lunch and maybe a massage because they were going to be hanging out at the mall for as long as it took.

"As long as it takes, Clark," Lala intoned with the sex-soaked inflections of a young Brigitte Bardot if that Gallic icon had suddenly learned to speak accent-free English. "Maybe go catch a movie after lunch. We've got shoppin' to do. Normally, I hate shopping. But today I'm feeling strangely serene and even a little enthused. Probably because I am already half in the bag. Isn't that great? Have fun, kiddo."

And then Lala leaned in further and kissed Clark square on the lips, which Clark deemed, "Excellent, Ms. Lala," to which Lala responded, "Please, call me Ms. Babe," before he sped off in a cloud of desert dust.

Helene's bachelorette gift to Geraldine was a new outfit for everyone to wear to the Cirque du Soleil spectacle they would be attending that evening, the tickets for which were also part of Helene's gift to Geraldine. Helene had chosen "Zumanity" for their Las Vegas show because, as she read aloud in the limo from the pages she had printed via their website, "This highly eroticized, cabaret-style spectacular has an array of unique characters whose performances are each themed by different elements of sexuality."

"I've heard about this show," Brenda said. "They call it Cirque du Soleil's sex show. That's how I've heard it described. This is so cool."

"I can't wait to see the sex show," Lala panted as they all sprinted toward the web of stores that seemed to be alive, and, if not actually alive, then surely seemed to be undulating like a living presence and definitely calling all their names like so many mythic sirens. "Did you see that guy? That picture of that guy in the show? The tall, really handsome one? He's mine. I saw him first. You know, Auntie Anne's really might serve booze. It's not entirely outside the scope of possibility. Should we stop there first to check before we head for the BCBG, does everyone know that stands for 'bon chic, bon genre,' store? Or I bet maybe Cinnabon at least serves wine. Should we check first before we start shopping? Why is everyone ignoring what I'm saying? Omigod, look at that shirt!"

The presumably seasoned sales staff at the BCBG store spun on the varying locations of their heels at the sound of four sets of palms shoving open doors that would have opened automatically, but apparently not quickly or emphatically enough for the bride-to-be and her entourage.

Lala lead the charge down a rack of evening wear.

"Normally, I don't even like shopping, but I bet this would look great on me, and Brenda should try this on, and I think Helene would look amazing in this, so—"

"Gimme that, gimme that, gimme that," Geraldine ordered.

She snatched all the clothes Lala had grabbed and was distributing only moments earlier and handed the pile to a saleswoman who was following them all to offer mute assistance.

"Hey, hey, hey, those were cute! Give those back!" Lala demanded.

"Hush," Geraldine said. She did a grand, confident sprint up and down all the aisles and returned laden with finery. She handed out armfuls of designer clothes to Lala, Brenda, and Helene, keeping a sizable portion for herself.

"You try this on and you try this on and you try this on. Don't start whining, Lala."

"Awwww, this color is gonna look terrible on me! I don't wanna try this on! I wanna try on what I picked out!"

Only half an hour later, Geraldine executed a victory stroll outside their four adjacent dressing rooms. She was wearing a flowing silk dress with blocks of tangerine and turquoise and white and grey. It hit just below her knees in the front and fell to her ankles in the back.

Geraldine paused outside Lala's dressing room door to watch Lala look at herself in the mirror.

"Never in my life would I have chosen sequins," Lala said. "But the pale rose makes these so subtle. I can't believe this works. Geraldine, you're a genius. P.S., I swear, if Helene looks as good in that black, strapless number as I suspect she does, I am going to stage a major snit."

"I don't know why you don't do this professionally, Geraldine," Helene announced from her dressing room.

"Geraldine, you are incredible," Brenda yelled from hers, which was at the far end of the row. "I would have bet money I would look like a clown in a leopard-print dress. I am never ever going shopping without you again."

Brenda poked her head outside her dressing room and saw Geraldine in her new clothes for the first time.

"Omigod, Geraldine, look at you. You look fabulous."

Helene and Lala ran out of their rooms.

"You do," Lala said. "You look fabulous. And Brenda looks fabulous, and Helene looks fabulous, and I look fabulous. Seriously, that's the only adjective I have left right now, that's how happy I am. I can't wait to go to the sex show looking like this. You wait and see if I don't get laid tonight. You wait and see if that guy in the pictures Helene printed from the website and I don't end up naked together somewhere. Somewhere with good lighting. And by 'good,' I of course mean 'forgiving.' Because he looks young, huh? I can't wait for the sex show. And sex! I can't wait for the sex show and the sex *après* show!"

"No. Seriously. How great is it to be away from home?" Lala brayed.

She did a running leap onto the sectional couch in the living room of their Prestige Bella Suite at the Palazzo Hotel on the Vegas Strip, the cost of which Lala and Brenda and Helene were splitting as a bachelorette gift to Geraldine.

Geraldine and Helene and Brenda started unpacking, and Lala started nearly bouncing off the walls and furniture with excitement.

Clark had pulled the limo up to the Palazzo and had helped the swarm of Palazzo valets take the luggage out of the trunk before the long car was whisked away to the hotel's subterranean parking. Clark then checked into the hotel along with the ladies, because Brenda's bachelorette gift included an all-expenses-paid room for their LA-based chauffeur at the hotel.

"He is so cute," Helene said. The four ladies had just dropped Clark off on his floor and were holding the elevator doors open so they could watch him walk down the long hallway. "That ass on him? Divine."

"I saw him first," Lala said.

And now they were in their suite, and Lala was ignoring her suitcase to act like a toddler who had eaten a ten-foot-tall tower of cotton candy.

"I feel so free! It's so great to be away from home and just be yourself and not overanalyze every damn thing and just have fun and just do what you feel like doing and not worry and just be true to yourself whatever that self might be."

*Wait a minute,* Lala thought.

Her face wrinkled up in concentration, but she did not stop bouncing on the sofa.

*Am I thinking of Manhattan Beach as home? Wow. Holy shit. That is way too weird.*

"Hey! Where's the wet bar?"

"Way ahead of you," Brenda said. Brenda had unpacked, located the in-house source of booze, opened a bottle of white wine, and poured four glasses while Lala was still doing her performance art piece titled "Lunatics I Have Known: A Grating Montage."

"Brenda, you are an angel," Lala said. "May I make the first toast? Pleeeze? Yeah? To Geraldine and Monty. Two of the kindest people I have ever known. I'm so happy you found each other, and, yes, I take full credit. Wishing you years and years and years of surpassing joy together. Auntie Geraldine, if you start crying, I will. And you know I look like shit when I cry. It's not conducive to the Vegas sexcapade I have planned."

"To my new mom, Geraldine," Helene said. "Thank you for bringing love back to my dad's heart."

"Wait a minute," Lala said. "Geraldine's like my mom too. That means Helene and I are kind of like sisters. Cool! We just need to understand that I'm the Alpha Sister, 'kay?"

"To love," Brenda said. "Eternal."

*Eternal,* Lala thought.

Lala smiled as she recalled the first time she laid eyes on her late husband. And the last time she saw him.

*Did you hear that, Terrance?* she silently asked him. *Of course you did. Love is eternal. You already knew that, right?*

Lala smiled at everyone and grabbed them into a circle so they could do a big group hug.

"Tissues," she said. "Seriously, where do they keep the damn tissues in this place?"

🍷

Brenda whispered to Lala as the four women made a grand

entrance onto the casino floor of the Palazzo.

"I'm sorry I made you cry."

"No, no, no, do not apologize," Lala said. "I like thinking about my husband. I'd rather think about Terrance and cry than not think about him. I appreciate you reminding me that love is constant. And forever."

"You sure?"

"I'm sure if my face doesn't look red and swollen anymore," Lala said. "Because I need to get laid tonight. Okay, one more time. Who's playing what for what?"

Lala's bachelorette party gift to her beloved aunt, in addition to covering the cost of all their food and drink in Las Vegas, was to more-than-amply stake the four revelers to the gambling venue of their choice, for the charity of their choice.

"Blackjack," Brenda said. "Habitat for Humanity."

"Damn, you're good," Lala said. "Superb cause. Superb. Auntie Geraldine?"

"Poker," Geraldine said. "Big Brothers and Big Sisters of America."

"Damn. Superb."

"Craps," Helene said. "Doctors Without Borders, and, yes, Lala, I know that's *Médecins Sans Frontières* in French."

"Superb choice and it is indeed that in French, God love you," Lala said. "As for me, I will be playing the slots because there is absolutely no skill required. And is anyone surprised that I will be playing for Dogs of Love? So what are we gonna do?"

"Win big!" Geraldine and Brenda and Helene cheered.

"And when are we gonna do it?" Lala roared.

"Now!"

❧

*I cannot fucking believe I am losing like this,* Lala thought. *Oh, shit, what are they all doing here? What are they all grinning about? What time is it?*

"Eighteen thousand dollars for Doctors Without Borders!" Helene crowed.

*Omigod, that is so fucking superb!* Lala thought.

"Eighteen grand?" Lala spit out, her eyes never leaving the spinning lemons and bells and number sevens that had never been more than a blink away from inducing an aneurism for the past three hours. "That is wonderful. Damn it, is there anything you're not great at?"

"You should see Helene play craps," Brenda crowed. "It is awesome!"

*Brenda, shut up,* Lala thought. *I'm concentrating on the randomness of cruel fate as manifested in gambling machines that require no skill whatsoever.*

"And what about our bachelorette?" Helene crowed. "A lot of kids are going to get the mentoring they need because of Geraldine. I mean, who knew anyone could take risks like that without blinking an eye? Without sweating a drop? Without shitting her pants?"

*Shoot me,* Lala thought. *If this entire farce of me losing while everyone else is raking it in, because I'm assuming Brenda won big too, isn't a metaphor for my life, then I don't know what is.*

"And then there's Brenda working the blackjack table like she owns the place. Wow!" Geraldine crowed. "A whole slew of houses will be built thanks to Brenda!"

*Seriously,* Lala thought. *Shoot me. Now. There must be a mobster around here somewhere carrying a loaded piece equipped with a silencer. Get him over to me. Stat.*

"We were looking for you—"

"Have you been here the whole time—"

"You missed a lot of fun—"

"Why didn't you come find us—"

"You haven't been sitting here the whole time, have you—"

"Listen, we need to leave right away, or we'll be late for the show, so let's—"

*Damn it!* Lala thought. *I'm going to miss the sex show!*

"Let's run up to the room and put our bounty in the safe and then we can—"

*This is stupid,* Lala thought. *If I had written a check for all the damn money I've pumped into this damn machine, the dogs would have been better off, and I could be drinking right now. And I wouldn't have such a stabbing headache.*

"Lala, we need to get going or—"

"Somebody give me a quarter," Lala whispered. "Please."

*You want metaphor, universe,* she thought. *I'll give you metaphor.*

"Lala, we don't have time—"

*I've got a feeling,* Lala thought. *I've got a feeling this time . . . Please, God, don't let me be the loser I'm afraid I might actually be.*

"Please," Lala whispered. "One quarter. Just one more."

The three women started fishing around in their exquisite and quite tiny evening bags that had been bought at the outlet mall along with the four pairs of exquisite and quite ridiculously high-heeled shoes. Helene pulled out a dime and three pennies. Brenda found nine nickels.

*What is she doing with so many nickels?* Lala thought. *Isn't that weird. What are the odds? I feel dizzy.*

Geraldine dug through her purse, which she had managed to stuff within an inch of its tiny life.

"Here," Geraldine said.

Geraldine kissed the quarter and thrust it at Lala.

The three reels began to spin. They picked up speed. Lala swooned on the chair.

One diamond.

*Is it me, or did they just lower the lights in here?* Lala thought.

The second reel began to slow down.

Another diamond.

"Uh oh," Helene said.

*Am I going nuts, or is it suddenly incredibly hot in here?* Lala thought. *And why is everything getting all wavy all of a sudden? Am I about to have a flashback?*

The third reel began to slow down.

"Come on," Brenda said.

"Come on," Geraldine said.

"You did it!" Helene bellowed. "You won! Look at those numbers go up!"

"They're not stopping!" Geraldine yelled.

"Wow!" Brenda screamed. "Wow! Wow, that is gonna be a

huge jackpot! Wow! Lala, you . . . Oh no, get some water! Is there a doctor anywhere in here?"

Lala slowly opened her eyes and gazed up from the richly carpeted casino floor at the three faces that were staring down at her with so much love and concern.

"We don't have time for water," she gasped. "We don't have time for a doctor. We have to get to the sex show."

"Sweetheart, you just fainted. You are going right upstairs, and you are getting in bed. You are in no shape to attend a lust-drenched Vegas extravaganza."

"Omigod, Auntie Geraldine, are you fucking nuts?" Lala whispered. "I have never felt better in my entire life."

*Omigod,* Lala thought. *Why haven't I tried lesbianism before?*

If the two stunningly gorgeous women, who were on stage executing a flowing series of sensuous poses together in a vast bowl of water that sat atop a stem in the guise of a massive champagne glass, had paused to look out over the audience, and if these genetically-blessed young women had happened to rest their gazes on the third row center of the theatre, they would have seen four women of various decades staring at them with wide eyes and dropped jaws and lips curled in slight and unwavering smiles.

"Are you thinking what I'm thinking?" Brenda whispered.

"If it involves girl-on-girl, then yes," Lala whispered.

"How did we miss that? College was so wild. So how did we stay stuck in such a rut?"

"Your loss, ladies," Helene whispered. "It's quite lovely. Not my daily cup of tea, but definitely something to sample."

"Indeed," Geraldine whispered.

The three younger ladies stared at their honored bachelorette.

"What are you looking at?" Geraldine asked.

"Does my dad know?" Helene whispered.

"Are you kidding? He loves hearing about the summer I studied cooking in Milan before I married my late husband. I could repeat the story of sharing a flat with Carmela and her boyfriend

Giuseppe and all the resulting permutations *ad infinitum* as far as your father is concerned, and it still wouldn't get old."

"Okay, thanks," Helene said. "I think I've got enough images to haunt me for a while."

"I wonder if it's too late for me," Lala mused.

"It is never too late," Geraldine said.

When the beguiling performers executed their final pose and King Kong's champagne glass slid off stage, Lala, Geraldine, Brenda, and Helene exploded in applause and cheers.

"Encore!" Lala screamed. She stood up and waved her hands in a kind of spastic recreation of British royalty's standard twisting of the wrists to greet the masses.

"What are you doing?" Geraldine giggled. "You look like Queen Elizabeth with a brain tumor. That's not what you're going for, is it?"

"Once more!" Lala yelled. "Are you taking volunteers from the audience? Take volunteers from the audience! Right here! Right here! Pick me! Pick me!"

And then Lala started trying to pull her beautiful dress up, and it was instantly clear to everyone that she was intending to flash her boobs at the stage.

"Sit down!" Brenda guffawed. Brenda, Geraldine, and Helene yanked at Lala's sequined dress and forced her back into her seat. Brenda sat on Lala's lap and pinned Lala down until Lala agreed to "stop acting like a fucking lunatic, and I mean that as a compliment."

A delicate, white curtain fell from the lights above the stage. The four friends watched as a man and woman—who were, Lala whispered, "Naked? Are they naked? I can't tell, I think they look naked? Or is that the lighting playing tricks? Anybody have a definitive opinion one way or the other? Anybody?"—descended from the air. The aerialist duo used the white curtain to perform a weightless dance together. The choreography was graceful, stunning, filthy.

"That is schmutz on wings," Lala gasped.

"Have I died?" Geraldine asked. "Am I in Heaven?"

"He is gorgeous," Brenda whispered.

"Gorgeous," Helene echoed.

"I saw him first," Lala declared.

When, far too soon, the last erotic interlude of the erotic evening—this one a gorgeous dancer with a guileless air doing a tantalizing routine on top of a television in an attempt to grab the attention of her football-focused partner—concluded, and the performers took their bows, and the lights came up in the audience. The four women reluctantly shuffled out, seemingly loath to abandon the site of this ephemeral sin palace.

Lala paused in the lobby of the theatre.

"I'm only slightly kidding when I say that I might need to run up to the suite and . . . and . . . well, you know . . . do something about this excess sexual energy that has enveloped my mind and body, so I don't take a flying leap onto the crotch of the first handsome man I see. I mean, of course, I still intend to have sex with someone tonight, but all in due course. So maybe I should just take a few minutes and go . . . hmm . . . what euphemism shall I employ?"

"Masturbate?" Geraldine suggested.

"That is not, dear Auntie Geraldine, strictly speaking, a euphemism," Lala said.

"It's not a euphemism, not strictly speaking," Helene added.

"Pleasure yourself?" Brenda offered.

"A bit Victorian bodice-ripper, no?" Lala said. "I mean that as a compliment."

"Jack it?" Brenda suggested.

"I've always liked that one," Helene said.

"Awww, what the hell?" Lala said. "Let's just go dance it off. And if I crash land on some poor schmuck's scepter and crown jewels, he'll have to fend for himself. Seriously, I gotta worry about him? What am I, Florence freakin' Nightingale?"

᠆

"I'm not a hundred percent sure, because I don't remember ever actually looking at his face, but I think the aerialist is up there in the balcony staring at you."

Lala spun around and looked up in the direction Helene had pointed. She peered at the figure peering down at her from the upper level of the small and intimate space.

The four women were dancing in a circle under a dome that was emitting a pulsating series of lights that alternately made Lala, Geraldine, Brenda, and Helene look like Disney princesses and Twilight Zone space aliens. They were at the coolest and coziest and most exclusive nightclub in their hotel, and Geraldine was giving the younger women a lesson on timeless, infinite stamina.

After Hour One, Lala had complained that her feet hurt and could they please sit for a little bit and maybe have some champagne?

"I wanna dance!" Geraldine declared. "I can't stop dancin'!"

"Yeah, yeah, fine, we'll dance again soon. Can we just sit for fifteen minutes? Pleeeeeze?"

They returned to their alcove in the patio, with Geraldine shimmying and shaking as they passed through the crowd.

"Come on! Let's go back in and dance!"

"Geraldine, my poor feet give up," Lala said. "A bottle of Dom Perignon, please."

The androgynous waiter smiled and winked at Lala.

"Have you had the Dom Perignon here before?" he asked.

"Nnnnnooo?" Lala said.

"You're in for a treat."

He sashayed away and the four women watched him depart.

"Me like," Brenda said.

"Me want," Helene said.

"Me getting married," Geraldine said. "But me not married yet."

"Me saw him first," Lala said. She leaned back on the cushions that were spread out in a fashion that suggested the nightclub might be shooting a cover for the Ikea catalogue's 'Moroccan Nights' edition and scanned the crowd. At the far end of the patio, Lala saw someone she thought she might recognize, flirting with someone she was sure she didn't recognize.

*Is that our chauffeur?* she thought. *Mother of God, is he cute.*

Before Lala could make any declarations that she was going to go hit on Clark because he was so freakin' cute, and she saw him first, the epic chords of the theme to the *Superman* movies began to thrust forth from the club's speakers. And then out of nowhere a man dressed in a Superman suit was being carried over to their table by a team of muscled men who had hoisted him above their heads to make it look like Superman was flying in with a bottle of Dom Perignon in hand.

"Look at that!" Lala screamed. "That is delightful! Don't shake the bottle or the bubbly'll be all over the damn place! My God, is that a presentation or is that a presentation?"

Lala smiled and sighed.

"Ahhh, champagne," she said. "Your explosive whispers are the demi-sec soundtrack of my life."

"I thought I was very specific about not ordering a stripper," Geraldine said, her eyes undressing every man within five feet of the champagne bottle.

"I didn't order a stripper," Lala said.

"Well, now I think I'm rather sorry I was so vocal about that. Maybe Superman could take off his uniform? Or maybe just drop his pants and give us a quick glimpse of his tushie?"

The Superman bearers halted in front of the ladies and gently lowered the hero of comic book and screen to the ground.

"Oh, hiiiiii," Lala gasped. "Are you adorable, or what?"

Superman smiled at the ladies, motioned for his crew to produce four glasses, and popped open the bottle.

"Ahhhh!" Lala screamed. "I knew the explosion was coming and still it caught me off-guard. It's a metaphor for my life."

And now, back on the dance floor, after having savored the delicious champagne, Lala was watching someone who might be the gorgeous aerialist staring down at their group.

*I'm not sure if that's him,* she thought. *Did I ever get an actual glimpse of his actual face?*

"Lala, whoever that guy is, he's staring right at you," Helene said. "Wow. That is some intense look he is giving you. You must remind him of an old girlfriend."

Lala stopped dancing and squared off at Helene.

"An *old* girlfriend?" Lala shot at Helene. "*Old?* Owwww!"

Geraldine had just hauled off and whacked Lala hard on both her shoulders with the flat palms of her hands.

"That hurt! Why did you do that?"

"I'm knocking the chip off your shoulder," Geraldine said.

"Both of them? I've got chips on both my shoulders?"

"Yes, apparently you have. What does 'old' refer to besides age?"

*Huh?* Lala thought.

"Come on, you're smart," Geraldine said. "Another meaning for the word 'old.'"

*Damn it*, Lala thought. *She's right.*

"I'm sorry, Helene. I somehow managed to forget that 'old' can also mean 'former.'"

"I understand," Helene said. "No problem."

"Really, I have no excuse other than the fact that you're younger than I am, and I sometimes feel so past-my-prime, but that is no excuse for being rude and for being a total putz, and I shouldn't be so AAHHHH!"

Lala stumbled over her feet as she turned around to face the person who had just startled her by tapping her on the shoulder. Then she spun back, once again stumbling over her feet, to challenge the other women.

"No one saw him coming?" she hissed. "No one could maybe have given me a warning that he was coming?"

"Sorry," Brenda said. "I was focusing on the lady brawl in progress."

"Excuse me for interrupting, but I had to come over. I've been watching you dance," the handsome young man said. To Lala.

"Yeah?" Lala said. "You have? Okay, I'm sorry, can we just pause for a moment? You are the aerialist from the show, right?"

"I am," the handsome young man said.

"I thought so," Brenda said. "But I wasn't sure."

"Apparently none of us took in much of the details of your face," Geraldine admitted.

"I get that a lot," the handsome young man said, smiling. "Ladies, may I join you?"

"Of course," Geraldine said.

"Indeed," Helene said.

"Please do," Brenda said.

"Duh," Lala said.

The handsome young man and the four lusting-to-various-degrees-with-Lala-being-the-odds-on-favorite-to-be-the-most-crazed-of-the-bunch-as-usual women began dancing together. In no time, there was almost no space between Lala and the handsome young man. He had moved in to single her out as his dance partner after only a few bars of music had played.

*Gosh,* Lala thought, *I hope I don't remind him of a friend's mother or a teacher he had a crush on in elementary school.*

The handsome young man smiled at Lala and very delicately placed his hands on either side of her waist.

*Thank God, thank God, thank GOD, I wore Spanx,* Lala thought.

"I like to find the slower beat in any kind of music," he whispered in her ear. "It's so much sexier, don't you think?"

*Gosh,* Lala thought, *I always assumed not having kids disqualified me. But maybe I'm an* ersatz *MILF! Wow, I bet there are some fun possibilities with that. Let's find out, shall we?*

"May I cut in?"

Lala looked in the direction of the deep, rich voice that had just startled her and her dance partner, and saw what the handsome young man would look like in about thirty years.

*Whoa,* Lala thought. *Did you win the DNA lottery, or what? Count your blessings, kiddo.*

"Dad!" the handsome young man whined. "Not right now, okay? We're having a really interesting conversation here."

The handsome young man's dad smiled at his son and at Lala.

"Josh, don't you have an early rehearsal for the new show tomorrow? Hadn't you better get some rest?" "Your father is right, Josh," Lala said, not looking at Josh at all anymore but, instead, staring into the eyes of his dad. "Go home and go to sleep. Sage advice from your elders."

🍷

"You have a lovely home," Lala said.

Lala's path to a spacious, opulently appointed, corporate-owned apartment with a killer view in the Aria Hotel that evening was paved with lascivious intentions mixed with a sturdy serving of female solidarity.

After Josh sulked off and Lala began dancing with Theo, Josh's father, Lala learned in the course of a myriad of songs—and so did Geraldine, Brenda, and Helene, because Theo expansively and happily included all the lovely women in the sphere of his newfound dance troupe—that Theo was Josh's boss as well as his parent, having been for many years a producer of a long list of Cirque du Soleil's extravaganzas across the globe. Josh's mother, they also learned, had been one of the managing directors for the Vegas shows until five years earlier, when she left the United States and Theo, "not in that order," to start a new life in Nova Scotia running a yoga retreat and bed and breakfast.

"We're great friends," Theo said, "as long as a continent separates us."

After many more songs, Lala emitted the first notes of a whimper and looked like she was about to drop kick her stiletto heels into the air, so Geraldine cut Lala off before her niece could unconsciously descend into the realm of the unsexy.

"Why don't we go sit for a bit?" Geraldine suggested.

The party continued on the patio, where Theo asked the ladies if he might be allowed to order them all a pitcher of margaritas because his buddy Sonny was behind the bar at the club that night, and "nobody makes margaritas like Sonny anywhere in the world, not hyperbole."

As soon as Theo was out of earshot, the four women went into a huddle.

"Okay, so, Brenda," Geraldine continued, "we finish the margaritas, and then we head back to the suite and leave the two single gals to wreak havoc."

"Stop reading my mind," Brenda said. "I am so on that page with you."

"But . . . But it's your bachelorette celebration," Lala said.

"Could you have made that sound more half-hearted?" Brenda chuckled.

"Yes, it is my bachelorette celebration, and I am having the time of my life, and I look forward to all of us convening for mimosas and brunch by the pool tomorrow sometime around noon to continue the festivities, but, in the meantime, Brenda and I are old married ladies, and we need to head up to the suite before we turn into pumpkins. Old married pumpkins."

*Wait,* Lala thought. *Is that . . .*

"Lala, where are you going?" Geraldine demanded. "Theo will be back any minute and you can't—"

Lala leaped up from the Moroccan cushions, an act which did not put her in her best light because there wasn't much traction to be had from the low-lying pillows, and she made several false starts that sent her tumbling back on her ass before she finally managed to get on her feet with the help of a boost from Helene.

*Damn it, where's Theo?* Lala thought. *Did he see me wobbling like a weeble? Okay, don't have time to obsess about that right now.*

Lala pushed her way through the tight crowd until she was close enough to pounce on their chauffeur, who was standing alone at the edge of the patio looking out onto the dance floor.

"Clark!" she brayed. "So great to see you! Come with me? Please? Okay?"

Lala grabbed Clark's hand, spared a moment to note that he was reacting by smiling and not by motioning for security to haul her away, and took that as permission to drag him back to their cushion cave with her.

"Look who I found!" Lala screeched.

"Hello, ladies," Clark said.

*Look how shy and cute Helene is!* Lala thought. *Is she blushing, or is that red glow coming from the strobe light out on the dance floor?*

Lala grabbed Helene's hand and pulled her up. She put Helene's hand in Clark's.

"Go dance, you two," Lala commanded.

"Would that be okay with you?" Clark asked Helene.

*God, is he adorable,* Lala thought. *All shy and cute and stuff. God.*

"I'd love to," Helene said.

"Good," Lala said. She gave them a nudge bordering on a shove toward the dance floor. "Excellent, go. Come on. Get going. More margaritas for me."

And now Lala was alone with Theo in the corporate apartment that had been his home since he and his wife split up and would continue to be his home, as Lala had learned over a fresh batch of margaritas that Theo had mixed himself when they got to his place, and that Lala had dubbed "way better than Sonny's, as outstanding as Sonny's were, I'm not kidding," until he left for Moscow to supervise the building of a new Cirque du Soleil theater complex in Red Square. Next week. For two years.

"Sheesh," Lala said. "And just when I was thinking that a long distance romance between LA and Vegas should be no obstacle to lifelong happiness and, forgive me for being forward about my now dashed fantasies, but in tequila *veritas* and what the hell anyway, you're leaving town. I seem to have that effect on men."

"Well, you know," Theo said, "I caught myself entertaining those fantasies quite a few times tonight."

"So, Theo, here's my thought. It seems to have occurred to me tonight, and I'm not sure when, probably around the time I started imagining you naked, that I may be in danger of veering into toying with out-and-out sluttishness—"

"Oh, do go on," Theo said. "I'm mesmerized."

"So I'm thinking maybe we just make out for a few hours tonight, and then I head home to my suite and send you off to Russia with my heartfelt best wishes and more than a little regret that fate has rendered us asunder so soon after rendering us . . . sunder . . . in other words, we don't full-on bonk tonight?"

"That sounds wonderful," Theo said. "Not that I wouldn't cast my vote for full-on bonking given half a chance."

"Ahhhh!" Lala screamed. Her cell phone, tucked into her fancy evening bag, was emitting a wail that could have woken the dead. "When did the volume on that damn thing get so screwy? Gimme a sec, I just want to make sure it's not an emergency with my aunt or something."

Lala grabbed her bag and pulled the offending communication device out of it.

"I kind of hate texting. I can't manage to text back without the results making me sound *meshugganah* because of all the damn typos I make and because of what autocorrect goes ahead and turns them into. Don't text me from Russia, okay? Let's just write actual letters, and then, years from now, they can be published in a collection that will inspire future generations of lovers. I just said that because I'm kind of hammered. I mean, but, you know, I would love to stay in touch."

Lala poked at her cell phone and got to the message that had just arrived for her. It was from delicious e-publisher James Lancaster.

*I feel sick,* Lala thought.

"Why aren't you checking your e-mail?" the text read.

"Theo, do you have a laptop handy and will you please, please, please excuse me for a few minutes?"

Lala sat at Theo's desk in his bedroom trying to will herself not to sweat right through the armpits of her lovely, expensive party dress. Theo had remained in the living room at her request because Lala told him, "I might get crazy depending on what this e-mail I've been waiting for says, and I think it's too early in our relationship for you to see me like that because it might not be pretty."

*There's no subject line on James's e-mail,* Lala thought. *I don't think I feel well. Oh, fuck it.*

She clicked on the link and the contents popped open.

"I swear, I didn't think it was possible . . ." Lala read.

*Uh oh,* Lala thought.

> . . . but your annotated *Say Yes to the Dress* had me cracking up the whole time I was reading it. And you have to do more entries for 'Lala Pettibone, Journalist to the Stars' because it's a hoot. I really loved everything you sent me.

*I feel dizzy,* Lala thought.

> Except for . . .

*Shit,* Lala thought.

> . . . 'These Bloody Awful, Bloody Marvelous, Bloody Bloody Streets'?

*True,* Lala thought. *That one was weird.*

Short stories set in a futuristic London where the unifying theme is dismemberment? And you seemed to be trying to be funny about it? What the hell was that?

*I have no idea what I was thinking,* Lala thought. *No clue. I got bupkis in terms of an explanation.*

I mean, I can see where you were maybe going for something Poe-esque, but, Jesus. Anyway, I predict we can make 'Dressed Like a Lady, Drinks Like a Pig' a big hit. It's a great piece. Call me.

♟

Theo looked up from the book he had been reading when Lala reentered the living room, wearing nothing but her stiletto heels and the string of pearls her late husband had given her for their tenth anniversary.

"Lean back," Lala cooed. "Close your eyes. And then say your prayers. Because I am gonna wear you out."

# THE DAWN

There were no meddling moms to make cutting remarks about their daughters' weight, no clueless fiancés to break one of the most sacred rules of wedding planning by insisting that they be part of the entourage. No self-centered bridesmaids to undermine the process by demanding that the bride "at least try on a mermaid gown, because, I mean, come on, what could it hurt to just try it on, for God's sake we came all this way so just try the stupid mermaid one on . . . I bet you'll look great in it, and then you'll be thanking me for making you try it on, okay?" after the bride repeatedly declared that she had always dreamed since she was a little girl of wearing a ball gown wedding dress on her special day. There were no pouts, no sneers, no tears. Indeed, the only time the shopping experience of finding Geraldine's wedding dress even came close to the heightened drama on *Say Yes to the Dress* was when Lala unintentionally hurt Helene's feelings while Geraldine, Helene, and Lala were combing the racks with the bridal consultant.

Brenda, who had flown home to New York directly from Las Vegas, would be joining in to offer her thoughts on the dresses via webcam once the top three contenders had been selected.

"How about this one?" Helene said, holding up a tiered lace gown in pale pink.

"You're kidding, right?" Lala brayed. "It's got a rose on it the size of an Aztec sundial, for chrissake! Oh no, Helene, I'm so sorry. I didn't mean it that way . . . I'm sure roses the size of Aztec sundials look great on certain brides . . . Seriously, please don't be hurt, I thought you were kidding . . . I'm a total idiot."

It turned out that there would not be three dresses vying for the honor of being chosen. And so Brenda's only function would be to confirm what the three women standing in the dressing room already knew.

"This is the one," Geraldine said. She had discovered the off-white silk organza gown in one of the most distant racks in the shop, on which this treasure was surrounded by a sad collection of fashion misfires.

Geraldine turned around slowly so that they could all see the dress in the three-paneled mirror. It had a slight train and three-quarter length sleeves and the fabric draped itself exquisitely over Geraldine's tall, trim body.

"You look gorgeous," Lala gasped.

"Gorgeous," Helene whispered.

Lala grabbed the price tag.

"How much . . . OMIGOD!"

Helene grabbed the price tag from Lala.

"That must be misprint—"

"What?" Geraldine demanded. "What? Where are my glasses? I can't tell if that's a seven or a—"

"It was originally seven thousand, and it is now marked down to a hundred bucks!" Lala crowed.

Afterward, cozily ensconced in a booth in one of their favorite restaurants, the four women—Brenda was with them via Helene's iPhone, which was propped up against the wall next to their table so that a picture of Brenda in her study in New York with a glass of white wine in her hand could be seen—agreed that the money Geraldine was saving on her wedding dress would be divided among four new charities.

"The ACLU is my choice," Brenda said.

"And I'll be donating to the Democratic National Committee," Geraldine said.

"It's Greenpeace for me," Helene said.

"I love that we're a girl group of clichéd liberals," Lala said. "It's like we're the Go-Gos of progressivism. It's like if the Bangles were made up of four Joan Baezes. And is anyone surprised that I will be donating to the Humane Society of the United States? Okay, wait, before anyone says another word, can we just go ahead and pretend that we traveled to Brooklyn to go to Kleinfeld's to get a wedding dress, and we're being filmed for *Say Yes to the Dress,* and I'm playing Geraldine's part right now, and I'm saying something I actually heard a bride say on the show when she was torn between two wedding dresses."

Lala pulled herself up in her seat on the bench of the booth and put on her best imitation of Geraldine's elegant voice with an added frantic edge.

"I have literally never been so confused in my entire life."

Lala bobbed her head and grinned.

"That's a quotation! About choosing a wedding dress! No decision in that dame's life had been as challenging as which wedding dress to pick. Which college to attend? Nuh uh! What career? Piece of cake. Which groom to marry? Could decide that in her sleep. But the dress! No, don't make me decide between two dresses. She actually said that."

Geraldine would never have said anything like that because Geraldine was the very antithesis of a high-maintenance bride. Geraldine and Monty's ceremony and reception would be in the courtyard of Geraldine's fourplex. The food would be catered by a friend of Geraldine's, whose area of expertise was creating sumptuous, yet low-calorie, vegetarian buffets. The caterer was also taking care of the open bar and would be serving Helene's favorite cocktail that Helene had reworked in honor of the bride and groom; this time it would be a blend of champagne, an infusion of peach, or *pêche,* as Lala insisted on calling it, and those delightful edible gold flakes—or flecks, as Lala had taken to calling them.

There would be no arguing over which style of dress would suit all three of Geraldine's attendants because the only guidelines Lala, the matron of honor, and Brenda and Helene, the bridesmaids, could get out of the bride were, "No, no, don't bother finding the same outfit, just wear whatever you want, maybe something with a little . . . I don't know . . . a little purple in it somewhere for a unifying theme. Just be comfortable. It's a party."

There would be no scanning of items into a bridal registry, in person or online, because Monty and Geraldine had everything they needed to be happy for the rest of their lives, and if any of the guests were to insist on giving them a gift, a donation to "a cause that promoted kindness and caring" would be all they needed to be even happier for the rest of their lives.

"Suck on that, you social and political conservatives who hide your selfishness beneath a veneer of trumpeting classic American individuality, as though it is somehow anti-American to consider oneself one's brothers' and sisters' and other sentient beings' keeper!" Lala crowed at their favorite restaurant after her second vodka gimlet. The three other women nodded their approval.

"Even when she slurs," Brenda said with smiling admiration, "she makes her point."

"Especially when she slurs," Geraldine added.

Geraldine's attitude toward her big day was so profoundly leisurely and easygoing, it left very little, if indeed anything, for her matron of honor to worry about once the bachelorette celebration had become a treasured memory—other than, perhaps, whether she was in fact a matron or a maid of honor, given how long she had been widowed.

And so Lala found herself in the midst of a longish block of free time. She had decided to take a brief hiatus from her creative writing. She had an idea for her next project, which was to be a treatment and full episodes for the first season of a cable sitcom about Mata Hari's new career as an agent for Britain's MI-5 in the afterlife that she had given the working title "Double-Oh-Heaven," but she wanted to take some time to recharge her batteries before she began the foray into a "hopefully hilarious and mesmerizing journey through time, space, and the outermost boundaries of our preconceived ideas of Heaven and Hell, good taste, and narrative storytelling."

"I'm hoping this saga will lure Sean Connery out of retirement so he can play the lead role in drag because I think having Mata

Hari as an older and more masculine angel could definitely work," Lala shared with her precious dogs during their many relaxing and restoring hours on the couch together watching the most deliciously over-the-top television known to man or beast.

From the tone of the silent glares with which Petunia, Yootza, Chester, and Eunice were accosting Lala, the dogs were united in wishing that their mama would shut her pie-hole so their eighteenth hour of that day's napping could proceed undisturbed.

Though Lala was on vacation, she still had her laptop with her on the couch. Because Lala was maintaining a fevered, virtual *ménage à quatre* with three very desirable men, two of whom were at a distance and one of whom was not.

Lala was in frequent e-mail contact with Theo and James. And she continued to write daily messages to David, though she anticipated that they would never be seen by eyes other than her own, nor heard by ears other than her dogs' until her death and David's, and that they would then create a media sensation in the sphere of romance that would dwarf any renown Abelard and Heloise had managed to achieve over the centuries with quill and parchment.

"It's a blogary," Lala explained to her uninterested dogs. "Or a diablog, if you prefer. It's a diary, but it's not written by hand on lovely paper, get it?"

*When you think about it,* Lala thought, *I'm getting to be quite a hussy in my prime.*

"David, I am apparently quite a hussy," Lala typed. "I think about you all the time, and I relive our epic porn fest together, and I also have a huge crush on Theo, and then there's a guy in town who is adorable and loves animals and is my new publisher, and I get very stupidly shy and awkward when I think about him. Jesus, I feel like I'm back in high school, and I've got a crush on three guys in the theater department and maybe only two of them are gay."

"Theo has an ear for schmutz," Lala coyly confessed to Geraldine. "His e-mails are smokin', lemme tell you."

Lala and her aunt were sitting in the courtyard with the dogs enjoying a big pitcher of lemonade. With vodka.

"My philosophy on booze," Geraldine said, "is that I had an aunt who, starting at her eighty-fifth birthday, was potted from morning 'til night, and she looked great, and she felt great, and she was very active and very involved in life until she went to sleep one night shortly after her one-hundred-and-second birthday and didn't wake up the next morning. So I'm getting a head start."

Geraldine cradled Yootza on her lap and planted a big smacker of a kiss on his forehead. Lala refilled each of their glasses.

"I think Theo and I might be soul mates," she mused.

"That guy in Vegas? You're talking about that guy in Vegas?"

"Yeah," Lala said. "Theo."

"Are you moving to Vegas?"

"Actually, he's in Moscow for the next two years, but we write each other such lovely e-mails all the time, and I feel like we're getting to really know each other on a very deep soul level, and that he might be the one who can—"

"So you're moving to Moscow?"

"God, no," Lala said. "It's freezing in Moscow. It's worse than New York. My blood has thinned since I moved here. I'm starting to really like this weather. Jesus, I hope New York didn't hear me say that."

"What do you hear from James?"

"He's such a sweetheart," Lala said.

"I'd love to meet him sometime," Geraldine said.

"His e-mails crack me up."

"Remember the days when people who lived in the same town would actually see each other? And actually speak to each other? In the same room? In person? Remember that?"

"Vaguely," Lala said.

A few days later Geraldine was over at Lala's place, and they were watching *Casablanca*, which put their combined total of watching that film well into the three digits.

"James got me an online interview with one of the most trafficked international e-book web forums," Lala gushed.

Lala and Geraldine had been talking through much of *Casablanca*, as they always did, when they weren't saying the lines along with Humphrey and Ingrid and Paul and Claude.

"James timed it to appear just before the first installment of *Dressed Like a Lady* goes up on his website. Did I tell you James is planning to present my novel as a serialization, the same way Dickens's works came out? Isn't that cool?"

"You did tell me that, and it is very cool," Geraldine said. "I couldn't be more thrilled for you."

"James is such a nice man. We were instant messaging each other for hours last night, and he writes the goofiest things, and I was laughing and laughing and laughing—"

"Why didn't you just call him and talk to him? Or invite him over or something?"

"Umm . . . Well, he didn't bring up getting together, and I was feeling kind of shy, so I didn't say anything."

"You were what?" Geraldine said. "When do you ever feel shy?"

"Lots of times," Lala said. "I just don't act on it. Or mention it. Or consciously reflect on it. Most of the time."

Over the weekend, Lala and Geraldine had gone to the gym together to give "that maddening area under our arms and that infuriating tire around our waists a run for their money." Lala had adjusted her workout to avoid even the whisper of a hint of a chance of injuring herself again and was now an acolyte of the stationary bike and the elliptical machine, both of which she embraced with the obnoxious vigilance of a former cigarette addict enforcing a No Smoking sign.

"Non-impact," Lala droned to Geraldine as they worked their abs on neighboring inclined benches. "It's the only way to go. Hey, want to hear something funny? Did I tell you James volunteers at Dogs of Love?"

"Yes, you did," Geraldine said.

"Seriously, how sweet and adorable is that? So I was at Dogs of Love at noon, and then I heard from one of the other volunteers that James showed up at three o'clock right after I left, and so the next time I got there at three, and, apparently, he had been there at noon that day, and I thought that was the funniest—"

"Why don't you just suggest that you both meet there one day and volunteer together and then maybe go out and have dinner and—"

"Well, he didn't mention that, and I didn't want to sound—"

"Sound what?" Geraldine said. "Interested?"

"I don't know; I guess I'm just going through a shy phase or something."

The following Tuesday Lala and Geraldine treated each other to a vegan lunch and an afternoon at the spa and then capped off their day with cocktails on the terrace of an oceanfront restaurant. Lala chuckled at the crashing waves.

"I have to send you a copy of an article James wrote," Lala told Geraldine. "I swear, you talk about layered, non-bullshit analysis of what it means to tell a great story? You talk about conveying an idea with astronomical intelligence and somehow managing to do that without sounding like a patronizing prick? James is the gold standard. He sets the bar so high I don't know how anyone . . . Geraldine, why are you making that hideous face?"

Geraldine seized Lala by the elbow, hoisted Lala up out of her seat, and proceeded to shove Lala through the crowd on the patio, into and through the restaurant toward the bar area and the front door.

"Tony," Geraldine called out to the bartender. "We need our check, please, dear!"

"Comin' up," Tony said.

"I haven't finished my cocktail!" Lala wailed.

"You've got until Tony runs my credit card," Geraldine hissed. "So I suggest you start chugging."

"Oh sure, good timing of the crazy outburst for you," Lala muttered. She downed a series of gulps until she made herself sputter. "You were between drinks. Nice for you."

Geraldine left Tony a big tip, as she always did, winked at Tony as they were leaving, as she always did, and pulled Lala toward the exit.

"'Bye, Tony!" Lala yelled over her shoulder, still gulping her drink. "We'll see you soon!"

Lala handed her empty hurricane glass to the hostess just a second before Geraldine shoved the doors open and thrust Lala out into the cool night air.

"Sheesh," Lala grumbled. "Here's my hat. What's my hurry? Don't let the door hit me in the tuchus on the way out."

Geraldine hustled Lala into the passenger seat of her car and slammed the door. She ran around the car, got into the driver's seat, slammed that door, and turned to face Lala.

"I didn't want to embarrass you by lecturing you in public. I have officially had it up to here with you!"

"Had it with what—"

"Be quiet!" Geraldine yelled. "I'm speaking!"

"Okay," Lala silently mouthed.

"Do you remember the first time you introduced my beloved late husband and me to your beloved late husband?"

There was a pause, during which Geraldine drummed the console between their two seats.

"Do you?" she demanded.

"I can talk now?" Lala asked, and made the mistake of betraying an oblique reference to a smile.

"Very funny!" Geraldine yelled. "I am serious. And, yes, you may speak now."

"I remember," Lala said.

"Hugh and I were visiting New York and, of course, we were so eager to meet our beloved niece's new boyfriend, so we took you two out for dinner at the Sazerac House in the Village—I can't believe it's not there anymore we all loved that place so much, remember how much fun we had there that night?"

"I remember."

"Do you remember what Terrence said?" Geraldine demanded.

"Uhh . . . You're going to have to be . . . Can you be more specific?"

"Over dessert. You were waxing on and on about how Terrence was the one and how it had been so painful to kiss . . . I don't think that was the verb you used—"

"It definitely probably wasn't," Lala said.

"Shush," Geraldine said. "Kiss so many frogs before your prince came and Terrence said no amount of pain and risk is too much on the path to finding your Truest Love."

"He was right," Lala whispered. "No amount. Terrance was

worth all of it and more."

"So what do you think your beloved late husband would have to say about this bullshit with you being shy around guys who live in the same town you do and only fucking men who are about to go trekking on Mars for the next decade?"

"Okay, wait . . . That's where you're going with this? Because that is an absolutely absurd misreading of what I've been doing since Terrence—"

Geraldine started ticking a list off on her fingers.

"That guy from Dubrovnik you were gaga over for years. That guy who lived in Juneau where you were even considering a long-distance marriage with him with no mention of anybody relocating."

"Okay, but that was just the booze talking," Lala said.

"And then of course the winner, whatshisname from New Zealand. You wouldn't stop blathering about him for three years."

"Danny from New Zealand was adorable, and that was a long time ago, and I was very aware of what I was doing because I didn't want to replace Terrence; I just wanted to have lots of great sex on the occasional weekend visit, which I did with full awareness, and if we're going to continue this ridiculous line of conversation, can we at least go back inside and ask Tony if he'll make us a few to-go cups of dirty vodka martinis?"

"So what's changed now?" Geraldine said. "You're having romances with a guy in Moscow and some animal doctor who's in a boat on who knows what ocean—"

"If I had known you were going to use my diablog-slash-blog-ary against me like this, I would never have told you about my love letters to David—"

"While James is here, in town, and you two, despite never being in the same room together, seem to get along famously. Why are you still refusing to have a relationship with someone who lives in the same damn town you do?"

"What?" Lala sputtered. "What are you talking about? Have you forgotten about Gérard? Gérard happens to pitch your thesis into the dustbin of history, dear Auntie Geraldine. Because Gérard and I both lived on the Great Island of Manhattan!"

Lala threw her words down with the triumphant air of a brand new multimillionaire who had just watched the bobbling white ball for his sixth Lotto number roll out the big spinning drum down the tubular plastic pathway to victory.

There was a pause, during which Lala savored her feeling of superiority and during which Geraldine knit her brow.

*That's right,* Lala thought. *You don't have a counterargument for that, do you, you self-righteous demi-Evita.*

"That's right," Lala said. "You don't have a counterargument for that, do—"

"Who the fuck is Gérard?" Geraldine said.

"Gasp!" Lala gasped.

*I just literally said the word "gasp" in a gasping tone*, Lala thought.

"You're not talking about that French guy?" Geraldine said.

"*Bien sur!*"

"You know why I couldn't place the name?" Geraldine demanded. "Because you weren't in a relationship with him!"

"I would have been," Lala spat. "He looked just like Terrance, and I was clearly at a new stage in my life, and I was ready to be in a full, committed, fully committed—"

"Yeah, Brenda told me all about how shocked she was that Frenchie looked exactly like Terrence. You didn't even see that they could have been twins until Brenda pointed it out to you. So don't even bring that up as a denial of your immeasurable denial that you won't get into a relationship with anyone who lives in the same zip code you do."

"Brenda's such a blabbermouth," Lala muttered.

"Brenda is not at all a blabbermouth. Brenda and I are concerned about you. Brenda and I want you to be happy."

There was another pause while Lala stared out the window and frowned.

"I said 'gasp' aloud," Lala finally admitted. "In a gasping voice. I suspect that might possibly, in some perverse reading of the universe and all the perverse forces surrounding us, indicate some level of my subconscious agreement with your perverse, barfy thesis. Well, Auntie Geraldine, I have to tell you that you and my subconscious are grinding my last gear right about now."

Y

"Wow, I wish we had more volunteers like you," Andrew said. "You've been cuddling those puppies for hours. Look how happy they are. And thanks for helping me wash the older dogs. That oatmeal shampoo makes their dry skin feel so soothed."

Lala had walked over to Dogs of Love very early that morning. During the leisurely stroll to the shelter, she had carried on an angst-filled running commentary.

*I don't know how I'm going to explain this to David,* Lala silently fretted. *He'll be so disappointed. I mean, in the future I'm creating in my mind, he'll be disappointed. In reality? Who the fuck knows? I'm not even sure reality is relevant right now.*

Lala stopped for an iced tea on the way. She sat at one of the tables outside Starbucks and didn't realize that she was making exaggerated facial expressions to punctuate her internal conversation with David. The concerned stares of the passersby might have alerted Lala to this, had she been looking at anything other than her caffeinated beverage.

*I don't know what to say, David. Shit, I wish I had brought a notepad with me because I am never going to remember any of this for my diablogary to you. Maybe I can get my cell phone on "record," and I can whisper my thoughts into it. Fuck it. Like I could ever have a prayer of getting that damn device to do anything I want it to do. David, I don't know how to tell you that I maybe just need to have a relationship with someone nearby right now. Maybe I'm at that stage in my life. Maybe that's growth. Maybe I'm hopeful again. I don't know. I've got to try something different. Maybe James is my something different. I'm sorry you're not here, David. I'm sorry the timing wasn't right for us. I swear, I will never forget you. Hmm, I'm going to have to formulate a very gentle e-mail to Theo, too. I think he really likes me. I really like him. He's in Moscow. Fuck.*

Andrew was the only person at the shelter when Lala arrived.

"Look at you walking again!" he said when Lala tentatively entered and scanned the room hoping James might already be there.

"Andrew, you are an adorable angel, and it has been way too long since I've been here, and I'm paying for your college education. I'm not on painkillers anymore, so you can take me at my word. And you should definitely apply to Wesleyan. I'll write you a recommendation. Though I'm not entirely sure if that will advance your standing with them."

Lala didn't have the courage to ask Andrew if James was expected.

*I prefer to wallow in a haze of nervousness*, Lala thought. *It seems to have become my permanent go-to state.*

Several other volunteers had shown up throughout the morning, and Lala had treated everyone to a vegetarian lunch buffet that was brought in by a nearby restaurant. And now it was late afternoon, and there had been no sign or mention of James. Lala sat on a bench with two tiny terrier puppies on her lap. Every few seconds, she would pick them up and kiss their little faces as they napped.

*Kids, your Auntie Lala is about to jump out of her skin,* Lala silently told the precious babies.

Lala buried her nose between their smooth heads and took a deep, long, comforting breath of puppy smell.

"Andrew, sweetheart, I think I'm going to head home," Lala called out to Andrew, who was in the kitchen filling up the dishwasher with dog bowls. "But I'll plan to come back tomorrow so we can—"

Lala clutched the puppies to her chest and jumped up as the door was suddenly thrust open and an invasion force consisting of James, Candace, and Ruby's baby carriage breached the shelter's fortifications.

James had one arm around Candace's waist and his other hand was grasping the left side of the carriage's handle. Candace was his mirror image with her arm around his waist and her free hand holding the right side of Ruby's ride. They were laughing about something that had been done or said outside.

*Oh, no,* Lala thought. *Seriously?*

"Lala!" Candace bellowed. "Great to see you!"

*No, come on, seriously?* Lala thought. *This is happening again? My timing is supremely sucking yet again? Seriously?*

"Uh huh!" Lala said.

*Stay calm*, Lala silently told herself. *Don't freak out. Get out of here before you go bat shit.*

"You look great!" Candace said.

"Thanks! You too!"

Candace unzipped the mesh around Ruby's carriage and lifted the sleeping dog.

"Come here to Mommy," Candace said.

*I would estimate that I'm a blink away from going bat shit*, Lala thought. *Must get out of here. Now.*

Candace cradled Ruby like a baby and cooed at her.

"Isn't it nice that Lala's here, Ruby? Mommy loves Ruby. Lala, you're like our guardian angel. None of us can thank you enough for all your financial support."

"Yeah! Okay, well, you know, it's my pleasure to help! Great to see you all and isn't that funny because I was just telling Andrew that it was time for me to leave so, okay, I'll be back soon. Have a great rest of the day, everyone, okay?"

*Don't run out of the place like you're going bat shit*, Lala silently ordered herself.

Taking deep breaths that she fervently hoped were not audible or visible, Lala tried to appear calm as she took what she fervently hoped were slow and dignified and maybe even attractive steps toward the door and the vista beyond the door where she could manage to get herself home, so she could go bat shit in solitude, with only the judging eyes of her dogs to witness her meltdown.

*It's not like Petunia and Yootza and Chester and Eunice haven't seen me at my worst before*, Lala thought. *Repeatedly. God, get me out of here.*

Lala opened the door to the shelter. Her shoulders relaxed a little when she felt the cool air from outside surround her. She turned back to the room and smiled.

*Pretend you're on stage again*, she silently advised herself. *Pretend you're acting again. But not badly this time, okay?*

"Yeah! Okay! Bye!"

Lala waved to the room and turned and walked out and let the door shut behind her.

*Okay*, she thought. *Worst is over. Almost home. Oh, no. Jesus. Shit, James, don't follow me.*

"Lala! Let me escort you to your car!"

Lala forced herself to turn around to face the echo of the door opening and shutting again and to face James, but she kept moving.

"It's okay, I walked here."

"Oh. So how about I drive you home?"

James stopped on the sidewalk in front of the shelter and gave Lala a smile.

"Aren't you nice, gosh, no, thanks. I want to walk. I need to walk. Listen, if we're going to continue talking, which we absolutely don't need to do, can you please walk beside me because I am not at all good at moving backward. Unless it's metaphorically."

James sprinted to catch up with her.

"Are you okay?"

"I'm fine."

They walked together in silence for a block.

"I've gotten to know Candace in the past few weeks," James said.

"Mmm."

"I hope we can all go out for a drink sometime so you can get to know each other."

"Absolutely. You know me. Any friend of the animals—"

"Sure," James said. "She . . . I guess she swept me off my feet. Apparently I needed that. You know, with my wife leaving me, turns out those wounds were still there. Vividly there. Candace made it very clear that she knows what she wants, and she goes after it, and, apparently, what she wants is me."

*That's sweet*, Lala thought. *Fuck me, there's no denying that that is sweet.*

"That's a lovely thing," Lala said. "I'm so glad you're happy. I'm so glad you found someone to be happy with."

"So, you're doing well?" James asked.

"I am. I'm really looking forward to that interview you scheduled for me."

"First of many."

"I really like working with you, James."

"Me, too. And more than that. I'm very glad we're friends, Lala."

❦

Lala and Geraldine were on Geraldine's couch with their feet up and with lavender masks that had been heated in the microwave covering their eyes. The curtains were drawn. The muted sounds of a piece by Brahms were almost inaudible in the background.

Each of them held a champagne flute that was never empty. Geraldine was able to fill their glasses from a bottle of Veuve Cliquot chilling in a standing wine cooler without taking her mask off, as though she had the mystical sensory powers of a science fiction epic's hero.

Geraldine had gone into emergency mode and created a peaceful and calming atmosphere in her home as soon as Lala arrived at her door and gave her a painfully insouciant summation of what had happened that afternoon.

"He's got a girlfriend. I snoozed. So I losed. I slept. So I wept. It's only fair."

Geraldine refilled their glasses and, also without benefit of eyesight, patted the top of Lala's head.

"I'm very proud of you," Geraldine said.

"It means a lot to me that you're proud of me," Lala said, "but I'm not sure I deserve much credit. I didn't have nearly as much time to obsess about James as I did about Gérard. I didn't even know I was obsessing about James. I needed you to point that out to me."

"You honestly didn't lose it when you got home?" Geraldine asked.

"No. Honestly. I took a shower, and I kept expecting to lose it at any moment, and the moment never came."

"You're not mad at me for pushing you to give it a try with James?"

"Of course not. You didn't know he was dating a very large and attractive blonde steamroller. You didn't know he had found exactly what he needed, and you didn't know that exactly what he needed was not, in any way, me. How could I be angry with you for advocating hope? For urging me to keep trying? For insisting that I never give up?"

"Oh, sweetie, what a lovely thing to say. I'm so relieved because—"

"Okay, yeah, I am kinda pissed off at you for being the catalyst that launched me into having to go through this shitbag of a day. Wow, did I have fantasies on my way over there. Like James was going to be my date for the wedding, and I was going to catch the bouquet . . . Oh, well, Helene can be my date. I shouldn't be so pessimistic. I should look on whatever positive sides there are, here. We'll have a blast, just two single gals hanging out and getting toasted, and I promise not to trip her or elbow her after you pitch your flowers to the unmarried—"

"Ummm . . . Helene is bringing Clark to the wedding. Our chauffeur from Vegas? He's her plus-one."

"Jesus. Love is in the air, huh? Fuck. Well, I think that's great, and I'm also taking all the credit for her happiness since I practically shoved them into bed together, and I will be reminding Helene of that at every available opportunity for decades to come."

"You want to get gussied up and go out for a fancy dinner?"

"Can I have a rain check? What I'm itching to do is get back upstairs and get back to work. First day of the rest of my life blah, blah, blah, blah. I've got some new ideas for that Mata Hari in Heaven series I told you about."

"Honey, I think you might want to rethink that concept a little? Or at least revisit the casting? I just can't quite envision Sean Connery in a silver lamé evening gown."

🍷

Lala was back home in her bathrobe. She had just finished a bowl of delicious spaghetti and was sipping the last of a glass of lovely red wine. All the dogs were asleep in the living room. With her laptop in tow, Lala settled herself next to Yootza on the couch and flipped on the TV.

*What to watch, what to watch, what to watch?* she silently debated.

"Ohhhh," Lala gushed when the offering on Turner Classic Movies appeared on the screen in sumptuous black and white. "Who's in the mood for *Now, Voyager*? I am! I am! Transformation! Rebirth! Heartbreak! Multiple Second Acts! And, yes, of course I realize that I own this fabulous film on DVD, and so I could watch it whenever I want, but isn't it more reassuring when fate takes a hand in our joy?"

Lala thrilled as she watched frumpy Bette Davis struggle to find her way in an unkind world.

"She doesn't feel pretty! Or safe! Or hopeful! I know exactly what she's going through. Isn't this fun? We can't wait until the part where she feels pretty and safe and hopeful, huh, kids?"

Lala absentmindedly opened her laptop, not with the intention of beginning to work, but with the hope of finding something additional to divert her attention so that she could procrastinate on a second front.

Lala's first stop was in her e-mail's in-box. She scanned the long list of left-wing, virtual schmoozefest communiqués and listings for local meet-up groups to practice French. Her eyes landed on a subject line that read "Dressed Like a Lady, Drinks Like a Pig" and in the instant before she shifted to the "From" column, assumed that the e-mail had been sent to her by James.

When she saw the source e-mail address, Lala immediately remembered the name of Helene's literary agent.

*Oh, come on,* Lala thought. *I don't feel rejected and disappointed enough today? You want to remind me how one-dimensional my characters are? I'm not opening it. I am not. Fuck.*

Lala clicked on the e-mail and winced.

"Hi, Lala," she read.

*Bitch,* she thought.

"Sue me. I was wrong," Kelly Franklin Adams had written. "I got an advance copy of your novel. Where did all that quality stuff come from? It's like *Bridget Jones's Diary* for women over 40 if Nancy Meyers and Erica Jong had written it."

*Head spinning,* Lala thought. *Eyes can't focus. Wow. This is a very good feeling.*

"I'll be out in LA at the end of the month, but I really don't want to wait that long. When can we set up a Skype appointment, so we can talk about how we're going to work together?"

Lala stared at the screen. She took a controlled sip of wine. She gazed down at Yootza, who had his upper lip curled within his lower teeth and looked like an adorable, old, grey-bearded troll.

"My heart is racing," Lala whispered. "I must get you a teeny little stocking cap, Yootza. That would be a hoot. I am really enjoying this. I never want to forget this feeling."

Lala began typing. And reading aloud.

"Dear Kelly. Thank you so much for your e-mail. I'm very pleased to hear that you enjoyed my novel. But, at the same time, I have to tell you that my immediate reaction to your suggestion that we work together is to point out that it might benefit us both if we were to acknowledge that you and I didn't seem to have the same opinion of my work when this story existed in screenplay form. And, while I do understand and happily admit that the comedic novel form seems to be much more suited to the telling of this particular tale, I fear that we could not—given what I can only describe as your somewhat harsh and dismissive reaction to my earlier efforts—hope to establish a working relationship that would have much of a chance of being mutually respectful and . . . Oh, for heaven's sake."

Lala hit the delete key with a demonic smile.

"The poor woman doesn't deserve to have her ear bent off," Lala told her dogs. "And, by the way, I'm choosing to keep my finger on the delete key for the whole shebang rather than just blocking the text and hitting delete once because it's much more satisfying this way. Much."

*Okay,* Lala thought. *Succinct. Cogent. Concise. Every antonym you can think of for "longwinded."*

Lala sat back and watched *Now, Voyager.*

"Let me tell you something, Bette. Your Act Two is just around the corner. And it's gonna be a doozy. Trust me on this."

Lala smiled and relaxed. And then, out of nowhere and unbidden, the image of one of her eternally favorite cartoons from *The*

*New Yorker* popped into her head. It was of an executive in his office. The man was talking on the phone while he was consulting his datebook that he had open on his desk.

*Pithy, indeed, but not terribly gracious,* she thought.

Lala read the last line of Kelly Franklin Adams' e-mail aloud.

"When can we set up a Skype appointment, so we can talk about how we're going to work together?"

*Fuck gracious,* Lala thought.

"Dear Kelly," she typed. "How about never—is never good for you?"

# THE SUN'LL COME OUT TODAY

The caterer made sure there was a bottomless pitcher of signature champagne cocktail waiting in Geraldine's bedroom for the bride and her entourage.

The ladies had awakened early and were gathered at Geraldine's place to get ready. Lala's four dogs would also be participating in the ceremony. They were all asleep in the bedroom, all wearing special outfits for the occasion: tee shirts that had stencils of tuxedoes on the ones for Yootza and Chester and stencils of old-fashioned wedding dresses on the ones adorning Petunia and Eunice.

Benedict the Great Dane was to be Monty's best man. He would be wearing an actual doggie morning suit that a Beverly Hills neighbor of Helene's had made for him.

Lala and Brenda and Helene had surprised Geraldine with matching dresses that they had picked out together at Macy's because Lala had a coupon for twenty-percent off everything for one full day of your choice, and "they have amazing sales anyway, so with the coupon added it's a steal, and there's also a Wetzel's Pretzels at the mall, and I've been having a yen for one of those buttery salt bombs lately."

The dresses were in a delicate floral pattern of very pale purple on an even paler purple background, tea-length and with cap sleeves, v-neck, belted natural waist, and pleated skirt.

"So classic," Helene had said when they were trying them on together in the dressing room.

"So flattering," Brenda had agreed.

"So fuckable," Lala had concluded. "Can you believe what they're doing with polyester nowadays? Keep your fingers crossed. I should only get lucky in this dress."

Geraldine cried when the three of them appeared in front of her, grinning in their finery, and clutching their lovely, simple, white rose bouquets. Lala lunged for a box of tissues. Helene and Brenda immediately began frantically fanning Geraldine's face.

"Watch your makeup!" they cooed.

"You all look so gorgeous. My little angels."

"Stop crying!" Lala ordered. "Like anyone's going to be looking at us. You are the most beautiful bride in history. No one is even going to notice we exist. Omigod, why are our glasses empty?"

Lala grabbed the pitcher of signature champagne cocktail and began pouring.

"Nobody move! Nobody start crying again! The Maid-tron of Honor is on it!"

"Maid-tron of Honor," Brenda whispered. "I like that. You made that up?"

"Mmm hmm," Lala whispered. "I mean, probably not, but it was new to me when I thought of it."

Lala and Brenda and Helene were standing in the middle of the courtyard of Geraldine's fourplex, next to a new, white metal garden archway that would be serving as the huppa for the ceremony. Lala looked around the beautiful grounds and smiled. The windows of all the apartments were festooned with yards of flowers strung together in cascading strands. Five rows of eight white rattan chairs were arranged in a semicircle around the archway, and they were filled with close friends and family of the bridal pair.

Clark was in the front row, and he couldn't take his eyes off

Helene, who also never stopped smiling at him.

"On the East Coast?" Lala said to Brenda and Helene. "An outdoor wedding? Nonstop anxiety. Nonstop checking of the weather report up to the very last second before the ceremony, and, *oy vey*, what if there's rain predicted? Better rent a tent just in case. Here? Nice. Every damn day. God love Southern California."

Resting in their places immediately by Lala and Brenda and Helene were Lala's dogs. They had been the escorts down the very short aisle leading from Geraldine's front door, through the center of the rows of chairs, to the archway. Helene came in first, leading Chester on his leash. Then Brenda walked down with the two gals, Petunia and Eunice. Finally, it was Lala with Yootza, who had a small, white lace pillow tied to his back that had the two white gold wedding rings attached to it.

Standing beneath the archway was Rabbi Denise, the head of the LGBT reform congregation in El Segundo and a friend of Lala and Brenda from high school.

And then there was Monty, standing with Rabbi Denise and his beloved Benedict. Monty looked like an ambassador to the Court of St. James in some Lifetime adaptation of a thriller-cum-romance. Lala caught Monty's eye and winked at him.

"You look devastatingly handsome," Lala said.

Helene waved at her father.

"Love you, Daddy," she said. Monty started to sniffle.

A lone violinist sounded a single note, and all eyes turned to Geraldine's apartment. Geraldine's door opened, and Geraldine appeared on the arm of Thomas, her dear "Salman Rushdie."

Monty gasped when he saw his beautiful bride.

"Great reaction, Uncle Stepdad," Lala gushed. "I love you so much for loving her so much."

Lala smiled at her beautiful aunt. The violinist began to play again. After the third note of the piece, Lala got confused.

*Is that the Wedding March?* she thought. *That's not the Wedding March. Is that . . . wait a minute . . .*

Beside the violinist, a young singer from one of the local amateur theater groups began to sing in a slow, operatic voice, maintaining lyrically that she had fooled around and fallen in love.

The song had the words about fooling around and falling in love repeated in the verse, in case anyone had missed the point the first time that fooling around had lead to falling in love.

Had Lala or Brenda or Helene or Monty or probably even one or all of the dogs been drinking a signature champagne cocktail at that moment, there would have been a geyser of spit-takes.

"You know why she picked that song," Lala said through clenched teeth as she desperately tried not to go on a giggling jag. "So we wouldn't all be blubbering right now. Auntie Geraldine's a flippin' genius."

The singer's voice reached a deafening crescendo as Thomas gave Geraldine's hand to Monty and retreated to his seat in the front row next to Clark. The words "fooled" and "around" were sung more times than Lala could accurately tick off on her fingers and still hold her bouquet without getting entirely confused and having to start counting all over again.

Rabbi Denise smiled as the song ended. She cleared her throat.

"Dearly and eternally beloved, we are gathered here today because it may sometimes be too wonderful to imagine, but it is never, thank goodness, too late to believe in happy beginnings."

"Well, this dress didn't do me much good."

"Oh, the night is young," Geraldine said.

Lala and Geraldine were taking a break from the dance floor and were standing together at the bar. Monty was still shaking it, solo, to the beats of a Beatles block spun by a young man the universal opinion held as the best DJ ever.

"Where did you find him?" Lala asked. "He's fabulous."

"Craigslist," Geraldine said.

"Wow," Lala said. "A secular miracle. Such a good omen for you and your adorable husband."

They watched Monty on the floor. He was surrounded by a love battalion of couples, including Brenda dancing with her husband, Frank, and Helene and Clark making out under the camouflage of slow dancing to a ballad.

Then a new song began a moment before the old one had ended, and Geraldine's new husband just as seamlessly shifted from what had been—if a best educated guess was anywhere near discerning what was going through Monty's head—a variation on a highland jig to moonwalking to Paul McCartney singing "My Love."

Monty shimmied his shoulders as he slid backward and waved at Geraldine and mouthed, "My love does it good."

"God, I envy you," Lala said. "He is adorable."

"He is, isn't he? Your time will come. Trust me. It's never too late."

"Yeah, I need to remember that. You know, I have been flirting shamelessly all night. Whorishly. I think if I catch the bouquet, Monty's friend Mr. Shaughnessy from the VA Hospital might choose that as exactly the right moment to pop the question."

"What time is it?" Geraldine asked.

"I don't know. You in a hurry? You're not leaving on your honeymoon until next week because you agreed to plan it that way so I could drink all night tonight and not have to—"

"Yes, yes, I remember," Geraldine said. She turned to the bartender. "Dear, do you have the time?"

"It's just after eight o'clock."

"Oh, excellent, thank you," Geraldine said. She turned back to Lala. "You're still writing those lovely blog diary thingamajigs to David, aren't you?"

Lala's whole body deflated a little.

"Way to ruin my buzz, Auntie. I stopped after the whole James-has-a-new-girlfriend-and-it's-not-me fiasco. I haven't even sent an e-mail that consists of much more than 'Busy, can't write much now' to Theo. I think I've lost my *joie*. For *vivre* at any rate or, dare I say it, even for sex. I mean, sure, I can still flirt a good show at a wedding, but if it were to come right down to it, I don't think I'm up for—"

"Nonsense," Geraldine huffed. "Stop talking crazy. It's like riding a bicycle. You'll be up on that seat again in no time."

"You sound bizarrely confident in that prediction, Auntie Nostradamus."

"Let's just say I have a hunch that good things are right around the corner."

Geraldine waved to Stephanie and Chuck, who were on the opposite side of the dance floor trying to waltz.

"Stephanie! Chuck, dear!"

The two of them scurried over to Geraldine and Lala and stood before them bobbing their heads in unison.

"It's just after eight o'clock," Geraldine told them.

"We know," Stephanie leaned in and whispered.

"We've been checking," Chuck said, his head next to his wife's and his voice just as low. "We didn't want to say anything."

Lala watched them as they bounced out of the courtyard without saying another word. She shook her head to clear her focus.

"They are so nutty, those two. Adorably nutty. Do you know what that was all about?"

"No clue," Geraldine said. "Let's get back out there."

Helene joined them at the bar before they could return to the dance floor.

"Where's Clark?" Lala asked.

"Bathroom."

"Good, because I've been wanting to accost you about the bouquet, but I didn't want to do it in front of him, and there hasn't been a moment that you two haven't been joined at the lips since Rabbi Denise pronounced your father and Geraldine husband and wife. Listen, technically I think you should just let me have the bouquet. As a gesture of gratitude for hooking you up with Clark."

Helene furrowed her brow and wrinkled her nose. She seemed to be fighting a mighty internal battle. At last, she exhaled.

"You're right. It's yours."

"Ha ha! Sucka!" Lala crowed. "Hadja goin'. Look, since I don't have a boyfriend, I've decided I'm going to leave the bouquet for you. With my affection and my best wishes."

Helene moved to hug Lala, but she stopped herself midgesture.

"That's not a ploy is it? To get me off my guard and the next thing I know I'm on the ground with your foot on my neck and the bridal bouquet in your sweaty little paws?"

"Oooh, nice narration," Lala said. "You better use that in one of your books, because if you don't, I swear I'm gonna."

Before Helene could answer, Clark came back and whisked her off to the dance floor. Geraldine and Lala followed close behind. They spent the next hour dancing in a big group to the better part of the Bee Gees' oeuvre and were interrupted only when the caterer came over and loudly asked Geraldine if it was time to bring out the wedding cake.

"Oh! No! Not just yet!" Geraldine yelled. She waved to the DJ, who promptly ran into her apartment. "First I've got a surprise for my Maid-tron of Honor."

Lala and the guests watched as the DJ ran out of the apartment with a cart ferrying a multi-component setup that he quickly assembled next to the bar. It included several microphones, a squat black monolith, and a flat screen.

*Whoa!* Lala thought.

"Whoa," Lala said. "Karaoke! Wicked cool!"

Geraldine hustled Lala to the performance area and shoved a microphone in her hand.

"But you and Monty should sing a duet together first," Lala protested.

"We'll sing one. We'll sing it last. You go first. I've picked out a song just for you."

"But what if I don't know it, and what if I can't—"

"You know it!" Geraldine barked. "We just danced to it."

"Okay, but I really think the bride and groom should be the first ones to—"

"You go first!" Geraldine yelled. "Jesus!"

Geraldine kissed Lala on the forehead and scrambled away to stand between Monty and Thomas.

"You think it's a good idea to let her sing alone?" Thomas whispered.

"She won't be singing alone for long," Geraldine said. She smiled and gave a nod to the DJ.

Lala squinted at the words that appeared on the screen.

*Oh, cool!* she thought. *I know this one! I love this one! God, I'm gonna start bawling.*

And once again the '70s came alive with the iconic work of the

254 • Heidi Mastrogiovanni

Brothers Gibb about love and everlasting smiles, as essayed by the delusional song stylings of Lala Pettibone.

Many of the guests looked at Geraldine with confusion and others winced at the sound of Lala trying to hit the right notes, and the sight of Lala blithely being unaware that she wasn't coming close.

"Geraldine," Thomas began. "I think you should—"

"Here it comes," Geraldine whispered.

Lala was about to continue with the second verse when a male voice from outside the walls of the courtyard joined her to salute in song the power of love and everlasting words.

Lala continued to sing as she watched David walk into the courtyard with a maniacally grinning Stephanie and Chuck following at his heels. And then David was right next to her with his wireless microphone, and they were singing together that only words could take your heart away.

"How does she manage to harmonize like that when, forgive me, she's really quite a dreadful singer," Thomas whispered to Geraldine.

"Blissful ignorance," Geraldine said.

And then the song was over, and Lala was staring at David and Stephanie and Chuck were in a lather.

"It's so cool!" Stephanie giggled. "We had to call the caterer and tell her we were outside with Doctor David, and then she had to come over and tell Geraldine, in code, that we had called. For the timing! To work out the timing for the surprise. Get it? Cool!"

"He's been here since yesterday," Chuck chuckled. "In Manhattan Beach! Since yesterday! He's back. Doctor David's back!"

"Uh uh uh," Lala said. "Uh uhhhhhh . . ."

She looked at Geraldine and pointed at her and then pointed at Stephanie and Chuck.

"You knew he was here? You all knew?"

Geraldine grabbed Lala and hugged her.

"David called me last week and said he was a landlubber again," she explained.

"Doctor David got Geraldine's number from us!" Stephanie crowed.

"Because Doctor David was able to find our e-mail addresses because we're listed with the American Veterinary Medical Association," Chuck gushed. "Isn't that cool! Doctor David has our e-mail addresses now!"

"You don't think shit this magical just happens, do you?" Geraldine asked.

🍷

"What's this?" Lala asked.

Lala and David had been hidden behind one of the pillars dividing the walkway surrounding the courtyard since maybe five minutes after their duet had ended. The party continued at a distance, and their conversation was punctuated by kissing jags that all included at least a few moments of Lala hiking her dress up and wrapping her legs around David's waist.

David had just handed Lala a box wrapped in silver paper. She put down the bottle of Veuve Cliquot they had been drinking directly from and tore open the package. Inside the box, Lala found a book. She looked at the first page, which had only "For Lala" written on it by hand.

"I printed all the e-mails I wrote to you, and I had them bound as a book. It's what I would have sent to you every day if we hadn't agreed we wouldn't do that. And if the Pacific Ocean had wifi."

"Oh, David," Lala said.

She turned the page to the first entries. And frowned and flipped through the rest of the pages.

"David, these are all in French. I mean, I'm entirely enchanted, but it is going to take me fucking forever to actually understand all this stuff."

David laughed and said, "I'll help you."

*Yeah, you can help me,* Lala thought. *You can read to me while we're naked, 'kay?*

"This is an amazing coincidence," Lala said. "I've written a diary. Well, I'm calling it a diablogary because it's not written on paper and stuff. It's written to you. I wrote to you every day while you were away."

"You did?" David said. "That's wonderful."

*Shoot*, Lala thought. *I am such a blurter. And such a broad interpreter of the phrase "every day." Now unless I stay up all night while he sleeps and excise every reference to James and Theo and also write entries for all the days I haven't been writing to him, I'm going to look like a major liar. And a major slut.*

Lala grabbed David and kissed him.

*Oh, well*, she thought. *Worry about that later.*

"Lala?" Geraldine called from the courtyard.

"Hang on one sec," Lala told David. She poked her head around the corner of the pillar and saw the assembled wedding party and guests standing together staring in her direction.

"Yeah?"

"We were thinking we might cut the cake and throw the bouquet now?" Geraldine said.

"Okay," Lala said. "Excellent idea. Can you hang on for maybe five more minutes? David and I are mashin' somethin' fierce back here."

"Sure," Geraldine said. "Take your time."

"Hey, Helene?" Lala said.

"Yeah?"

"Friendly warning. I will do what it takes to catch that bouquet. I. Will. Do. Whatever it takes to make that sucker mine. Do we understand each other?"

"You're on."

"Excellent! We'll be out in five."

Lala began kissing David again and after a minute she pulled away.

"David, not to bring the room down, but I have to ask. Where will you be living now? That is to say, and if I may wax nautical once too often, are you planning to drop anchor anywhere in particular for the foreseeable future?"

David shrugged.

"I'm flexible at this point in my life. I mean, I've got some conferences in Europe next year, but other than that, no set plans."

*God, I love Europe*, Lala thought.

"Are you . . . Were you going to move back to New York sometime?" David asked.

Lala shrugged.

*Gosh*, Lala thought. *I don't know . . .*

"Well, I'm making a lot of money subletting my apartment. And that's letting me do a lot of . . . you know . . . not to toot my own horn too much unless of course you find self-confidence very arousing . . . charitable stuff that's making me feel very good. And the weather here is really nice, huh?"

"Yeah," David said. "I think I could like living in Manhattan Beach. I think I could like it very much."

David grabbed Lala and kissed her, and Lala hiked her dress up once again and wrapped her legs around his waist and wondered if maybe that sharp twinge she suddenly felt in her left leg meant she might have done damage to the damn thing yet again, and then decided she really didn't have to waste time worrying if she had injured herself, because even if she had, she knew she would heal. Eventually.

*Wow*, Lala thought. *I bet this is definitely the Act Two that Auntie Geraldine had in mind for me.*

Lala's adventures continue in:

# Lala Pettibone: Standing Room Only

# ABOUT THE AUTHOR

Heidi Mastrogiovanni is a dedicated animal welfare advocate who lives in Los Angeles with her musician husband and their three rescued senior dogs, Chester, Maggie, and Squeaks. She loves to read, hike, travel, and do a classic spit-take whenever something is really funny. Heidi is fluent in German and French, though she doesn't understand why both those languages feel they need more than one definite article.

Heidi is a graduate of Wesleyan University and was chosen as one of ScreenwritingU's 15 Most Recommended Screenwriters of 2013. The comedy web series she writes and produces, Verdene and Gleneda, was awarded the Hotspot on the Writers Guild of America's Hotlist.

*Lala Pettibone's Act Two*, Heidi's first published novel, embraces the themes found in all of her work . . . It's never too late to begin again, and it must be cocktail hour somewhere.